Will these doctors be tempted up the aisle…?

MILLS & BOON®

Winner at

2001

IDEA

INTERNATIONAL
DESIGN
EFFECTIVENESS
AWARDS

0402/AWARD

Doctors
Down Under

THE BABY AFFAIR
by
Marion Lennox

UNRULY HEART
by
Meredith Webber

MUM'S THE WORD
by
Alison Roberts

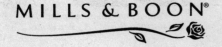

MILLS & BOON®

*All the characters in this book have no existence outside the imagination
of the author, and have no relation whatsoever to anyone bearing the
same name or names. They are not even distantly inspired by any
individual known or unknown to the author, and all the incidents are
pure invention.*

DOCTORS DOWN UNDER
© by Harlequin Enterprises II B.V., 2002

The Baby Affair, Unruly Heart and *Mum's the Word*
were first published in Great Britain by Harlequin Mills & Boon Limited
in separate, single volumes.

The Baby Affair © Marion Lennox 1999
Unruly Heart © Meredith Webber 1995
Mum's the Word © Alison Roberts 1999

ISBN 0 263 83155 8

05-0402

*Printed and bound in Spain
by Litografia Rosés S.A., Barcelona*

Marion Lennox was born on an Australian dairy farm. She moved on – mostly because the cows weren't interested in her stories! Marion writes for Medical Romance™ as well as Tender Romance™. Initially she used a different name for each category, so if you're looking for past books, search also for author Trisha David. In her non-writing life Marion cares (haphazardly) for her husband, teenagers, dogs, cats, chickens and anyone else who lines up at her dinner table. She fights her rampant garden (she's losing) and her house dust (she's lost). She also travels, which she finds seriously addictive. As a teenager Marion was told she'd never get anywhere reading romance. Now romance is the basis of her stories; her stories allow her to travel and if ever there was an advertisement for following your dream, she'd be it!

In 2001, Marion Lennox was nominated for a prestigious Romance Writers of America RITA award, for Best Traditional Romance.

Don't miss **THE DOCTORS' BABY** by
Marion Lennox, the climax of her emotionally
compelling *Parents Wanted* mini-series.
On sale May 2002, Medical Romance™

THE DOCTORS' BABY

As Bay Beach's only doctor, Emily Mainwaring is too
busy for distractions. Unfortunately, there are two
large ones heading her way! The first is an orphaned
baby boy, whom Emily longs to adopt. The second
is Jonas Lunn, a gorgeous surgeon from Sydney. Jonas
is more than interested in a passionate affair – but
what Emily needs from him is marriage…

THE BABY AFFAIR
by
Marion Lennox

CHAPTER ONE

'THERE'S one baby too many in this nursery.'

Sister Ellen Silverton looked up from her desk at sister's station and sighed. Oh, dear. This had to happen. She'd juggled babies and cribs for a week now, but Dr Jock Blaxton wasn't stupid.

In fact, Jock Blaxton was anything but stupid!

Still, maybe she could hang out a little longer. She owed it to Tina to try. Tina Rafter was Gundowring's newest doctor, and if things went wrong then Tina's job could be the briefest in the hospital's history. Ellen thought back briefly to the conversation a week ago. Tina, white-faced and desperate, had been close to breaking point.

'I'll resign, Ellen,' she'd told the charge nurse. 'I can't manage. I can't bring a baby into work.'

'Of course you can,' Ellen had said roundly. 'No one will notice an extra baby.'

No one except Jock Blaxton. Drat the man. He was too intelligent for his own good. The man had eyes in the back of his head. So how could she distract him?

'What on earth do you mean, Jock, dear?' Ellen asked, and then it was Jock's turn to sigh.

'Ellen, don't come the "Jock, dear" with me,' Jock retorted. Gundowring Hospital's obstetrician held up a fistful of patient notes and waved them accusingly at the senior charge nurse. 'There's something going on, and I don't know what. Just because you're twenty years my senior...'

'And I knew your mum.' Ellen sniffed and tried to dredge up a tear, hoping desperately to deflect Jock's

5

attention from one too many cribs. One too many babies...

'Jock, your mother was the nicest lady! She was my very best friend...'

'Ellen!' Jock intensified his glare by a notch or two. 'Stop trying to divert me. Sister Silverton, I want to know what's going on in this nursery, and I want to know *now*!'

'Why, what on earth could be going on?'

What, indeed?

Dr Jock Blaxton frowned at his mother's best friend in frustration. Was he imagining things? Gundowring Hospital was the last place in the world where things 'went on'. It was a busy enough hospital, nestled on the coast of New South Wales and serving a district of over four hundred square miles, but Gundowring was placid and sun-soaked and peaceful.

In fact, Gundowring was too peaceful for Jock Blaxton. Jock had spent the first ten years of his life in Gundowring before his mother died, and he'd returned twenty years later to take the job as hospital obstetrician.

Jock had returned partly because of memories of a happy, sand-and sea-filled childhood and partly because his friend, Struan Maitland, worked here as the hospital's medical director. Struan had been desperate for an obstetrician and hadn't hesitated to twist Jock's arm. And also... Jock had been restless in the city. Searching for something he couldn't even name...

Well, whatever he was searching for he hadn't found it in Gundowring. Jock had tried hard to settle, but twelve months into the job he figured if Gundowring grew any quieter *he'd* grow mould! He'd just returned from a holiday in London, and London was looking good. Dr Jock Blaxton wanted action in life, and he was about to move somewhere he might find it.

For now, though, if Jock wasn't mistaken and he

didn't let Ellen distract him, there was a problem to be dealt with. Action of a sort. One baby too many... What on earth was Ellen playing at?

'OK, if you won't tell me...' Jock lifted the pile of patient histories. 'Let's go through these, shall we, Sister? First.' He read the name from the top history. 'This history belongs to Jody Connor. Jody Connor is two days old.' He looked around until he found the matching crib. 'And Jody's here.' He placed Jody's notes on Jody's pink bassinet and moved on.

Uh-oh... Ellen swallowed and thought fast. Things were getting serious. It was starting to look like Tina was in major trouble.

'I'll...I'll just take little Benjamin in to his mother,' she said, heading for the nearest crib to collect a baby. 'He needs a feed. And Lucy Fleming should go back under the ray lamp...'

Jock placed a hand on Ellen's shoulder and stopped her. 'Leave every single baby where he or she is,' he ordered. 'Ellen—sit!'

'Well, I...'

'*Sit*!' Jock's powerful hands brooked no opposition. He propelled the senior nurse into her chair.

Defeated, Ellen sat. She glowered. 'You make me sound like a spaniel.'

'You're more like a beagle.' Jock's irresistible grin flashed out, his blue eyes twinkling. 'I know you, Ellen Silverton. You're stubborn, you're wilful and you're very good at playing the innocent. But, Ellen...' He shook his head as Ellen started to rise again. 'No. This nursery's my responsibility. Every night nurse in the place has been sidelining me and I want to know why.'

'If by sidelining you mean avoiding, then I can tell you why,' Ellen muttered darkly. 'Your reputation...'

'My reputation?' Jock was placing a history on each

crib but he was still listening. 'What do you mean—my reputation?'

'If you don't know about your reputation then you have fewer brains than I gave you credit for.' Ellen sighed all over again as she watched Jock move from crib to crib. She'd done all she could. He was going to figure this out. And if he blew the whistle...Would he? Who knew? Certainly not Ellen. After twelve months of working with Jock Blaxton Ellen still didn't think she knew Jock at all.

Once she'd known him well. Jock had been a great little kid, she remembered. Jock's mother had been a real friend of Ellen's, and Jock had grown up with her boys. But at ten his mum had died and his dad had taken it hard. Jock was an only child, dark and intense and deeply troubled by his mother's death. They'd moved to the city. Ellen hadn't seen Jock for twenty years—but then he'd come back to Gundowring, a fully qualified obstetrician, but even more dark and intense than she remembered.

And much, much larger...

He asked about his reputation and Ellen almost groaned. Jock Blaxton was six feet two, with a body to die for. Muscles, muscles and more muscles... Deep black hair. Strongly boned face. Blue-black eyes that were almost shadows. The eyes of an eagle. And a mouth that quirked when you least expected it into laughter so infectious you had to join in.

His patients loved him and every unattached nurse in the hospital was pining for Jock Blaxton—and wondering why he held himself aloof and disappeared to Sydney or overseas every chance he had. He had shadows, Ellen thought sadly. Ghosts from the past that were haunting him. He held himself too far apart. It was as if he was afraid of committing himself to life. To love...

Still, none of this had anything to do with Ellen's

immediate problem. How to explain one extra crib…
She couldn't.

'If I can't take Benjamin to his mother, then I'll just
tell his mother what's going on,' she managed, trying to
rise again. 'She'll be awake and wondering…'

But Jock wasn't to be deflected. He had one last set
of notes in his hand and he'd spotted the matching crib.

'Jason, here are your notes,' he told a week-old baby
boy—who wasn't the least bit interested—and then he
looked around. There was one crib left over. He was
right. There was definitely one baby too many.

'I'll just go—'

'Ellen, stay!' Jock growled—and he walked over to
stare down into the one pink crib that didn't have a history on top of the bedclothes.

'I knew I could count,' Jock said in satisfaction, his
eyes crinkling in automatic pleasure at the pink-wrapped
bundle. 'My maths isn't *that* bad. So, who are you, little
one?'

The baby was a tiny girl, maybe four or five weeks
old, and she took no notice of Jock at all. Her tiny face
was concentrating fiercely on sleep. She had a fuzz of
fiery hair, she was finely boned and she was just perfect.

'Ellen..'

'Dr Blaxton, I really must go.' Ellen edged sideways
toward the door.

'Nope.' Jock put his big hands into the cot and
scooped up the baby. 'Not until you've performed introductions. Who do we have here?'

'I'd have to look at the—'

'History?' Jock finished for her, and his eyes twinkled
again. 'Nope again. I've looked at all the histories. There
isn't a history for this little one.'

'There must be.'

'Ellen…'

'Look, if you think I have time to waste, trying to…'

Ellen took two steps forward and tried to bluster her way past, but Jock was having none of it. His muscular body blocked her exit.

'Ellen, are we indulging in a spot of moonlighting here?' he asked gently, the twinkle fading. 'Are we doing some child-minding on the side?'

'Don't be silly.'

'Ellen, there's no hospital name-tag on her wrist.' Jock's voice was implacable. 'There's no history and I don't know her. As far as I can remember, I've never seen this little one before.'

'She's Gina's patient,' Ellen gasped, knowing as she uttered the words that she was inviting disbelief. Boy, she was clutching at straws!

Gina was Dr Gina Buchanan—Gundowring's paediatrician. Gina was married to Struan Maitland, the hospital medical director. And Gina and Struan were on holiday.

To fob Jock off by saying this little one was Gina's patient didn't make one ounce of sense. Ellen was, indeed, desperate. Jock shook his head.

'Ellen, you know very well that Gina's away. She and Struan left on long service leave two weeks ago, and before she went Gina handed over to me. She told me of every single patient she has. And she didn't say one thing about a four-week-old girl.'

'She's five weeks old…'

'Five.' Jock nodded, his big hands weighing the baby in his grasp. He had the gentlest hands, Ellen thought. The kindest…

Would he be kind now?

'So you *do* know her,' he said softly. 'Does she have a name?'

Ellen tilted her chin. Daniel facing the lions. It wasn't a bad comparison, she thought. Jock Blaxton was *some* lion.

'Her name's Rose.'

'Rose.' Jock considered. The baby stirred and stretched in her sleep, and her tiny face puckered into a windy smile. Her rosebud lips twitched and Jock smiled despite himself. 'Yeah. I can see why she's called Rose,' he said softly. 'It's a beautiful name for a very beautiful young lady.' And then his voice firmed. 'Ellen, will you tell me just what the hell is going on?'

'I don't—'

'Cut the nonsense, Ellen.' A snap. When Jock meant business he meant business, and Ellen knew the time for dissembling was over. 'I want to know who she is, and I want to know *now*. I want to know what's wrong with her, and if there's nothing wrong with her I want to know why an apparently healthy baby is sleeping in our nursery. Tell.'

'But—'

'Ellen.'

Ellen sighed. And sighed again.

Then, finally, she lifted her face and met Jock's stare. Sister Silverton wasn't intimidated by anyone, lion or not, and she'd known Jock since he was in short pants.

'OK, Jock,' she said softly. 'As I said, her name's Rose, and we're looking after her for Tina.'

Tina.

Jock nearly dropped his bundle. He stared down at the baby in stunned incredulity, and then he stared at Ellen again.

'Tina... You mean Dr Rafter?'

'I mean Dr Rafter,' Ellen said miserably. 'We agreed—'

'Who agreed?'

'Well, I agreed—'

'You agreed to look after Dr Rafter's baby?'

'She'll have to resign as night casualty officer if I

don't,' Ellen told him. 'Jock, you don't understand. Tina's desperate. She can't afford to pay—'

'She can't afford to pay for child-minding?' Jock's voice was still incredulous.

'Jock, you don't understand,' Ellen said again. 'Tina's—'

She got no further. 'Too right, I don't understand.' Jock's face was as black as thunder. 'Of all the nerve. Dr Rafter's only been working here for two weeks. Ellen, we interviewed five applicants for the locum position. There was no mention of a baby.'

Ellen squared her shoulders. 'No. But would it have made a difference?'

'Of course it would. If we'd known she was dependent on us to look after the thing…'

'Dr Blaxton, Rose is *not* a thing!' Ellen's Irish temper was rising fast. 'This baby's called Rose and she's lovely. And you're not to blame Tina. I told her it'd be fine for me to keep Rose here. I also told her not to mention the little one…'

'Why the hell…?'

'Because you know that Wayne Macky will never agree to Tina having the baby here. Not without Struan's say-so, and Struan and Gina are away for three months.'

Jock's eyes widened. 'But Ellen, Tina's just a locum. She has no right to take on a short-term job like this if it involves us looking after her kid.'

But Jock's indignation was met head-on by Ellen's temper. 'That's enough! Tina isn't *just* a locum. You know she's a local girl. We all know her.'

'Well, I don't know her,' Jock said grimly. 'Tina's twenty-eight. She's six years younger than me, which means she would have been all of five years old when I left the district. So, unlike you, I'm not looking at her through rose-coloured glasses.'

'And you don't like her…'

'And I don't like her,' he snapped. 'I've told Struan already that I'm concerned about her having the job. She has no commitment. Even if it is just a locum position I expect dedication, and she's arrived at work late twice already...'

'Jock, Tina has family here. They need her. That's why she wanted the locum position...'

'She said she was between jobs.'

'It's true,' Ellen said desperately, 'but she also needs to spend time with her family. And to look after the little one...'

'And she thought we'd be a soft option.'

'No,' Ellen said flatly. 'Tina knows Wayne Macky, the hospital accountant, would never agree to this. When she took the job she didn't think she'd need child-minding at night, and when she figured it out she wanted to quit. But...' Ellen flushed. 'Well, I knew how much she needed the job and so do all the nurses who work on this ward. We've known Tina for ever. And if you blow the whistle on us...'

'To Wayne, you mean...'

'Yes.' Ellen put her hands on her hips and glared. 'You know Wayne will take it to the hospital board and they'll harrumph about it being irregular and—'

'And kick Dr Rafter and her baby straight out of here.'

'That's right. And if you want to be held responsible—'

'So what's happening here, then?' Jock interrupted grimly. 'Is the staff looking after Rose every night?'

'That's right.'

'The woman's got some nerve.'

'She's got some need!' Ellen snapped. 'I know you don't like Tina, but I don't know why. She's a dear girl. If you were a bit more sympathetic...'

'Ellen, we're not a babysitting service,' Jock said flatly. 'You know we're often tight for beds. And if this little one gets a hospital-based infection like golden staph...'

'Jock...' Ellen bit her lip, unable to defend herself here. It was a definite weak link in her argument. Golden staph was a worry and it had troubled both Ellen and Tina—but, then, Tina really didn't have a choice. Tina knew the risks and it had been sheer desperation which had made her bring Rose in.

'It's not on,' Jock said wearily. 'Hell, Ellen, I won't be responsible for keeping a healthy baby in hospital for the three months of Dr Rafter's term. And it's not fair of her to expect it of us. We pay her a decent wage, and she's old enough to know what she was taking on when she got herself a baby. So now she can just get herself a babysitter.'

'But—'

'No, Ellen.' Jock's arms tightened around the tiny Rose in his arms. 'I know your kind heart. You might not be able to tell her—but I have no such qualms. Cas. is quiet at the moment. I'll take her down and tell her myself.'

'Jock, why don't you like Tina?' Ellen asked Jock quietly, and Jock's mouth tightened into a grim line.

'Because she's a flibbertigibbet and she doesn't take her work seriously,' he retorted. 'And finding out about this little one's existence is exactly what I would have expected of someone like her. I might have guessed about the baby. There had to be a good reason why someone like her would want to leave the city. She'll have to go, and that's all there is to it.'

And he turned on his heel and stalked down the corridor before Ellen could say a word.

Tina Rafter...

Jock walked down the corridor with the grim look intensifying on his face as he walked. Tina...

He'd been against her appointment from the start. She seemed so young... Even though her résumé said she was nearly twenty-nine, it was hard to believe. She seemed too young to be casualty officer, even if it was only short term.

Why had she taken on the job? Jock had known there had to be some reason she was interrupting her career as an anaesthetist to take on a job like this, and it annoyed him that he hadn't been able to figure out what it was.

He couldn't ask her. Jock remembered the day two weeks ago when Struan had brought her into the hospital staffroom for introductions.

Tina had been happy and cheerful and eager to meet everyone, and at first sight Jock had been just as eager to meet her. Tina Rafter was *some* package. She was slight and curvy, with a smile that lit her whole face and with flame-coloured hair that tumbled in gorgeous curls around her shoulders. Her step was light and eager and she'd made an instant, glowing impression.

But then, as Struan had brought her across the room and introduced her to Jock, Tina's face had frozen. The lovely green eyes that faced him were suddenly ice-filled and full of contempt.

Her look had taken Jock aback. He wasn't used to women reacting to him like that. Time after time over the past two weeks he'd told himself that he was imagining it, but he wasn't. The woman had taken an inexplicable dislike to him, and the dislike bordered on contempt.

Jock had voiced his concerns to Struan. Maybe there were problems with the girl that they didn't know about. He'd been overruled. Struan, Wayne Macky and an older member of the hospital board had made the appointment, and they'd known Tina since she was a youngster. They trusted her, even if Jock didn't.

'We might even persuade her to make her position here permanent,' Struan had said as he'd made the last arrangements to take his family off on his long-awaited holiday. 'Her credentials are impeccable and we could use another anaesthetist. She only has the exam to go...'

'That's another thing I don't understand,' Jock had said. 'Why the hell is she interrupting her anaesthetic training to do a locum job?'

'Family problems,' Struan said curtly, and didn't elaborate. 'But see if you can work on her to stay. When Gina and I come back... Well, Gina's doing too much and Lloyd's overworked and there's too much anaesthetics for one person. We could stretch to another doctor.'

Jock could only agree. Especially when he was thinking he wouldn't renew his own contract. But Tina Rafter... The contempt in her eyes disturbed him, as he saw no reason for it. And now... For her not to tell them of her baby... For the woman to be a single mother and not tell them...

Well, maybe he could understand that. Wayne would be unforgiving and old Ron Sergeant, president of the hospital board, would be judgemental. Jock didn't mind the girl having a baby out of wedlock, he decided as he walked grimly down the hospital corridor toward Cas. But if she expected the hospital staff to look after it...

Jock's mouth tightened into a line of decision. He swung open the big glass doors of Cas. and strode in to face her. His timing was unlucky, to say the least. Tina was being solidly, thoroughly, and very, very, passionately kissed. Jock stopped dead and stared—and stared some more.

Who on earth was she kissing? He couldn't see. Tina was slight, five feet five or so, and finely built, with a lovely trim figure. Her skirt and blouse were covered by her customary white medical coat and she was being held against a large male body. All Jock could see of

Tina were her slim, stockinged legs and the mass of fiery red curls, flying free around her shoulders. The rest was enveloped by the man she was kissing.

And the man? He was a farmer at a guess. The kisser was big, rough and grimy, and looked like he'd come straight from the cowyard. As a passionate suitor, Jock thought he left a bit to be desired. Tina didn't think so. She was being kissed and she was kissing right back with heartfelt enthusiasm, and Jock felt his own body stir in recognition of the passion between man and woman.

Anger came to his rescue. Just in time!

'What the hell is going on?'

The kissing couple broke apart reluctantly. There wasn't a lot of guilt here, though. The man turned, Tina held fast within his hold, and Tina was laughing up at him, her green eyes alive with mischief and pleasure.

'Harry Daniel, that's not fair. I said a kiss. I didn't mean an out-of-body experience.'

'I pack a punch,' Harry said placidly, grinning down at the laughing young doctor.

'I'll tell Mary!'

'Yeah, right. You're our chief bridesmaid. She'd never believe you. Besides...' Harry grinned down at Tina in lazy contentment. 'As of next month I intend to spend the next fifty years being faithful to my lovely Mary. This is my last chance to sow wild oats.'

'And that's what I am? Wild oats?'

The big farmer considered and grinned. 'Well, wild... I'd definitely say wild...'

Jock might as well not have been there. He stared. Harry Daniel... He knew him. Local farmer. Local footballer. Engaged to be married to Mary Stevenson, a local schoolteacher.

'What the...?'

Finally he had their attention. They looked across the

room at him and Harry grinned. Tina didn't. As soon as she saw Jock her smile died as if it had never been. She hauled herself out of Harry's clasp and went stiffly back to the sluice tray.

'That's you finished, Harry, lad,' she told him, her voice suddenly tight. 'Come in on Friday and I'll take the stitches out. The scar will fade and we'll have you beautiful for the wedding.'

Jock's eyes swung back to Harry and for the first time he noticed a gauze dressing across the farmer's hand.

'What happened?' he asked, and his incredulity went down a notch.

'I had an argument with a power saw, Doc,' Harry said cheerfully. 'The damned thing won. You never can get the better of those infernal machines.'

'And Dr Rafter was kissing you better?' Jock's voice was tight with disapproval, but Harry didn't bat an eyelid.

'I told her I'd cry if she didn't.' Harry's grin deepened. 'Gave me courage to face the needle and all. She told me she'd give me a kiss better at the end of it if I didn't make a fuss, and I didn't squeal once. Our Dr Rafter's the best. I hope you'll keep her on when her locum's finished, Doc. She cheers the place up no end.' And he gave Tina a cheery wave of his injured hand and took himself off.

Silence.

Behind the desk Barbara, the casualty sister, looked curiously from Jock to Tina and back again. She'd been watching Harry and Tina kiss—and enjoying herself very much indeed—but now she figured that she wasn't wanted in the ensuing conversation. A smart lady was Barbara. She took herself off around the corner to check the reception area—but stayed close enough to the corner to be within earshot.

Tina was clearing the mess from the sluice tray, but

she'd now noticed what Jock was holding, and her hands were on automatic pilot. Her eyes weren't leaving the pink-wrapped bundle of baby in Jock's arms.

The door closed behind Harry, and Tina left her sluice tray and took a step forward.

'Rose,' she said softly, her arms reaching out for the baby. 'Is there something wrong?'

Then she stopped. Jock's face was cold and forbidding, and she had to find the courage to take another step. This wasn't going to work. Ellen had assured her it would. But Tina had known… Sod Jock Blaxton, Tina thought miserably as she looked up into Jock's disapproving face. Sod him! Sod him! Sod him! The man had done so much damage already and here he was, facing her with judgement written all over his face. Well, there was only one way to handle this. Tina was darned if she was going to stand here and face a lecture from Dr Jock Blaxton. No way! She'd told Ellen this wouldn't work, and it hadn't. So get out fast. Cut her losses and go.

'Would you like me to finish my shift before I resign, or would you like me to leave now?' she asked.

More silence.

She'd taken the wind right out of Jock's sails. He stood there without a darned thing to say for himself. He just stared.

'Well?' Somehow Tina made herself take the final steps forward to lift Rose out of his grasp. Rose kept right on sleeping. Tina looked down into the baby's tiny face and felt a surge of love so strong that it threatened to overwhelm her. And this man… He'd done so much damage….

'I'll leave now,' she said.

That made him stir. Jock stared, his anger building. Of all the irresponsible…

'Who's going to look after Casualty?' he demanded. 'Dr Rafter, your contract is for three months.'

'No.'

'What's that supposed to mean?'

'It means I have urgent personal problems, and urgent personal problems sometimes cause contracts to be broken,' Tina snapped. 'In the circumstances, no lawyer will hold me to my contract. And it also means I'm not expecting the least bit of sympathy from you, Jock Blaxton. Ellen told me I was wrong about you, and that you'd react with kindness if you discovered what we were doing. I was a fool to believe her.'

She took a deep breath. 'So... I'll take Rose home now and I'll forfeit my pay up to Thursday. It means you'll be overworked for a couple of days until you find another locum, but I bet that won't kill you, Dr Blaxton. In fact, it might do you good!'

And she turned on her heel and walked to the door.

Somehow Jock stopped her. He took three fast steps forward. As Tina's free hand reached for the brass pull-bar his hand landed on her shoulder and held.

'Just a minute...'

'I'm not listening to lectures from you, Jock Blaxton,' Tina snapped, without turning round. Her hold on the baby in her arms tightened. 'You've messed up this little one's life enough. I was a fool to let her anywhere near you. Now let me go.'

Jock's dark eyes snapped down in a frown. His grasp on Tina's shoulder tightened.

'I don't understand.'

'No. That's your specialty.' And she wrenched herself away.

'Tina...' Jock moved fast, shoving his body between the door and the angry young woman, and his hands swivelled her around to face him. Behind them, the casualty sister, peering round the corner, was practically pop-eyed.

'Look, would you mind telling me what the hell is

going on here?' he demanded. 'I find *my* staff looking
after *your* illegitimate daughter—as far as I know, you
took this job without even telling us of her existence—
and now *you* react with anger, as if we're in the wrong.
You've been angry with me from the time we met. And
you—'

But Tina was no longer listening.

'My illegitimate daughter?' she gasped. 'My...?'

'What the...?'

But Tina was beyond speaking. She was beyond any
reasoned thought at all. She raised her free hand and she
slapped him just as hard as she could, a stinging slap
right across his face—and then she pushed hard past
him, still cradling her little Rose against her breast.

Before Jock could recover, Tina had disappeared out
into the car park. Thirty seconds later he heard the sound
of a car being gunned into action, and Jock was left,
staring after Tina's disappearing tail-lights in absolute
bewilderment.

CHAPTER TWO

THERE was little time for Jock to think about Tina's crazy reaction for the rest of the night. He was just too busy. There was normally only one doctor on duty in the hospital overnight and the night casualty officer was it. Night casualty officer. Dr Tina Rafter, no longer employed. Specialists were called in at need. Tina's sudden departure meant that Jock had to act as casualty officer for the rest of the night, as well as perform his normal obstetric work if needed.

He was needed. So Jock fixed drips, coped with a heart attack, dealt with an old lady who was frantic because she couldn't sleep and didn't wish anyone else to sleep if she couldn't—and delivered a baby. The delivery was tricky, needing high forceps, and by seven in the morning Jock was close to exhaustion.

He finished stitching the new mother's perineum, and then ended up back in the nursery to recheck his new arrival just as Ellen was doing change-over, ready to leave.

Sister Silverton took one look at Jock and her normally benign face creased into disapproval and anger. In a small country hospital the nurse-doctor lines of authority were smudged, and the fact that Ellen had bounced Jock on her knee when he was tiny meant the lines here were non-existent.

Now Sister Silverton was angry, and the world was about to hear of it.

'Dr Blaxton, you had no need to dismiss Dr Rafter,' she snapped. 'Sister in Casualty told me what happened. Dismissing Tina out of hand, without even asking for an explanation… Jock, if your mother could see you now she'd be ashamed of you.'

Jock closed his eyes. He'd been up Sunday night with a delivery, he'd spent most of Monday consulting, Monday night had just finished and he was facing Tuesday exhausted beyond belief. He'd had enough!

'Ellen, I did not dismiss Tina,' he said through gritted teeth. 'She left. She walked out. Broke her contract and departed. And it's good riddance, as far as I can see.'

Ellen's breath sucked in fast.

'You don't mean that.'

'I do. She's flighty, she flirts with patients, she's not punctual, she's incompetent and, as well as that, she expects this hospital to look after her illegitimate child because she's too irresponsible to look after her herself. Or too mean to pay for childcare. Where the father is, I have no idea. I wouldn't be surprised if she doesn't even *know* who the father is!'

Ellen stared.

'Now, if you're quite finished, could you arrange for Mr Macky to contact the locum agency to find a replacement for Dr Rafter before you go off duty,' Jock said wearily. 'I need to have some breakfast and I have an elective Caesar booked in at eight.'

Ellen stared some more, and finally found her tongue.

'Did she hit you?' she asked softly. There were still four red finger-marks across Jock's cheek, but Ellen's voice wasn't the least bit sympathetic. 'Barbara said she hit you. Did Tina hit you hard?'

'Yes, she did,' Jock snapped. 'I could have her up for assault. Of all the—'

He got no further. Ellen Silverton walked straight over and gave Jock a ringing, stinging slap on the other cheek.

'That's from your mother,' Ellen told him harshly. 'And from me. And if you'd like to dismiss me, too, then go right ahead. I'm too old to pander to the likes of you, Dr Blaxton. Of all the arrogant, overbearing, judgemental... You should be ashamed of yourself.'

'*I* should...'

'Yes, *you* should.' Ellen put her hands up to grip Jock's shoulders and pushed him down hard onto her chair. He was so astounded that his long legs buckled under him—and he sat. 'You shut up, Jock,' Ellen snapped. 'Sit down and shut up and listen.'

'But—'

'Not one word until I'm through.' Ellen was small and broad and red-faced with fury. She stood before him like an avenging angel.

'One,' she snapped. 'Tina is a dear girl and what she's gone through... What she's facing...'

'I don't—'

'Shut up, Dr Blaxton,' Ellen said thunderously. 'Second. Rose Maiden is not Tina's daughter. The baby is Tina's niece. Tina's sister's child. If you accused Tina of being an irresponsible mother of an illegitimate child, when she's carrying the weight of the world on her shoulders, then it's no wonder she slapped you. And to accuse her of promiscuity...'

'She was kissing Harry Daniel in Casualty...'

Ellen took a deep breath, fighting for control.

'Yes, so Barbara tells me. She says you reacted like an outraged lover. Dr Blaxton, Tina and Harry have been close friends since pre-school, and next month Harry is marrying Mary, Tina's best friend from high school. So she kissed him. That makes her promiscuous?'

'But...' It was Jock's turn to fight for breath here. Things were spinning way out of control, and it was starting to look possible that he just might have made a fool of himself. 'But... If Rose isn't Tina's daughter...'

'I told you. Rose is Tina's sister's baby.'

'Then why isn't Tina's sister looking after her own baby?'

'She can't. Christie was admitted to hospital in Sydney a week ago, suffering from exhaustion and severe postnatal depression.'

'I don't—'

'You don't what?' Ellen snapped. 'You don't believe it? You'd rather believe that our Tina is a promiscuous, unreliable tramp? Is that it?' Ellen shook her head. 'And I thought you were a decent man, Jock. I'm ashamed of you, and your mother would turn in her grave if she could see how you'd turned out.'

And Ellen turned on her heel and started to walk away.

'Ellen…'

Jock's voice stopped her dead. There was weary desperation in Jock's voice. And also…also horror.

'Ellen, I think you need to tell me what's going on,' Jock said slowly. He fingered his bruised cheek and winced. 'OK,' he admitted, as she turned back to face him. 'I may have jumped to a few conclusions. But… Ellen, if I'm to avoid bruises all over me, maybe I need to know what's really going on.'

Ellen pursed her lips, still angry. 'Dr Blaxton, it's not my business…'

'Ellen.'

'Yes?'

'Sit. And tell. Please. Who is Tina's sister?'

Ellen sighed. OK. Jock's 'please' had had real desperation behind it. Maybe everything wasn't lost here. Maybe if she made an effort…

'Tina's sister is a woman called Christine Maiden,' she told him. 'She lives just out of town.'

'I see.' Jock didn't yet, but he was trying hard. 'So…Christine had her baby—Rose—here five weeks ago?'

'Yes.'

'That must have been while I was on holiday in London.'

It still didn't make sense, though. Jock frowned. As the only obstetrician in the district, he knew all the pregnant ladies around here. Or he'd thought he did. And he hadn't heard of a Christine Maiden.

'So...did Henry Roddick deliver her?' Henry was the relief obstetrician to whom Jock paid a fortune to look after his practice while he was away.

'If you didn't deliver her, then I guess Henry must have,' Ellen told him. 'I'd assumed you had. Tina told me it was you. But I was on leave then too.'

'But...' Jock shook his head, as if trying to clear a fog. 'If she had the baby here—if Christine's a local— then why don't I know her? I was only away for two weeks. If she lives near here, who did her prenatal checks?'

'Well...she might not have had any,' Ellen said diffidently. 'She was in trouble from the start.'

'Why?'

Ellen shrugged and sighed. And then spread her hands. 'It's a bit of a long story.'

'So try me.'

'Well, I don't know it all,' Ellen said slowly, 'but I gather... Tina says Christie's husband walked out when she was two months pregnant. They live on a farm about ten miles out of town and barely make ends meet. There's already a four-year-old and a two-year-old. Instead of trying to find help, Christie struggled on through the pregnancy by herself. Hardly anyone in town knew she was pregnant. I didn't. We never saw her.'

'But she ended up in Henry's care for the delivery?'

'I guess.'

'Do we have notes?'

'They'll be with your patient files,' Ellen said diffidently. 'You can look them up—if you want.'

'You don't think I will?' Jock's frown darkened. 'You don't think I give a toss?'

'I didn't say that.'

'I figured your opinion out all by myself.' Jock fingered his aching cheek with a rueful smile. 'I'm clever like that. Hit me hard enough and I'll figure you disapprove. Hell, Ellen, you could have told me all this before... So where does this leave Tina?'

'She's taking care of all of them,' Ellen told him. 'All the children. She took the locum job here because she was worried about her sister, and then when she arrived Christie just fell in a heap. So Tina had her admitted to hospital for rest and recuperation. Which leaves Tina with sole care of the children. I gather Tina's paying a girl to live in so she can get some sleep during the day, but the girl won't get up to a five-week-old baby at night. So Tina's bringing Rose with her to work.'

'And who knows about it?'

'Only the nurses on this ward.'

'Not Gina and Struan?'

'No. At least... Struan knew why Tina came home, but he didn't know she was bringing Rose to work.'

'Why not?'

Ellen shrugged. 'Christie wasn't in hospital when they left. And, anyway, Tina thinks the less people who know her sister's in a psychiatric hospital the better. This is a small town and it's judgemental.' She shrugged again. 'Well, maybe not so judgemental but Christie's afraid of stigma. Apparently, she wouldn't even go to a doctor here to seek help. Tina had to take her to Sydney.'

'Hell!'

'It is, isn't it?' Ellen said mildly. Flatly. Not letting him off the hook one bit. 'And you've just made it much, much worse. Now, if you'll excuse me, Doctor, I'd best be off. If you want me to contact the locum agency before I go home to bed…'

'Leave it,' Jock said heavily. He raked his fingers through his thick black curls in a gesture of absolute weariness. 'Can you…? Ellen, can you ask Tina if she'll come back? Say I understand about the baby?'

'No.' Ellen shook her grey head decisively.

'Why not?'

'Because if you want her to come back, I have a suspicion that it's you who'll have to ask her to return,' Ellen told him. 'She's a proud girl is Tina. You sacked her, Dr Blaxton. You fix it.'

It was five o'clock that afternoon before Jock found time to get to Tina's sister's farm. He'd found the address from the patient notes, but the address was vague and it took him half an hour to reach the farm. Even then he wasn't sure he was at the right place. Jock climbed from his car to open the farm gate and he looked up at the house in dismay. Surely no one could live here?

The house was a ramshackle cottage set high on the ridge where the coastal plains turned to rugged mountains. Here the bush was fast encroaching on the cleared land. The cottage was fenced off from the bush but there were eucalypts suckering everywhere, and masses of bracken clustering closer and closer to the house.

There were scrawny chickens on the front verandah and one sad-looking cow, staring moodily down the track at Jock's neat little sports car. Was he in the right place? Jock nearly turned away, but then there was a shout of laughter from the back of the cottage. A girl's chuckling voice calling out.

'I spy Ally…'

And Tina burst from behind the cottage. This wasn't the neat, white-coated and professional doctor Jock had seen in the hospital, though. Tina was dressed now in scruffy jeans and T-shirt, with a bundle cradled against her breast. She was barefooted and her flame-red hair was flying. With one hand steadying her bundle, she raced up the verandah steps to the front door, where she thumped the panels with a resounding bang.

'Home. *Out!* That's it, Ally Maiden. Tim and I have found you and now you're *It*!' And then she swooped back down the steps to the side of the house to where a child was toddling after her. Still steadying her bundle, she scooped the little boy up onto her hip with her free arm and hugged him hard. 'How about that, Tim, boy?' She gave a war whoop of triumph and spun toddler, bundle and herself in a circle. 'We've found Ally.'

But Tim had seen Jock. The little boy stared out at Jock's sleek little Alfa sports car and his jaw dropped.

'Car, Aunty Tina. *Car!*'

Aunty Tina turned to look—and froze. Unlike Tim, she didn't see the sleek little sports car. She only saw Jock. Dr Jock Blaxton. In person. Jock Blaxton here! This was her worst nightmare come to haunt her. Then Ally came racing round the house—a little girl of about four with hair the same flaming red as her aunt's.

'I thought you'd never find me,' the child was crowing happily. 'I hid for ages and ages...'

Then she, too, saw Jock. She stopped and stared—and then she headed straight for Tina and grabbed her hand, which left Tina standing stupidly on the verandah steps, one baby slung in a papoose against her breast, one child on her hip and one child clutching her hand—all of them waiting for Jock to approach.

When all Tina wanted to do was walk inside and slam the door. If she did slam the door, the whole place would fall down, she thought ruefully. There wasn't anywhere secure you could hide around here. If ever a big bad wolf could blow a house down, this was the house.

Jock was walking up the track, the warm wind ruffling

his thatch of deep black hair and his blue-black eyes creased against the afternoon sun. The big bad wolf in person. Tina backed up the steps, the children clutched close. She looks afraid, Jock thought suddenly. Why on earth…?

'Tina?' He stopped at the foot of the steps and looked up at the little group, standing by the front door. Tina didn't blame him one bit for not coming further. The steps looked like they might collapse at any minute.

'That's me,' she said, her voice carefully neutral. Then she turned to her niece, forcing herself to make an effort. To try and find *something* to say. 'Ally, this is Dr Blaxton. He's the man I told you about who was so horrid to me this morning. Dr Blaxton, this is my niece, Alison—better known as Ally—and this is my nephew, Timothy.'

Jock found himself being regarded by four large, very interested and totally judgemental eyes. Ally's small chin tilted straight up, defiance in every inch of her person. Dr Blaxton. She knew all about Dr Blaxton.

'You made my Aunty Tina cry,' she said severely. 'We don't like you, Dr Blaxton. Even if your car *is* nice, I think you'd better go away from here.'

Jock swallowed. This wasn't getting any easier.

'I didn't mean to make your Aunty Tina cry.'

'Then why did you?'

'I made a mistake.'

Six eyes were watching him. Maybe eight if you counted the baby, swathed snugly against Tina's breast. All were the same intense green, with the same light behind. All were redheads. You could have sworn these children belonged to this girl.

'Did you come to say you're sorry?' Ally asked curiously, and Tina made a sharp little movement backwards.

'He doesn't need to say he's sorry, Ally,' she said grimly. 'I don't want him to apologise.'

'He made you cry.'

'I was silly,' Tina said flatly. 'Silly to let him upset me. Dr Blaxton doesn't have anything to do with us. He shouldn't be able to make any of us cry.' Then she tilted her own chin and the eyes that met Jock's were cold and hard.

'Please leave,' she said flatly.

'Tina, I'm sorry...' Jock's voice was getting a bit desperate. He didn't know what he was fighting here, and he wasn't enjoying the sensation one bit. 'I shouldn't have implied that Rose was your daughter... It was—'

'Is that all you've come to apologise for?' Tina asked incredulously. 'Is that all? Implying that I might have an illegitimate daughter? You hurt us in every way possible and that's all...' Her voice broke off, strangled in impotent fury, and there was a long, drawn-out silence. Not even the children spoke. Finally Jock found his voice.

'Tina, I don't have a clue what you're talking about.'

Tina stared, and stared some more, as if she couldn't believe her eyes. 'You mean you don't know what damage you've done?'

'No.' There was nothing else to say to her question, but that one word was enough to open the floodgates.

'You don't know...' Tina's green eyes flashed fire. 'You don't know! You admit my sister into hospital, deliver her baby and discharge her twenty-four hours later—*twenty-four hours!*—because she's a public patient and you can only charge the set amount for delivery no matter how long she stays in hospital. And she's exhausted almost to death, she's starving herself, she's depressed beyond measure and she has no one at home to help—*no one*! But you send her away because you can't make any more money out of her, and you don't give a damn.'

Tina might only be five feet five inches high, but what she lacked in stature now she more than made up for in venom. She was practically spitting.

'And you don't even follow through. Not even with the easy things. You don't contact the maternal child care centre and send a home visitor. There's no one to care. My sister came home here after one night in hospital and the neighbour handed back these two and left her. No one even contacted me until two weeks later, and then I flew down from Brisbane to find...'

Tina gasped and choked and then closed her eyes, remembering a nightmare. 'Well, it was just as well that I came.' She pulled the two little ones closer. 'Mummy was ill, wasn't she, kids? But now she's in hospital and she'll be better soon. But we don't need your apology, Dr Blaxton. My sister needed a caring doctor and she didn't get one. So now... We don't need you now. We don't need you at all. So I think you'd best leave before I get even angrier.'

Silence. More silence. It stretched on for ever. A mopoke called from high in the gum trees around the house. The call was high and mournful, accusing. The whole world, it seemed, was accusing Jock Blaxton.

Maybe the bird was right to be accusing. Maybe Tina was right. Hell! Jock's feeling of weariness intensified almost past bearable limits. He was responsible here, horribly responsible. Maybe he wasn't as responsible as Tina believed, but he was responsible enough. He'd badly wanted a holiday and he'd hired Henry Roddick without any guarantees as to the man's competency. He'd expected Gina and Struan to keep an eye on him— but maybe they'd been just too busy.

'Tina, I didn't deliver your sister's baby,' Jock said softly, his voice laced with exhaustion. 'I've been away, overseas. Did your sister tell you definitely that it was me who delivered her?'

Tina's eyes widened.

'That's crazy. Yes, she did. Dr Blaxton...'

'Are you sure she didn't find out who the obstetrician here was some time during her pregnancy, and then just assumed Dr Roddick was me? If she was so distressed...' Jock's voice softened still further. 'If she was so distressed when she was having the baby, maybe she didn't listen to introductions during labour.'

'I don't...' Tina looked blank. 'I guess...'

Jock's voice firmed in the face of her uncertainty. 'Tina, it definitely was Dr Roddick who delivered her. After Ellen told me Rose was your sister's child, I looked up your sister's history. Christie hasn't been near me. I haven't seen her once through her whole pregnancy. According to Henry's notes, there was no prenatal history at all. Her delivery caught Henry by surprise. She delivered normally, and requested discharge twenty-four hours later. He saw no reason why she shouldn't be discharged.'

Tina's mouth dropped open. Her huge eyes practically enveloped her face.

'You mean... It wasn't you.'

'It wasn't me.'

Tina's eyes closed in denial.

'Oh, no... Oh, no!'

'I think...maybe we've both done ourselves an injustice here,' Jock said wearily. 'Maybe we should start again and figure out just what happened.'

Tina's eyes opened cautiously. 'But... I made you stay up all night,' Tina said slowly. 'You had a woman in labour, and you had all my casualty patients as well. You must have been so busy...'

'I survived.'

'I hit you.'

'I deserved it.'

'No, you didn't,' Tina said honestly. 'I had no right to take Rose to work. Ellen talked me into it. But—'

'But I should have found out the whole story, before flying off the handle.'

'Excuse me!' It was a virtuous voice from waist height. Four-year-old Ally had been looking from her aunt to Jock with increasing impatience. 'Excuse me, Aunty Tina, but are you making friends with Dr Blaxton?'

'I don't know.' Tina managed the ghost of a smile. 'I'm thinking about it.'

'I thought we hoped Dr Blaxton got something… something with pox in it.'

'Never mind, Ally,' Tina cut in hastily. 'We don't hope any such thing any more. I might have made a mistake about Dr Blaxton.'

'Does that mean we can have a ride in his car?'

Tina gasped and choked. Suddenly the smile was flooding back—the smile that Jock had seen directed at other people but never at himself. The smile that had had him entranced from the moment he'd seen it and had made Tina's contempt all the more hurtful. And now her smile was flooding straight at him.

'Oh, Ally… Oh…' Tina shook her head, and there was the glimmer of tears behind her smile. 'Oh, heck…' She put her nephew down on his two sturdy little legs, the baby swaying against her breast as she bent, and then she straightened and held out her hand towards Jock. 'Dr Blaxton, you can't know how good it feels not to need to hate you,' she told him.

Ditto.

That smile was doing strange things to Jock's solar plexus. He took Tina's firm, cool hand in his, and the things kept on happening, only faster. This was a girl unlike any he'd ever met before. Tina wasn't wearing a scrap of make-up. Her eyes were clear and bright and honest, and she was up to her neck in domesticity. There were milk stains on both her shoulders and the baby slung against her breast looked like she belonged there. This was the sort of scene that would normally make Jock run a mile!

'How's…how's Rose?' he managed, and his voice sounded only slightly hoarse. Only slightly out of kilter…

'As you see.' Tina smiled fondly down at her bump. 'She'll let us do anything as long as we take her along. Very sociable, our Rose. But at the moment she's fast asleep. Long may it last.'

'Why…?' Hell, how to get his voice working properly? 'Why isn't she in hospital with her mother?' In cases of severe postnatal depression it usually made things worse to separate mother and child. 'I don't understand,' Jock complained. There was so much here he didn't understand, not least of which was the way the girl in front of him made his legs feel—sort of like jelly. It was those eyes… But Tina's face was closing again, pain washing back.

'I don't think…' She sighed and the light faded from those brilliant eyes. 'Maybe you don't understand just how ill my sister was when I found her,' she said softly. She flicked Ally's crimson curls. 'Ally, can you take Tim and collect some eggs? If we make Dr Blaxton an omelette and treat him really well, then maybe he'll give you and Tim a ride in his car.'

'Really?' Four avid eyes looked straight up at Jock, their faces a picture.

Who could resist? Jock spread his broad hands and let his eyes crinkle into a smile of agreement. This little group was like a fine silk net, drawing him in. He should go straight home to bed, but these matching sets of green eyes…

Irresistible.

'Really.' Jock grinned, caving right in. 'For a farm-egg omelette, a car ride is a small price to pay.'

'Oh, boy!' Ally gave a war whoop to match Tina's. She grabbed her brother's hand and both children swooped off toward the hen-house.

Jock was left with Tina…and one baby…

CHAPTER THREE

THEY stood in the late afternoon sun, neither knowing where to start. Tina's bare toes shifted uncomfortably on the dusty verandah boards while Rose stirred and then settled against her breast. Tina winced. She loved the feeling of Rose, but Jock made her feel... He made her feel young. Gauche. Out of her depth.

'Come in and have some lemonade,' she said at last, and her words were strained. 'That is...well, I seem to have hijacked you for dinner. Can you bear it?'

'To have a home-cooked omelette and take two kids for a ride in my car?' Jock's lazy smile swung back into action. 'I can bear it.' He followed her inside the cottage, and part of him was acknowledging that at least some of his willingness sprang from Tina's neatly packaged body. She looked great in jeans and bare toes. Immersed in domesticity, with or without baby, she looked just great!

Inside, the cottage was much like outside. Grinding poverty stared at him from every angle. Jock stopped at the kitchen door and stared around him. There'd been attempts to keep it neat. The house was clean—but that was about all that could be said for it. The furniture was almost non-existent. There was a table, of sorts, but no chairs. The seating consisted of a pile of wooden fruit crates. The floor covering had given up the ghost long ago. A strip of linoleum lay before an ancient wood stove, but the rest of the floor was bare, scrubbed boards.

A bunch of bottlebrush in a jam jar gave the room its only colour—a bright splash of crimson that went perfectly with Tina's wondrous hair. It made the place seem as if someone cared. Someone did. Tina was watching Jock's face and she saw his eyes rest on the bottlebrush.

'We change the flowers every morning,' she said, her hand soothing Rose with semi-conscious strokes. 'It makes us all feel better.'

'Why...?' Jock shook his head and lowered his frame gingerly onto a fruit crate. 'Tina, why is your sister living like this? This is dreadful. She surely doesn't need to. There are social agencies who can help. They'll give her furniture at least.'

'They will.' Tina's mouth set into a tight line. 'They will now. But they haven't been allowed to.'

'Can I ask why not?'

Tina shrugged. She filled the kettle and placed it on the stove, then pulled up her own fruit box to the table, settling herself and the baby to face Jock Blaxton. To share a truth that hurt.

'My sister's proud,' she told him. 'She's always been stubborn and strong and totally in control. Only now...'

'Now?'

'Christie's husband has been having an affair with another woman,' Tina said bluntly, meeting Jock's eyes head-on. 'With a teenager, for heaven's sake. Christie found out when she was two months pregnant. Ray...Christie's husband...wanted her to get an abortion, even though the baby was planned.'

'And she refused?'

'Of course Christie refused.' Tina looked down at Rose as though the thought was totally abhorrent. Which it was. She smiled softly at the downy little head and bent her head to give the faint tinge of red hair a soft kiss. 'Christie wanted this baby. She loves her kids. She loves... She loved Ray.'

'So?'

Tina sighed. 'So Christie took the children away for a few days to give her time to think. In retrospect, it was a stupid move. I think she'd expected Ray to panic—to come after her. But he didn't. And when she finally came back Ray had stripped the place bare. He'd sold everything that was of any value at all. Everything. Even the floor coverings. He'd cleared out their bank accounts. He'd run up debt on their credit cards and he'd gone. He even took every single light bulb in the place.'

'Oh, no...'

'And, instead of calling for help, Christie just froze,' Tina went on sadly. 'Our parents died some years ago. I was up in Brisbane, working, and she didn't tell me anything was wrong.'

'But you must have known...'

'How could I know?' Tina's eyes clouded with pain. 'I was so busy with my own life—with my medicine— and I thought... Well, Christie didn't even tell me she was pregnant. I hadn't seen her since last Christmas. I'd ring her and she'd chat normally about Ray and the kids—as if there was nothing wrong.'

'So what did she do for money?'

'I don't know,' Tina said grimly. 'As far as I can see, she didn't even apply for social welfare. She had the poultry and the cow so at least the kids had eggs and milk. But she didn't go near the neighbours, and the few friends she had she wouldn't see. Because she was so embarrassed...'

Jock closed his eyes, thinking it through. A woman struggling with the emotional turmoil of pregnancy as well as a whole life shattered. If ever a woman had needed a caring doctor, Christie had. But Christie had used no doctor at all.

'And then she had Rose...'

'She had to ask for help then.' Tina's voice was bleak, and Jock knew she was kicking herself for not being here. For not having guessed something was wrong. 'She didn't have a car—it had been leased and there was no money to meet the payments—so when she went into labour she walked over to the nearest neighbour and asked her to take her to the hospital. The neighbour isn't particularly kind, but when she saw the state Christie was in...well, the woman knows me a little. When Rose was two weeks old she managed to track me down and said...just that I ought to come.'

'And you did.' Jock's eyes were open again now. He was watching Tina, watching her haunted face. Watching the pain behind her eyes. Watching the expressions flit from bleakness to despair.

'I did—and Christie was almost dead,' Tina told him, and Jock knew she was hardly registering that he was there at all. She was only seeing Christie. 'Christie was feeding them all but she was doing nothing else. She was barely talking and she wasn't feeding herself. I tried to take her to hospital here but she just disintegrated. So I took her down to Sydney.'

'Without the baby?'

'There's no problem about Christie bonding with Rose,' Tina said bleakly, 'But...what she desperately needs is time for herself. Time to recover her strength and start thinking about the future. Time to figure out that there is life after what's happened to her.'

'Time to figure that there's life after pride,' Jock said softly, and Tina's eyes flew to his face.

'You understand,' she said wonderingly. Her eyes met his across the table, and Tina found herself fighting an unexpected feeling of warmth. She'd been alone with this nightmare for so long and now... Now comfort was coming from a source where she'd least expected it.

More than comfort. A feeling of... A feeling she didn't understand in the least, as though this man was part of her.

Good grief! She shook her head as if she didn't understand herself. She didn't. 'It's just...it seems crazy,' she faltered, trying hard to get a grip on herself. 'But Christie's always been so strong. She's always been a mover and shaker. For this to happen... It shook her foundations, brought her crashing down. She's so ill...'

'How long will she be in hospital?'

'I might bring her home next week,' Tina said doubtfully. 'The kids and I are going to see her on Sunday.' She hesitated. 'Though I guess I could take them to see her now... Now I don't have a job.'

'You do have a job.' Jock reached over the table and gripped her hands. The feeling of her soft hands in his was...well...great! 'Hell, Tina... You're as bad as Christie. To not tell anyone...'

'I did tell people,' Tina told him. She looked down at their linked hands for a long moment, as if trying to figure out where the warmth was coming from. From where the comfort was flowing. Finally it seemed to register that her hands had been there too long, and she hauled them away reluctantly. And Jock was just as reluctant to release them.

'I told Ellen and Struan and Gina,' she continued, only a slight flush of crimson showing that she had been aware of the warmth between their hands. 'Struan knew why I wanted the locum job and then, when Christie had to go into hospital, I told Ellen what was happening. She told the rest of the night shift nurses. Christie will hate it, but people have to know.'

'You could have told me.'

'Not when—'

'Not when you thought it was me who'd treated Christie like this,' Jock said grimly, meeting her look directly across the table. 'Discharging her without checking...'

'I'm sorry.' Tina took a deep breath, forcing herself to concentrate on the man before her rather than on her sister's troubles. And forcing herself to concentrate on what he was saying rather than on the strange sensations she was starting to feel.

'Jock, I'm so sorry I thought it was you,' she told him in a voice that wasn't quite steady, 'but Christie was definite that it was you who delivered her. And... Well, whoever it was, he needs to be struck off.' Tina's voice was tight with pain. She looked across at Jock, willing him to understand.

'Jock, Christie was anorexic. She weighs seven stone, for heaven's sake. They weighed her when she was admitted in Sydney. For him not to see... And you hired him,' she added, a flash of the old fire shooting out Jock-wards.

'I know. I accept responsibility there.' Jock gave a rueful grimace. 'Hell, Tina, I didn't get it right. But tell me how I can get it right now.' He looked searchingly over the table at her. She seemed such a slip of a girl to have this burden thrust on her—to be inundated with kids and responsibility. He kept on looking and his gut gave a savage twist. For him to have caused such pain... What price a holiday to London? 'How can I help now?' he asked.

Tina's response was fast and to the point.

'Give me my job back.'

'Of course.' Jock frowned. 'But... Tina, should you be working at all? You have your hands full.'

'I do,' Tina admitted, 'but I'm almost as broke as Christie.'

'I don't understand.' Jock's frown deepened. 'You've been qualified for a while now. You won't have been earning peanuts.'

'Would you believe I have massive gambling debts?' Tina's irrepressible twinkle flashed out and Jock blinked. For her to laugh... For her to have all this on her shoulders and to *laugh*!

'No.' He barely managed a matching smile. His gut

was doing strange wrenching things that he didn't understand at all. 'I wouldn't believe it. So tell me the truth.'

Tina hesitated but only for a second. Her finances had nothing to do with Jock. Her family had nothing to do with Jock, but the warmth behind his dark eyes told her that he really wanted to know, and his concern was irresistible. In fact, Jock Blaxton was irresistible.

Outside, they could hear the children laughing together as they carried the eggs toward the house.

'We've got seven,' Ally was shouting. 'Seven!'

'Car!' said Tim. 'Car.'

'We'll put the eggs down here and have a look at the car,' Ally said seriously. 'But just for a minute, Tim, 'cos Aunty Tina's waiting.'

So was Jock. Waiting for Tina to tell him everything.

'Our parents died I was sixteen and Christie was nineteen,' Tina told him slowly, her eyes still on his face. 'I worked my way through medical school, but I couldn't cover all my expenses. Christie helped—which is one of the reasons I feel so bad now. So responsible that she's broke. But I also had to borrow and I'm still paying off loans. Much as I'd like to spend the next six months with Christie and the children, I can't afford to.'

'Let me help.'

Tina looked oddly across the table at him.

'With another loan?' She shook her head. She found that easy enough to resist. 'No. Thank you, Dr Blaxton, but no.'

'What would you like to do now?' Jock demanded. 'If money was no object.'

'That's crazy. I can't—'

'Just tell me.'

This man... He had such a magnetic, powerful personality. It was as if somehow he could wave a magic wand and make everything better. Which, of course, he couldn't. No one could, not even the great Jock Blaxton. But Jock was waiting for an answer to his ridiculous question.

'I guess... If I had my druthers, I'd take the children to Sydney until Christie is well enough to come home. And then I'd continue working here the way I have been.'

'Taking Rose into work with you? Paying someone to be here?'

'That's right.'

'It won't work.'

'I know. I can't afford—'

'Regardless of what you can and can't afford, you can't take Rose back into the hospital,' Jock said firmly. 'Christie doesn't want a baby with golden staph, and I don't want a nursery of children infected by a child who's in and out of the community. No. This is what you'll do.'

'I beg your pardon—'

'Tina, the locum I hired helped cause this mess.' Jock was watching the girl on the other side of the table intently, as if trying to figure out the workings of a strange and unfamiliar piece of machinery. Some machinery! 'If you were a different sort of person then you could sue the pants off me.'

Good grief! Tina's eyes flew to Jock's face and she gave an involuntary choke of laughter. Suing the pants off Jock Blaxton... It had its appealing points. *Good grief!* Her colour rose.

'I wouldn't—'

'No. But you could sue Henry for negligence and unprofessional conduct, and that would embarrass me professionally. As you say, I hired him and I'm responsible for his actions. So we'll settle out of court.'

'I told you, Dr Blaxton, I won't—'

'Tina, I'm settling with your sister. Not you.'

'But—'

'Shut up, Tina,' Jock said kindly. 'You might not have much money, but I do. I've been qualified for years and I'm single. I spend my money on cars and not much else. So... There's a lady living a couple of miles down the road from here and she's looking for a job. She has an outdated mothercraft nursing qualification. She's only just moved here and she came into the hospital last week to see if there was any work. Until she upgrades her qualifications there isn't work for her at the hospital, but there is here. So...'

'Jock, I—'

'Shut up,' he said again. 'I'm not doing this for you, Tina Rafter. I'm doing it for your sister, and you have no right to refuse on her behalf. So I'll employ Marie to work here. Full time, sleeping over as needed. She'll do it and she'll love it. And the kids will love her.'

'But—'

'You take the kids down to Sydney, bring Christie home and settle everything down. Make sure you're happy with Marie. Then come back to work.'

'I can't take time off.'

'You resigned,' Jock said firmly. 'You resigned in front of witnesses. So now you can't come back until I say so. And that's not until everyone's ready. Until Christie and Marie are coping with the children.'

'You can't take my workload...'

'I'll share your workload with the others.' Jock gave an inward shrug. So much for spending time searching for a replacement for his own job, as he'd intended. Somehow it didn't matter so much now. Not when Tina's eyes were watching him with a trace of hope behind her despair. 'We've coped with a shortage of medical staff before and we'll do it again. Don't argue, Dr Rafter. Just do it.'

'Jock, I can't.'

But Jock simply reached across the table and took her hands in his again. That one simple action took her breath away. It stopped her protests dead.

'Yes, you can,' he said gently. 'You can, Tina. Your responsibility is to your sister and to her children. And, because of my dreadful locum, I share that responsibility. So move over and let me share.'

'Jock…' Tina looked helplessly up into Jock's eyes and was lost, hopelessly, bewilderingly lost. Half an hour ago she'd hated this man. And now… Now he was gripping her fingers and her body was doing all sorts of strange things in return—and she didn't know whether she was Arthur or Martha. Martha, she thought suddenly, very definitely Martha. If Jock was Arthur.

He was expecting her to speak when it was as much as she could do to get her mouth open. Worse, she had to think of something intelligent to say. Ally and Tim saved her. They'd obviously finished their car inspection. They burst through the door, bearing a bowl full of eggs, and they stopped short when they saw their Aunty Tina holding hands across the table with this interesting man, the owner of the wonder car.

'You're holding hands,' Ally said, and she frowned, working things out. 'Does this mean you're going to be friends?'

Tina tried to drag her hands away, but Jock would have none of it.

'Yes, Ally, it means just that,' Jock said solemnly, and it was as if he were taking a vow. His grip on Tina's slender fingers tightened. 'It means that from now on your Aunt Tina and I are definitely friends. For just as long as it takes to get you guys all back together again as a family.'

Or maybe longer?

Family.

After eating a wonderful omelette and taking the two

children for a drive along the track leading to the house—he'd sat them on his knee one at a time and let them steer, and the kids were now friends for life—Jock drove home from Tina's dilapidated cottage, and for some reason the word kept resounding in his head.

Family.

It sounded good. No, it didn't, Jock told himself savagely, hauling his head back into line. It sounded claustrophobic. It sounded like prison. Family meant committing yourself to one person, and committing yourself to one person meant kids, mortgage, school fees—the full catastrophe. And then something would happen, as it had for Christie and as it had for Jock's parents. One partner walks away. Or one partner dies...

Jock thought back to the last time he'd seen his father, nearly fifteen years ago. Jock's father was a man who'd committed everything he had to his marriage. When his wife died, Sam Blaxton had been left with nothing but a hard, bitter shell, with no capacity to love at all.

He'd made his son's life hell.

Jock bit his lip and steered his little car out around the headland, enjoying the feel of the sea breeze against his face. He wanted none of it, the love bit. Marriage. Babies. He didn't want a bar of it.

This was what he wanted. Freedom. The wind in his face. The freedom to pick up his life and move on, as he would as soon as he had Tina and her tribe back on their feet again. How would it feel—to be as committed as Tina was to her family? He thought of the burden the girl was carrying and blenched inwardly. Debt. A sister totally dependent on her, and those three little lives...

Maybe it would have been better for Christie to abort the baby, he thought savagely. To bring another little life into this mess... Tina didn't have one baby too many to care for. She had a whole tribe too many. But then

he thought back to Rose's perfect little face. Her red
hair. The baby was going to have flaming hair, just like
the others. Just like Tina's.

Hell, what was he thinking of?

Just get back to work, and start organising, he told
himself savagely. The one thing he did not want was to
involve himself emotionally, not now, not ever. He'd
seen what lay down that road. All it led to was disaster.

Tina came back to work a week later. Jock didn't hear
about it. He was suffering serious sleep deprivation after
two nights awake, and the night of Tina's return he hit
the pillow at seven p.m. At five in the morning she called
him. Funny how a voice could get under your skin.
Tina's voice, soft and melodic, sounded down the phone
and it was like an extension of a dream.

'Jock?'

Jock had to shake himself to convince himself the
voice was real. Tina calling to him through sleep was
surely a dream. He lay on the pillows with the telephone
receiver in his hand and thought really hankering
thoughts about Tina.

'Jock?'

That woke him up. There was urgency in the way she
spoke his name for the second time. He hauled himself
back to being a doctor on call.

'I'm here, Tina!'

'Jock, I'm sorry,' she said, and her voice said she truly
was sorry to have to wake him. 'But Mrs Blythe's just
come in and we need you right away.'

Mrs Blythe...

Jock frowned. Julie Blythe was a young primigrav-
ida—a mum giving birth for the first time. He'd expect
that if she'd just presented there'd be a long wait before
delivery. It wasn't normal to call in the consultant as
soon as a woman arrived in labour.

'Is there a problem?' He knew the answer before Tina spoke.

'Yes. Posterior presentation and she's waited too long to come in.'

'Posterior...'

'She really is in trouble, Jock. I think... Maybe a Caesarean, but she may have left it too late.'

'Ring Lloyd, then, and give him warning,' Jock snapped, his senses now fully tuned to medicine. If they had to do a Caesarean then they needed three doctors. He could do the delivery and Tina could do the anaesthetic but they needed another doctor for the baby.

'I don't know if a Caesarean's possible,' Tina faltered. 'Jock, hurry. I'm out of my depth here. This lady... She needs you now, Jock.'

So do I, Tina thought as she put the phone down and wondered how long it would take Jock to get to the hospital. So do I...

Jock was there in four minutes flat, breaking all legal limits and a few illegal ones to cover the half-mile trip from his beachfront house to the hospital. Tina's voice had been urgent and distressed, and he knew enough of Tina by now to respond. She wouldn't put that urgency into her voice if there wasn't a need.

One look at Mrs Blythe and he knew that Tina had been dead right when she'd made her voice urgent. It was the admitting officer's job to assess all patients as they arrived during the night. Jock's workload was too heavy to assume total care of patients through a long labour. The hospital was set up so that the admitting officer—casualty officer at night and thus Tina—checked the mothers as they arrived, did what had to be done and then called Jock as needed.

Tina had called Jock the moment she'd seen Julie Blythe, and then she'd sent the nursing staff to set up Theatre. He went to Labour Ward and was redirected to

Theatre—so Tina was still thinking Caesarean. He pushed through the swing doors of Theatre with a frown.

'What on earth…?' A posterior presentation didn't mean an automatic Caesarean, but Tina must have reasons for bringing Julie here. She did.

'Dr Blaxton, Mrs Blythe's been in labour for twenty-four hours,' Tina said, without looking up. She was setting up a drip, her face tight with strain. 'Mrs Blythe's husband was away and she didn't think the contractions were strong enough to worry about. Then, after her husband came home, things just got out of hand.'

'OK.' Jock walked swiftly over to the table and gave the frightened young mother's hand a reassuring squeeze. 'You have the full complement of labour staff here now, Mrs Blythe. Let's just see what this youngster of yours is doing.'

Julie Blythe was almost past responding. Her eyes were dulled with pain and she looked exhausted almost to death. As well she might. Two minutes later Jock's face was as strained as Tina's.

The baby was fully into the birth canal—as far down as it could go—but its posterior presentation meant that it could go no further. The relentless rhythmic contractions were causing swelling to the baby's head, meaning every moment the baby was in that position it was less likely to be born naturally. And it was so far down…

'I don't know if you can do a Caesar,' Tina said hesitantly. 'The baby's so close. But I thought…'

Her eyes flickered to the monitor. Leads ran from Julie's distended abdomen and the monitor showed how the baby was managing its fight for survival. It wasn't managing well. The heartbeat was faltering, and there was meconium staining adding to the overwhelming impression that whatever was to be done had to be done *fast*.

And Jock moved!

His orders came thick and fast, and Tina barely had time to be stunned. She'd expected a dead baby out of this. One look at this presentation and she'd almost given up hope. The imperative had to be to save Julie's life, but to get a live baby as well... Jock was going for it, and Tina followed orders with a gratitude that made her feel physically weak. Thank heaven for technical expertise. Thank heaven for specialists.

Thank heaven for Jock.

Under Jock's orders, Tina administered a pudendal block and then she watched as Jock's lubricated fingers carefully examined...felt the resistance, carefully probing for any room at all... Surely he couldn't deliver it normally, Tina thought, astounded. Surely...

'I want Kjelland's forceps,' Jock snapped, and then he was carefully adjusting the forceps...and then easing...forcing...the baby back, using all his strength and skill to rotate and push the baby back up the birth canal. Tina could only gaze in bewilderment as she followed Jock's snapped orders. She'd never seen this before. To push the baby back...

Whatever Jock was doing was working. The relentless contractions were easing, and Jock was pressing the baby away from the outside world.

'It's OK, Julie,' he murmured, through no one could know how much the young mother was taking in. 'We'll get this youngster out yet to meet his mama.' Jock didn't tell her that what he was doing was just the opposite to delivering a baby—forcing the child away from where it most wanted to be. 'You just hang in there...'

Then, to Tina, he added softly, 'Where's the father?'

'He's out in the waiting room. I thought...'

Jock nodded. He knew what Tina thought. Most obstetricians removed onlookers if things looked complicated. To work under this type of life-and-death stress was bad enough, but to work under stress with terrified relatives watching was worse. But Julie Blythe was fading. Her breathing was rapid and shallow, and shock was setting in.

'Sister, ask Mr Blythe to come in,' Jock said. 'Julie needs all the support she can get here.'

A moment later a white-faced young man stumbled into the room. He made it to his wife's side, gripped her hand as if he were drowning and sat down hard on the chair that the nurse provided. Tina had the overwhelming impression that he was sicker than his wife. Jock waited until the young man was seated to speak to both of them.

'We're going to perform a Caesarean section,' he told them. 'Now.'

His eyes signalled his staff and Tina and the nurses moved swiftly to set up screens across the woman's breast and begin the process of anaesthetic block. Tina was working on automatic pilot, following Jock blindly. Had he moved the baby high enough to perform a Caesarean? She wouldn't have thought so.

'Mr Blythe, I want you to support your wife,' Jock was saying. 'Julie, can you hear me? Focus here, Mrs Blythe. You're OK and we're nearly there. The baby will be here soon, but we need to perform a Caesarean. You know what that is. We make a small slit in your tummy and lift the baby out. The baby's head's too swollen to deliver normally. I'll deliver the baby now, but I don't want to give you a general anaesthetic. I want you to be wide awake to greet this baby.'

What Jock wasn't saying was that he was doubtful whether Julie—or the baby—were in a fit condition to cope with a general anaesthetic. Tina figured it out for herself—and then blocked it out. She forced herself to think solely about her anaesthetic skills. Only that. She had to focus solely on her job and ignore the anxiety of the young man and his wife.

'I think I might be sick. I...I don't know if I can stay,' the young man faltered, but Jock was having none of it.

'Julie has no choice and she needs you beside her,' Jock growled. 'Just hang on tight, and concentrate on caring for Julie. Talk her through this, Mr Blythe. You're all she has and she needs you.'

He turned to check monitors again.

'Lloyd's not here yet,' Tina told him. 'He was out at a call when I rang. Sally said he'd be here in ten minutes.'

All eyes were on those monitors. Jock's eyes narrowed. It was a risk to bring a baby into the world without another doctor ready to receive it to resuscitate if necessary. But another look at the monitors told him that the risks were worse if they waited. He gave Tina a grim, silent message with his eyes and Tina read the monitors and knew.

There was simply no time left at all. Those monitors had to keep up their message that this baby was still alive until Tina's anaesthetic could work, but that was all they could wait for. They must... And somehow they did. The anaesthetic took over. Jock waited until a last weak contraction passed—almost non-existent now. He checked the position of the baby's head once again— now as far back up the birth canal as he could get it— and then he took a deep, steadying breath—and cut.

Two minutes later a tiny sliver of a baby girl emerged to greet a new world, and after that suddenly everything was magically, wonderfully, OK again.

Lloyd burst in as the baby emerged, just in time. He cleared the baby's airway and checked the little one while Tina kept tabs on the anaesthetic and Jock stitched the wound. By the time Jock put in the first stitch their new arrival was wailing her lungs out. Lloyd was hardly needed.

'Is this all you kept me out of bed for?' he demanded,

but his eyes twinkled. Lloyd had babies of his own and Lloyd loved babies. He wasn't a paediatrician, he was a physician, but he was thoroughly enjoying looking after Gina's paediatric practice while she and Struan were away.

'One healthy baby? One gorgeous little girl?' Lloyd beamed at both parents. 'Congratulations to the pair of you, but I'm back to bed. Your daughter doesn't need a doctor and I only have an hour or so before my tribe wake up.' The physician grinned at Jock and Tina, sketched them a mock salute and took himself back to bed.

Jock finished his suturing and turned to check what Tina was doing.

'I want two million units of penicillin in that drip,' he told Tina, and she looked up from adjusting the drip stand and stared.

'Two million...' She frowned. 'Surely not. It was a straightforward Caesar—'

'Two million,' Jock snapped, and there was a sudden tense silence in the room.

'OK.' Tina shrugged. She hadn't meant to query him. It wasn't her place as anaesthetist to question the obstetrician, but the dosage was certainly high. It couldn't do any harm, though. It would certainly stop any hint of infection in its tracks, and the tension cleared again. With the drip adjusted, the orderly wheeled Julie off to Maternity, her husband following her trolley like a puffed-up lion. Bill Blythe had grown a full six inches with the advent of fatherhood. Ellen took the baby off to the nursery to be washed and dressed, and Jock and Tina were left alone.

CHAPTER FOUR

ALL of a sudden the silence was deafening. Awkward even. There was a tenseness between them that Tina couldn't fathom. It was as if there was a frisson, running back and forth. An electric current that had nowhere to go except between their two bodies.

'I'm sorry about the antibiotic,' Tina said awkwardly. 'I didn't mean to question you. It's just that it's not the usual dose.'

'I like to be sure,' replied Jock.

'I guess…'

It had been the dosage Tina would have given if the Caesar had been done in less than aseptic conditions, though. There had to be a reason for it. Still… Hers not to reason why. She was the junior doctor here, and Jock's obstetric skills were certainly not in question.

'I guess you should go back to bed, too,' Tina said slowly as she crossed to the sink. 'I'm sorry I had to wake you.'

Jock's frown cleared. 'Don't be sorry. It's worth waking to get a result like this.'

'If she'd left it any longer she could have died. And the baby almost did.'

'Yes.'

Both of them fell silent, knowing just how close they'd come to the edge. If Jock hadn't been so skilled…

'I wasn't expecting you to be back at work so soon,' Jock said brusquely, shoving unwelcome scenarios aside. 'I thought Sally was looking after the hospital tonight.'

'She was, but we arrived back from Sydney yesterday

in time for me to attend Mary's kitchen tea—I'm chief bridesmaid, you know, so I have an obligation. Then I rang in and said I'd take over for the night.' Tina gave a prim little smile. 'Christie's come back with me, and Marie's every bit as competent as you promised in looking after Christie and the children. So I'm back. I like to carry my own workload, Dr Blaxton.'

'I can see that.' Jock hauled off his theatre gown and hurled it down the laundry chute with more force than was necessary. The gesture helped get rid of some of the damned electricity he was feeling. Electricity? Whatever it was. Whatever... 'How's your sister?'

'Better.'

'Define better.'

'She's not at death's door any more,' Tina said, and Jock looked up from turning on the taps, startled.

'Was she ever? Isn't that being a bit melodramatic?'

'Meaning she wasn't at death's door when she went to Sydney?' Tina shrugged. 'I think she was. She'd stopped eating. Things were way out of control.' Tina took a deep breath. 'The real reason I insisted on her being admitted to a psychiatric hospital was that she needed medical care but I was afraid of suicide.'

'And now?'

'Now she's eating again. She's rested. She's talking sense. So it's up to me...to me and the kids to bring her back, and we will.'

Jock's frown deepened. 'If she really was that bad, then it'll take months.'

'I know that. I have months.'

Jock's eyebrows furrowed, concerned. 'But what about your own life during these months?' he asked gently, watching Tina's face as he washed the talcum from his ungloved hands. 'Tell me. What were you doing in Brisbane when you dropped everything to come here?'

'You already know some of it,' Tina said doubtfully. It was weird, standing at the sinks beside this man. Weirdly intimate. She'd spent heaps of time in operating theatres in her medical career, but with Jock it was a whole new feeling. Weird! She took a long, slow breath, trying to sort sense from her jumbled thoughts. 'I imagine you saw what I've done from reading my résumé when I applied for the job here.'

Jock nodded, remembering Tina's curriculum vitae. 'I remember. You'd just finished your first part anaesthetics—for which Julie Blythe, Bill Blythe, young Blythe junior and I are profoundly grateful. That was a skilled anaesthetic job you did there.' Ignoring Tina's flush of pleasure, he kept right on probing. 'So you hadn't found a registrar position for your anaesthetic second part?'

'I... Yes, I had, but—'

'But you abandoned your plans—and your job—to come here.' Jock nodded. 'That's what I thought. With the skills you have, finding a registrar job would be no problem. But to give it up... That means a year out of your career plans. The registrar jobs don't come up again until early next year.'

'Someone might drop out and create a vacancy.' That's what Tina had told herself. She'd agonised for a whole two minutes about giving up her job. There hadn't been a choice, but she'd known what she was losing. 'I might be lucky.'

'But you might not.' Jock looked at her curiously across the sinks. 'And how about your social life? Do you have a boyfriend?'

Tina flushed again. Drat the man, he really had the power to unsettle her. 'That's none of your business.'

But Jock was reading her face and to Tina's disgust he did it with ease. 'So there is someone waiting patiently in the wings?'

Tina thought of Peter, waiting patiently back in

Sydney. That was exactly how she'd describe him. Peter waiting patiently in the wings for some spark to ignite between them. She and Peter suited each other—they had heaps in common but maybe not enough for marriage, and both of them knew it. Peter was a sweetheart, a patient sweetheart. It was a pity he was a sweetheart who didn't make her toes curl.

'If you must know, I do have a boyfriend,' she said, and she couldn't make her voice sound the way she wanted. She was willing her voice to sound warm, definite and sure. Instead, all she sounded was defensive. 'His name's Peter.'

'Peter's another doctor?'

'He's a surgeon.'

'Bully for Peter.' Jock's voice wasn't quite under control either. There was a growl of anger underneath that neither he nor Tina understood. 'Is he coming to see you next weekend?'

'No.' Tina flashed Jock a startled glance. 'Why should he?'

'Did you see him in Sydney?'

Good grief! Tina glowered and backed away from the sinks. 'Of course I did. What is this, Dr Blaxton? A private grilling? Me and Peter—'

'You and your Peter are nothing to do with me,' Jock agreed, and he flashed out his smile again. The smile that had Tina's toes doing the sorts of things she wished Peter could make them do. 'I know it's none of my business,' he added. 'It's just...'

Then Jock hesitated, as if he was suddenly about to do something that might not be wise. Then he shrugged. 'Tina, the hospital dance is on Saturday night. I need someone to come with me.'

Tina's eyebrows rose. Her stomach was turning somersaults and so were her toes, but she managed to keep her face straight. 'Really?'

'Really.'

'Well, I can't see the problem. I imagine there'll be a queue,' she managed dryly.

'What's that supposed to mean?'

'Meaning, according to the nursing staff, finding a date has never been a problem for you.'

It was Jock's turn to raise his eyebrows. 'Tina, are you accusing me of being a playboy?'

Tina considered. 'Yes,' she said at last, and managed a grin. 'I've heard that's exactly what you are. According to the nurses, you never take anyone out more than twice.'

'Is that a problem for you?'

'Oh, not for me, it's not,' Tina said cheerfully. 'But, then, I'm not in the market for a long-term relationship.'

'Because you have one with Peter.'

'Because I have one with Peter,' she agreed flatly, trying to ignore the weird sensation still coursing round in her toes. 'What's your excuse?' As she watched Jock's face, Tina frowned. 'There really is a reason, isn't there, Dr Blaxton? There's a reason you don't take women out more than twice.'

'I...'

'You're not gay, are you?'

Jock stared, and then he choked.

'No, Dr Rafter, I am *not* gay. Do I seem gay?'

'N-no.' She looked sideways up at him and managed a grin. Good grief! Masculinity—sheer arrant sex appeal—oozed out of every pore of this man. 'I guess not.'

'*You guess...*'

That got her laughing out loud. There was no way she could keep a straight face before his incredulity. 'No.' Then, at the look of Jock's affronted face—and as he took two threatening steps toward her—she held up wet hands to fend him off. 'OK. I know you're not. But...'

'But what?'

'Why don't you take women out more than twice?'

That was easy. 'They fall in love with me,' he complained.

'Oh.' Tina grinned. 'Silly me. Now why didn't I think of that for an answer?'

'You're laughing at me.'

'Yep.'

'Dr Rafter...'

She backed another step. 'You don't think you just might sound a touch conceited here?'

It was Jock's turn to smile then. 'I guess I do at that,' he conceded. 'I'm sorry. I'm just not in the market for "serious".'

Tina considered. 'So what's so appalling about someone getting serious?' she demanded. 'You might just like it.'

'Nope.'

'That's very definite.'

'It is.'

Tina's laughter died as she heard the note of gravity beneath his words. 'Do you want to tell me why?'

Jock's laughter faded as well.

'Let's just say I don't wish to share the experience.' He shrugged. 'However... Seeing you're nicely settled with your Peter, but your Peter's in Sydney... Seeing you're not in the market for a long-term relationship... How do you feel about coming to the dance with me on Saturday night?'

He smiled again, and Tina's heart did a backward somersault. Which it had no business doing, she thought crossly, not with Peter waiting patiently in the wings. So what should she do here? Ignore the somersaults? Ignore the curling toes?

If she *could* ignore them then maybe it would be fun, Tina thought. Life had been altogether too serious for too long now, and Christie was feeling guilty about Tina

being here. Apart from Mary's kitchen tea, Tina had had
no social life at all since she'd returned here to live. With
Marie living in, there was nothing to stop her enjoying
herself now. If Christie could see that she was getting
out...having fun... It would be fun to go out with Jock.

Jock Blaxton... He was smiling at her, waiting for an
answer, and his eyes were dark and kind and warm.
Involuntarily, Tina's toes did their curling bit again and
she struggled to straighten them. For heaven's sake—
what was happening here? Keep it light, keep it casual!

'Well...' Tina's face grew thoughtful. How to keep
this as casual as possible... 'Maybe. But...'

'But?'

Jock was using her, Tina decided, using her as a date
to serve his own ends. So she could use him just the
same.

'The dance is an after-dinner affair,' she said thoughtfully. 'So... I'll be your date for the dance if you come
and have a picnic first with Christie and the children and
me.'

'What, out at the cottage?' he asked, startled.

'Yep.' She grinned. It was time Christie had a bit of
company—time she saw other people—and Tina knew
Jock well enough to know he'd be empathic. 'If I work
every night until then, I'll be off duty from Friday. So
Saturday afternoon I'll be raring to go, and so will the
children. There's a big dam out behind the ridge. Bring
your bathers, we'll take the children for a swim, have
tea and then come in to the dance.'

'Take the children...'

'You don't mind a bit of domesticity, do you?' Tina
asked demurely. 'Or is that what you're running from,
Jock?'

'No.' Jock shook his head and smiled. 'I don't mind
a bit of domesticity. As long as it's not my own.'

'That's OK, then.' Tina smiled straight back at him,

ignoring the odd lurch in her innards. 'We have a date. I'll see you on Saturday. About four?'

'About four. I'll look forward to it.'

But suddenly Jock wasn't sure whether he was looking forward to it or not. The same old fear reached out to clutch him. Usually it was after the first couple of dates that he felt like this, like running a mile. But now... With this girl the fear was striking early. Tina was *not* interested in him, he told himself savagely. *Not!* She had a life to lead. As soon as she had her sister back on her feet she'd be off back to Sydney. Off to her boyfriend. There was no risk to him to take her out. So why did he feel as if his foundations were shifting from under him?

'Babies permitting,' he reminded her, and suddenly he thought that babies might be just what was called for here. He needed a good long labour next Saturday afternoon to get him out of this swim and dinner. Then he needed to free a couple of hours to collect Tina and make his token appearance at the dance. Then he needed another labour to follow.

That's what he needed. It was unfortunate that he couldn't make babies come on demand.

'I hope you don't get a baby, then,' Tina said lightly—and Jock could only agree with her.

'I don't know about you going to this dance with Jock.'

Tina was in the nursery with Ellen, before going off duty. Tina hadn't been able to resist having a last look at young Laura Blythe. Two hours old and already making her presence felt from one end of the hospital to the other, Laura was *some* baby. She was gorgeous. Unable to resist, Tina lifted her out of her cot and cuddled her close.

'Listen you, your mummy's asleep. You give her a

couple of hours' grace before you start demanding tucker.'

The baby gave an indignant wuffle and snuggled her face into Tina's breast. Two hours old and she already knew exactly what she wanted. No wonder she'd survived. This little one had taken a huge battering. She was a survivor in anyone's books.

'You like babies, don't you?' Ellen said softly, and Tina smiled.

'Isn't it obvious?'

'You'd like to have your own one day?'

'Well, of course.'

'I don't think Dr Blaxton does.'

'No?' Tina cradled the little one closer, trying not to be too interested. There was no reason for her to be interested—was there? 'He likes babies, though.'

'He does.' Ellen compressed her lips in disapproval. 'He likes them from a distance—but not for keeps. He's not in the market for a long-term relationship. Anyone can see that.'

'Well, neither am I,' Tina managed lightly. 'So we should suit.'

'That's what all my nurses say before they go out with him.' Ellen sniffed. 'One after the other, I see 'em go out. One date is all it takes with *that* man. They come back with stars in their eyes. After the second date they come back and their feet don't touch the floor. Then he asks someone else out and they howl for a month—or pine, which is worse. I've had so many lovesick nurses...'

'Surely not,' Tina said, startled. 'For heaven's sake, Ellen... You make him sound like James Bond without the gun.'

'Yeah. Maybe it's a good comparison. Move over, Sean Connery.'

Tina giggled. 'It doesn't fit. His car doesn't have as many gadgets.'

'No.' But Ellen didn't giggle, and even her smile faded as she watched her young friend.

'Ellen…'

'All I'm saying is be careful,' Ellen said sternly. 'You're young and impressionable…'

'I'm twenty-eight, for heaven's sake. Nearly twenty-nine.'

'Then you're mature and impressionable. But Jock is dangerous, Tina. You mark my words.'

'Ellen, I'm going to the dance with him. That's all. I'm not about to fall for a pretty face.'

'If I thought Jock was just a pretty face I shouldn't worry.'

'Then what are you worrying about?' Tina fixed her friend with a look. 'For heaven's sake, Ellen, just what is worrying you about Jock?'

'He has ghosts.' Ellen grimaced. 'And the ghosts hurt him and everyone around him.'

'Ghosts?' Tina smiled, refusing to match Ellen's grimness. 'What sort of ghosts?'

'His mother's ghost for one. There may be more. But I doubt if any girl will get close to him. Ever.'

'So…how come Dr Blaxton has his mother's ghost tagging along for the ride?' Keep it light, Tina told herself. Keep it light, even though you desperately want to know.

Ellen shrugged. She hardly spoke of Jock's mother now. She hardly even thought of the woman who'd once been her best friend. The pain from years ago had faded. It was only when she looked at Jock's face…saw the traces of pain still lingering there…that she remembered.

'Jock's mother had an emergency Caesarean to give birth to Jock,' she said softly. 'She wasn't well looked after. She had a huge pelvic infection.'

'I see.' Tina nodded, thinking of Jock's attitude to Julie's antibiotics. 'I can understand that.'

'I'm not sure that you do,' Ellen said sadly. 'The infection didn't disappear without damage, but caused adhesions. Jock's mother needed operation after operation to correct the problems, but each operation made things worse. She was in and out of hospital for the rest of her life. She wasn't able to have more children, and she was in constant pain. The adhesions got worse and worse—and finally when Jock was ten years old they caused a complete bowel obstruction. She died just before Jock's eleventh birthday.'

'Oh, no…'

'There's worse,' Ellen said grimly. 'All of us…all of Jock's mother's friends… We wanted to help Jock so much. But Jock's father was a hard, unforgiving man. He loved his wife very much, loved her past reason. I think…watching her die, he went a little bit crazy. If she had to die, then someone had to be to blame.'

'Not Jock.'

'Jock.' Ellen closed her eyes, remembering past pain. The pain was all around her again. How could she have thought she could forget? 'Yes, Jock. Sam Blaxton blamed his son totally for his wife's death. According to Sam, they'd had one baby and that baby was one baby too many. Jock should never have been born and he was never allowed to forget it.'

'Oh, Ellen…'

'So you keep a hold on your heart when you're around Jock, my girl,' Ellen went on grimly, 'because, charming as Jock is, there are some wounds that can't be healed. He's grown up thinking that there are too many babies in the world. It's been drilled into him that even his own birth was a mistake. He's an obstetrician, and I'll bet part of the reason for his career choice was to ensure what happened to his mother doesn't happen to anyone

else. But I can't ever see him having babies of his own.
Can you?'

Jock arrived at Christie's farm right on the dot of four
o'clock on Saturday. No babies arrived to hold him up,
and when he saw Ally and Tim, hanging over the verandah rails, he couldn't be sorry he'd arrived in time to
take them for a swim. Nor could he regret it when Tina
came out the front door, wearing a scanty yellow bikini
and a baby pouch, and nothing more.

The sight of Tina acted like a hard kick in the guts,
he thought breathlessly. She looked stunning, standing
behind the verandah railings, practically naked, but with
a tiny baby pouch cradled against her naked skin…
Whew…

'Hi!' Tina came lightly down the steps toward him,
the baby bouncing happily before her, and the kicked
feeling in his gut only got worse. He was finding it hard
to breathe.

'Hi.' Jock managed to make his voice normal—but
only just. He checked her out from the toes up, but closer
inspection only got better. He was starting to feel like
he needed a ventilator. 'Are we all going swimming,
then?' he managed. 'Even Rose?'

'Silly. Rose can't swim yet.' It was four-year-old Ally,
swooping down on Jock's car and dragging Tim behind
her. 'Rose's staying with Mummy. Will you drive us to
the dam in your car?'

'Ally, we'll walk,' Tina said, laughing. 'This little car
can't drive over paddocks.' Her voice made it quite clear
what she thought of Jock's ridiculous car.

'It will so,' Jock said, offended. 'It doesn't mind the
odd bump.'

'What about tree stumps?'

'It's good at dodging.'

'There are only two seats.'

'If we're not going out onto the road, then we can all squash.'

'Oh, yeah? And come back all muddy, and squish our mud down on your leather upholstery...'

Jock glared. It was as if Tina was finding malicious enjoyment in telling him how unsuitable his car was, and Jock rose right to the bait.

'My leather will wash.'

'Are you sure?'

'Yes!'

'Well, that's great, then.' Tina gave Jock a grin of unholy amusement, and she swung Tim's small body up and plonked him in the passenger side. 'Great. You're right, Dr Blaxton. It's really too far to walk, but I don't want to get *my* car full of mud so it's very nice of you to offer your car's services.'

Then, as Jock choked in indignant laughter, Tina looked back at the house—to see a woman emerge from the front door. Jock's gaze followed hers. This must be Christie. It had to be Christie. The woman was a pale, frail echo of Tina. Same vibrant colouring—same flame-coloured hair—but on Christie the colouring looked all wrong. As if her body wasn't strong enough to support it.

Christie was painfully thin, and the hand which clung to the verandah rail had skin stretched tight and was blue-veined from emaciation. She was dressed, simply, in a cotton frock which hung on her too thin body, but Jock knew how much effort it cost severely depressed people to dress. Dressing was a sign of recovery. Christie's hair had been brushed until it shone and she was managing a tremulous smile.

'So this is your Dr Blaxton, Tina.'

'He's not my Dr Blaxton.' Tina swung her lithe body up the steps to her sister and stood beside her, gazing down at Jock. Her eyes were still twinkling mischief. 'I have him for two dates. He only ever concedes two invitations to each of his lucky ladies. Then he's off to the next conquest. So it's up to me to get as much as I can out of him on each visit.'

'Tina!' Christie sounded shocked, but she kept up her smile as Jock unwound his long body from the car and strode up the verandah to meet her. 'You'll have to excuse Tina,' she told Jock in a voice that wasn't quite steady. 'She was brought up badly.'

'I was not!' Tina grinned. 'I just have bad genes. Christie did what she could with me, but you can't make a silk purse out of a sow's ear, no matter how you try.'

Both sisters chuckled and Jock looked from Tina to Christie in astonishment. Tina was gorgeous. Tina and Christie were both gorgeous. They were all gorgeous, Jock thought desperately, looking around at this little family. They were embedded in poverty up to their ears, Christie was ill, they were fighting to stay afloat and yet they could still laugh.

Christie. Concentrate on Christie, he told himself. And block out the thought of Tina's long bare legs right there beside you!

Jock took Christie's fragile hand in his, held it hard, and concentrated. 'Hello, Mrs Maiden. I'm so glad I'm finally meeting you. I'm glad that I'm finally able to say I'm sorry I wasn't here to look after you when you had Rose.' His smile reached out to this frail woman and held her. 'I'm so sorry my locum treated you as he did,' he added gently. 'I have a lot to apologise for.'

'But…it wasn't your fault,' Christie said faintly. 'The whole thing was my fault. Tina said I should have been seeing you all through my pregnancy and you never would have let me get in this state. I know she's right, but—'

'But sometimes depression is a downward spiral, with relentless pressure keeping you down,' Jock said softly.

'There's no way you can climb out of it without help. I know. You were in shock and then you copped postnatal depression on top of it. Postnatal depression is a physical illness. It's an imbalance of hormones that we don't fully understand yet. That meant you had physical illness on top of mental strain. It's a wonder you didn't go all the way under—and yet here you are, smiling!'

'Tina makes me smile,' Christie said simply, and Jock nodded, and looked down at Tina's legs. Yeah!

'Tina would make anyone smile.'

'Does that mean I'm a joke?' Tina said huffily, hoisting Rose higher against her breast. 'Hey, Rose, do you hear that? They're accusing your Aunty Tina of being a clown.'

But Jock was back concentrating on Christie, avoiding Tina's bare toes.

'Mrs Maiden, now you're home…now you've got child care…'

'Thanks to you,' Christie told him.

'Providing child care is the least I can do after my locum's cavalier treatment of you,' Jock said bluntly. 'You're not to feel grateful. Paying Marie gets me off the hook, guiltwise. But for the rest… You're not to stop treatment now that you're home from hospital. Would you let me see you professionally?'

He heard Tina's sharp intake of breath beside him but she didn't say a word. Nothing. The whole world seemed to hang on Christie's answer.

'I don't know,' Christie said dubiously, looking up into Jock's face with doubt. 'I don't really need a—'

'You don't trust doctors,' Jock finished for her, deliberately twisting her irresolution. 'Given your experience with Henry—with my locum—I don't blame you. But I would ask for you to trust just one more time. Come and see me.'

Jock's smile was gentle—beguiling—and beside him

Tina held her breath. He lifted a notebook from his shirt pocket and flipped open its pages. 'What about Monday morning at eleven a.m.? Can you see me then? Marie could bring you in. Would you trust me that much, Mrs Maiden?'

'My name's Christie,' Christie said blankly, and Jock's smile broadened. He kept his eyes on hers, refusing to break the moment.

'Christie, then. Do you trust me?' Then he motioned to where Ally and Tim were piling water-wings, a rubber duck and various floaties into his car. 'You're trusting me to take care of Ally and Tim and Tina. How about yourself?'

'I don't—'

'Christie, please. I'm going to feel bad for the rest of my life if you don't let me help.'

Christie stared, and finally that shy, tentative smile peeped out again—an echo of Tina's smile. The promise of what might come again. 'Oh, heck... I can see why Tina says you're dangerous, Dr Blaxton,' she said softly. 'You could talk blood out of stone. Very well. I'll come in and see you on Monday morning.'

Jock caught both her hands and his smile lit his whole face.

'Hey, Christie, that's great,' he said. 'With me looking after you medically, with Tina bludgeoning you domestically, with Marie to help with the kids and with your inner strength we'll conquer this damned depression. You just see if we don't!'

'I don't think this damned depression stands a chance,' Christie said faintly. 'Not with you and Tina working on it. You two make a powerful team! You take my breath away.'

CHAPTER FIVE

'YOU were great.'

Squashed beneath children, water-wings and a vast beach-ball, it was all Tina could do to make herself heard as they bounced across the paddocks, but somehow she did and Jock grinned. This wasn't his normal sort of date, he decided. Once he'd seen Tina in her gorgeous bikini, he very much fancied having her beside him in his little car. He didn't even mind Rose cradled against her breast. But they'd left Rose with Christie.

'Marie will be here in an hour and it does Christie good to have time alone with her baby—I wanted her to come with us but she's not quite ready for that,' Tina had told him. She had organised everyone else into the car and now Jock couldn't even *see* Tina, much less appreciate her gorgeous body. But he could react to the warmth in her voice.

'How do you mean—I was great?' he asked cautiously. 'And you used the past tense. Does that mean that once I was great but now I'm a poor squirming excuse for an obstetrician and gynaecologist?'

'I meant with Christie.' Tina grinned herself and wriggled happily under a couple of squirmy bodies. Ally and Tim were holding onto the windscreen and bouncing up and down on her lap with excitement. 'How did you know she's still reluctant to see doctors?'

'I guessed. Do you think she'll come and see me?'

'Now she has a definite appointment and she's met you, she'll come. The hard part's over.' Tina's smile faded and she sighed. 'I just wish... I wish you'd been here for her when she had Rose. I wish I'd been here.'

'Don't think about it,' Jock said gently. 'We're here now. She has all the support she needs and she'll make it. She's on the other side of the abyss now, Tina.'

'Maybe.'

'She must be.' Jock steered around a tree stump and the little car bounced. 'Who's the psychiatrist who looked after her in Sydney?'

Tina told him and Jock nodded with recognition.

'She's great. If Pat Morgan said Christie's OK to come home then she's OK to come home. She wouldn't let her out of her sight if she didn't think she was recovering.'

'Yeah, well, I still want to thank you,' Tina told him, her voice distant and pensive. 'After all the bad-mouthing I did... You really were...well...great!'

The word echoed on the breeze and Jock gave himself a fast mental shake. For Tina to give him such praise when he hadn't earned it... How on earth was it possible for one slip of a girl to get under his skin like she did?

Keep it light.

'Well, what did you expect?' he demanded. He made the words smug, shoving away sensations he didn't know how to deal with and concentrating fiercely on humour. 'Great is in the job description of medical specialists,' he told her, chuckling. 'You wait. The minute you qualify as an anaesthetist you'll be great, too. The only people greater are surgeons. You call them mister and you practically have to tug a forelock every time they glide their imperial presences into your orbit.'

Tina chuckled with him, the tension eased and they set about enjoying their afternoon, which they did. They all did. The dam was just under the rise to the mountains beyond the coastal plains. It was a tiny hollow, forming a catchment for the crystal clear mountain run-off. Vast gums towered overhead, and at some stage—millions of years ago—this whole coastal plain must have all been under the sea. The remnant still remained. Magically, the north end of the dam was a sandy beach, with soft white sand and a littering of ancient sea shells.

Jock stopped his little car just before the sand and gazed in awe.

'Wow!'

'It is wow, isn't it?' Tina said softly, and then she flung open her car door and gave an Indian war whoop in glee. 'OK, kids. Last one in the water is a one-legged yabby. Let's go.'

Her bubble of excitement lasted all afternoon. Jock lay on his back and floated in the sun-warmed water, shaded from sunburn by the canopy of the vast gum trees and content to watch Tina playing with her niece and nephew.

She let him be, and that, in itself, was a novelty. Most girls Jock Blaxton dated were all over him. They'd never let their attention be deflected by two small children.

Tina was different.

He'd never met anyone like this, he thought, wondering, as he watched her. Tina took life in both hands and she wrung every last ounce of enjoyment from it. She held these two little children in thrall, towing them around the dam in their water-wings, diving under them and coming up as a 'Tina shark'. Laughing, always laughing.

She served out a picnic tea she'd made that morning and got more cream on her nose from her cream cakes than either of the children did, not being the least embarrassed when Jock pointed out her creamy nose. In fact, Tina promptly turned it into a competition, daubing each of their noses with cream and seeing who could make the best job of licking it off.

She even had Jock stretching his tongue out as far as he could, joining in their ridiculous game with the chil-

dren and Tina yelling encouragement as he finally
reached the offending cream.

'Jock's got the biggest tongue. Jock's got the biggest
tongue,' the children yelled, as Tina convulsed in laughter. Then Tina tried the same trick—and her tongue
neatly reached up and removed her cream in one dex-
trous swipe.

The children were spellbound.

'You've been practising,' Jock said accusingly, and
Tina gave him a bland smile.

'Yep. All my life. It's my one claim to fame and now
it's finally paid off. I'm not a medical specialist yet, but
I'm more great than you are at cream-licking, Jock
Blaxton. Beat that, Mr Specialist!' Then she grabbed a
child in each hand and whirled them around back into
the water. 'OK, kids. One more lap of the dam to de-
icecream and then it's time for me and Jock to dress up
and head for the dance.'

Her lovely, lithe body knifed down into the water,
with the children tumbling after, and Jock was left staring after her as if he'd been struck dumb. Good grief!
He didn't follow. He couldn't. His body seemed overcome by inertia—or was it that he just didn't trust himself to join her? To be near that lovely, near-naked
body…

So Jock lay in the sunlight on the soft sand and stared
at her in amazement as she played with her niece and
nephew, trying to figure out what he was feeling. What
was happening to him here? This was a crazy, out-of-
body experience. This girl… It was the setting, he told
himself savagely. Only the setting. This must be one of
the loveliest places in the world. But it wasn't the setting, it was Tina.

Hell!

Jock looked out over the water and watched as Tina
towed her two little charges around the dam. She was

floating on her back, her feet kicking her on strongly, and she had ropes attached to her wrists and then to a child apiece. The children were laughing and whooping and Tina was laughing and whooping right back. They were a lovely, laughing family. What would it be like? To have a family like this of his own?

Oh, yeah, sure! What was he thinking? Jock gave himself a harsh mental shake. One beautiful setting, one gorgeous girl and a couple of nice kids, and all of a sudden everything he'd promised himself for the last twenty years looked like being thrown out the window. No way. Jock let his thoughts drift back to his father. To the overwhelming bitterness his father had carried to the grave.

'You let your heart go ônce and you're stuffed for life,' his father had told him over and over. 'I wish I'd never met your mother. I fell for her and that was that. Nine months... Nine months of pregnancy and then ten years watching her die. And then having to see you every day of my life... See you in her...'

The bitterness had been all around them. It would stay with Jock for ever.

'If you fall for a woman then you're a fool,' his father had told him. 'You're not in control for the rest of your life. It's a hard lesson, boy, but if I can teach you that then it'll be a lesson well learned. Don't lose control. Not ever...'

Jock looked over the water, and he knew for the first time what his father had been trying to tell him. Because for the first time in his life he felt totally out of control.

The feeling grew worse. They took the children back to the house and showered and changed for the dance. Jock took first shower and then chatted easily to Christie, Marie and the children while he waited for Tina. He lifted Rose from her crib and played with her—hey, she was smiling already—and the time flew. And to Jock's astonishment Tina took only fifteen minutes.

Fifteen minutes to be ready for a dance! Jock had resigned himself to wait for an hour. As she came out the bedroom door he stared in incredulity. And kept on staring.

'What's wrong?' Tina smiled across the room at him, her laughing eyes mocking. She twirled. 'Is my dress too short?'

Too short!

It was short, Jock acknowledged. It was tiny. It was a tiny wisp of crimson, with pencil-slim shoulder straps, a plunging neckline front and back, figure-hugging form at the waist and then a skirt that flared softly out around her thighs. Soft silk, diaphanous folds which ended just below her…just below…

Jock swallowed.

Just below her hips. Just! And her legs… Tina was all legs and they were *some* legs! She was wearing shimmering silver stockings that showed her beautifully curved thighs and calves to perfection. She wore high, high stilettos and she looked… She looked a million dollars.

'Your hair's still wet,' Marie said blandly. The middle-aged mothercraft nurse was watching Jock's face with interest. 'You'll catch your death!'

'It takes ages to blow-dry and it'll dry by itself in Jock's car,' Tina retorted. 'If he leaves the roof down.' Tina swung her mass of damp curls around her shoulders and smiled down at Jock. 'Does your little car have hair-drying in its job description?'

Gorgeous! She was gorgeous! Jock cleared his throat and rose from where he'd been sitting at the table with Christie and Marie. He didn't look too bad himself, Tina thought as she watched him rise. In fact… In his deep black dinner suit Jock looked downright stunning. Smashing! And holding Rose in his arms… He looked so right. he was so good with babies! What a waste that he wouldn't consider one of his own.

He was born husband material. Born lover material!

Whoa... Where were her thoughts leading her? Tina couldn't afford to think what she was thinking, she told herself severely, because this was her first date with this man and after the second date there was nothing more. She knew that. She'd heard it from everyone, Jock included. She could still think he was good-looking, she told herself. Just...just not that he was desirable.

'Tina, do you think that dress is short enough?' Christie was asking dryly. 'You don't think you should hitch it up a bit at the shoulders?'

'It'll be a shirt if I do.' Tina chuckled. 'It's only just hiding my knickers as it is.'

The wind was right out of Jock's lungs. He was finding it harder and harder to breathe. Marie and Christie were watching his face and he was finding it harder and harder to keep an expression on his face which wasn't completely facile. He felt like a fawning Labrador puppy, dearly wanting to wag his tail.

'You want to leave now?' Tina glanced down at her wrist-watch—the only piece of jewellery she'd allowed herself on her creamy skin. 'It's seven-thirty. Hand Rose back to her mother and let's go, Dr Blaxton, while that bleeper of yours stays silent. We don't know how long we have before another baby comes along. So let's enjoy what time we have.'

Jock thought fleetingly back to his wish that he be called out tonight to a couple of complicated deliveries. If he was called now, he'd slit his throat, he thought. Tina was coming to the hospital dance as his partner— *his partner*—and the thought took his breath away.

The dance was wonderful.

Tina enjoyed herself immensely, but afterwards Jock

could remember only snatches. Snatches of memory, such as his colleague, Lloyd Neale, meeting Tina for the first time out of her doctor's uniform and staring at her as if he'd been struck as dumb as Jock. And Sally coming up and tucking her hand possessively in her husband's arm.

'You're a happily married man, Lloyd Neale so you can take your eyes off Tina's dress—or rather, lack of dress—and leave her to Jock.' Then Sally, gorgeous herself in a soft cream dress that suited her figure to perfection, smiled happily at Tina. 'Though I'd think something was wrong with my Lloyd if he didn't look. You look fabulous, Tina. Take her away, Jock, and hold her close or we'll have to put blinkers on every other man in the room.'

So Jock did just that. He whirled Tina onto the dance floor and placed his hands on her slim, compliant waist and drew her in to him... The room spinning... Being tapped on the shoulder more times than he cared to remember.

'Give over, Doc. Doc Rafter's a single lady. Give us a turn.'

The local bachelors vying with each other for Tina's attention and vying with Jock.

'Don't you devote yourself solely to Doc Blaxton, Doc Rafter. You remember me? I used to borrow your pencils way back in grade three. If I'd known you were going to turn out like this, Tina Rafter, I'd have given you all my pencils, no sweat. Give us a dance, Doc, and we'll talk about how many ways I can pay you back.'

Tina smiling and laughing, tossing that glorious hair and letting her own slim hands hold firmly onto Jock.

'Not tonight, guys. I'm partnering Dr Blaxton until his next baby comes along. Leave us alone!'

How could Jock have wanted a baby to intrude on tonight? But, of course, he got one. About midnight, just as the music started to slow and the dancers moved closer—and Jock's senses were starting to swim way off to some distant point in a tropical horizon—the tiny electronic buzzer at Jock's waist chirped into life.

'Hell.' Jock hauled himself back to reality with a huge mental effort. He drew back from Tina, flicked open his pager and swore again.

'I need to find a phone,' he told her. 'Sam Hopper's on call tonight but this message says he wants me to call him. Hopefully he just needs some advice. Will you wait for me?'

Famous last words. Wait! Jock had gone no more than two feet from Tina's side before she was whisked away in the arms of Kevin Blewitt, the local pharmacist.

I want to be a pharmacist, Jock thought bitterly as he searched for a phone. Nice regular hours. A shop I can shut at six o'clock and go home...

He swore again. How he was going to retrieve Tina after the phone call? The pharmacist was already holding Tina closer than Jock liked. But there was no call for him to retrieve Tina from her pharmacist's hold. Sam Hopper, one of the town's general practitioners, was terse and anxious and Jock just had to listen to the man's voice to know he'd be needed.

'Jock, I'm sorry, mate, but I've had a prolapse.'

A prolapse...

Jock closed his eyes. Hell!

This was a hard call. Sam was a general practitioner who insisted on doing his own deliveries. There were competent general practitioners in the district who delivered their own babies, but Sam wasn't one of them. First, he had a tiny practice and he only delivered five or six babies a year. That meant that he simply didn't have a wide enough experience to keep his hand in.

Second, the man was arrogant and he loathed asking for help, which meant that he always waited until the situation was a total disaster before he called Jock in. A prolapse...

It must have been a hell of a delivery to make that happen so why hadn't Sam called Jock out hours ago? He hadn't, though, so there was nothing Jock could do about it now. It was too late to do anything but sigh and go and tell Tina that he had to leave. Maybe Lloyd and Sally could run Tina home when the dance ended? Maybe her pharmacist would. Tina elected neither.

She stood within the proprietary hold of the pharmacist and looked at Jock in concern. 'Oh, Jock, that's too bad.' Her eyes creased in understanding. Like all doctors, Tina knew what it was like to be interrupted at every conceivable wrong moment. Then she smiled apologetically up at Kevin the pharmacist.

'Kevin, if you'll excuse me, I'll go with Jock,' she said softly, and Jock had to pinch himself to believe he was hearing correctly. 'He might need an anaesthetist.'

'But—'

'No.'

Kevin and Jock spoke in tandem. Kevin's hold tightened.

'You're not a doctor tonight, Tina,' Kevin growled. 'Unless you're on call... Mark's the full-time anaesthetist. Jock can call on him.'

But Tina looked over to where Mark Spencer was dancing cheek to cheek with his wife, and shook her head. Her fiery hair swung free, doing strange things to the way Jock's knees operated.

'Nope.' She disengaged herself from Kevin's hold and tucked her arm into Jock's. 'If my date's going to play doctors then so will I. I only have him for two dates, you see. I'd best make the most of it. Goodnight, Kevin. Let's go, Jock.' And she led him out of the hall, with Jock feeling as if he could be pushed over by a feather.

*   *   *

'You didn't have to come.'

They were almost at the hospital before Jock found the strength to speak, and even then his voice sounded odd. Tina threw him a very odd glance.

'Yes, I did,' she said frankly. 'Kevin's got body odour and his hands sweat. Also he's got only one thing on his mind, and I'm not interested.'

That produced a grin.

'You don't want me to run you home, then?' Jock asked, hoping like hell she'd say no. 'Or call you a cab?'

'Nope. I'm coming with you.' Tina smiled. 'You asked me out, Jock, so you're stuck with me for the evening, like it or not.'

There was the beginnings of a disaster in the labour ward.

Heather Wardrop was a middle aged mother of six children. She'd expected a complication-free delivery, like the other five, but, weakened by multiple births, the uterus had simply inverted. Now Heather was appalled and distressed by the mess she was in, she was in the beginnings of shock, her husband was frantic and Sam Hopper was bleating like a helpless nanny goat.

'Hell, Jock,' he said as Jock walked through the door, and his voice was defensive. 'How was I supposed to guess this might happen? It all just happened so fast. I've never had one do this. God, it looks awful...'

'It looks bad but it's not awful,' Jock said firmly, making a fast visual examination and seeing the fear escalate by the second in Heather and her husband. First step here was to get the shock under control. 'Can you set up an IV line, please, Tina?' Heavens, Sam might at least have done that. 'This isn't all that uncommon as a complication of delivery, and it's easy to fix.' He moved to Heather's side and took her hand, then ignored the bleating doctor behind him to concentrate solely on allaying her terror.

'Hey, there's no problem here, Heather,' he said softly. 'There's no need to look like that. Your body's just a bit too efficient. It's getting so good at pushing out babies that it's pushing out everything else as well. But it's OK. You know when you take off a sock and sometimes it turns inside out. All you need to do is turn it right way around again. That's my job now. Turn you the right way out again.'

'But—'

'Where's the end product here?' Jock asked, his eyes gently smiling and sending out reassurance in waves. From Jock's face you'd think there was no problem at all, and Tina felt a sense of relief start to creep back into the room. The terror ebbed. 'Where's the cause of all the trouble?' He looked around for a crib. 'All this fuss and no baby?'

'Sister...Sister took her to the nursery,' Heather faltered.

'So it's a little girl?'

'Yes.'

'And what are you and Michael going to call her?' Jock was acting like there was all the time in the world. His eyes sent an urgent message to Tina to get the fluids going fast, but his actions were steady and unhurried.

He moved to the sink and scrubbed, ready to do a full examination, then came back, still waiting for an answer. The urgency faded even further, and Heather's terror-filled eyes softened. 'What are you going to call her?' he asked again, and finally the woman focussed on her baby rather than on her fear.

'Marguerite. We'll call her Marguerite,' she whispered. 'After Michael's mother...'

'That's a lovely name. I'll make myself known to

Marguerite very soon,' Jock promised, 'but first we'd better turn this sock back to rights.'

'How…? How…?' It was Michael Wardrop, his face as white as death as he watched what was happening to his wife.

'It's a simple procedure,' Jock told him, 'but it's easier—pain free, in fact—if Heather's asleep while we do it. So if it's OK with you, Heather, Dr Rafter here will give you a quick anaesthetic and then I'll do my sock turning. I'll pop a couple of stitches in to hold you in place while your body heals, and then Bob's your uncle. You'll be fine again.' He smiled. 'OK, Heather?'

'OK.' The woman was sagging with relief, terror giving way to absolute exhaustion. She'd had enough. Fear was fading and exhaustion was taking over.

'I guess I do need to ask, though,' Jock said thoughtfully as he examined the damage and suppressed a wince. 'Is it in your plans to have any more babies? I can do a better stitching job here if I know there's no more coming out the way this one did.'

'Oh, Doc, there'll be no more babies,' Heather breathed wearily. 'We wanted this one, but six…well, six is a nice even number and I'm forty-three and Michael's forty-seven. I reckon we'll call it a day. Don't you, Mike?'

'Too right we will,' her husband agreed fervently. 'We hadn't really planned this one. She just sort of slipped through. But now…' He gripped his wife's hand and stared at Jock, with hope building in his eyes. Who knew what Sam's terror had done to these people? Tina thought. In the face of his fear they must have thought Heather was dying. 'You just fix my Heather up, Doc,' he pleaded. 'Please?'

'You don't think we should send her to Sydney?' Sam said nervously from behind them. 'Hell, Jock, this looks…it looks ghastly…'

'It looks a lot worse than it is,' Jock snapped, and his voice was cutting. Sam would have them all in hysterics if he wasn't stopped. Jock turned his back on the man and smiled at Michael and his wife.

'Now, I know Dr Rafter and I look a pretty unlikely pair of doctors,' he told them, 'but underneath the party clothes and Dr Rafter's silk stockings we're extremely competent. Tina's a fine anaesthetist and I've dealt with more prolapses than I'd care to mention. We can fix this if you'll let us. I can send you to Sydney, Heather, but it'll be a long and uncomfortable journey, and there's no need. Do you trust us?' He faced Michael head-on. 'Do you trust us, Mr Wardrop?'

'Gee, I dunno.' For the first time Tina saw the flicker of a smile enter Mike Wardrop's anxiety-ridden eyes. Jock's solid confidence was having its effect. He looked from Tina in her crazy, skimpy dress to Jock in his dinner suit, and then Michael managed to smile down at his wife. 'Do we trust you to these two gladflies, Heather, love? They look like something off the cover of *Vogue*.'

'Oh, yes,' Heather breathed, and she managed a smile herself. Her head sank back wearily on the pillows and she closed her eyes. 'I've always had a thing for men in dinner suits. Sexy as anything, they are. You just leave me be, Michael Wardrop, and let Dr Blaxton do whatever he likes with me. He's more than welcome. Just as long as no one expects me to help!'

She started drifting toward sleep before Tina could even begin to think about an anaesthetic.

It wasn't quite as simple a procedure as Jock had implied. It took two hours in Theatre before they were sure all the damage had been rectified, and Jock was really glad the Wardrops had said it was the end of babies for Heather.

'Because with this amount of stitching the next one's a Caesarean or not at all,' he said grimly, as he stood back from the table. 'Maybe this one should have been a Caesarean anyway. With such a big baby, Sam should have sought specialist advice. If not mine, then someone else's.'

Jock's anger was almost palpable. Tina had been aware of it, barely suppressed, from the time Dr Sam Hopper had yawned as they'd wheeled Heather into Theatre and announced his intention of heading back to bed and leaving Tina and Jock to cope.

'He's just not interested,' Jock had said through gritted teeth. 'Sam closed his books after medical school and he makes no pretence of keeping up with modern knowledge.'

That was all he'd said, whispered through gritted teeth while the nurses were occupied with Heather, but now...with Heather wheeled back to the ward and Jock and Tina alone at the sink, Jock made no effort to control the blast of fury.

'The man's incompetent. Incompetent to try and deliver babies. Doesn't he know the damage he can do? Doesn't he realise the consequences?' Jock's voice was laced with fury, laced with exhaustion and laced with pain.

Jock took Heather's danger seriously, Tina thought. Deadly seriously.

'Jock, Heather's OK now,' she said gently. 'Thanks to you...'

'But what if she'd had a ruptured uterus? Or... So many things to go wrong... Doesn't he know the risk with multigravidas is more than the risk with first-time mothers? According to Sam's notes, Heather's had five big babies... Every single baby over nine pounds, and two of them over ten pounds. This one's ten and a half pounds—Sam must have known it was huge at prenatal checks—and he sails in at the last minute with not the least fear of complications.

'And you know what would have happened if she'd died?' Jock's face was white and drawn as he continued. 'Sam would have shrugged and said "these things happen". They don't *just happen*. Not now. Not with the precautions that should be taken. But I can't be in every place at once to make sure they are, and if doctors won't refer...'

'Is that what you want to do?' Tina asked gently, watching his face. 'Be everywhere at once?'

That stopped him. Jock lifted his face to Tina's, and stared. Then he shook his head, shaking off a nightmare, and, at last, he managed a smile.

'Hell, that makes me sound like a conceited...'

'Like the great obstetrician that you are.' Tina grinned and hoisted herself up to sit on the bench beside the sink. She was wearing a theatre gown over her skimpy red dress and was feeling almost demure. Only her stockinged legs swung free, hinting at the sexiness of her outfit underneath. 'Hey, Jock...'

'What?' The strain was still in his voice. He looked up, but Tina knew he was hardly seeing her. He was seeing catastrophe—six children without a mother, Michael Wardrop without a wife. He was seeing his own mother. Tina's heart lurched. Jock's heart was on his face. There was anguish in his eyes. Who'd have guessed it? she thought. Who'd have guessed...? The great Jock Blaxton... With a heart big enough to take on the whole world. Dear heaven, she was starting to love him.

Love? The word flashed through her mind like lightning, flashing to illuminate the sky. That one simple thought showed things which had always been there but had been hidden in the dark until now. It showed her that she was falling in love with a man who had no intention in the world of committing himself to anyone, much less her.

'Hey, Jock...' Unconsciously, Tina's hand reached out to stroke Jock's hair. Her fingers slid through the tangle of deep black curls in an age-old gesture of comfort. A woman, giving comfort to her man.

'There's a new little person in the world because of what's happened here tonight,' she said softly. 'A tiny little girl called Marguerite Wardrop, who has a mother who's going to be fine, thanks to you, Jock.'

Her fingers kept right on stroking, trying desperately to ease his pain. 'You might not be able to save the world, Jock. You might not be able to be everywhere. But you've done your bit for the Wardrop family tonight. You've done your bit for my sister as well, and I think you're wonderful. So, what else do you expect of yourself?'

No answer. Jock was stiff and silent under her fingers, standing before her, not moving, and still his face was etched with pain. Suddenly Tina couldn't bear it. There were ghosts in this man's past, dreadful ghosts. Ghosts that meant he couldn't live with himself, couldn't go forward.

What sort of parents had laid this awful sense of guilt upon his shoulders? she wondered. To blame a child for a mother's death... To bestow on him a guilt that meant that he had to face this pain alone, for ever. There was nothing to do to ease the pain but...but to comfort him in the only way that seemed to make sense. Tina let her other hand drift up to his hair so both sets of fingers were stroking through those magic curls. Thick and thatched and curling, the feel of his hair sent erotic shards through her whole body. Stroking. Stroking.

Then she pulled him forward so that his head was almost on her breast. Tina lowered her face to his, and tilted his unresisting chin up to hers. And kissed him.

CHAPTER SIX

IT WAS supposed to be a kiss of comfort, nothing more. Ha!

Whatever was between Jock and Tina—whatever was between this man and this woman—wasn't comfort, but a full-blown volcanic explosion. The moment Tina's lips met Jock's the whole world changed. Or stopped. What was happening here? This was crazy, Tina thought desperately as she felt passion surge between them. Here she was, feeling content that everything had turned out well, and feeling warm and weary and sorry for this big man with his damned handsome face and his lovely thatch of hair and his caring eyes and his ghosts...

But that was all! she told herself. She'd felt sorry for him. Sorry! Sorry wasn't the emotion that slammed into her now. It was naked, fathomless lust. Tina's lips descended onto Jock's and he hadn't wanted to be kissed—she was almost sure of that. It was just that he was numb and exhausted and in no condition to argue—and all of a sudden this lightning bolt hit him and it hit her at the same time and it fused them together like glue.

Heat! The heat was overpowering. Tina was melting inside. There was fire, starting in her lips and working its way downward—sweeping its way downward—burning straight down to her toes and back up again. Sweeping back and forth, washing wave after wave of fire from her toes to the tips of her ears and back down again. And her thighs... Her thighs were screaming a need she'd never known she'd had.

Jock's hands were moving. They rose, almost of their own volition, and they were now holding her waist, bringing her body closer, moving her thighs against him. Tina was somehow sliding off the bench, sliding down to be held against his body, her lips never moving except to open—to deepen the kiss—to demand that Jock's mouth took hers. Her tongue came out all of it own accord. Searching his mouth. Demanding an entry into his moist, wonderful recesses.

Jock. Jock! Her toes were curling upward at the thought of him, at the feel of him! Tina's whole body was curling. Like a burning match, she was flaming beside him—being consumed—taking him to her and offering the heat of her body in return. Jock... Dear God, Jock...

What was happening to her? She knew. She knew! Without doubt, she knew. This feeling had never happened to Tina in her life before, but it was unmistakable. This was her man, this was where she wanted to be.

Jock...

But he didn't want her, he didn't want anyone. Somehow... Somehow Jock pushed her back, an inch...two inches...with Tina whimpering a protest. But she didn't follow. Somehow Tina managed to grip onto that much pride. She let herself be pushed away—held at arm's length and watched by those dark eyes.

Jock watched her with eyes that were almost accusing, but Tina's eyes didn't leave his for a second. She stared straight back and her look didn't falter. She wasn't ashamed that she'd kissed this man. How could she be ashamed? Something was happening to her here that she didn't understand—that she had no hope of understanding because it was so new to her—and she was starting to wonder where it would take her.

This might be a path she'd never travelled before, but Tina knew for certain that whatever she was feeling she wanted it to continue. She'd walk down this path with joy.

But… 'No,' Jock said, and his voice was ragged.

'No?' Amazingly, there was laughter in Tina's voice, though her voice wasn't the least bit steady. 'No? You don't want to ravish me on the theatre floor, Jock, darling? Rats! That's what it felt like for a moment there, and it would have been a first, too!'

Jock's eyes flared. His body stiffened and for a moment Tina thought—hoped—that he'd seize her again, and do just that.

But Jock—somehow—was back in control again, and he didn't want women. Not seriously. Not ever.

'Tina… I'll… I'm sorry.'

'Sorry you kissed me?' Tina chuckled and leaned forward to kiss him again lightly on the lips. He didn't respond, didn't move. Simply stared with those blank, fathomless eyes. 'That's not very nice.'

'I'm not meant to be nice. It's just…'

'I know. You're not in the market for a serious relationship.' Tina nodded, forcing her voice to sound light, making a Herculean effort to keep her voice light. 'I know that. And neither am I, of course. Remember… Remember Peter?'

That got to him, reached through the blankness. Some of the anger flooded back and saved him.

'Peter…'

'Yep, Peter.' Tina's eyes dared to smile up at him and his anger grew.

'You mean, you kiss a man like that when you're going steady with another man?'

'Only when it's you.' There, she'd said it now. He could shove that in his pipe and smoke it.

Jock's eyes narrowed, and blazed with a mixture of anger and passion. 'What the hell's that supposed to mean?'

'Just what I said,' Tina retorted. 'Meaning I never have kissed a man like that, and I don't know why I kissed you like that and if you can explain it then you're welcome to try. I'm all ears.'

Silence.

Tina finally managed to find the courage to kiss him again, lightly, but not with passion.

'Jock, leave it,' she said, and only she knew the effort it cost her to keep her voice light. She was starting to believe she was falling heavily in love with this man, but admitting it... Heavens, admitting it would make him run a mile. 'We're obviously good at creating electricity. So maybe we could interest the State Energy Board. Or maybe...' She sighed at the look in his eyes. 'Maybe we could just check that Marguerite Wardrop's OK and then maybe we could go to bed.'

'Bed...' Jock's tone was blank.

'I mean our own separate beds,' Tina said, and there was a tiny spurt of anger in her own voice then. How dared he! she thought suddenly. The man was behaving like a moralistic prig and now he was making her feel like a tramp. 'What else would I mean? What else when I'm happily settled with my Peter?'

Only, of course, she wasn't.

There was no talk of another date. Tina was left under no illusions that Jock wanted anything further to do with her. But she couldn't let it rest there. She couldn't. Tina spent the next week, trying to figure out just what she was feeling. Trying to avoid Jock Blaxton and failing. He had a night delivery of twins and a woman with a miscarriage while she was on duty, and both times they had to work together. Jock was stiff and formal and distant—but by the end of the week Tina figured she was going quietly nuts.

Dear God, she was in love. She was totally, absolutely and irrevocably in love—with someone who wanted nothing more to do with her. But it wasn't in Tina's nature to go quietly nuts. If she was going nuts, then she'd do it in style, and do it honourably. There was no way she could continue to go out with Peter—not now. Not now she knew what it was to be kissed by a man like Jock.

Sure, there was a strong possibility that Jock would never kiss her again in his life. He'd certainly try not to. But she *knew* now. She knew what it felt like, and Peter's kisses were going to be a pale comparison. Peter telephoned her on the night after the dance and she tried to be interested in the news from Sydney. She tried. Then Peter tried to be interested in what was happening in Gundowring and that didn't work either.

So Tina took a deep breath and said since they'd be spending so much time apart maybe they should feel free to date other people—and was only faintly piqued by the trace of relief in Peter's voice as he agreed. Yeah, OK. She and Peter really didn't suit long term, but it had been a comfortable relationship for two busy people. So where did that leave her now?

It left her here. It left her in Gundowring with Christie and the children. They were all that mattered.

At least things were good on that front. But Christie thought Jock was wonderful and that was a bit hard to take when she was trying hard to tell herself that Jock wasn't so fantastic.

Christie went to see Jock on the Monday of her appointment and came back bubbling. For the first time since Rose's birth she was smiling, without Tina working on it.

'Oh, Tina, Dr Blaxton's just lovely,' she told her sister. 'He's made me see things in such a new light. He's found out who Ray's with now.' Christie shook her head in astonishment. 'And he made me laugh about it!'

'Laugh?'

'I couldn't believe it myself,' Christie admitted. 'But…well, Ray's forty-seven and Skye…the girl Ray's with…is seventeen. He painted such a picture of what Ray must be going through! Dr Blaxton's idea of purgatory would be taking a teenager to discos when he's forty-seven. He says Ray's chosen his own punishment and I should count my blessings.'

'I did try telling you that,' Tina said cautiously, and Christie's smile widened. She gave her sister a hug.

'I know. I know you did, Tina, love, but maybe I wasn't ready to hear it. Or maybe I needed an outsider to lay it on the line. And Dr Blaxton has such a way with him…' Her smile turned to a downright grin, mischief included. The old Christie was flooding back.

'And I'll tell you what else. Dr Blaxton rang the Department of Social Security and they say they can garnishee Ray's wages. That means support for our children comes out of Ray's wages and is sent to me before he even sees what he's earned. And that happens no matter where in Australia Ray goes.'

'Is that right?'

'He says it is. Oh, Tina, Ray left because he hated paying for the kids… But now… As well as supporting Ally and Tim and Rose, he'll be paying the expenses of his seventeen-year-old lover.' Christie's smile faded. 'I don't think that'll be all that much fun—do you?'

'You don't feel sorry for him, do you?' Tina asked incredulously, and Christie nodded.

'I do. Tina, for the first time I do—and that's a healing in itself. For the first time I feel not just anger and hurt but disgust with Ray that he could do this. And sorry for what he's lost.' Christie's lovely smile flashed back. 'But that's not stopping me applying for garnishment.'

'Oh, Christie…'

'I think he's the best doctor,' Christie said happily. 'When are you going out with him again?'

'He hasn't asked me,' Tina confessed, and Christie stared.

'So when has that ever stopped you with a man?' she demanded. 'Ask *him*, then. For heaven's sake, Tina. If I wasn't sworn off men for life—or at least until my stretch marks fade—I'd ask him out myself. Tina, Jock is seriously wonderful. Go for it.'

'He isn't serious.'

'So he's just plain wonderful. You get serious for both of you. Ask him!'

Ask him… Easier said than done.

Tina spent a few days working on her courage and telling herself she was a dope for even attempting such a thing. But every time she talked herself out of it she'd turn a corner in the hospital corridor and there Jock would be, stethoscope dangling across his white coat, his dark eyes twinkling at some joke a nurse was making…. The man was seriously wonderful…

Christie was dead right, Tina decided. Jock was the most desirable man she'd ever met in her life, and she wasn't going to get one inch further with the man unless she did the running.

So ask! Ask, Tina Rafter. Ask! So she did. Tina waited until she had him alone—no mean feat itself in a busy hospital—in the nursery. He was checking his charges—four lusty babies—and Tina watched him through the windows, moving from crib to crib, before she entered.

He did love babies! The look on his face as he lifted young Marguerite Wardrop up into his arms… There was no real need for him to lift her but as Jock looked down at her, unaware of anyone watching, Tina could see for herself what was written in his soul. It was nonsense that this man didn't want a family, she thought. Sure, he was afraid. But his desire was written in his eyes. He wanted one of these babies for his own. There wasn't one too many babies in the world for Jock. There were too few!

He'd make the best father, Tina thought as she watched his gentle hands—and his smile which had her heart doing back flips. He'd make the best lover! Tina's thighs started heating up all by themselves.

Ask him!

She took a deep breath and swung open the nursery door. Before her thighs started flaming right here in the hospital corridor!

'Hi.'

Jock looked up from Marguerite and his smile faded.

'Hi.' He placed the baby back gently in the cot, adjusted her covers and then looked at his watch. By which time he had his face nicely under control. Stiff and formal. 'What are you still doing in the hospital?' he asked.

As a welcome it was about as warm as a bucket of cold water.

'I work here.' Tina managed a smile. 'You employed me again. Remember?'

Remember? How could he not remember? Jock's face closed even more. 'I meant you're due to go off duty at seven a.m.' He scowled at his watch, as if it had betrayed him. 'That's an hour ago.'

'I know,' Tina told him. 'I waited. I wanted to see you.'

If it was possible for his face to close any more it did then. It shut down all over the place. As far as his face was concerned, Jock was out for lunch!

'Why?'

'Gee, you sound friendly.'

'I'm busy.'

'Yeah, I can see that.' Tina grinned. 'So busy you have time to cuddle each of these babies in turn. Frantic schedule, Dr Blaxton.'

'What did you want to talk to me about?'

'Our second date.'

That reached him. Tina saw an expression flit behind

his eyes that she wasn't the least sure she understood. Like a lion suddenly unsure that the prey he was about to kill didn't have tusks. Sharp tusks that could kill.

'Hey, it's only a wedding,' she said hurriedly. 'I need a partner, and I can't take Peter.'

'Why can't you take Peter?'

'We've split up,' Tina said mournfully. 'Isn't that sad? We've been going out for nearly a year, and now we find we're not suited.'

'Why aren't you suited?' The wariness was there in force. Tina felt she was practically *wearing* tusks. So what answer would take the wariness away?

'Peter wants a wife and babies and I don't want to be a wife and mother,' she said. It was true. Not with Peter, she didn't. 'I want to have some fun, Jock, while I'm still young enough to enjoy it.'

'Yeah?'

'Yeah.' Tina leaned over young Cameron Croxton and stopped looking at Jock, taking the heat right off him. When in doubt refer to work.

'Hey, Cameron's jaundice looks almost better,' she said. 'He just looks tanned now, instead of like he's been eating too much saffron. That's great.'

'His bilirubin levels are way down and still dropping.'

'He'll be able to go home, then?'

'Yes—except his dad wants him to be circumcised. I can't talk him out of it.'

'Straight away?'

'He says his son's not complete until it's done,' Jock said morosely. 'I guess I'll have to do it or they'll get some backyarder to operate, but I hate it. Especially when he's been so ill. We're only just on top of the jaundice.'

Tina nodded in sympathy. Once little boys had been circumcised as a matter of course in the days immediately after their birth, no matter what condition they'd been in. The old belief had been that it didn't hurt new-borns—but it did. It hurt them very much and in some it induced shock. Occasionally—rarely, but often enough for most doctors to have seen a tragic example—it caused infection and death.

So, if it had to be done, it was best to be done by a competent doctor, using local anaesthetic. Most doctors now asked that it be done when the babies weren't so new, but if Cameron's parents insisted then there was little for Jock to do but perform the operation. As he said, if it meant that much to them, if Jock didn't do it someone else would.

Tina lifted young Cameron from his cot and gave him a hug. 'It's a hard world out there,' she told the fuzzy little head, and hugged him again. 'But Dr Blaxton's good. The best. He'll look after you.' She looked over to Jock and his wary look was back again.

'About this wedding…' she said.

'Tina…'

'Jock, are you afraid to go out with me?' she demanded, and Jock's eyes widened.

'Well?'

Despite his wariness, Jock found himself smiling. 'Tina, in the circles I was brought up in it was impolite for young ladies to ask men out—and if the man refused it was even more impolite for her to call him a coward.'

'It's just lucky I'm not a young lady, then.' Tina's eyes locked on his, challenging. 'This wedding is this Saturday at four o'clock. You're not on call. I checked. The church and reception are both close enough for you to leave if there's a baby needs delivering. I'm brides-maid so you'll get to mingle with the other guests while I do my duties. I only need a token partner to sit in the partner spot while I eat my dinner. A token partner, Jock Blaxton. That's all. And who knows? You might even end up having fun.'

He might. Maybe. But maybe that was just what Jock was afraid of.

Jock didn't have fun, but it was no fault of the wedding. The tension between himself and Tina was almost palpable.

The wedding itself was great—a huge affair to which the whole district was invited. Harry was a local farmer. Mary was the local school teacher. Harry played football and cricket and darts and Mary played netball and tennis and hockey, and every sports club was there in force. As well as that, both families were huge and even the district dogs were showing a fair representation.

The church was out on the headland and the little chapel was overflowing. The reception was in a nearby shearing shed, and the bush band was quite simply the best Jock had ever heard. But, as Tina had promised, he really was only her token partner. He got to sit beside Tina at the formal part of the dinner but afterwards the tables were hauled back and Tina, as chief bridesmaid, was whirled around and around the shed in the arms of one man after another. It was almost as if she was avoiding him.

She was.

Tina was dressed much more demurely today than at the hospital dance in her simple white bridesmaid's dress that fell in soft folds to her ankles, covering her nicely from the neck down. Demure, but still wonderful. She was tense, though.

It had been a mistake, Tina thought sadly, inviting Jock. The man looked at her with the eyes of a man stepping into a river full of piranhas. Jock might have agreed to accompanying her, but he hadn't agreed to anything else.

Damn the man! Somehow she had to let him see she wasn't about to launch herself at him. She wouldn't cling like a limpet and threaten his damned solitude. He made no move to stay with her as the evening progressed and, short of making herself seem a lovesick fool, Tina had no choice but to let him be. Drat the man!

He had to dance with her once. After the bridal waltz there was a dance where people were expected to stay with their partners so Jock couldn't escape. Tina danced well but Jock held her rigidly in his arms and she knew that, given the choice, he'd be home like a shot.

Tina had her pride. Two circles of the dance floor and she was getting angry. It helped. And then she found something to distract her, which helped even more. A group of teenagers was drinking heavily outside the shed, and Tina was suddenly more concerned with them than she was with Jock.

'They're only just eighteen,' she told Jock. She'd allowed herself to be deliberately diverted by the teenagers, but now she was truly troubled. 'I wish their parents would intervene. They're drinking far too much for their own good.'

This was a new sensation for Jock. Sure, he hadn't wanted this dance, but now... To have a woman in his arms and not have her full attention... He'd meant to stay aloof, apart. The fact that it was Tina calling the shots now made him want to haul her in close and make her pay attention. Or maybe that's what he wanted to do anyway.

But Tina was still watching the teenagers. He followed her gaze, and some of the tension he was feeling found a vent in anger. The teenagers were drinking like idiots, mixing spirits with beer and generally becoming louder and more aggressive by the minute.

'Their parents are here,' Tina said. 'Why don't they stop them? I wonder if I should do anything.'

'What could you do?'

'I don't know. Say something...'

'It's not our business,' Jock said brusquely. God, she was lovely. 'And they won't be stupid enough to drive.' His eyes rested on the teenagers for a long moment. 'Stupid fools. If they were my kids…'

'They won't be, though, will they, Jock?' Tina said, and her voice was infinitely sad. Infinitely weary. The hands holding her were still rigid and formal. Giving nothing. 'Not ever. Responsibility isn't your scene.' She bit her lip—and suddenly pushed herself away. 'No. I'm sorry, Jock. Maybe…maybe tonight was a mistake.'

Heavens, if he held her like this one moment longer she'd burst into tears. 'I…I need to dance with somebody else.'

That was it! End of dance, end of allocated time with Tina. But Jock found his eyes following her around the shed as he whirled his own succession of partners across the worn shearing-shed boards. Hell! This was driving him nuts. This was *it*, he told himself. The end. The last time he'd spend any time with her at all except at work. She couldn't possibly ask him out after this—not if he was distant enough—and he wouldn't ask her. He wouldn't—because it was too damned dangerous.

He could start thinking about that London job again. Set things in motion so he could leave as soon as Gina and Struan came back. London seemed a long way away. And then the Pride of Erin had him changing partners yet again and Tina was suddenly beside him again, laughing in his arms. Soft. Delicious. Desirable.

'Having fun?' Her lovely eyes teased him, as though there was nothing between them at all, and Jock couldn't begin to guess the effort it cost her.

'Mmm.' That was one stupid lie. 'You?'

'I love weddings.' She did so it wasn't a lie.

'Yet you won't marry your Peter?'

'No.' She twirled out from him as he spun her around, and then pulled back into his side. She seemed to fit, as if there were a niche specially built in his ribs to accommodate her.

'You really don't want to get married?' he demanded, unbelieving, and she shook her wonderful hair.

'I really don't. At least—that's my story and I'm sticking to it.'

'Why?'

'Because every time I look twice at you, you get twitchy—like you're being pursued by a killer shark,' she snapped, her smile fading. 'So let's not get paranoid, Dr Blaxton. Just relax and have fun.' She managed to smile up at him and then took two steps forward to her new partner—and was whisked on in the dance circle, and Jock was left with all the wind knocked right out of him.

Tina avoided him completely after that for the rest of the night. Or he avoided her. Or maybe both. But they had to drive home together. Tina had come in the bridal car so she had no other way of getting home. They left at two in the morning, and both were so tense as they left that Tina was close to screaming.

The few stayers were still dancing but Mary and her Harry had left, tin cans and horseshoes trailing in a clattering stream from the back of Harry's farm truck. The oldies had long since packed up and gone home. Tina took a deep breath and tucked her arm possessively into Jock's arm. Reclaiming her man?

'OK, Prince Charming. Cinderella's about to turn into a pumpkin. Bring on your glass coach.'

'Isn't that a glass slipper?'

'Whatever. But I'm done with slippers.' She yawned, kicked off her bridesmaid shoes and walked barefoot with him over the paddocks to the car, trying to act casual.

They weren't the only ones leaving. In the distance some teenagers were fighting about car keys. They could hear them in the distance as they approached. It was the same teenagers they'd watched drinking.

'Hell, Andrew, you're not fit to drive. Leave the car here. We'll get a ride.'

'I'm fine. I've only had a couple of beers.'

'A couple! A couple of dozen more like. Plus the whisky.'

'Look, there's damn-all taxis out here. Shut up and get in!'

Tina and Jock heard their voices, carrying clearly across the paddocks, and looked at each other in alarm in the moonlight.

'Hi,' Jock yelled, and started forward, but it was too late. They were still too far away. The teenagers had piled into the car and the ancient vehicle lurched erratically towards the gate.

'Hell,' Jock said, and reached into his pocket for his mobile phone.

'What are you doing?' Tina stared after the car in consternation. She didn't need to be told that this was a disaster waiting to happen.

'I'm calling the police,' Jock said bluntly as the teenagers' car squealed onto the highway on two wheels. 'If that mob of young idiots aren't stopped, they'll kill themselves—if not someone else. Where the hell are their parents?'

It created even more tension, but there was nothing they could do about the teenagers. They were driving at such speed there was no way Jock or Tina could catch them. Tina settled into the passenger seat of Jock's lovely little car and was silent.

So was Jock.

Nothing had happened between them, Tina thought sadly. Nothing! Maybe she should have clung to him tonight. But... She knew that clinging would make this man run a mile. So...nothing had happened. Jock was telling himself the same thing. He'd been worried that he'd make a fool of himself tonight. Take things too far. Give Tina the wrong idea…

But nothing had happened. That was what Jock wanted, he told himself savagely. So leave it that way. Just get this girl home, leave her there and get on with his life. It was what he wanted—wasn't it? He stared ahead bleakly at the ribbon of highway—and then the night erupted in a ball of fire before them and the thought of what he wanted from his life suddenly had no relevance at all.

CHAPTER SEVEN

JOCK'S foot hit the brake as a boom with the force of a vast bomb smashed across the soft music of Jock's car stereo, and fire lit the sky. All Tina and Jock could see was flames. The fire was so huge it was practically towering above them.

Dear God. Without speaking, Jock put his foot to the accelerator again and his little car crept forward. Fearful of what they would find at the source of the flame, they drove forward three hundred yards, slowly around the next corner, and then there was a hill, rising to a crest... There was no way they were driving up that crest. Beyond was the fire. There were flames, leaping a hundred feet into the sky, on the other side. Without exchanging one word—there was just nothing to say to each other, nothing in the face of such fear—Tina and Jock left the car and ran up the hill to reach the unspeakable horror on the other side.

Before they reached the crest Jock had collected himself enough for priorities. He fell one step behind Tina as he fumbled in his inner pocket for his phone. Tina could hardly hear him for the roaring of the flames.

'Kate... Doc Blaxton here. I'm on Slatey Creek Road near Black Hill. There's been a major crash. I need ambulance and fire engine...fire engines. There's a major fire. Police, too, Kate. Send everything you've got. No. There have to be casualties but I don't know how many. Assume the worst. Fast, Kate. Now!'

Jock clicked closed the mouthpiece and reached the top of the crest two seconds after Tina, and stood beside her for one long moment, appalled. What they saw took their breath away. There was a petrol tanker…vast and burning out of control. It must have veered off the highway, before exploding, because it was thirty yards from the road on their right. It was now a massive, roaring ball of flames, consuming the night.

There was a car below the crest, on their left. It was lit by the flames but it wasn't alight. The car had a crumpled, mangled rear but it was still whole. Still safe. It was on the other side of the highway to the burning truck, and the same group of teenagers Tina and Jock had seen not five minutes before were struggling from the car, dazed and shaken.

Tina swung around to face the truck again—and stared. Dear God, that couldn't be the driver! Could it? There was a man, staggering across the paddock toward the road. His body was a black shadow lit by the inferno behind. A man… A man alive from that awfulness.

Jock had already seen him and was running, striding out with a speed Tina could never match, down towards that blackened figure. Tina was left to follow. Miraculously the man appeared to be almost unhurt. He was singed around the edges. He was bleeding from a gash on the face but he was still on his feet, and the fact that his shirt was still intact on his back meant that the singeing was only minor.

Tina practically sobbed in relief as she reached him. Jock was supporting the man, helping him away from the fireball. The heat was unbearable. Tina shoved herself under the man's other shoulder and together she and Jock half dragged, half carried him back toward the road.

'Is there anyone else in the truck?' Jock was asking urgently across the roar of the flames. The heat was catching in his throat, making speech almost impossible, but the question had to be asked. 'Anyone?'

The man shook his head, unable to make his mouth frame the word 'no'. His legs were sagging under him.

Released, he would have crumpled where he stood. Who knew what massive effort he must have made to get clear of the burning wreck? Another boom echoed across the paddocks and the blast of heat was like a physical blow, knocking them forward.

Tina lurched and regained her balance, the heat searing through the thin fabric of her bridesmaid's dress. This was not *de rigueur* fireman's clothing, she thought grimly, but it was all she had. She had no choice but to stay and help. The heat was growing more intense by the minute. Jock didn't falter and neither did Tina. Finally they had the man on the other side of the road near the teenagers' car where the fire was just a vast menacing presence, close enough to heat way past comfort but not close enough to damage.

They lowered the driver onto the grass verge and Jock knelt to give him a decent examination. Tina stayed standing and looked around her, taking her time now, missing nothing. She was performing triage, assessing priorities. Tina's training slipped back into force and, crazy bridesmaid's dress and satin sandals or not, she was now every inch a doctor.

Jock could manage here. The driver was so shocked he couldn't speak. The gash on his face was bleeding profusely but Jock was already ripping off his jacket to form a pressure pad. The man was shaking like a leaf and sobbing, but there seemed no sign of anything more life-threatening than the gash and some burns. So check the teenagers.

How many were there? One. Two. Three. Four. There were four kids huddled around the car in various stages of distress. Tina thought back to the group she'd seen by the car back at the shearing shed and she did a mental head count of her memory. Four. Yes. Four.

Good grief. Relief hit her with almost physical force. Did this mean they were going to get out of this night

without major casualties? If the driver of the truck was
OK and these four were accounted for…

But then… Tina looked closely at their car and felt a
surge of fear as she looked. This didn't make sense.
There must be… No. Maybe she was wrong. Dear God,
she'd never hoped so much to be wrong in her entire
life.

'Are you OK?' she asked the first teenager as she
reached his side. His girlfriend was vomiting in the
dust—a mixture of drunkenness and shock, Tina
thought—and let her be. 'Are any of you hurt?'

'Doc…'

The boy recognised her. Tina looked closely at the
boy's face in the firelight and recognised a lad she'd
treated for a football injury a week before. 'Oh, Doc…'

'Simon, is anyone hurt?' she asked sharply, and
gripped his shoulders, forcing him to focus through the
shock.

'Andrew thinks he's broken his arm, and Syl…Syl's
hurt her chest and she's sick. But the car… There's people…in the car…'

'Is there someone else in the car?' Tina demanded,
trying to block out the fearful thought that had slammed
into her head a moment before. She took two steps towards it before Simon stopped her.

'Doc, no. Not…not our car. The…the car that hit the
tanker.'

There are moments in life best forgotten. This was
one of them.

Tina turned slowly and stared at the tanker, and then
she stared some more, willing Simon to be imagining
things. Willing him to be wrong. There was no other car
that Tina could see. There was no other crash site than
this car here and the burning tanker. Nothing. She turned
slowly around, her eyes searching the fire-lit scene.

Nothing from this angle! Just a tanker, alone and burning. But... But...

Another look at Simon and she knew the boy wasn't imagining it. Simon's face was a blank reflection of her own terror, and the teenagers' car wasn't badly enough damaged to explain this carnage. To explain why the truck was smashed and burning on the other side of the highway. Dear God...

There must be another car, then, she thought, and her stomach gave a sickening lurch of horror. But where was it? She knew. There was only one answer. And then she was running back to the grass on the other side of the road, lurching crazily in her silly satin sandals as she ran. She couldn't rip them off—not when there were bits of burning debris flying through the night, setting off small sparks of fire in the grass.

Tina ran on regardless. Not straight towards the tanker but behind it. She couldn't go close. The heat was far too intense. She heard Jock yell from somewhere behind her as she ran, but she ignored him and kept on running. If she was right... If she was right, there would be nothing she could do. She knew that.

But she had to know...

Behind and back so she could see the other side of the fire. Running. Holding her hand to her mouth to block the debris from blowing against her, from breathing in ash and petrol vapour. Running so she could see... And it was there. The full horror. The crumpled, mangled mess of a family sedan, wedged in somehow against the side of the tanker as it burned, burning as part of it.

And what she could see... Dear God... Tina sank down onto the grass and closed her eyes. And it took her a long time before she could find the courage to open them.

*　　*　　*

Jock and Tina worked steadily, numb with shock but working with the sheer force of need. The rest of Gundowring's medical community turned out in force, and it seemed they were all needed.

The driver had second-degree burns to his face and hands. He'd lost some hair and too much blood, but he'd live. Recovering from shock, he'd live.

'He deserves to,' the police chief told Tina as he came into the hospital to get statements from the teenagers. 'You know, he slammed into the car and if he'd stopped—if he'd slammed on his brakes and stopped— then there'd be seven dead instead of three. The kids' car would have burned too.'

'As it was,' the police chief went on grimly, 'by the look of the tyre marks, he realised his load would most likely explode after such an impact so he accelerated again. Got the truck thirty yards off the road and then jumped clear. It wasn't his fault that the other sedan was smashed and caught against the side. His rig was so big it just dragged the car with it.'

'Were they…?' Tina had to ask. 'Were they…?'

The police chief shook his head, knowing without her finishing the question what she'd wanted to know. 'I reckon they were killed instantly,' he said. 'Sure, they were burned but the car was so badly smashed first that they couldn't have been aware… I'd say it was instantaneous.'

'But how did it happen?' Tina shook her head in horror. 'How…?'

'Bloody kids,' the policeman growled. 'It's early days yet—the police accident investigation squad are on their way now—but by the look of it the kids pulled out to overtake the Croxtons on the crest. The Croxtons had been to a family christening party for the baby and were coming home late. They were travelling too damned fast as well. The kids came up over the hill and pulled out

to pass them. When the kids saw the tanker they just
veered straight back in front of the Croxtons' car. The
Croxtons' car will have clipped theirs and been swung
sideways in front of the tanker. End of story.'

The big man's voice cracked. 'Bloody kids. Bloody
alcohol. We got Doc Blaxton's call from the wedding,
warning us the kids were driving drunk, but we couldn't
reach them fast enough.'

Tina bit her lip, closed her eyes on the sickening
memory—and went back to work. There was nothing
else to do. When the world comes crashing down just
pick up the pieces and start over... Lloyd and Mark
came in and took over with the truck driver. Tina and
Sally coped with the teenagers.

They stabilised Sylvia and readied her for transfer by
air ambulance to Sydney. She had broken ribs and a
punctured lung, and their fear was pneumothorax.
Maybe if she hadn't been so drunk they could have operated at Gundowring, but as it was, they'd have to wait
for the alcohol to wear off, so they may as well use the
time getting her the best surgeon possible.

'And it's not me,' Sally told Tina in a voice that
shook. 'Not tonight. I can't operate. Liz Croxton is...
Liz Croxton was my friend.'

Sally choked on a sob and Tina thought for the hun-
dredth time how hard it was to be a doctor in a small
town. You were too damned involved. And she thought
about Jock. As an obstetrician, after the initial first aid
there had been little for Jock to do here. Lloyd and Mark
and Sally and Tina had their hands full, coping with
shock, fractures, burns and drunkenness, but there was
a worse job to be done—and Jock had volunteered.
Someone had to do it.

Jock had stayed at the scene to supervise the removal
of the dead couple from the wreck. The dead couple and

their tiny baby, Cameron Croxton, the baby Jock had delivered only two weeks ago.

Tina worked on steadily, but her thoughts were on Jock, lifting what remained of that tiny baby from the burned-out wreck...

She inserted a saline drip into the second girl in the teenagers' car—the girl had been dry-retching non-stop for an hour and the retching showed no sign of abating. Dead drunk, the girl abused her and tore the drip out— and Tina still knew who had the worst job of the night.

The teenagers' parents began to arrive, terrified, appalled and angry in turn. Tina settled them as best she could. Somehow the town had to come to terms with the fact that these young people had caused three deaths. All the teenagers would desperately need the support of their parents in the face of the town's anger. Without it, they could well go under.

So Tina and Sally talked and talked—talked each set of parents through their shock and saw them reunited with their teenagers—and each of them held back the anger burning inside. What were eighteen-year-olds doing, driving dead drunk? These parents must have known the kids had been drinking, and yet they'd left them...

Recriminations were useless. Anger was useless. The dead were dead. Take care of the living.

By five in the morning there was no more to be done. Tina borrowed the hospital car and drove home as weary as she'd ever felt in her life before. She didn't make it home. In the end, she couldn't make herself go. At home Christie would wake if Tina arrived at five a.m. and get up and ask her how her night had gone, and Tina couldn't bear telling her. Not yet. She'd have to tell it calmly, matter-of-factly, so as not to risk Christie plummeting back into that well of depression she was only just climbing from.

And there was Jock...

Tina hadn't seen Jock since she'd gone with the burned driver in the ambulance. She'd left Jock at the scene, facing the unfaceable. Jock, the strong one. Just how strong was he? Unconsciously, Tina turned her hands on the steering-wheel until her little car was facing west, facing the beach where Jock had his cottage. She had a choice here, but there was suddenly no choice.

To distress Christie or to comfort Jock... To comfort Christie or find comfort in Jock? It was no choice. No choice at all.

Jock was home, his car in his driveway. For a moment Tina hesitated, but only for a moment. The lights were on inside the house so he'd be awake. Tina sat outside for a long moment and let her thoughts drift over what Jock had faced tonight.

Jock might be strong, but there was only so much strength a man could show without breaking. Underneath, he bled. Jock might show the face of a man who stood alone and was so strong he needed no one—but Tina knew better. How, she didn't know, but she knew! Now she couldn't bear that he was alone so Tina parked the car and went right on in.

There was no answer to her knock on the front door. Tina gave a tentative push and the door swung wide.

'Jock?'

No answer.

He couldn't have been home for long, she thought, and he surely couldn't be asleep yet. Not after this night. Slowly Tina walked from room to room, calling. No one. She shouldn't be here, she thought bleakly. She was trespassing, intruding on his personal space, but she couldn't bear to go.

'Jock?' She swung open the back door and walked outside.

He was there. The little house was set on the beachfront, its front door facing the road but its back doors and windows leading straight down to a sandy cove beneath the headland. The first rays of the dawn were tinging the horizon, and Tina could see Jock's long, lean body pacing the foreshore. Alone.

He must always have been alone, Tina thought suddenly. He'd spent ten years with a dying mother and a father who blamed him for everything, and then the rest of his life accepting that blame. So, of course, Jock had learned to be alone. But he wouldn't be alone now. Not now! Not if she could help it.

Tina slipped off her crazy bridesmaid's sandals—heavens, she was still wearing the stained and ruined chiffon—and ran lightly down across the sand to meet him. Her heart was beating crazily in her chest. He must let her close. He must! She needed him so much.

'Jock?'

'Tina?' Jock stopped and stared up the beach at the approaching figure. 'Tina.'

It wasn't a welcome. The way he said her name was flat, devoid of any emotion at all—drained.

'Oh, Jock.' Without the slightest trace of self-consciousness, Tina went straight up to him, took his hands in hers and held on hard, whether he wanted the contact or not. She desperately needed the link. 'Jock, I had to come.'

'What are you doing here?' Still there was no emotion. Nothing.

'I need you,' she said softly, and closed her eyes and swallowed. She gripped his hands even tighter, but kept her eyes closed and said a thousand silent prayers in her head—all the same prayer.

'Jock, we've finished at the hospital,' she said in a voice that faltered. 'The driver's stabilised. His wife's beside him. Except for Sylvia, the teenagers are all OK. They're with their parents. Sally's gone home with Lloyd. Mark's gone home to Margaret. Meg Preston's come in to take over for the rest of the night and to-morrow she'll go home to her Rob. But... But I couldn't wake up Christie and I needed someone. I needed you.'

Silence.

There was only the sound of the gentle surf, the waves washing back and forth across the sand. In. Out. It surged in time with Tina's breathing. Tina gripped Jock's hands and held hard. She was fighting here for something she hardly understood. Fighting for him to need her as much as she needed him.

'Jock...' She let her head fall forward and touch his chest. He'd worn a dinner suit to the wedding. Heaven knew what sort of state the dinner suit was in now. His coat was gone, used as a pad to stop the driver's bleeding, and his shirt was open halfway down his chest, ripped and stained.

'I'm so sorry it had to be you who coped with...who coped with the little one,' she whispered. 'It must have torn you apart.'

'It didn't... I'm OK...' Jock's voice was harsh and cracked. 'Hell, Tina, I don't need—'

'You don't need anyone,' she murmured, and her fingers moved within his hands. His hands were rigid, not responding at all to her clasp, but her fingers still stroked, pleaded. 'Jock, don't. Don't try to do this on your own. You deliver a tiny baby two weeks ago and you love him. You can't disguise it from me, Jock, no matter how much you hide it from the world. Somehow you love each and every one of the babies you deliver and you use it to compensate for all the love you should have been given yourself.'

'I don't—'

'It's true,' Tina said harshly, and her eyes flew open to look up at him in the faint dawn light. 'I know. Because I love you, Jock. God knows why. But some-how...I've fallen for you hard and I can read you like a book. So tonight…I know what you'll have gone through when you had to lift Cameron Croxton from that car. It'll have torn you in two. And now… Now you come home alone and you pace the beach and you shove it all inside, like a physical thing that can be swallowed and got rid of and forgotten. Only it can't, Jock, it can't. All the hurt… You have to share. You must.'

Slowly—infinitely gently—she released her hold on his hands. She placed her arms around him and held him close—her slight body moulding itself to his. Whether he willed it or not, she was giving him comfort in the only way she knew. And Tina knew exactly what she was doing, with blinding clarity she knew. She was offering her body in the age-old way of women. Some hurts were just too deep for words.

For some hurts there was only one comfort, there was only one's body. One's home. Jock was her love, her home, and she must be his. Somewhere here the line became blurred and indistinct. Whether Tina was offering comfort or pleading for it herself she didn't know. Who knew? It suddenly didn't matter at all.

'I should have done something,' he said in a voice that cracked. 'Tina, we saw they were drinking…'

'I know. I've been thinking that over and over… But, Jock, there was no way we could have expected them to drive. That was their parents' responsibility.'

'They shouldn't be allowed to have kids if they won't accept that…'

'I know. But that doesn't mean the whole world has to be bleak, Jock. What happened to your mother… What happens to the rest of the world… Jock, don't let it destroy you. Let me close. Please…'

She slipped her hands up under his shirt and ran her fingers along the hard contours of his back. She felt him shudder but she didn't falter.

'Jock, let it go,' she whispered. 'Let it go. Just admit

that you need me. I need you as much as you need me. God knows, I need you more. I love you, Jock. And I can't… Jock, I can't handle tonight…without you.'

And she stood on tiptoe in the sand and she kissed him.

CHAPTER EIGHT

FOR one long moment Tina thought Jock wouldn't respond. For one long moment she thought that he really
would stand alone. He'd reject her body and her longing,
as he'd learned to reject his own emotional need. But
the night had been too long. Too long and too dreadful,
and Tina was holding him, kissing him and longing for
him to respond—aching for him to respond. He could
feel the ache in her lips, and the coldness that was piercing his body right to the bone was warmed by her. The
ice was slowly thawing, whether he willed the thaw or
not.

He had faced death tonight—he had faced horror—
and Tina was offering life. She was offering him a way
to go on and he'd have to be superhuman to resist her
loveliness and her comfort tonight.

So with a moan that spoke of sheer desperation—of
the coming to the end of a cold and lonely road—Jock
gathered her yielding body to his and kissed her back.

Not softly. Not that. Jock kissed her fiercely, with a
burning, searing need that shook both their bodies with
its intensity, and the moment he let his mouth respond
to hers both of them knew where this would lead. There
was only one possible ending to this night if both of
them were to find some measure of sanity.

Somehow they managed to get back to the house,
though afterwards Tina was unsure how. She must have
been carried, she thought, but if she had been, her mouth
never left Jock's, not for an instant. Somehow they made
it across the sand, through the back door and into Jock's
bedroom, where the big, barren bed lay waiting.

It didn't have long to wait. They were breathless, frantic with passion and frantic with desire. Tina clung to Jock as if she were drowning and he was melting into her. Burning into her. There was no hesitation now. They were one force, united, one body. Jock's mouth devoured her, his hands claiming her, stroking the smooth, soft curves of her breasts, moving down to cup her thighs and lift…

To bring her body close… Closer…

Their clothing was in the way. It was stupidly, frantically, in the way—of no import at all—only there to act as a barrier, and the last thing these two lovers needed was a barrier. Tina heard the chiffon rip as it came away from her body and she didn't care at all. Her hands were frantically doing the same undressing of Jock and she'd rip too if she must. She was searching… wanting…fighting to get her body next to his.

They must both have been a little mad, she'd thought later. A lot mad. But now… For tonight there was no thought but their mutual need, no thought but the fire that was consuming them both. There were no words, no laughter, just burning, searing need that could only…must only…have one end.

Tina's breasts were twin peaks of want. Her body was arching, and still her mouth was locked onto Jock's. Their tongues were moving backwards and forwards, seeking, searching and devouring, and the want in their mouths was echoed and magnified a thousand times in their loins.

'Oh, God, Tina, I want you.'

It was the only thing Jock said, and that was a harsh, passionate whisper that she hardly heard. It was the only thing he needed to say, and even that was superfluous. They were gloriously naked by now, skin against skin, fire meeting fire, and Jock was over her, poised, and Tina was arching…up…up…her body pleading…

If he didn't come into her she'd surely die of wanting.

Then he entered her. Magically, wondrously, he entered her, descending straight into her like an arrow into fire, into the moist recesses between her thighs. The joy was indescribable. Jock's body was filling the dreadful emptiness of the night. He was uniting their two bodies as firmly—more firmly—than any wedding vow could ever do, making two into one.

As Tina felt him inside her, the last of her reason—the last of her sanity—disappeared on the soft night air. There was no reason in this, but this was where she wanted to be. All her life she had been waiting to feel like this, and she hadn't known it until now. She hadn't known a man's body could feel like this, could smell like this, could taste like this.

Tina's hands linked urgently around Jock's broad shoulders and she held him down to her, held him into her. This was her man, her heart. Her body arched and arched again, sending messages of love and desire and pure animal passion straight back to him.

The glorious rhythm began. Over and over he drove into her, drowning his need in her loveliness. Down... further and further, deeper and deeper into her body, deeper into her soul.

There was only Jock. Nothing else in the world could matter at all but this man and his body. The horror of the night receded to a dreadful blur that was now far away, a horror that could be assuaged by love. Anything in the world could be faced with this love, with Jock inside her.

'Jock... Jock...'

Whether she called his name out loud she didn't know, she didn't care. Maybe it was her voice, or maybe it was just her heart, but the word was a vow as binding as any marriage vow. Jock...

Jock.

Then the night exploded into a blur of love and mist and stars, and there was nothing, nothing but Jock. Nothing but the link between this man and this woman.

And nothing could ever be the same again.

'Coffee?'

Tina opened one eye and peered up at a world that was way too bright.

The morning sun was flooding in from the beach. From the bedroom windows there was a view straight down to the waves for the house was practically on the beach and the French windows opened to sand and sea beyond.

Tina winced at the brilliant light and glittering water. She rolled over in the bed—to find Jock standing in the doorway.

The rat was fully dressed. Dressed! Jeans, open-necked shirt and bare feet, but dressed for all that, and grinning like the cat that had caught the very fattest canary.

Tina hauled the bedclothes up to her neck and glared.

'What gives you the right to be so damned decent, Jock Blaxton?'

'I like playing superior.' Jock crossed to the bed and bent to give her a light kiss on the nose. 'I know I don't *need* to play superior—I am already—but you'll just have to indulge my whims. Being up and dressed and bringing breakfast to naked women in my bed is one of my very favourite pastimes.'

Whoa...

Tina flinched. Naked women... Just how many naked women was he talking here?

Keep it light, she told herself desperately, keep it as light as Jock wanted. Last night she had bared her soul to this man. She'd told him how she felt. She'd told him she loved him.

If he wanted her on those terms…well, it was over to him now. She couldn't say it again, she had to play it his way.

'Are you feeling better, then?' She managed a smile and reached out a hand gratefully for the coffee.

'Is that what last night was all about?' Jock asked, settling his long body onto the bed beside her, putting his hand into her riot of curls and letting his fingers drift. 'Making me feel good?'

'Of course.' Her eyes laughed up at him and her hand reached out to the crotch of his jeans and gently kneaded. 'Did I succeed?'

'Did you succeed?' He groaned and hauled back the bedclothes, nearly spilling her coffee in the process. She shoved the mug on the bedside table as his mouth went straight to the valley below her breasts and he kissed her just above her heart. Who could drink coffee with this happening?

'You can't imagine how you succeeded,' he told her. 'Or how awful I felt before you came.' Jock hesitated and gently started stroking the flatness of her belly, sending shivers from her toes right up her body and back again. And then some!

Then his voice grew serious, and his arms held her as if he was still seeking comfort.

'I don't know how you can work full time in a casualty department,' he told her. 'That's why I chose obstetrics. So I don't have to handle catastrophes like that every day.'

'You still get tragedies in obstetrics.' Tina twisted her fingers in his hair and stroked, but at the same time she was trying hard to hold herself aloof from the seductive tenderness of his arms. A little bit aloof so that when he put her away from him—as put her away he must—she could still continue. Naked *women*, he'd said. Remember that! Women, plural!

But Tina had no power in her to resist this man, naked women plural or not. Her fingers sifted through and through his thick black curls, holding his head to her heart, and every moment she was falling deeper and deeper in love with him. 'And... And I can't take tragedies alone either,' she whispered.

'That's why you came last night? Because you didn't want to be alone?'

Had he forgotten that she'd told him she loved him? Tina thought bleakly. Did he think it had been just a line—something she said to all her other lovers, the same way he reacted to all his other naked women...?

But... Despite how she felt, she couldn't say it again. She couldn't say the words 'I love you'.

The words had been right last night. It had been needful to make him love her last night and their emotional need had been raw, but this morning it would be blackmail to throw her emotional dependence on him.

'That's right,' she said, and if her voice was a little stiff he didn't appear to notice. 'That's why I came. I couldn't go home to Christie. Not after that.'

'Speaking of Christie, won't she be worried now?' Jock glanced sideways at his watch and then went back to what he was concentrating on—drawing circles with his fingers on the bare skin right above her navel, and then below. The sensation was driving her wild. 'Tina, it's nine on a Sunday morning,' he said softly. 'You don't think she'll fret when she wakes and you're not home?'

'I'm twenty-eight years old and last night I went out with a very attractive single man,' Tina said. Dear heaven, if he didn't stop stroking her there she'd just die! Or maybe she'd die if he did stop stroking. 'If she can't guess where I am then she's a dingbat. And Christie's not a dingbat.'

'I see.'

But he didn't, Tina knew. He was thinking… He was thinking she always did this. Slept with her dates. Said she loved them and threw herself at them. Good grief! She was no virgin, but…

'I guess…I guess I should go home now,' Tina said in a brittle, strained voice, 'and see if I can get a bit more sleep. I'm on duty tonight.'

'Do you have to go?'

'I should…' But Jock's hand was still doing its magic stroking and Tina's resolution was turning to melted butter.

'Tina..'

'Yes?'

Jock's mouth was following his fingers, his lips leaving a trail of kisses downwards from her breasts, and she was burning up all over again.

'It might have been a mistake for me to get dressed,' he admitted, in a voice husky with passion. 'Hell, Tina. Last night was our last date. Does it have to finish already?'

And, of course, it didn't.

But as Tina lay in her lover's arms an hour later, and waited for the day to start and the world to overtake them, she felt cold and sick to the core.

Because Jock's voice had been firm and sure.

'Our last date,' he'd said, and his voice had been absolutely sure.

Tina left at eleven and Jock went swimming. He swam for close on two hours, back and forth across the bay as if his life depended on it, trying to burn off some of this damned energy. Some of this damned restlessness.

God, she was lovely. What would it be like to have her in his bed every night for the rest of his life?

'So, what are you proposing here, Jock, boy?' he growled into the surf. 'Marriage? Kids? The full catastrophe? That's disaster country and you know it. You're already playing the fool. Hell, Jock, you didn't even take precautions last night.'

He'd asked her about that. As she'd showered and dressed in a borrowed shirt over her tattered brides-maid's dress, he'd brought it up with some trepidation.

'Tina, last night... I didn't even think. I should have worn a condom, but things just got out of hand. Do we...? Are you...?'

'It's OK.' Tina's voice from under the shower had sounded strained and tired. Flat. 'It's the wrong time of the month, and even if it wasn't there's always the morn-ing-after pill. I'm a big girl, Jock Blaxton. I can take care of myself. So relax—unless you've got something nasty I should know about?'

She'd made a joke of it, for which he was grateful, but it could have been a catastrophe. He did not want to go down that road. Pregnancy? No way! So why had he let his hold on his senses slip?

It had been the night, he told himself, and the horror.

But it was more than that. There had been this inde-scribable urge this morning... When he'd walked into the bedroom with her coffee and seen Tina, lying glo-riously naked and fast asleep in his bed with her won-derful hair sprayed across the pillows... Her body... Her lovely body...

He'd wanted her so much it had hurt, and to let her go, without making love to her again, had been impos-sible. There'd been an urge to hold her to him for ever.

But that was the way of madness. It meant misery, as his father had known and as his father had taught his son to expect. He had to let her go. He must. He didn't want to get any more involved than he already was.

Damn, he was too involved now.

So... He'd never given Tina false promises, he told himself bleakly. She'd known from the start he didn't want to get involved. From now on the relationship must be purely professional, he told himself as he swam on.

'And, Jock, boy, if I were you I'd contact London tomorrow about that job. Because the sooner you get out of this place and remember your resolutions the better for all concerned.'

'You slept with Jock Blaxton?'

Christie eyed her sister's extraordinary outfit with stupefaction. One wrecked, bloodied bridesmaid's dress with one man's shirt over the top. She looked like something out of a horror movie. 'Good grief, Tina. Your dress is ripped all up the back. He didn't rape you?'

'Rape...? Why on earth...? Of course not.'

'There's blood on your dress. And it's in tatters.'

'Oh, yeah...' Tina looked down at her bridesmaid's dress and grimaced. 'Oh, heck.' She shook her head and managed a smile. 'No, Christie, he didn't rape me. It's been one hell of a night, and I'll tell you about it soon, but...'

Despite the horror of the night before—soon she would have to find the courage to tell Christie about it—Tina couldn't quite keep a tiny note of pleasure from her voice as she said the words. The night hadn't been all horror. 'I slept with Jock all of my own accord.'

'Well, well...' Christie shook her head in disbelief and hauled her baby closer to her breast. It was lunchtime for Rose and Rose was only interested in one thing. The love life of Aunty Tina was a matter of supreme indifference to young Rose Maiden. 'Well, well,' Christie said again, a little smile playing at the edges of her mouth. 'Does that mean Rose's Aunty Tina has found herself a decent man for a change?'

'What do you mean, a decent man?'

'Peter's a wimp,' Christie said bluntly. 'A cheque book on legs, and you can't say that about your Dr Blaxton. He's testosterone on legs. I don't know if he has money but it doesn't matter. He's not just a cheque book.'

'No.' Tina managed a smile as she shook her head. 'I guess you can't say he's just a cheque book, and I'd have to agree with the testosterone. But he's not *my* Dr Blaxton, Christie.'

'What do you mean?' Christie's eyes narrowed and she subjected her sister to a searching glance, seeing the troubled look behind Tina's smile. 'You *did* sleep with him. Tina, one-night stands are hardly your style.'

Tina had to agree. 'No.' She shook her head. 'They're not but, sadly, they're all Jock wants. And if a one-night stand is all I can have of Jock...' She spread her hands in resignation. 'Well, Christie, I'm taking crumbs! Or I've taken crumbs. I don't think Jock has any more to give.'

The repercussions of the accident on the night of the wedding blasted outwards through the valley with an almost shattering force, and the valley doctors were frantically busy for the next week. In a small community everyone was affected by such a tragedy.

The trauma was deep and far-reaching, and guilt and sorrow showed itself in all sorts of ways—from severe angina in an elderly uncle to a teenager presenting with eczema from head to toe. It didn't make any sense at all, but with sedation and counselling the eczema eased and so did the angina. Stress had inexplicable ways of showing itself.

The week finished with the teenage driver of the car attempting suicide, by which time the valley doctors were close to desperation themselves. Tina found herself so busy she hardly had time to think about Jock.

Hardly.

She didn't actively think about him—she was too busy to do that—but Jock was in the back of her thoughts all the time, a constant, overriding presence. Tina's life had been changed for ever, whether Jock was aware of it or not. Tina was absolutely, irrevocably, in love, absolutely, irrevocably, committed, no matter what Jock intended to do with that love.

Nothing, Tina thought bleakly as the awful week wore on and she saw nothing of Jock at all, he intends to do nothing. He's finished with me. Now he'll move on to the next of his two-date stands.

Ellen eyed her at the end of the week as she finished her shift. It was dawn, the time when human defences were at their weakest. Ellen bided her time—the girl looked just plain exhausted after a hectic night of duty and Ellen had been eyeing her sideways all night—and finally she pounced.

'Dr Rafter, are you going to tell Aunty Ellen what's going on here?' she asked.

'What do you mean?'

'I mean between you and Dr Blaxton.'

'Then no. I'm not saying a word.' Dawn or not, Tina wasn't stupid. She was adjusting a drip in a baby she'd admitted during the night with dehydration, and her fierce concentration wasn't solely to avoid Ellen's eyes. A tummy upset in a two-month-old baby could lead to death if the fluids weren't maintained, and little Brie had been losing fluids for twelve hours now. 'Ellen, I need electrolytes done here.'

'I've already ordered them.' Ellen moved her ample body around to block the door to the nursery as Tina turned to leave. There was a glint of resolution behind her glasses. 'Now, Tina, lass, you've been wandering round, looking miserable, ever since the night of the crash. I thought it was just the horror and then young Andrew's attempt at suicide...'

'It is.'

'It's not,' Ellen said firmly. 'You've coped magnificently with everything, and as for the grief…well, we've all had to go through that. But, Tina, you've coped with hysterical relatives and stomach pumps and the lot. You've counselled the kids who survived and you've done it well. The horror's fading—but the shadows under your eyes are getting darker.'

'I don't know what you mean.'

'It wouldn't be Dr Blaxton's announcement that he's leaving, would it?' Ellen demanded—and watched her.

'Leaving?' Tina's eyes flew to Ellen's. 'Oh, Ellen…'

'I wondered if you'd heard.' Ellen's eyes softened at the look of pain that washed across Tina's face. 'I was right, then. I thought as much. The man's been avoiding you all week and—'

'Avoiding me?'

'I watched you both last night,' Ellen said softly. 'Dr Blaxton delivered a baby and he had to come in here afterwards and check her—but you were in here, working on this little one. I heard him come down the corridor and had a bet with myself that he'd be distracted when he saw you were here, and sure enough…the man stopped at the door, saw you and left again. He decided to go find himself a cup of coffee. He came back an hour later when you were gone.'

'Ellen…'

'If you think it's natural that he stays up an hour longer just to have a cup of coffee in the middle of the night, I don't,' Ellen said solidly. 'You and I are on night shift and we go home now and to bed. Dr Blaxton is due to start his day in about an hour—but it's my bet he won't start until five minutes after you leave.'

'Ellen…'

'I'm not imagining it, am I?' Ellen went on mercilessly. 'There's things going on here between the pair of you. And now Dr Blaxton tells me that he's starting a new job in London as soon as Gina and Struan get back.'

Ellen's kindly eyes perused her young friend's face. 'He looks as bleak as you do, Dr Rafter,' she said softly. 'So...'

'So nothing.' Tina shrugged. 'So nothing, Ellen. You're imagining things. There's nothing between us.'

'Except?'

'Except nothing.'

There had to be nothing. If Jock was leaving for London then there had to be nothing. Except...

CHAPTER NINE

EXCEPT she was pregnant.

Tina was staring with horror at two blue lines. Then she shook the strip of lined plastic, as if somehow it could possibly be wrong. Somehow.

She wasn't wrong. The two lines stayed firmly blue. Immutable and absolute. One positive pregnancy test. Oh, no.

Tina sat back on her bed and stared down sightlessly at her lap. She'd suspected this. For the last week she'd been telling herself she was crazy. Sure, she was tired and her breasts were sore but, then, she'd been working too hard, she'd been disturbed a few times by Ally and Tim when she was supposed to be sleeping during the day, and her period was due. That was why her breasts were tender.

Only now... As of last Monday her period had been overdue and the tenderness in her breasts was increasing. So, telling herself all the time that she was stupid, there was no need to worry and that she was overreacting, she'd popped a pregnancy test in her bag and brought it home.

To this.

Dear God... What now? One thing was for sure, Jock wouldn't want to know about this. It had been nearly four weeks since the night she'd slept with Jock, and in those four weeks Jock had scarcely spoken to her. Their conversation had been limited to professional need, and she'd heard he'd taken out Sister Jackson, the sister in charge of the nursing home. Twice.

Had Sister Jackson turned into the next of Jock's naked women? Tina thought bleakly. Who knew? If she had then Jock would have moved on to the next lady by now. Tina turned numbly back to the strip of plastic and stared, willing the second line to go away. It didn't. The blue line seemed to be carved in stone. The test said that she, Tina Rafter, was one hundred per cent pregnant.

How could she have been so stupid? It had been the wrong time, she thought desperately, her period had barely finished on the night she'd slept with Jock. She shouldn't have ovulated for at least a week after that, she should have been safe. She couldn't possibly be pregnant. She was.

'Never discount pregnancy,' she heard the echoes of her old obstetric professor intoning. 'Even in a nunnery, never discount pregnancy. Sperm has a way of getting through walls three feet thick. It gets through vows of chastity and through pills and condoms and vasectomies. There's no known hundred per cent successful birth control method for a fertile woman except abstinence, and even abstinence has to be strongly suspect.'

Dear God.

She should have taken the morning-after pill. She should have—but, then, in the days after the crash she'd been frantically busy, and taking the morning-after pill...well, she'd had no samples. She would have needed to walk into the pharmacy and say to Horrible Kevin, the pharmacist of the sweaty hands and big mouth, 'please, I need a morning-after pill' and handed over a script written to herself. Kevin would have looked at her and smirked, and spread the word...

'This is stupid,' she told herself fiercely. 'It was your damned pride that stopped you asking for a morning-after pill. You know you should have. It was dumb stupidity. And now...'

Now what? Abortion?

Unconsciously Tina's hand dropped to her abdomen.

It was flat and tight and hard, but the blue line told her that somewhere in there a tiny life was stirring—a life created by the love between Jock and Tina, a life created by their mutual need.

Only Jock no longer needed her—he'd moved on.

'It's just a foetus,' Tina said aloud, as if calling it the hard anatomical name would make it less than it really was. 'A foetus, not a baby. It's no bigger than a tadpole. And it's going to wreck your life. You're only five weeks pregnant, you can abort...'

No.

No. The word slammed into her heart and it stayed there. Unwittingly her hands formed a link across her stomach and held, in the age-old gesture of a woman protecting what was most precious to her.

She had turned twenty-nine last week. Twenty-nine.

'I'm twenty-nine years old and I'm going to have a baby,' she whispered, and suddenly it didn't seem such a disaster. Suddenly there was joy flooding through the terror, and the link of her hands across her stomach grew tighter. A baby...

How could she get rid of a baby that was part of her and part of the man she loved? she asked herself.

She couldn't. No way! No matter what Jock wanted, this baby had been created with love, it was here to stay—and she'd welcome it with joy. As for the practicalities...

There was a knock on the door and her sister peered around, her face anxious. Baby Rose was in Christie's arms, and Ally and Tim were stalking behind.

'You've been in here for ages,' Christie said. 'Is there something wrong?'

'Maybe. Maybe not.' Tina took a deep breath. She had to start some time; she had to plan for a future here, a future for all of them. 'Christie, you know...you know I said that I'd only stay here for a few months?'

'Yes?' Christie was no longer watching Tina. Her eyes were on the little piece of plastic, lying on her sister's lap, and the box it came in beside her on the bed. PregTest, the label on the box said in demure blue letters, the blue the same colour as the two blue lines on the plastic.

'I…I think I might be staying longer,' Tina said, and her voice shook. 'Christie…' She looked up at her big sister and the tables were suddenly turned. For the past two months she'd cared for Christie, hauling her slowly out of her well of depression, but it was Christie who was the strong one now. It was Christie who gathered her little sister in a bear hug and held her close, with Rose somehow squashed between them. 'Oh, Christie.' She gulped on a sob of fright. 'How on earth will we manage with four babies between us?'

'You have to tell him.'

Four cups of tea later, Christie and Tina were still staring at each other over the table. The change in Christie was astounding. If any good was coming of this, it was starting with Christie, Tina thought wryly. The dejected woman who'd had trouble raising a smile and who'd been content to let Tina and Marie run her life had disappeared. Now she was taking up cudgels; she was going to war on Tina's behalf—and she'd love doing it.

'Jock has a responsibility here, Tina, he made you pregnant. He'll have to pay child maintenance at the very least.'

'I guess.' Tina stirred her tea and looked sightlessly into its depths. 'I did tell him I was safe. I can't hold him…'

At the look on her face, Christie hesitated.

'Tina, are you so sure there's nothing left between you?' she probed gently, changing tack from anger to

sympathy. 'Nothing that can be salvaged? I mean…you
and Jock. You make a lovely couple. He'd make a lovely
husband.'

'No.' Tina put down her mug with a thump. 'That's
one thing he wouldn't, Christie. He makes a wonderful
doctor and he makes a good friend. And…' Her face
turned pink. 'And he also makes a great lover. The best.
But Jock will make no woman a husband—he's vowed
that all along. He slept with me with no promises at all
and now he's taking out someone else. He doesn't want
this baby, Christie, and he doesn't want me.'

'But you'll still tell him you're pregnant?'

'I think I must,' Tina said bleakly. 'He is the…he is
my baby's father, and when he goes…' Tina's voice
faltered. Jock was leaving for London and there was
nothing she could do about it. 'When he goes away to
London,' she said slowly, 'he needs to know he's leaving a little part of him behind.'

'He's leaving his baby.' Christie's voice softened almost to a whisper. 'Oh, Tina, what if he wants it? What
if he wants to be a daddy?'

'I don't think there's any chance of that,' Tina told
her sister, and her voice was bleak. 'One baby too
many… Boy, there surely is one baby too many now.'

'She went to sleep before tea and woke up hungry so I
made her a peanut-butter sandwich. She ate it and suddenly…suddenly…'

Midnight, a peaceful night in Casualty—until now.
The woman's voice was hoarse with terror. She was
standing in the entrance to Casualty, holding her toddler
in her arms and clutching her close in fear. She wouldn't
release her, and it took all of Tina's strength to prise the
woman's arms away so she could see the child.

And the child was in deadly trouble.

At a silent, urgent eye message from Tina, Barbara,

the casualty sister, came forward and took Mrs Hughes's arm, pulling her gently aside but brooking no argument.

'Let her be, Mrs Hughes. Let Dr Rafter examine her.'

But Claire Hughes was past reason. She started to sob, a harsh, piercing sob that racked her whole body, and she pulled away from Barbara in terror.

'She's dying. She's dying... I had to leave the other children with the neighbour. My husband's at work and I couldn't find... Oh, dear God...'

'Claire...'

Claire wasn't listening. She had a hysterical personality at the best of times, and this was the worst. The woman slumped forward, crumpling to the floor in overblown passion, and grabbed Tina by the leg.

'My baby. My baby. My baby...'

The baby was turning blue. Tina looked down at the child, trying to balance against the woman hauling at her leg and hold the child and see at the same time. She didn't need to see much—Tina knew instantly what was happening.

The mother had said she'd eaten a peanut-butter sandwich. Peanuts. It must be the peanuts. The child's whole body was swelling. Her eyes were puffy, swollen slits and there was an angry red rash over her arms and face. Her breathing was shallow and painful and...

Suddenly, the breathing was non-existent, and through her sobs Claire heard the breathing stop.

She screamed, grabbed Tina's other leg and tried to drag her down with her.

'No. No. No!'

'Let me go.' Tina hauled herself backwards but the woman still held on. 'Mrs Hughes, let me go!' Tina pulled back with all her strength, but her arms were full of unconscious toddler. The nursing sister bent over to try and take the woman away, but Claire lashed out. She was way beyond reason, way beyond thought.

'Claire!' The harsh, male voice shot out over the room, catching them all. Jock had been passing the door. One glance in had told him what was going on, and three fast strides took him to Claire.

He asked no questions. He lifted the woman bodily into his arms, hauled her away from Tina and dumped her unceremoniously in a chair beside the door.

'Stay there and don't you move an inch,' he snapped, in a voice that would have stopped an army in its tracks. 'Barbara, stay with her and don't let her move. Call Security if you must. Tina, bring the little one in here.' He held the door of the examination cubicle wide and Tina practically ran in. A flick of the lock and the hysterical mother was Barbara's concern, safely locked on the other side of the door. At last they could concentrate on what was happening. The child was still not breathing, and the awful blue was fading to a ghastly white.

'Intubation,' Tina gasped. 'There's no time...'

The child's throat must have swollen completely shut. There was no way they could do artificial resuscitation without a tube. There was no room for the air to get through the swollen throat and there was no time for antihistamine to work. But Tina didn't have to tell Jock what was needed. Before she'd settled the toddler onto the couch Jock was at the crash cart, sorting out what he needed. It took him seconds.

He moved like lightning. One fast swipe of lubricant on the intubation tube and he'd turned back while Tina was still lowering the little one onto her back, tilting her head and lifting her jaw. They moved like two parts of a whole. As the tube was readied Jock deferred to Tina. She was the anaesthetist, and she had the skills to intubate. He took over positioning the jaw so Tina could insert the laryngoscope and carefully, carefully, position the tube.

The vocal chords were so swollen...

Jock tilted the jaw further, his hands rock-steady, and Tina slid the tube down. Almost before she had the tube in place Jock was moving again, injecting adrenalin. Before she needed to ask he'd readied the bag for ventilation. In seconds—less—they had it connected. Then, as Tina breathed gently into the limp little body, Jock started to set up the IV line for antihistamine. Dear God, let them be in time...

One puff of the ventilator bag. Another and then another. Please... And then the child took one long harsh, grating breath, and the little chest moved of its own accord. Tina practically sagged in relief.

Medicine! Who'd be a doctor? she thought grimly as the child started to breathe again. One minute she'd been sitting having a coffee with Barbara and the next she'd been fighting for a little life.

She held the tube carefully in place, mindful of the child's natural reaction before they had the chance to sedate. Without sedation she'd gag on the tube. But Jock was already organising antihistamine and sedation. She may well have lost this life without Jock, Tina acknowledged. With an uncontrolled, hysterical mother on her hands and with a baby not breathing...

Peanuts, Tina thought bitterly as she and Jock worked on to stabilise the little one's breathing. Ban all peanuts! They were so dangerous. Hardly anyone knew how allergenic they could be—except the people who reacted like this.

Little Marika Hughes would be fine now, but she'd spend the rest of her life being careful about her food, reading ingredients, and carrying adrenalin and antihistamine wherever she went because there were foods made with compounds of ingredients where peanuts weren't listed.

There was a knock on the door and there was time

now for Tina to answer it. Barbara stood there, her face
creased in concern. One look at little Marika's face, fast
regaining its colour, and Barbara's own face flushed.

'Oh, thank God. She'll be OK?'

'I think so.' Tina managed a shaky smile. They had
come so close... She gestured to Jock who was still
working. They'd keep the tracheotomy tube in place for
several hours until the last of the swelling had gone
down. The toddler would have to be sedated to hold it
in. Still, that was the least of their problems now. 'How's
her mum?' she asked. 'Quieter?'

'I had to knock her out,' Barbara said. 'I'm sorry.
There was no other doctor in the hospital, and as soon
as you guys locked yourselves away she went bananas.
More bananas. She kicked Eric right where it hurt most,
and if we hadn't stopped her she would have broken this
door down.'

Tina grimaced. Thank heaven Eric, their security
guard, was large.

'What did you give her?'

'Valium intramuscularly. Eric held her down while I
gave it to her. Oh, and her husband arrived and he helped
administer it.' Barbara nursed a bruised arm. 'She'll
probably have us all up for assault.'

'You may well be able to put in a counter-charge.'
Tina frowned down at the ugly bruise on Barbara's arm.
'Are you OK?'

'Yeah, well, I'll live. And I won't do that—she really
was terrified.' She hesitated. 'The husband's still here,'
she added, with another look at Marika. 'Do you have
time to talk to him? He's going out of his tree—only
not so volubly as his wife.'

Tina flashed a glance at Jock. His hands were still
working on the IV line. He had such skilled hands, Tina
thought inconsequentially. And his face...

He did love babies, Tina thought, and the idea was

like a kick in the stomach. He did. And he *should* want them. He *should* want babies of his own.

He should want a wife, too, but he didn't, and now… Now, like it or not, Jock's child would be coming into the world, and he wouldn't want to know about it.

'I…I'll come back in a few minutes, Jock,' Tina said aloud, and if her voice shook surely it was because of the tension of the last few minutes. Surely! 'If you can stay with her…'

'I'll stay.'

He would—she hadn't needed to ask. Wild horses couldn't have dragged Jock away from a baby whose life was on the line. So how would he react to a baby of his own?

It was half an hour before Tina found Jock again. She'd had to calm Barry Hughes, reassure him that things were OK and then see to his wife. They'd settled her in a single room and Tina wrote her up for admission overnight. Barry had more children at home and he had enough on his plate, without sending Claire home with him.

Now she had to write up retrospective orders for drugs. In theory, Barbara had no business giving drugs without doctors' orders. In practice it had been a choice of drugging her or calling the police and having her dragged away, screaming.

Now… Claire was close to sleep, medicated almost to oblivion. She was tucked firmly into bed, with metal guard rails on either side of the bed to keep her safe and a junior nurse in attendance. She managed to open her eyes as Tina came in, and kept them wide long enough to get out her most important question.

'I'm… Oh… Marika…'

'Marika's safe,' Tina said firmly, crossing to take the woman's hand. 'She's fine. She's fast asleep. Dr Blaxton is looking after her and the swelling's already going down. You'll see her in the morning, but she really is OK.'

'Oh, Marika… Oh, I'm so sorry…'

The woman let a weary tear slide down her face, and then slid into sleep.

Jock was sitting in the children's ward with Marika when Tina went to find him. He was alone. Barry had been and gone—home to care for his two other small children. The man had a heavy weight on his shoulders, Tina thought—three tiny children and a wife who re-acted to emergencies with hysterics was no one's idea of a picnic.

This could well have been fatal. If it hadn't been for Jock…

Tina stood at the door of the darkened ward and watched him for a couple of moments before she en-tered. Unaware of her presence, Jock sat. He was totally still, calm and watchful, his total attention on watching the gentle rise and fall of the little one's chest.

It was as if he wasn't tired in the least, Tina thought. It was as if he had nothing better to do in the whole world than to watch the steady breathing of this child. He loved. He was a man capable of so much love…

Unconsciously, Tina's hand dropped to her abdomen and fleetingly stayed there. She was eight weeks preg-nant. In five more weeks Jock was due to leave—to take himself off to the other side of the world. Would he ever look down at his own child with the same tenderness with which he was watching this little one?

No way. One baby too many… But she had to tell him, and there was no easy way.

'Jock?'

Jock glanced up and smiled, but his smile was ab-stracted. His attention was only on his little patient. There was no way he would focus his attention on Tina, not now. She'd had her allotted two dates with this man. Jock had moved on.

'She's fine,' he said softly, turning back to the bed. 'The nurse will come in soon and take over obs but I thought I'd sit here for a bit, just to make sure she's stabilised. There's no need for you to stay.'

She was dismissed. There was no mistaking the finality of his tone. He didn't want her here, but Tina had something to say. It had to be said, and there was never going to be a better time than now—in this darkened room and in the intimacy of a shared success—in the time before the world broke in again.

All she needed was courage, a trainload of courage. She needed the courage to ignore the dismissal and say what she needed to say—to say what he least wanted to hear, what he'd spent a lifetime avoiding. She took a deep breath, wiped her suddenly moist palms on the sides of her white coat and crossed to sit on the chair on the other side of the toddler's bed.

'Jock, I need to talk to you,' she said, and her voice gave a definite wobble. 'I need—'

'Do you have a medical problem?' There it was again. The blunt, harsh dismissal. Medicine or nothing.

'In a way.' Courage, Tina, courage. She tilted her chin and met Jock's look head-on over the bedclothes. The only sound was the faint whistle of Marika's breathing through the tube—nothing else.

'I'm pregnant.'

Then there was nothing, no sound at all. It went on and on, the silence stretching into a minute. Two minutes. Three. Finally Tina could bear it no longer. Jock's face was totally impassive, and he sat like a man carved in stone. There was no warmth at all in his look, nothing except blankness. Say something, Tina's heart screamed, say something, but he said nothing at all. She couldn't bear it. She couldn't. So... Where did she go

from here? She didn't know, but wherever she went Tina
knew she would be travelling alone. She'd said what
she'd had to say, and now she had to leave.

'I'll...I'll leave you to it. I need to go back to
Casualty.' Tina finally found the strength to rise to her
feet. One more look at that cold face and she shuddered
and turned away. There was pain shooting through and
through her. It was a pain worse than any physical agony.

Dear God, she loved this man, but he wanted nothing
to do with her—nothing to do with her or with his child.
'I'm sorry, Jock,' she whispered, 'but I thought you
ought to know.' And she turned and walked straight out
of the room.

One of the night nurses was just coming in as she
left—Penny, the nurse who was taking over Marika's
obs from Jock. She smiled at Tina and then turned in
astonishment to watch as Tina walked straight past her.
There was no answering smile, nothing, as Tina made
her way blindly along the corridor toward Cas.

Tina was known for her laughter and her friendliness
and her bounce. There was no bounce in her tonight.
Something dreadful must have happened. Fearfully the
nurse walked on, swinging open the door of the children's ward and expecting the worst. Sister Silverton had
told her that little Marika Hughes was recovering, but
by the look on Dr Rafter's face she expected to be walking in on a dead baby.

She wasn't. Marika Hughes was sleeping soundly and
breathing steadily—it was a good result. But Dr
Blaxton... Penny stared down at him in amazement for
Dr Blaxton had the same look on his face as Tina had
had. It was a look the young nurse had never seen before, and Penny had been out with him twice.

'Thanks, Penny,' Jock said blankly. He rose and
stretched his long frame, but the look on his face didn't

alter. 'Don't leave her alone for a minute,' he ordered, handing over the chart. 'Ten-minute blood-pressure checks, keep an eagle eye on that tube and give me a ring the minute there's any change. But I don't expect there to be. The swelling's reducing already so I'll leave you to it.'

He walked out of the room in the same trance-like state in which the nurse had just seen Tina.

CHAPTER TEN

TINA was writing patient histories when Jock arrived. Her red curls were falling over her face, her head was bent and she was concentrating fiercely on what she was doing. She was concentrating as if it was the most important thing in the world to record what had happened to Marika Hughes on this night.

Sister Roberts was cleaning the examination cubicle at the far end of Casualty. The door to the cubicle was closed so, working in a pool of light in the dimmed casualty area, Tina seemed totally isolated. Jock felt his heart wrench. Dear heaven, she was so alone, and she was so lovely. She was pregnant with his child.

How was he supposed to feel? he wondered. He stood in the entrance and stared across at this enigmatic child-woman, this laughing, lovely creature who'd bewitched him from the moment he'd seen her, and he felt the old irrational fears surge through and through him. And some!

Tina. Pregnant.

He hadn't wanted this. He hadn't! How could she possibly be pregnant? How was he supposed to cope with this? But Tina was bent over her work and her hair was falling forward and... Dear God, he loved her. But hell! Pregnant!

He was going to London, he thought savagely. Leaving. The job overseas had been confirmed. He didn't want to be in love with anyone, he didn't want to feel like this about Tina and he didn't want to be a father to this child. He didn't want...

Tina looked up at him and smiled, and Jock's thoughts

144

stopped in mid-sentence. He didn't know what the hell he didn't want—or what he did want. In the last five minutes his orderly world had been turned upside down and the rules had all changed. Or maybe it had been turned upside down the minute Tina had walked into his life.

'It's OK, Jock,' Tina said steadily, the smile still on her face and the pain in her face almost hidden from the outside world. Almost. 'It's fine. There's no need to look like that.' God, was his panic so obvious? 'There's no call for you to marry me or worry about us or for you to have any part in this. I'm not holding you to me. I…I just thought…you have the right to know about the baby before you leave.'

'Tina, what the…?' With one explosive oath Jock was over the other side of the room, shoving his palms flat on her desk and bending forward to meet her head to head. 'What the hell is happening here? I don't understand. You told me you were safe. You told me you'd take precautions, and you're not stupid.'

'That's just it. I was stupid.'

'No. You're not a dope, Tina. If you're pregnant then you wanted to get pregnant.'

She didn't flinch, not outwardly at least.

'No, Jock, I didn't want to get pregnant,' she said steadily. 'No matter how it looks, I didn't set out to trap you. You have to believe that. I thought…I really did think it was the wrong time of the month. It was—but I should have made sure. I know no time is completely safe but it was just that…I couldn't bring myself to take the morning-after pill so maybe subconsciously… Maybe…'

She spread her hands, trying to make him see, trying to make sense of things herself.

'You see, to me this baby's not a disaster, Jock,' she managed.

'Not a disaster?' He stared down disbelievingly. 'Of course it's a disaster. It's a total, unmitigated disaster. On a scale of one to ten it ranks about a hundred and fifty. Of all the stupid, senseless...'

But Tina had had enough. These words meant nothing and she didn't want to hear them. *Stupid. Senseless.* This was a baby they were talking about here. A baby whose mother was Tina and whose father was Jock. A child. She rose and backed against the wall, standing as far away from him as she could without walking past him and leaving. Her hands knotted behind her back—a gesture of defence against the emotions flooding through her—and her face was deathly white.

Senseless? Jock's baby? No and no and no.

'Jock, I have to tell you...' She closed her eyes for a long moment, and when she opened them she knew exactly what she wanted to say. She needed to tell him what was in her heart. She needed to give him the truth, stupid or not—and let him do with it what he willed.

'Jock, my stupidity has nothing to do with this pregnancy,' she whispered. 'Not now. It's time to look forward, not back.'

'But—'

'No, just listen. Jock, I'm twenty-nine years old and I've fallen in love. Stupid or not, I've fallen totally, blindly, absolutely, in love with you. I'm more in love than I've ever been in my life. I've never felt this way about anyone and I've lived for twenty-nine years. But...you're leaving and I know...I know the odds on me feeling like this about anyone else are impossible. So the thought of carrying your baby fills me with joy.'

The hard incredulity was still on Jock's face. 'You mean you *did* want to get pregnant,' he said flatly.

'No.' Tina's voice was as flat as his. As hard. Negating his accusation. 'I didn't. But now that I am...I can no sooner have an abortion than I can fly. Unlike you, I don't think there's one too many babies in the world. I can care for this baby. I'll give this little one all my love. All my love…'

'You're broke,' Jock said bluntly, cruelly. 'How the hell do you intend to care for it?'

Tina's chin went up then. Practicalities she was good at; plans were what filled the void.

'Christie and I have talked about it. If Struan will give me a permanent job—and when I took the job he said he'd like me here permanently—then I'll stay in Gundowring. Christie will sell the farm, move into town and we'll live together. We'll manage—we don't need much. Christie will be at home while I work, and my wage will support us all.'

'You have it all planned.' Anger was riding through and through him as Jock watched Tina speak. They had it all worked out, these women, but where the hell did that leave him?

'Jock…'

'Why the hell?' He swore and turned away from her, staring bleakly out the window into the darkness. 'Hell, Tina, am I supposed to just walk away? Walk away from my child?'

'So what do you want to do?' she asked gently. 'What do you want to do with fatherhood, Jock?'

Silence. Nothing. Then Jock made a decision. It felt hard and leaden and dreadful—and flew against everything he had ever been taught. He felt trapped. But this was Tina. Hell, this was Tina! He'd walked right into this trap and maybe it was time to let the door swing shut and accept his fate.

'We'll have to get married,' Jock said heavily. 'I can't see anything else for it.'

'He proposed.'

'Yep.'

'Oh, Tina...'

'Now, before you start getting carried away and planning weddings, let's get one thing clear,' Tina told her sister. 'I am not marrying Jock. Pregnant or not, marriage is out of the question. There is no way I am trapping Jock into marriage.'

'But—'

'Christie, he said, "We'll have to get married. I can't see anything else for it." And he looked as sick as a horse.'

'Oh,' Christie said doubtfully, and her face fell. 'I see.'

'I knew *you* would, but *he* can't see it. He doesn't understand why I won't.'

'You mean he still wants—'

'He wants to be honourable,' Tina burst out. 'He wants a wife and baby like a hole in the head, but he's going to do the right thing by us, by golly. So now he'll marry me if he has to shove me down the aisle in front of a shotgun.'

'It's supposed to be the bride's father, shoving the groom down the aisle with a shotgun when you're in this condition,' Christie said dubiously. 'I don't think I've ever heard of a groom doing it with a bride.'

'Yeah, well, you're not about to see it now,' Tina told her. 'I told him to take his wedding and shove it.'

'And he said...'

'He said we'd talk about it tomorrow when we're more rational.'

'Oh.'

'"Oh" is right. Oh, no!'

'We'll get married on the seventh of November.'

'Pardon?'

It was seven o'clock the next night. Tina had been at work for a whole five minutes. She'd barely had time to put her white coat on and hang her stethoscope around her neck before Jock came striding through the doors.

'It's the first date that we can legally do it,' Jock said bluntly. 'I've checked. There's a month's cooling-off period, between applying for a licence and marrying.'

'I'm sorry.' Tina dug her hands deep into the pockets of her white coat and glared. 'You'll have to explain. I seem to have missed out on part of the conversation here.'

'Like?'

'Like the hero going down on bended knee and laying his heart on his sleeve. And the heroine—that's me, by the way—turning a blushing shade of rose and coyly saying, "Oh, really, Dr Blaxton, you'll have to ask my father".' She managed a shaky smile. 'And then the hero—that's you—producing a diamond worth enough to take my breath away and sweeping me into his arms and against his heart—for ever. I've read my romances, Dr Blaxton. I know what's what.'

'Don't be stupid.'

'You see, that's just it,' Tina said sadly. 'I am stupid. You said it yourself. Stupid to get myself pregnant. Stupid to be in this mess in the first place. Stupid even to love you. So you don't want a stupid bride, Dr Blaxton, you don't want a bride at all.'

'Tina…'

'You don't want to be married, Jock,' Tina said, and her voice was flat. 'And, baby or not, I'm not marrying any man who doesn't love me.'

Jock took a deep breath, steadying himself. 'Tina, that's blackmail.'

'Well, it's a strange kind of blackmail,' Tina snapped. 'There's a common misconception that love comes before marriage. I might love you, Jock Blaxton, but there is no way on this earth I am marrying you if you don't love me right back.'

'Tina...'

'I have a customer,' she said coldly, as a car swept into the entrance. 'Don't you have any babies to deliver?'

'Not at the moment.'

'Then go away and annoy someone else,' she told him. 'Or check out Sarah Page, the new nurse down on Two East. She's only been working here for two nights so maybe she's escaped your attentions so far. A whole new nurse, Dr Blaxton. That's two great evenings, seeing if you can make someone else fall in love with you before you leave for London. But go away. I'm working and I'm not interested in your crazy plans.'

He didn't go far away at all. Jock hovered, stopping to speak to the cas. sister before leaving, unsure whether to go or stay—unsure just what the heck to do. His head was spinning. Hell, she had to marry him. He couldn't leave now. But...

Then he paused as he saw Barbara, the cas. sister, helping a middle-aged man out of a car and onto a trolley at the entrance to Casualty. The man was naked from the waist up, bent double, unable to straighten. Tina was crossing quickly to see what the trouble was, and Jock figured he'd stick around and check he wasn't needed.

It beat going back to his lonely house with things still undecided. It beat letting himself think any more. There was a woman rushing from the driver's seat of the car to help the man onto the trolley, and Jock recognised her. It was Lorna Colsworth, head of Gundowring's ladies bowling team, member of the hospital board, upholder of the town's moral principles. Wife of the local undertaker, Simon Colsworth.

Jock glanced at the trolley, expecting to see Simon, but it wasn't Simon. It was Reg Carney, the town's butcher, red-faced, overweight and with his features contorted in agony. Lorna was nearly as red-faced as the

man on the trolley. She was carrying a heap of clothes—
a shirt, a jacket and tie, socks and shoes. These she practically threw into Jock's arms as he stepped forward.

'Here. Take these and give them to him when he…
when he… Look, I have to go. I can't…'

But Jock put his hand on Lorna's arm, and his grip,
although gentle, was suddenly far too strong for her to
break from.

'Lorna, what's wrong?' From where he stood, Jock
couldn't see what the problem was. Tina was bending
over the man on the trolley, trying to get him to speak.
The man looked almost beyond speech.

If he'd eaten something—poison maybe—or taken
drugs or been injured, it was imperative that Lorna told
all she knew before she left. She mustn't be allowed to
leave. She certainly was desperate to go.

'I don't… Look, I really have to get home. These are
his clothes…' She took a frantic step back but Jock's
grip tightened.

'Tell us, Lorna.' He glanced at Tina, who had given
up trying to get the man to speak and was now prising
his hands away from his groin. The man was moaning
in agony, swaying from side to side on the stretcher.
'What's wrong?'

'It's his… It's his…' Lorna's crimson colour was now
close to purple. She looked like she was about to suffer
a stroke all on her own, and Jock hauled her sideways
and propelled her onto a chair. He needed to know, but
he didn't want her dropping dead on them before she
could tell.

'Lorna! Tell me!'

Lorna groaned, and groaned again. 'It's his…his…his
willy,' she burst out, and her voice was an agonised
whisper. 'It's stuck. Oh, you have to let me go. Please…'

Jock swung back to Tina and stared, just as Tina managed to haul away the man's hands. Tina gazed down

and her jaw dropped. For one moment—a fleeting second only—Jock saw the creases of Tina's green eyes wrinkle upward in an involuntary choke of laughter, but she didn't make a sound. Somehow her laughter was caught and held, and Jock abandoned Lorna and stepped forward to see.

Reg was caught in the most invidious position known to man. His penis was stuck firmly in the zipper of his pants, the teeth of the zipper cutting into the foreskin, and underneath... Underneath the heavy twill of his pants, surrounding the penis, was a frothy, frilly scrap of red and white...knickers? It was embedded in the wound, cutting in. Reg must have hauled at the thing with force to make it cut in so deeply.

Tina touched it and shook her head in disbelief. 'What...?' She looked back to Lorna. 'Mrs Colsworth... Mrs Colsworth, what is this?'

'They're my panties,' Lorna groaned, and she covered her face with her hand. 'At least...Reg just gave them to me tonight, as a present. They're...they're crutchless knickers from one of those adults-only shops. It was just a bit of fun, like, and he bought them for me for a laugh.'

Her face was flushing from puce to white and back to puce again, but somehow she kept on speaking. 'But... we were fooling around and...and I made Reg put them on—just to see what he'd look like, you know, for a bit of a giggle—and we heard a car. We thought it was Simon coming home, even though it's his Masons' night, and Reg got such a fright. He grabbed his pants and hauled them on too fast and...and he caught...and we couldn't get... We tried, but he couldn't. Then I tried but he screamed almost loud enough for the neighbours to hear. And it wasn't even Simon—it was only someone coming next door.'

It was all too much. Lorna's voice died away into a humiliated sob.

'Hey.' Somehow Jock kept a straight face, though afterwards he could never figure out how. He'd never been so close to losing it in his life. 'Hey, Lorna…' He bent over the distressed woman and took her hands.

'I don't… I can't bear…'

'*You* can't bear?' Reg moaned from the trolley. '*You* can't bear…? It's *me* who's stuck in the dammed things, woman. You damned near hauled me dick off when you pulled. Get me out of here.'

'Lorna, go home,' Jock said gently. 'Now we know what's wrong we can fix this. Believe it or not, it's a fairly common accident. Go home and ring later to check that Reg is OK.'

'But…' Lorna looked wildly up at them. 'Simon… Everyone… They'll know. They'll all find out.'

'Dr Rafter, Sister Roberts and I will know,' Jock said firmly. 'But that's all. We promise that nothing…no information at all…will go out of this room. That's a promise, Lorna. We'll even burn the panties.' A muscle at the side of his face twitched but he managed, somehow, to keep it under control. 'They're too damaged for further…further use. Now go home and get yourself under control before this husband of yours does come home.'

'You mean…'

'Lorna, go.'

It took them twenty minutes to free Reg from his entrapment—nineteen minutes for them to calm the man down and stop him writhing long enough for Tina to inject a tiny amount of local anaesthetic, and one minute or less for Jock to put a tiny nick in the foreskin and pull the whole zip down.

The lacy confection ripped as he brought it down with the trousers. Tina and Jock helped the man off with his pants and what was left of his knickers, without saying a word. Tina handed them back to Barbara. Barbara choked and left swiftly, her face strangely still.

'Can I telephone someone to bring you in fresh clothes?' Tina asked, managing to keep a straight face with an almost superhuman effort.

'No!' The moment Jock had finished dressing the wound Reg staggered to his feet. 'I'm going home. Lend me one of them hospital gown things.'

'Wear a hospital gown home? What…?' Tina took a deep breath. 'What about your wife, then, Reg?'

'She's at cards,' Reg managed. 'I gotta get home before she does. Call me a cab…' Then he had second thoughts. 'No. The taxi driver… Hell, it'll be Ted Farndale. It'll be all over town if he finds out…'

'How did you get to Lorna's?' Jock asked curiously.

'Walked. It's only two blocks and I wasn't going to risk parking the car outside, now was I?'

'I suppose not,' Jock said gravely. Then he rose to the occasion, as all men did to support each other in times of greatest need. 'Come on, Reg,' he said, his dark eyes twinkling. 'I'll drive you home. I'm off duty here. We'll leave Dr Rafter to deal with any more emergencies that chance in tonight.' He lifted a hospital gown and helped Reg into it.

'But don't go away, Dr Rafter,' he said softly, so softly that only she could hear it. 'There are things you and I still have to settle. One marriage, for instance.'

CHAPTER ELEVEN

JOCK returned ten minutes later to find Tina writing again. She looked up as he entered but this time there was no strain. Her face was creased into a wide smile, and Jock knew she'd been in a bubble of laughter ever since he'd left.

'Did you get him all the way home, without anyone seeing?' She grinned. 'I had thought of trying to rustle up a false moustache and dark glasses.'

'He would have taken them if you had.' Jock's grin matched hers. 'Boy, if those two are ever unfaithful again I'll be a monkey's uncle—and how I'll buy my sausages in future and keep a straight face...'

'Ditto.' Then Tina's smile faded a little. 'This may have one good outcome, though.'

'Which is...?'

'Lorna Colsworth is one of the biggest prudes in this town, and she's on the hospital board. As a single mum, I'd expect a pretty hard time from Lorna. She may even want me sacked, but I can't see her giving me a hard time now—can you?'

Jock's smile died as if it had never been, died to nothing.

'Tina...'

'I've been trying to figure out what to put on Reg's history,' Tina said, ignoring Jock's discomfort. 'It's unethical, but maybe it'd be kinder not to include it at all. If any doctor down the track asks him what this was all about, he'd die of heart failure right there on the spot.'

'Tina...'

'What do you think?'

'I think we need to talk.'

'I thought we were talking.'

'About us.'

Tina shook her head and bent over her work again. 'There's no "us", Jock. There's you and there's me and there's our baby, but there's no "us".'

'I think there must be.'

'Why?' Tina didn't lack courage. She met his look, her eyes defiant. 'To fulfil your obligations? I don't think so.' She shook her head. 'Jock, you don't want to marry me. Be honest and admit it—you don't.'

Jock stared down at her for a long minute, and then he sat heavily on the chair on the other side of the desk. This girl... She made him smile as no one else had ever made him smile. She made him feel like all he wanted to do in life was to be with her, laugh with her, love her. Protect her...

But...marriage?

'That's just it, Tina. I don't know what I want.'

'If you don't know then you don't want marriage.'

'Hell...' Jock ran his hand through his hair and stood. He walked to the other side of the ward and then returned to sit again. He raked his hair some more while Tina sat as still as a stone and looked on, trying hard to contain her churning emotions and keep her look sympathetic, interested but unemotional. The very opposite to how she was feeling.

Finally she laid down her pen and closed her eyes on his pacing, closed her heart. Enough was enough—she couldn't bear it any more.

'Jock, go home and go to bed,' she said softly. 'I have work to do and you're tired. Keep this until tomorrow. Don't let it disturb your sleep tonight.'

'Damn it!' Jock exploded, and his hand came crashing down on the desk, making Tina jump. 'Damn it, woman, is that all you can say? That I have work to do and you're tired? Keep this until tomorrow—as if it's a piece of your damned paperwork?'

'What am I supposed to say?'

'I have no idea, but...' Jock shook his head despairingly. 'Tina, this love thing. Hell...'

'It's not hell, Jock.'

'It is.' He swore. 'Love... It's something I've been trained since birth not to feel. Don't get close or you'll damage. You'll destroy, and be destroyed in turn. But it's crazy. Other people have happy marriages, just not my parents. They were the exception—not the rule—and it's time I learned that. So why can't I marry?'

'Do you want a happy marriage?'

'Yes... No! Tina, I don't know.' Jock looked over at her and his eyes were desperate. 'I only know... Tina, I only know that if I do want marriage I want it to be with you. I've never met anyone like you before. You sit there. You're tired, you're broke, you have the cares of the world on your shoulders—and I've made you pregnant and I'm leaving for London. But do you dissolve into hysterics? No. Of course not. You sit there and take all the responsibility for our child onto yourself, as you took on the responsibility for your sister and her children.'

'I don't see what use hysterics would be,' Tina said mildly. 'And as for my sister... Christie would have done the same for me.'

'That's just it.' Jock's voice was so intense that Tina blinked. 'She would have done. I know that. Because she loves you as you love her. But not the likes of me. I'd never do that—accept responsibility—because I'm running scared.'

Jock sighed and stood, walking around the desk until he was behind her. His hands came down on Tina's shoulders and he held on, gripping her hard. For a moment—for a long, life-changing moment—Tina let herself lean back against him and feel his strength. She let herself be cradled against him. In that minute she knew that she was lost—that if he said now that he'd stay, she'd hold him to her no matter what the future held, no matter how much against her better judgement it would be.

Jock was her love, she told herself bleakly. She loved him as she could never love another. So... If she could hold him... Take him up on his offer to do what was honourable... Surely in time she could heal the scars? Surely she could teach him what it was to love and be loved in return?

Jock bent and kissed her on the top of her curls, and his eyes were troubled.

'Tina, you must marry me,' he said gently. 'I know... Oh, hell, no, I don't. I don't know anything. But one thing... I do know that I can't walk away. I know I can't go to the other side of the world and leave you to raise our child by yourself. I know I'll have to change, Tina. I'll have to learn to give...learn to love.'

'Jock...'

'No.' He placed a finger on her lips, silencing her. 'Tina, if there's anyone who can possibly do that...teach me to love... If you're willing to take a chance on me then I want you to marry me, and I'll even go down on bended knee to ask you to do it.'

'Oh, Jock...'

How could she refuse this chance? It was only a chance, she knew, a small chance of happiness and an enormous gamble. But what was at stake here? What would she lose if she didn't gamble at all?

'You'll try to love me?' she whispered, and her hand came up to touch his, to feel his strength and his tenderness.

'I'll love you,' Jock said, and if his words were a trifle strained, please, God, she didn't hear it.

If I can, his heart whispered, if I can.

The wedding took place two months later.

As Gundowring weddings went it was small, but by Jock's criteria it was huge. 'We'll invite only our close friends,' he'd said, but everyone in Gundowring thought they were close friends and it was impossible to ask one and not others.

The medical community was out in force. Struan, back from his holidays in high good humour, employed a team of locums from the city for the weekend so no emergency could mar the celebrations. And it was some celebration. The locals *en masse* thought it was just the most romantic wedding they'd ever seen.

Tina... Well, Tina was exquisite. She refused to wear white—though 'everyone does nowadays; it's not as if marrying when you're pregnant is a disgrace any more,' Christie had told her—but she'd compromised by wearing palest gold shantung with white ribands threaded through.

The dress—made by Christie, to whom the wedding had provided a new lease of life and had launched her straight back into bossy big sister mode—was simple and flowing and lovely, fitting Tina's figure to perfection. Christie had allowed room for a tummy bulge but had taken it in at the last minute as there was still no bulge.

Christie was matron of honour, wearing matching gold and looking serene and lovely herself. She'd gained weight and was smiling fit to burst. Ally and Tim were flower girl and page boy respectively, strutting down the aisle proudly as if they'd planned the whole thing.

Christie and her children were right behind this wedding, and they had more reasons than just their fondness

for Jock. Jock and Tina had found a farmlet on the outskirts of town, overlooking the bay. It was truly lovely
and its best feature was that it had two houses a couple
of hundred yards apart.

'We need you to live near us,' Jock had told Christie.
'Tina wants to keep on working at least part time so we
need you—and if you could find it in your heart to need
us back, we'd be very grateful.'

Jock always knew the right thing to say, Tina thought
to herself as she stood at the entrance to the church. He'd
behaved wonderfully all through their engagement.
Bought her an engagement ring that had made her gasp,
took her out searching for a home, made love to her as
if…as if he meant it.

Now he was marrying her. Her beloved Jock was
waiting at the end of the aisle, impossibly handsome in
his dark suit—impossible for her to refuse. Her Jock.
Her love. The first strains of the bridal march trumpeted
forth, and Tina stepped forward. Jock turned and smiled,
his face alight with love and pride, and Tina would have
followed him to the ends of the earth.

Her Jock was waiting. Dear God, she loved him. But
if she hadn't loved him so much—if she hadn't known
him as she knew herself—she would never have seen
the trace of panic still lying behind his eyes and the
pervading sense of being trapped.

He loved her, but he didn't want this. As Tina stepped
forward to be married she knew that she still had a long
way to go before she found true happiness. If she
ever did.

CHAPTER TWELVE

IT WASN'T going to work.

It was Tina's last day at the hospital. She stared at her desk in increasing gloom. Five more minutes and then she'd close her drawer, take herself home and face motherhood. Alone. That's what it felt like. Loneliness. Tina had been married to Jock for four months now. In four weeks their baby would be born and they'd be a family, but they couldn't be a family the way Jock was acting.

'Ready to go?' Ellen Silverton walked into the ward, her arms full of bootees. 'Here you are, then. This is the entire production of the women's section of the nursing home for the past month. They're starting on matinée jackets now. If you don't hurry and have this baby, you'll need to have quintuplets to fit all the clothes.'

Tina smiled but her face was strained, and Ellen's sharp eyes noticed.

'Tina, what is it?'

'Nothing.'

'Tell Aunty Ellen.' Ellen perched herself on the opposite chair and frowned. 'Come on, Tina. As of now, you're no longer Dr Rafter to my Sister Silverton. You're an expecting mum on maternity leave, and I have eyes in my head. All's not right with your world.'

'It is.'

'Liar.' Ellen shook her head. 'So what's causing the shadows? Are you worried about the baby?'

'No.' Tina sighed. 'Of course I'm not. I don't have to be—Jock's worried enough for both of us.'

'Now that I don't understand. You've had every test known to man, and your husband's the best obstetrician

161

this place has ever seen. He's organised a locum to back him up during the delivery and the locum's qualifications are almost as good as his. He shouldn't be worried.' Ellen hesitated. 'Or maybe I do understand. His mum was so ill. Maybe it's inevitable that he'll panic.'

'As long as the panic stops,' Tina burst out. 'As long as one day it stops. It's irrational and I can't bear it.'

'You can't bear…'

'He's always watching me as if I'm about to disappear in a puff of smoke.'

'And that worries you?'

'It does.' Tina sat back in her chair and sighed. 'I know. I'm the luckiest woman in the world. I love him so much and he's so good to me. But, Ellen, you don't know what it's like…'

'Is he paranoid?' Ellen asked bluntly.

'Oh, no, nothing so simple. I mean—he's not over the top afraid that something will happen. It's just…it's just that it seems like he expects it. He knows that one day this will end—what's between us—so he doesn't give…'

'What doesn't he give?'

'Himself.' There, she'd said it. Tina bit her lip. She had no business discussing her husband with anyone else, but Christie worshipped the ground Jock walked on and couldn't see past how wonderful he was. Accustomed to a husband who didn't care, Christie thought Jock's caring was magic so Tina couldn't talk to her sister. Whereas Ellen… Ellen had known Jock forever. Maybe she could understand.

'Don't get me wrong,' Tina said slowly. 'He's doing…Jock's doing just the best he knows how. He loves me. He says he does and I believe him. If I didn't believe that I never would have agreed to marry him. I know it's true. And he's kind and gentle and we laugh at the same things and he makes love…' She blushed and man-

aged a faint grin. 'Well, there's no problem in that direction.'

'I'm glad to hear it.'

'But he holds himself...' Tina sighed. 'Heck, Ellen,
it's so hard to explain. It's like marriage is his duty, his
job—and, by golly, he's going to do it right. When we
joke... Like last week, a possum came down the chim-
ney. We thought it was a burglar and Jock armed himself
to the teeth with an umbrella and a rolling pin and in he
went—into the fray—and all there was was a possum,
sitting on the mantelpiece looking silly. Even when we
were laughing at three o'clock in the morning at a stupid
possum Jock was watching me. As if...he'll enjoy this
now, soak this up, because tomorrow...'

'Tomorrow you'll be gone?'

'That's it. Like I'm some lovely bit of porcelain,
worth a fortune but with a built-in time bomb and he
doesn't know when I'm going to self-destruct.' She grimaced. 'I tell you, Ellen, it puts some strain on things.
And when I yell at him—'

'You yell at him?' Ellen asked, startled, and Tina gave
a shaky smile, her indestructible sense of humour twinkling out.

'Yeah, I do. Sometimes I do. Don't you sometimes
yell at your husband?'

'Well...'

'Oh, come on, Ellen. Like when he does something
absolutely unforgivable, like leaving the toilet seat up
for the third time in a row, or just because he's being
too damned nice and I'm too damned pregnant... Don't
you, Ellen?'

'I might,' Ellen said cautiously. 'I'm not saying.'

'And if you might,' Tina went on mercilessly, 'what
happens then?'

Ellen stared, and then she blushed. 'He... Bob yells
right back,' she admitted. 'Tells me there's too many

women in our house and he wants his own toilet. And we get louder and louder, and then we end up with the giggles and often in bed... Though once he emptied a whole packet of frozen peas down my back before he made me laugh and hit the sheets...'

She chuckled in remembrance.

But Tina wasn't smiling. That was what she wanted, she thought, that was what it *could* be like. 'See?'

'But... Isn't that what happens to you?' Ellen probed, and Tina shook her head.

'No way. If I get crabby Jock humours me, as if I'm ill and I'm precious and I'm about to vanish in this puff of smoke—and if he doesn't relax soon I will!'

'Will what?'

Tina jumped, and turned to find Jock, standing in the doorway—white-coated, stethoscope swinging and so handsome he made her heart turn over just as it had the first day she saw him. He was smiling but his eyes were concerned. 'Are you OK, Tina? You sound upset.'

'I'm fine, Jock.' Tina managed a smile but it was a shaky one. 'Ellen was just presenting me with twenty-seven pairs of bootees.' She held a handful for him to inspect. 'Look. So if junior is born with fifty-four feet we're prepared. Any more than fifty-four and we're in trouble.'

He didn't smile. 'Tina, our baby will be perfect,' he said softly, as if to reassure her—as if Tina really was worried about fifty-four feet. He crossed and stooped to give her a swift kiss. 'He'll be perfect, just like his mother. All the tests have told us so. Are you ready to go home now?'

Tina sighed and gave up her attempt at humour. 'Yes. I guess I am. All ready. I'll miss this place.'

'At a guess you won't be away for very long,' Ellen told her, her face troubled as she watched Jock. There was enough in that little interchange for her to see what

Tina was getting at. 'And you have your anaesthetic exams to study for in between nappy changes.'

'There's that.' Tina managed a smile. She pushed herself to her feet. Jock moved to help her and it was all Tina could do not to slap his hand away. 'I'm OK.' She glanced at her watch. She'd gone onto day duty for the last two months and was finishing early. 'It's only five. The shops are still open. I'll do the grocery shopping on the way home, Jock, and I'll see you about seven. Your babies permitting.'

'Mrs Arthur's in labour now but she's slow.' Jock glanced at his watch. 'I should have time. I'll drive you home now and then come back.'

'No,' Tina snapped, but tried to keep her voice civil. 'I'll drive myself home, Jock Blaxton. I'm a perfectly capable adult, you know. Healthy even, believe it or not.'

Tina fretted all the way around the supermarket and half the way to the farm. This was stupid. This was really, really, stupid.

She knew how Jock could be. Relaxed and happy, Jock was the man of her dreams, but he was never relaxed, apart from maybe the times when they were between the sheets and he had her in her arms. There was that, she thought, the sides of her mouth curving into a rueful smile. Maybe they'd just have to spend more time in bed.

Maybe he'd relax more when the baby came, when he knew everything was fine. Maybe. Or maybe he'd worry twice as much.

'Why is everything so complicated?' she demanded of the road ahead. At the edge of town the road twisted upwards into the hills. There were a few scattered farmhouses, the last one on the road being theirs.

'And why am I so miserable?'

It was a gorgeous day. The sun was glittering on the sea and the air was warm and still. She was finishing work to bear the child of her husband, the child of the man she loved. She was protected and cherished and loved...

'So I'm just being selfish,' she muttered. 'I shouldn't want more.'

But she did. She didn't want to be Jock's cherished, protected and beloved wife.

'I want to be his friend, damn it,' she told the road. 'I want to be his lover and his mate. I want to have fun—not be stuck in cotton wool for the rest of my life!'

And then her thoughts ended abruptly. The road moved.

It was a good clothe. Tina was glittering on the sun and her eyes were dazzled. She was finishing smaller than she had before. Tina knew she chided the ball. She could take a breakfast and then into ran tycoon
to all had in a while...thoughts here muttered. I thought I

CHAPTER THIRTEEN

FOR a moment Tina thought she was imagining it. Accustomed to her baby doing infantile aerobics inside her, she thought the jolt was just another internal kick. Then it happened again, but this time the steering-wheel jerked under her hands and the car slewed sideways. Tina hit the brakes and stared ahead in stupefaction.

The road was twisting, buckling like an enormous stiff ribbon being turned at each end. Roads don't twist. They don't! Tina's hands gripped the steering-wheel desperately in panic. *They don't!* This one was. The whole world was moving, as if the earth had a giant case of indigestion. A tree ahead tilted at a crazy angle and crashed down across the road, sending a spray of leaves up over her windshield.

Dear God! Tina's breath was coming in frightened gasps. She'd come to a halt on the grass verge at a twenty-degree angle to the horizontal, and the car—and the road—was still moving under her. Should she get out or stay in?

Stay in. Stay in! At least there were no more trees near her and the one in front could fall no further. The bucking went on for ever—or at least two minutes. It was probably the longest two minutes Tina had ever known. With the dramatic twist of the roadway as the tremor started, Tina half expected worse to come—chasms to open, the sky to fall.

'It's an earth tremor,' she told herself, trying desperately to stay calm, to stay rational. 'An earth tremor. Like the one up at Newcastle...'

There had been people killed at Newcastle. The

Newcastle earthquake, just south of Sydney, had been catastrophic.

'This one's out in the open,' Tina told herself. She twisted around to stare out of the car's back window at the town she'd just come from. Gundowring looked placid and peaceful in the sunlight. The sea was calm and still. Nothing had changed.

'So...so it's a localised earth tremor,' Tina whispered. 'It's nothing to be afraid of at all.'

The road wound down to sea level again before home. From here sea level looked good, undamaged. That meant Christie and the kids would be OK. If the only damage was here... But was it? Cautiously Tina climbed from the car, distrusting the solid ground under her feet, expecting it to wobble at any minute.

Nothing happened. Apart from the angle of the road, the crashed tree and the vast crack along the centre of the bitumen, she might well have imagined the whole thing. What now? She couldn't drive on—that was for sure. Apart from anything else, there was a tree blocking her path and the land behind her was more densely wooded than here. If the tremors were still happening she'd be silly to go back that way. She put a hand on her car phone and then hesitated. Telephone? Telephone who?

Jock?

No. No way. He'd come tearing up here like a mad-man, she told herself. He'd mobilise the fire brigade and the ambulance and the emergency services to rescue his wife, who didn't need rescuing at all. The emergency services could well be needed elsewhere and would waste their time, coming to her aid. She had no guar-antee this was just local.

It was only about a mile to the farm. If she walked wide of any tree that looked remotely fallible— Then her thoughts stopped abruptly. Somebody screamed.

Tina hesitated for one second—only one. The scream had held sheer terror and it had been close. She hesitated only long enough to grab her doctor's bag and then started running as fast as her pregnant body would let her.

She didn't get far. A hundred yards from the car— just past the fallen tree—a boy burst from the undergrowth near the road. He was about twelve or so at a guess, in jeans, grubby T-shirt and sneakers. His face was scratched and bleeding, his arm was hanging oddly and his eyes were frantic. He took one look at Tina and headed straight for her—straight into her arms.

Jason Calvert. Town toughy. Tina knew him by sight—and by reputation. He and his mate, Brendan, swaggered round the town acting as though they were sixteen years old. He wasn't sixteen years old now; he was one terrified little boy. Jason grabbed Tina, held her hard—and burst into tears.

'Hey… Jason…'

Somehow Tina managed to pry him loose. She held him at arm's length, not breaking the contact but stooping to meet his eyes. 'Jason. What is it? You've hurt your arm…'

'Oh, miss..' He recognised her then and gave a ragged sob of relief. 'Doc…' He went for the huddle again and she gave in, holding him tightly against her—no mean feat with baby in between. 'Oh, Doc…'

'It's OK, Jason,' she told him. 'It's fine. It was just an earth tremor. Were you hit by the tree? We'll take you down to the hospital and get that arm fixed—'

'No!' He shoved himself away then, fighting for control—fighting back pain and terror. 'No! Miss, it's not me. It's Brendan… Brendan…'

'Where's Brendan?' Tina's voice sharpened. Jason was badly enough hurt, and if he was the one running for help… 'Jason, where is Brendan?'

'We…'

'Calmly,' Tina ordered. 'Three deep breaths first and then tell.'

Finally he did.

'We've…we've been wagging school, like.' Jason gulped. 'There was supposed to be some stupid camp so we told our mums we were going, but then we came up here for the night. Brought some food. We even got some beer…'

Tina knew. Before Jason went on she knew. Why had the boys come here? She'd spent her childhood here so she knew.

'Brendan's in the cave?'

'Yeah. He is. But the whole end… We were just sitting there, trying to get a fire going, and everything shook and roared and the rocks…they just caved in. A rock hit my arm and I ran, but Brendan… When the rocks stopped falling I went back to see… There's a whole heap of stuff lying on his legs and I can't move him.'

Eight months pregnant and on maternity leave, Tina's emergency medical mode still worked on automatic. She clicked straight in, and even Jason's hysteria was checked in the face of her calmness.

'Right. First rule, Jason, and it's the most important one. Don't panic. I need you and you *must* keep a clear head. He's in Bosun's cave?' Bosun's cave was the big one—the one the local kids had labelled a smugglers' cave generations ago. Tina had wagged the odd school day, too.

'Yes… But he's right up the back…'

'I understand, and I know the cave. I'll go there now.'

'I'll show you…'

'No. Your job is to stay here,' Tina said, checking his forward movement. With that damaged arm he was liable to collapse at any minute. She managed a smile. 'I

was a school-wagging twerp when I was your age so I
know the caves. There's locals that don't, though, so
you'll have to bring them when help arrives.'

'But... How...?'

'I want you to go back to my car,' she told him. 'It's
not locked. Pick up the mobile phone and dial 000.
Rhonda will answer. Tell her calmly—and I mean
calmly, Jason, not a tear in sight, mind—everything
that's happened. Stay on the line until you've answered
every question she has. Then stay in the car until the
ambulance comes so you can guide them to us. Wind
the driver's seat back so you're lying down and stay
there and wait. I'm depending on you, Jason, and so is
Brendan. Don't let us down.'

The tremor was felt at the hospital but only as that—a
minor tremor. A crack appeared in the plaster in the
corridor, a painting crashed in Ward Four and crockery
rattled. Mrs Dobson thought she was having a 'turn' and
rang her bell in panic.

Waiting between interminable contractions—good
grief, this was Mrs Arthur's third baby, you'd think
she'd be better at it by now—Jock wandered along to
Reception to talk about the tremor—and found semi-
organised panic. There were two ambulance officers in
the foyer and four men in state emergency gear and...the
fire brigade chief?

'What the hell...?' The room off the hospital recep-
tion doubled as the region emergency control room.
There were men arriving by the minute. Jock turned to
Rhonda, the receptionist. 'Rhonda, what's happening?'

'The tremor wasn't as mild as it felt,' Rhonda told
him. 'Not up in the hills. So far we've had reports of
four houses collapsing—two lots of injuries and there
may be more. Telephone lines are down...' Then she
hesitated and pointed to the first ambulance. 'Jock, if you

have time... I was going to call Dr Buchanan to see if she'd go, but if I get her to look after Mrs Arthur instead you might like to go with Ambulance One. Brendan Cordy is stuck in a cave up on the ridge. And...'

'And?' By the look on Rhonda's face, Jock knew there was worse to come.

'Tina's with him,' Rhonda told him. 'She's OK,' she said hurriedly as she saw his eyes widen, 'but as far as I know, Tina's in the cave with Brendan.'

The cave entrance was as spooky as Tina had ever seen it. Only the boldest of kids ever went in here, Tina remembered. Torches were OK near the entrance, but inside their beams were swallowed up by the darkness and Tina wasn't as brave now as she'd been when she was twelve. So she stopped at the cave mouth and called.

'Brendan? Can you hear me?'

Maybe if there'd been no reply she'd have waited. Maybe. But from inside the cave came a faint, pain-filled moan.

Spooky or not, Tina was in there fast. She carried a flashlight in her doctor's bag and she paused only long enough to find it. Then, carefully, mindful of her clumsiness—heavens, she wasn't as fit as she'd been when she was twelve, and there was the extra difficulty of the baby—she walked forward, bending her head so she wouldn't hit the rocks she remembered being at head height. Or at shoulder height—heck, she must have grown.

Then she gave up walking as too dangerous and started to crawl, ignoring the loose rubble biting into her knees, holding her torch under her arm and shoving her bag before her through the dust, until she found him.

Brendan was about fifty yards down into the cave and his legs were pinned under the rock-fall, but he was conscious. His eyes focussed on the beam of light as he watched her come closer. When she reached the point where she could touch him he gripped her hand, held on as if he were drowning and burst into tears.

'Oh, Doc.. Oh, Doc...'

'You'll be all right, Brendan.' The fact that he'd recognised her and was talking so strongly was a wonderful sign. She flicked the torch beam upwards. The roof here seemed stable enough. If she could just haul away the rocks on his leg...

'Help's on its way,' she told him, feeling more confident by the minute. 'I'll give you something for the pain and then we'll set about getting you out of here.'

And then the earth moved again.

There was one sickening upward jolt. The rocks at the entrance came crashing down, and the world turned to thunder.

'Where did you say this cave was?' Jock's voice was hoarse with fear.

'It's here...' Jason looked wildly around him at the freshly tumbled rocks. 'Somewhere...' But nothing looked familiar any more. Nothing! 'It must be here. I swear. I'm sure the entrance was just by the redgum. But the redgum's fallen...'

'He's right, Doc,' one of the ambulance men said heavily. 'I know this place. This is where the cave entrance used to be.'

Jock stared down with sickening incredulity. There was nothing. No cave. No Brendan. No Tina. Just one vast mound of settling, unstable rocks.

CHAPTER FOURTEEN

Saturday, May 5th
Two missing, feared dead

A young boy, injured and trapped by falling rocks, and the pregnant doctor who went to his aid are to-day listed as missing after yesterday's earth tremor north of Gundowring. The tremor, measuring 4.1 on the Richter scale, was felt as far north as Bateman's Bay but damage was confined to a small area...

'Oh, God. They must be alive... They must...'

'Jock, let's face it, the chances are slim, to say the least.' Struan's face was nearly as strained as his friend's. 'There must be two hundred tons of earth came down on that cave.'

'They must still be down there... One way or another... Why the hell can't they dig faster?'

'They're digging as fast as they can. The earth's un-stable. If they go in fast they risk more rock-falls. And they're flying in electronic sensing equipment from Sydney. If they're alive, we'll find them.'

'When...? But when?'

Sunday, May 6th
Hopes fading for missing pair

Rescuers are conceding the chances of finding anyone alive in the rock-fall north of Gundowring are now

174

exceedingly slim. Sniffer dogs and sophisticated sensing equipment today failed to find any trace...

Monday, May 7th
Despair among rescuers

There is still no sign of life from the rock-fall north of Gundowring. Rescuers are privately admitting that twenty-nine-year-old Dr Tina Rafter, her unborn baby and twelve-year-old Brendan Cordy, the lad she went into the cave to rescue, are probably dead. There are now more than two hundred workers at the site...

'Jock, go home and get some rest.'

'No.'

Christie placed a hand on Jock's shoulder and gripped hard. 'Come on, Jock, This is doing you no good at all. I think it's time we accepted that she's gone—don't you?'

'I...'

'Jock, I'm feeling the same way you are.' There was no denying that. Christie's face was drawn and haggard and she looked as if she hadn't slept for a week. 'But...' She hesitated. 'Jock, we can move on from here. Tina wouldn't want this to destroy us. All I want to know now... All I want to know is that it was quick...'

But Jock was shaking his head.

'There's no moving on,' he said dully.

'Yes, there is.' Christie stared down at him and she saw what was in his heart. She'd been talking to Ellen and she'd seen enough. She wasn't stupid. Jock had expected this. His mother's death had effectively ended his father's life, leaving only bitterness in her place. It mustn't happen to Jock.

So, despite how she was feeling herself—despite the

hopelessness washing over her in waves—Christie had to try. She lifted his hands and pressed them hard.

'Jock, Tina loved you, loved you absolutely. She would have died for you, and that love... It doesn't end with death. We had her for a short while and we were blessed. She lived her life to the full and we loved her for it.'

'Christie, don't...'

'Jock, you have to listen. You must! Jock, if Tina hadn't lived so much maybe she'd be standing here with us today—mourning one little boy who was buried alone. If she hadn't lived so much she wouldn't have taken risks—but, then, she wouldn't have been the Tina we loved. She gave herself, Jock, totally, and that's why we loved her. That's why she'll stay with us.'

'No.' Jock was almost past hearing. He was unshaven and filthy and weary past belief, and he stared at Christie with eyes that hardly registered. He'd dug with his bare hands, desperate, and then, as the digging teams had become organised, he'd dug alongside the miners until he'd been ordered off.

He was in no state to think. But still Christie tried—she had no choice.

'Jock, Tina wasn't a precious thing to be idolised and kept safe. We loved her but now it's time to let her go. Please... For Tina, you have to keep on living. Loving...'

Then Christie's voice faltered. Her voice fell to a whisper and she put her hands to her face. Dear God, she wasn't made of stone. 'Just...just as long as we know that it was quick!' she whispered. 'Please, God...'

Her voice was laced with despair, and Jock was shaken enough to look swiftly at her. For the first time he saw past his own misery. He saw Christie's total exhaustion, and he saw the love that made her reach out, past her own despair, to try and help him.

Tina was right, he thought slowly, wondering. Life did go on, and he knew then what Tina would want him to do. It was as Christie had said. His father had let his mother's death destroy his life, destroy his son's life, but Tina... Tina would want him to live on, to love as he'd never been able to live and to love before—even when he'd had his Tina at his side.

Suddenly he saw the gift Tina had given him, and it was like the lifting of a black, cold fog, letting in the light that had been outside all along. Dear God, that Tina could only live to know...

'Come on, Christie,' he said softly, and he rose stiffly from the log where he'd been sitting for hours. Days. 'I'll take you home. And then I'll come back here and wait some more. But, Christie...' He shook his head, as though trying to shake off a nightmare. 'Maybe you're right,' he managed. 'Whatever happens... Maybe we can still let her live.'

Monday 7th—Evening Extra
ALIVE?

Sensitive electronic probes today detected signs of life deep under the ground in the rubble from the Gundowring quake. Rescuers are cautious of raising hopes at this stage, but manpower on the site has been increased. It is believed that three hundred men will be digging through the night...

Jock was the first to see her. There had been pressure on him to stay back—pressure because they were unsure of what they would find. But then there had been a voice—husky at first and incredulous, as if the thought that someone could hear her could be nothing but a dream. Tina. After three days buried, unbelievably it was Tina.

The probe picked up her calls as faint echoes and then, almost not daring to breathe, the technicians adjusted the probe, moved it and adjusted it again. They heard words, faint but true.

'I'm OK. I'm hungry as a horse, my legs are so stiff I can hardly move—even if there was room—and I'm so thirsty that my tongue's swollen, but Brendan and I are fine.'

'Brendan?' Beside Jock, Brendan's parents were close to collapse.

'Brendan's broken his leg.' Tina's voice cracked with dryness. 'It took us a while to get him clear of the fall, but the leg should be OK. He still has circulation. We're in a crevice about five feet square, and Brendan wants his mum and a can of Coke like nothing else on earth, but we're OK.'

'And what do you want?' The captain of the State Emergency Service was grinning like a Cheshire cat. This was an ending everyone had ceased even to hope for. 'What do you want, Dr Rafter?'

There was silence, and then the voice fell to a shaky whisper.

'Please, God... Please, God, I just want my Jock.'

'Hold on there, Tina. He's on his way.'

It couldn't be that easy—and it wasn't. It took five more hours of digging and all the skill in the world—they didn't need another rock slip at this stage—to reach them.

Then Jock was allowed over the pile of rocks—down through the shored-up tunnel which had taken so much manpower to build—and he was there, squeezed in with the miners, when the final rock between them was moved... And there was Tina. She was battered and filthy, but she was unbelievably alive in the torchlight—and, unbelievingly, she was managing to smile.

'Jock,' she whispered, and her hand came through the gap and gripped with a strength he wouldn't have believed possible. She held on as if she were drowning.

'We'll get you out,' Jock managed, his voice breaking with emotion. 'Oh, Tina..'

'That'd be appreciated,' she said hoarsely. 'And…and make it fast. Because…Jock, I have the most dreadful back pains…'

'Back pains.' Visions of a fractured spine flooded through him, and the tension in the group of miners increased to breaking point. Jock could feel the men around him tense. 'Hell, Tina, don't try and move. We'll get you out flat on a stretcher…'

'I'm waiting for no stretcher,' Tina told him, her voice strengthening. 'No way. You just get this hole a bit bigger—a lot bigger—and I'm coming out anyway I can because, Jock…'

'Tina?'

'I'm coming out and so…' She gave a ragged gasp of fear. 'Oh, Jock, so's our baby, and I don't think Brendan fancies himself as a midwife.'

Jessica Christine Blaxton was born at three a.m. in the morning at the mouth of the most makeshift tunnel Jock had ever seen—and if Struan Maitland as doctor in charge hadn't ordered screens to be placed around the cave entrance the world press would have watched the birth.

There was no time to get Tina to hospital. As Christie said laughingly about it later, there had been no time for anything.

'You're a paddock breeder, my dear,' she said. 'A month premature with your first baby and there was barely time to catch her.'

But Jock had caught her. He stood in the still night

air while rescuers cheered and wept and hugged each other around him and he knew… In that one crystalline moment, which would stay with him for ever, Jock Blaxton knew that he was truly blessed.

CHAPTER FIFTEEN

'ARE you ready to come home, Mrs Blaxton?'

Tina stretched out in her hospital bed like a cat, moving every one of her limbs in turn. Even two weeks after being released from her underground prison it still felt unbelievably good to move.

'Convince me.' Tina smiled happily up at her husband. 'In hospital I have menus for every meal, nurses to change Jessie's nappy, my friends around me and you seemingly on tap. What does home have to offer that this place doesn't?'

Jock's eyes glinted. He bent and kissed his wife on the lips—a long, toe-curling kiss that had her heart doing handstands.

'How about a double bed?' he whispered.

Tina's delicious chuckle rang out through the ward.

'Sold. I'm convinced. Grab the baggage and the baby. Take me home immediately. Or on second thoughts...'

Her own eyes twinkled. Tina's arms wrapped themselves around her husband and she hauled him backwards onto the bed. 'Can I wait that long? A single bed is fine...'

'Not with a glass insert in the door it's not,' Jock retorted. But he wasn't completely refusing. Regardless of passing nurses, he held her close and let his long body relax on the bed, moulding her lovely body against his. 'Hell, Tina...' His smile died.

'No.' She placed her finger on his lips. 'No, Jock. Don't think about it.'

He shook his head and his hold tightened. 'I just can't believe that I have you back.'

The whole world was still marvelling about their escape. Apart from healing cuts and fading bruises, Tina was fine. Brendan was recovering as well. He was trussed up in traction in the children's ward, sitting up in bed to boast of his exploits to all and sundry. But holding his parents' hands—hard. There were still scars, Jock knew, and he knew, when Tina held him close, that she couldn't shrug everything off.

They'd been so lucky. Lucky that the roof had held, that one huge slab of granite had fallen right in front of them and they'd been protected. Lucky that so many people had been prepared to work around the clock against seemingly hopeless odds.

And lucky that Tina had had her doctor's bag, with antibiotics, intravenous saline and morphine to keep Brendan's pain and dehydration and infection at bay. She'd held Brendan and comforted him and had told him over and over that they'd be rescued—and she'd been right.

Eventually.

Jock felt himself shudder and he looked up to find Tina watching him, her face troubled.

'What is, love?' he asked.

'Jock...' Tina hesitated. 'I know... I know this is silly, but...'

'But what?'

'How are you going to keep me safe from earthquakes?'

Jock's face stilled.

'Tina...'

'You were frantic about me before,' she whispered. 'What now?' Then she moved to look down into the crib beside the bed. Jessica Christine Blaxton was almost due for a feed and was starting to stir. 'Will you let us...?'

'Let you what?'

'Let us be...us?'

Silence.

Jock closed his eyes. He held his wife in his arms and let his fingers run though her fiery curls—and he knew what she was asking.

'Tina—'

'Jock, you never wanted us,' Tina burst out. 'All the time I was trapped I kept thinking…this…this awfulness is just what you expected. This is what you were most afraid of, and I've done it to you. You didn't want to love me, Jock, you didn't want a family. I've caused you such pain, and I'm so sorry.'

'Don't!'

Jock straightened on the bed, and his eyes blazed. He held Tina at arm's length and anger surged through him. 'Don't, Tina. Don't you ever dare be sorry. Not ever.'

'But—'

'I said no! No way! Because you're apologising for being you,' he told her roughly, and he pulled her into his arms again, holding her in a grip of iron. 'Tina, it's me who's been so unfair. It's me who hasn't seen straight. Christie said it. When you were down that hole and we thought you were dead. And I'd been so blind…'

'What…?'

'Christie said that you give yourself. She said that's why we love you and that's why you'll stay with us, dead or not. You'll always be with us.

'Tina, I've been a fool,' he said softly. 'A blind, stupid fool. I've almost destroyed the thing I hold most precious in the world. Christie's right, Tina. I can never lose you—you're part of me.' He put his mouth against hers and he kissed her. 'You're part of my life, you've made me whole again and one day… God forbid but one day if death divides us then that part will still be with me.'

He kissed her again, tenderly, gently, and there was wonder in his voice.

'I want eighty years of married life with you, my love. My heart. Or more if I can wangle it. And I'll keep on protecting you and our little Jessie, but not because I'm terrified of losing you. Not that. Because I know now that I can't lose you. You're a part of me, and because of you I'm a different person. For ever.'

'Jock...'

'Tina, I'll protect you and cherish you because I love you,' he said softly, holding her close to him, close to his heart. 'And we'll have fun, my lovely Tina. We'll enjoy life to the full.' He shook his head, his eyes firm and sure, telling her that he spoke the truth.

'My love's changed,' he told her. 'For ever. From now on... From now on you'll be my wife and my lover and my friend. I want you to marry me, Tina. Not like before. Properly. For ever. Please, Tina...'

All of a sudden his eyes were anxious as if, even now, she could say that it wasn't on, that it was too late, that he'd killed her love.

But nothing could kill her love. Nothing.

Jessica stirred and whimpered in the cot beside the bed, and Jock released Tina long enough to lift his daughter and place her in Tina's arms. Then he held them both. And Tina held her tiny daughter close and thought her heart would burst.

'But...what about our little Jessie?' she said softly, her eyes not leaving her husband. Her eyes loving him, loving her family, and her heart full of wonder. 'Is there still one baby too many in the world, Jock? Is our Jessie one baby too many?'

'No way.' Jock pulled his wife and child closer into his arms and held them as if he'd never let them go. 'Did I ever say there was one baby too many in the world? I must have been mad.'

He looked down at his wife and his infant daughter and his face told Tina all she would ever want to know.

All that a woman could dream of. She was right where she wanted to be, and she was truly loved.

'No way in the wide world is our Jessica one baby too many,' Jock said softly. 'In fact…'

He held Tina slightly away from him, his eyes glinting with pure devilry, pure love of living. Love of life and love of the two lovely ladies in his life.

'I'd say she might be one baby too few.'

'One…'

'Or two or three? What do you think, Mrs Blaxton? Shall we work on it?'

Previously a teacher, shopkeeper, travel agent, pig farmer, builder and worker in the disability field (among other things), the 'writing bug' struck **Meredith Webber** unexpectedly. She entered a competition run by a women's magazine, shared the third prize with two hundred and fifty other would-be writers and found herself infected. Thirty-something books later, she's still suffering. She says, 'Medical romances appeal to me because they offer the opportunity to include a wider cast of characters, and the challenge of interweaving a love story into the drama of medical or paramedical practice.'

Out this month in Medical Romance™ is Meredith Webber's latest book, A WOMAN WORTH WAITING FOR, in the *Dr Detective – Down Under* mini-series where you can experience the fascinating world of forensic medicine.

A WOMAN WORTH WAITING FOR

After five years Ginny is still the beautiful, caring woman Max remembers, and a wonderful emergency nurse. But she clearly hasn't forgiven him. It takes a murder investigation to bring them together! Their new-found closeness convinces Max that he'd wait for this woman for ever…

Recent titles by the same author in the *Dr Detective – Down Under* mini-series

HER DR WRIGHT
MARRY ME
LOVE ME
TRUST ME

UNRULY HEART
by
Meredith Webber

CHAPTER ONE

MELANIE listened with something approaching awe as Jan Stevens gave brief outlines of some of the repatriation cases UniversAid had handled. The strange tingling sensation flooding through her body told her how much she wanted the job, but outwardly she remained composed, her excitement only visible as an extra gleam in her soft brown eyes, and a straining whiteness in her tensely clasped hands.

'We need people with common sense,' Jan continued. 'Cool, unflappable operators who will be able to handle frightened people shrieking abuse at them in a foreign language from half a world away.'

'I can understand that,' Melanie assured her. 'I've had some experience in unusual situations and I know that staying calm and thinking rationally is the safest course to take.'

Jan nodded, rifling through the pages of Melanie's application and rereading the page that Melanie knew was a reference from her field manager during her work as a volunteer in Botswana.

'Yes,' Jan confirmed at last. 'With your language skills and broad nursing experience, I do think you're the person we've been looking for, although——'

Melanie held her breath. Could there be some computer link-up between medical repatriation services? Would a case from eight years ago make lights flash against her name when it was typed into the data base? She could feel tiny beads of perspiration forming

around her hairline, and unclenched her fingers to raise
one hand and push the thick blonde hair back from her
forehead.

'—you're younger than most of our nursing staff. In
the past, we have tried to employ more mature
women.'

'I'm twenty-six,' Melanie objected, sighing with
relief yet fearful that she might now lose this fantastic
opportunity because of her age.

Jan smiled.

'I was talking forty-plus maturity,' she said wryly,
shuffling the papers back into a neat pile, 'but no one
in that age range who can speak Spanish and French
has applied, and the fact that you can throw in
Portuguese and a bit of Shona dialect is an added
bonus. With the trekking companies moving into
Africa and many young people working as volunteers
over there, we are operating in Africa more often than
we have previously. For the same reason, the South
American business is also increasing.'

Was that a definite maybe? Melanie wondered,
aware that she was finding it hard to breathe as she
waited for Jan's decision.

'You do understand that this full-time position
entails long, boring hours on the telephone. Some of
our part-time staff work specific shifts, some do only
telephone work, while our doctors and a few of our
nursing staff are only on call for emergencies and
repatriation trips. In this position, you'll be involved in
every aspect of UniversAid, not just a constant round
of world travel at company expense, a dozen missions
of mercy in a month!'

Did this mean she had the job?

She responded quickly. 'Of course I realise that. I

imagine being able to provide immediate reassurance to people by phone would prove as rewarding as physically bringing them home. I believe the work UniversAid does is so necessary, so important to people in trouble anywhere in the world, that being even a small cog in the wheel would be rewarding.'

'I happen to agree with you,' Jan told her, a warm smile now lighting her eyes and transforming her placid face to one of glowing attractiveness. 'I also happen to think you'll make an excellent employee.'

The excitement became an excited, bubbling joy, and Melanie felt her face split by a huge, delighted grin that nothing Jan still had to say could totally erase.

'There is, of course, a two-month trial period during which time you can see if you like working for us, as well as our being able to gauge your suitability. You'll start by sitting in with one of our phone operators in the command-room, then progress to taking calls on the morning shift, which is the least hectic.'

Again, Melanie nodded, and her smile faded. Initial elation was turning to trepidation as she realised the responsibility that would be placed on her, taking calls from travellers in trouble, often in remote parts of the world, and organising help and support for them.

Then Jan was speaking again, and she forced the concern away and concentrated on what the administrator was telling her.

'In a few weeks, you'll do a stint of night duty, to make sure you can handle the isolation and function well with fewer supports. By the time your trial period is over, you should have a good idea of the scope of our work, and we'll have a good idea of your ability to cope. Any questions?'

'Only one,' Melanie said, nervous laughter making the words tremble slightly. 'When do I start?'

'Nine o'clock, Monday,' Jan replied. 'Now, if you've the time, I'll show you around and introduce you to the staff on duty.'

Rising to her feet to follow Jan from the neat office, Melanie resisted an almost overwhelming urge to skip and dance in sheer joyous relief. She had been granted this trial because she had shown herself sensible, mature, calm and efficient, which meant that any physical demonstration of her delight would have to wait until she was well away from the offices of UniversAid.

Jan led the way past empty glass-walled offices, explaining as she went, 'It rarely gets busy before eleven, so our airline specialist, Bill Gates, doesn't start work till ten. He makes all bookings, charters planes where necessary, and can tell you who to see in Bogata, for instance, if you need a plane that can land on a short strip, at altitude, but still hold a stretcher.'

Melanie shook her head in wonder at such encyclopaedic knowledge, then realised that the man was as much a specialist as any doctor or nurse who pursued further training in a particular field.

'The next office is that of our medical director. He may be in before you leave. He's supposed to be off duty after bringing back a heart attack patient from Riga yesterday, but UniversAid is his baby and I think it would take surgical intervention to remove him from it for long.'

'If he feels that way, he's probably better off here than pretending to relax at his home,' Melanie responded, picking up a faint thread of expectation —

or was it challenge?—in the air that made her sympathetic to the absent man's actions.

'And this is the heart of UniversAid,' Jan announced, throwing open the door to a wide, bright room. In front of the windows, two banks of desks faced a wide, curving wall that held whiteboards divided into columns, a huge map of the world, and flashing digital clocks announcing the time in New York, Los Angeles, Tokyo, Moscow, Athens, Paris and London.

Phones rang, computers hummed, and the operators' quiet voices murmured instructions and advice. The whole effect was of an orchestrated efficiency that made Melanie shake her head in wonder.

'The back row of phones deals mainly with domestic and vehicle insurance and car problems, as we provide a twenty-four-hour assist service for corporate clients. The front row is travel, with many of our callers seeking advice about medical precautions to take prior to setting out. "Should I have a smallpox vaccination?" is still the most common.'

'Because people won't believe their doctors that smallpox has been completely wiped out?' Melanie asked.

'Precisely!' Jan told her, introducing her to the room at large and naming the staff who were present, before turning back towards the door. 'I suppose I can understand it,' she added. 'It was a decade before health authorities who oversaw the massive vaccination programme could bring themselves to believe that they hadn't missed a tiny village somewhere in the world, where the scourge still lingered!'

They moved out into the passage and Melanie turned to pull the door of the operations-room closed.

'Ah, Peter has arrived,' Jan announced happily. 'Come in and I'll introduce you.'

Responding to a tugging hand on her arm, Melanie turned, her eyes caught by the movement behind the glass partition. Then her heart stopped beating.

It was impossible! It couldn't possibly be! Not after all this time! Not here in Brisbane, of all places!

'Come on,' Jan was saying, dragging at her arm, but her mind whirled in such chaos that she was unable to order her feet to move.

'You're not shy, are you?'

She could hear laughter, but also a faint edge of doubt in Jan's voice. A shy courier would be useless!

One foot moved forward, and the other followed, mechanical movements made through a thick fog of despair. They wouldn't need a computer to check on her, not when they had the man whose report would have provided the original details of her medical re-patriation from Portugal.

'This is Melanie Ashcroft, Peter. Melanie, this is Peter Wade, our founder, medical director, and rescuer extraordinaire!'

There was a note of almost possessive pride in the introduction that lanced through Melanie's confusion. Yet for a moment she still hesitated, her gaze flickering quickly over the thin, dark face of the man on his feet behind the wide cedar desk.

'I've met Dr Wade,' she mumbled through lips stiff with the realisation that he did remember her.

This dream job, so nearly hers, was not going to be saved by any lapse of his memory! Her one brief glimpse of dark eyebrows almost meeting above his long-lashed eyes, pinched nostrils and a thin slash of lips had told her that the anger she had provoked eight years ago was something else he hadn't forgotten.

'How are you, Melanie?' he asked formally, the melodious English voice overlaid with an austere politeness.

Berfore she could find the words for a meaningless response, Jan said quickly, 'I wonder if you'd mind waiting in my office for a moment, Melanie? There are a few messages I have to pass on to Peter, then I'll take you down in the lift.'

So even practical, sensible Jan had picked up on the explosive, atmospheric disturbance that her meeting with the boss had caused, Melanie realised as she hurried thankfully back to the sanctuary of Jan's panelled room. Would they conjure up some reason why Jan's decision was to be set aside, or would she simply be told she was unsuitable?

She sank into the comfortable chair beside the desk, her mind battling against memories she'd thought were buried forever. With grim determination, she forced them back, breathing deeply to regain her physical balance and settle her erratic pulse.

The distorted voices had been mere background noise, until she finally relaxed into the chair, the past under control and the present almost ready for review.

There are other jobs, she was assuring herself, when the sounds became words—words that she was not meant to be hearing.

'I tell you she was out of control,' the clipped voice was saying. 'A wild raver who'd run away from her host family and taken up with a bunch of kids who made your hair curl even to look at them.'

There was an inaudible rejoinder, then the deeper voice continued, 'She wasn't the first exchange student

I repatriated for Worldwide, Jan. I'd seen some pretty pathetic sights, but nothing approaching the behaviour of that young madam.'

Shrinking back into the chair, Melanie raised her hands to her ears, meaning to shut out the man's scorn and anger, but curiosity—or was it an instinct for self-preservation?—made her pause, and lean forward to try to pick up what the administrator was saying.

'—best qualified, in fact the only person who applied who actually met all the criteria—which you set yourself.'

There was a dark muttering noise, overlaid by Jan's calm reasoning. 'Support staff are my responsibility,' she was pointing out, 'and, after all, it's eight years since the girl was in trouble, and her references and recommendations are proof that she's got her act together since then.'

Melanie stood up and took a step towards the desk, trying to track down the source of the conversation. Hearing Jan's defence filled her with a guilty unease, and she studied the complicated phone, assuming it must have a conference function that was activated at the moment, making it an effective intercom. Her fingers hovered indecisively over the buttons.

It was patently obvious that Peter Wade was far from happy, although his next words were unclear. Had he walked away from the desk and turned his back to Jan as he voiced more objections? Were his fingers clenched into a white-knuckled fury as they had been with her once before?

'Well, I've already told her she's got the job,' Jan interrupted abruptly, 'but I did explain about the two-month trial. If you're convinced of her unsuitability we needn't keep her on, and, in the meantime, you don't have to have anything to do with her.'

The words had a finality that sent Melanie scuttling back to her seat. With any luck, Dr Wade would stay in his office and sulk for a while, and Jan would not realise that their conversation had been broadcast.

The excitement she had felt earlier vanished like mist beneath the rising sun and it was a strain to find a smile to hide her disappointment.

'Sorry to keep you waiting,' Jan said briskly. 'With people coming and going all the time, we have to grab any opportunity to pass on information.'

Melanie watched warily while the older woman reached for a set of keys on the neat desk. Surely Jan would want to know details of the long-past escapade!

'Come on, I'll take you down in the lift. I'm afraid all the security seems paranoid to new staff and visitors, but with the mass of data on our computers it's essential.'

She led the way back to the lift, summoned it, then activated its return to the ground floor with a special key that slid into a slot low down on the control panel. Melanie's stomach clenched into a tight knot as she waited for the questions that would probably end her career at UniversAid before it began.

'When you come in on Monday, go up to Reception on level one, and someone will go down and work the lift for you to access the control-room floor. This is standard practice for all our new employees while they are on trial, from the best qualified doctors down to the janitorial staff. You'll get used to it.'

'It does seem extreme, but I had assumed it was to protect staff on night duty.' Melanie struggled to sound as if nothing had happened to disturb her.

'That too,' Jan agreed. 'But data security is paramount. We can access the fourth-floor offices with our plates, but the fifth floor, where the computers are kept, is off-limits to everyone but our computer programmer and Peter. Once you're into the swing of things, you'll usually find someone working your shift will be coming in at the same time, and you'll come up with them.'

The lift came to a silent halt as Melanie ran through the words in her mind, trying to make sense of a reprieve she could barely believe. Jan ushered her out with a warm smile that effectively hid any consternation she might be feeling about her boss's disclosures.

'See you Monday, Melanie,' she said as the doors closed, and Melanie was left in the foyer, wondering if the words were a threat or a promise.

'It's a power struggle between the two of them,' her friend Kip announced a little later as they sat over coffee in a pavement café around the corner from the UniversAid offices.

She had listened in silence to Melanie's recital, and, after two fresh Danish pastries, had finally found a satisfactory solution to the question of why Melanie was still to be employed. 'She's in charge of the appointments and that's that! Maybe he's been throwing his weight around in her section for too long, and she's determined to put him back in his place.'

'But if he's the founder of the service, then he probably owns the entire business, which kills your power struggle theory.' Melanie squinted as sunlight from a passing car threw a dazzle of light into her eyes. 'Besides, he's not a "throwing weight around" kind of person—or he wasn't eight years ago.'

'I thought you told me he'd dragged you kicking and screaming back home——real caveman stuff!' Kip complained. 'I've always put your hang-up about the man—all men in fact—down to the fact that it was physically confrontational—something you'd never experienced before in your family of gentle, refined academics.'

She sounded so aggrieved that Melanie had to smile, in spite of the dismay still seeping through her. Long before Kip had obtained her major in psychology, she had constantly analysed her friends' behaviour, changing her theories with blithe good humour, and ignoring the often glaring inconsistencies in her arguments.

'Sorry, Kip,' she said, a slight smile playing about her lips as she fixed her eyes firmly on her friend's face. 'Peter Wade is *the* most civilised man I have ever met, and while I'm in denial mode I'd like to point out that I *do not* have a hang-up about him or men in general. I simply prefer the single state and an uncomplicated life. I'm a travel freak, remember!' she added with a laugh.

'As if I hadn't noticed!'

Smiling at the resignation in Kip's voice, Melanie pushed the plate containing the remaining pastry towards her friend, before adding, 'Not that any of this raking through my past or discussion of the present is helpful. It's the future I'm concerned about—specifically Monday, and the beginning of my "trial" at UniversAid.'

Kip looked perplexed, her blue eyes peering across the table at Melanie as if she hoped to read her unspoken thoughts.

'Do you want the job, Mel?' she asked, and Melanie looked away from her puzzled scrutiny, staring out across the traffic that filtered slowly past them in a steady stream.

'Of course I do!' she replied. 'It's like an answer to all my dreams—to be able to combine work and travel. And it's an opportunity to do more than ward nursing, to pit my ability and ingenuity against a different set of circumstances every moment of the day, and find solutions. It's a challenge, Kip!'

Hearing the ardent enthusiasm in her own voice, she shook her head, trying to regain the composure that had helped her through her interview. Drawing a steadying breath, she added, 'But if I'm not going to be officially appointed in two months' time, is it worth starting? I don't know if I can cope with learning the ins and outs of it, and making new friends—not to mention the inoculations!—knowing all the time I won't be appointed to the permanent staff.'

'You can't be sure of that,' Kip asserted, slapping a hand down on the table with such force that the coffee-cups rattled. 'OK, so you're on trial, but unless you're hopeless at the work, or blow all their computer fuses, they can't really put you off.'

'Even if the boss doesn't want me working there? Come on, my friend, let's have some realism here!' Melanie picked up a teaspoon from her saucer and twisted it in her fingers, watching the futile movement to avoid her friend's perceptive eyes. Would Kip hear the quiver of despair in her voice?

'Well, I don't think they can,' Kip said stoutly. 'It will be up to you to make certain that you're the best damn apprentice they ever had—then they can't possibly let you go. What's more, you've always said you'd like a chance to have that part of your life over again.'

There was a silence that dragged on until Melanie

was forced to look up at her. She found her eyes
caught, and held, by her friend's stern gaze.

'Well, this is it, handed to you on a plate. This is the
perfect opportunity to prove to that man, who totally
misjudged you at the time, from the little you've told
me——' there was a meaningful pause that Melanie
ignored; she'd kept her own counsel for eight years,
and was hardly about to pour out all the humiliation
and pain of that period now '—that you are an
extremely competent, capable, caring and utterly
worthwhile human being, beside being my best friend!'

She pushed back her chair as she finished this
accolade, and came around the table to drop an arm
round Melanie's shoulders and give her a quick hug.

'I've got to get back to work so I'll see you tonight.
Go out and buy yourself something. That never fails to
cheer me up!'

Melanie watched her friend's well-dressed figure
wend its way through the tables, and sighed as she
disappeared from sight. Advice always sounded simple
when it was spoken but she was well aware that the
reality was never as easy.

An icy shiver shook her frame as the ghost of the
past rattled up her backbone, and filled her with a cold
dread. Could Kip be right? Would contact with the
man who had witnessed her mad belligerence lay the
spectre of her time in Portugal forever? Had some
particularly malignant fate produced this twist in her
life as a test of some description? And if fates existed,
what benighted spirit had made that stiff and proper
English gentleman, Dr Peter Wade, desert his native
land and start his business on the other side of the
world in subtropical Brisbane?

'May I join you?'

The blood froze in her veins. She did not need to lift her head to know who had spoken, so she focused on the bit of dark suit in her field of vision and nodded mutely.

Here's your chance to find the answer to at least one question, a small imp of self-preservation whispered in her head as she heard the deep, English-accented voice again.

'I won't bite you, Melly!'

The words brought her head jerking up and the old retort, 'Don't call me Melly,' flew off her tongue before conscious thought could prevent it.

His eyes, a clear pale blue that reminded her of skies above deserted places, were fixed on her face, and his expression was unreadable behind the stillness of his face.

Had Kip been right? she wondered as her body reacted to his scrutiny with a wayward lurch of her heart and a skittering rush of blood through her veins. Peter Wade might not have used physical force on her, but there had been a physical element to their struggle, on her side anyway.

The blush started at her toes and worked its way up, burning through her body in an enveloping tidal wave of shame, as that one fleeting thought liberated another shred of memory she had completely blanked out until this moment.

'If you're the boss, I'd rather you sack me now than give me two months of a pretend trial,' she blurted out, as much to hide her embarrassment as for any rational reason.

He lowered his head, as if conceding her right to the tetchy statement, then turned to thank the waitress who had placed a cup of coffee on the table in front of him. His beautiful manners had shamed her once before!

Melanie watched his hand reach out, and his thin, bony fingers spoon sugar into the black brew, while the silence grew and grew.

'Jan showed me your application. I can't fault her selection based on your experience and qualifications,' he said eventually, his eyes lifting to meet hers, his face still expressionless.

A large 'but' seemed to hover in the air between them, and Melanie turned away, her heart hammering crazily in her chest. Was she 'hung-up' over this man, as Kip had suggested, or was her reaction to him all mixed up with the turbulent shame and horror of that bit of her past? He was speaking again, and she concentrated on the words to blot out the memories that his reappearance in her life had unleashed.

'It seems that once you settled back down at home you worked hard at becoming a responsible adult. If that's the case, I'll be happy to have you on the staff.'

A hint of doubt still shadowed the words, making them sound more like a reproach than a compliment, and Melanie felt a tiny spurt of anger, sharp and hot, stab through her, but she bit back a sniping retort, then wondered if he was deliberately testing her composure with his subtle provocation.

With a considerable effort she forced herself to act as the calm, composed applicant who had impressed Jan Stevens. A question usually solved a social hiatus, and besides, beyond her shock at finding him here, she was curious.

'What made you choose Brisbane to set up in opposition to Worldwide?'

'I set up in Australia so I wouldn't be in opposition,'

he told her, his eyes meeting hers over the rim of his raised coffee-cup. 'There was no medical repatriation service here when I started, and it fitted in with a loose network of affiliates Worldwide was gathering up, to provide on-the-spot support without too much expensive infrastructure or outlays on their part.'

A wintry smile plucked the corners of his mouth upwards as he added, 'I spent a few days in Brisbane once, after delivering a patient to a town not far south of here. It was the only city in Australia I knew!'

Her eyes had caught that flicker of movement and were held by the shapely lips, no longer thinned in disapproval. Irrationally, she wanted to see the smile widen, but the reference was too obvious a lure and she skipped hurriedly past it with another question.

'And what did Cynthia think when you dragged her halfway round the world to this remote outpost of civilisation?' Her mind had dredged up a vivid picture of the elegant brunette who had clung like a limpet to his side while they'd waited at the airport in London for their flight to Australia.

She saw those shapely lips tighten again and her eyes swept up, but his head was turning towards the traffic, and any expression that might have flickered in his eyes was hidden from her.

'Cynthia had very little to say,' he said quietly. 'She realised early in our courtship that the logistics of a job like this make even the most casual of arrangements difficult. The unpredictability is a great strain on relationships, as Jan has, no doubt, pointed out to you.'

'With so many people working in this business and other jobs that require frequent absences from home, there must be plenty who can maintain successful relationships in spite of the irregularity of their work patterns.' Melanie argued automatically, to hide a flicker of inexplicable pain, although relationships were something she avoided assiduously.

Study and work were both enjoyable and satisfying, and the opportunity to work in Africa had fired her with a determination to see as much of the world as she possible could—an ambition that seemed far more realistic and achievable than other young women's dreams of marriage and living happily ever after!

'Maybe the people who wrote such glowing references for you liked a pert little chit who argued with everything they said!'

It took her a few seconds to register the sniping words, as she'd been lost in her own stray thoughts.

'I don't argue all the time,' she said quickly, then chuckled, caught out in doing what she denied. Looking across at his face in the hope of seeing an answering glimmer of laughter, she was shocked by the deep lines of strain or tiredness beneath its blankness.

'Well, not normally,' she added lightly, to cover her dismay. 'Maybe it's a reversion to teenage habits caused by the shock of seeing you again after all these years.'

'The past coming back to haunt you, Melly?' he asked, his voice soft and so low, it sounded curiously husky. And now he smiled, but it wasn't the warm, spontaneous grin that lit up his craggy face, the smile she remembered vividly from the rare occasions she'd seen it. This was more a twisted puckering of the lips, with a hint of world-weary cynicism thrown in, and it shocked Melanie more than his sudden reappearance in her life had done.

'Did you recover completely from the hepatitis—no

recurrences or after-effects?' It was his turn to fill the silence with the cool politeness of a question!

'Completely,' she assured him. 'I had regular SGOT and bilirubin tests for years afterwards, and had the Hep B vaccine when I began nursing.'

'And obviously you've conquered the anorexia.'

She could almost feel his eyes on her lightly tanned skin as they took in the soft contours of her arms, and lingered on the fullness of her breasts.

'It wasn't a clinical case of anorexia nervosa, you know,' she told him carefully, her eyes fixed on his face as she put the facts to him in spite of his earlier comment about her arguing. 'It was a side-effect of the hepatitis! I may have been stupid, but I wasn't silly enough to punish my body deliberately.

'No?' he tempted softly, and again she felt the burning shame, and dropped her head to hide the wash of colour that would betray her.

'I've got to get back to the office,' he said abruptly, rising to his feet. 'Good luck on Monday!'

Then he was striding away, his tall figure erect, neatly suited—the essential businessman. He didn't sound as if he'd meant it when he'd said good luck!

She watched with an unfamiliar feeling of regret, as if she had lost something very precious.

Eight years ago, there'd been a brave and spirited adventurer beneath the façade of the proper English doctor, an intrepid man who loved the challenges presented by distance and medical emergencies, and who conquered them with all the determined zeal of an old-world explorer.

She'd fought him every inch of the way home, kicking and spitting as viciously as a trapped cat attacking a rescuer. He'd found her in the basic clinic at Monsanto where she'd drifted with a gang of 'no-hopers', as he'd called them, and somehow chivvied and coaxed her back to her home on the Gold Coast, an hour's drive south of Brisbane. Once home, he'd handed her back to her parents with a list of medical instructions and some harsh words about their methods of child-raising.

Poor loves! As if any of it had been their fault.

And what of Peter Wade? Did the adventurer still lurk beneath that civilised exterior, or had the cynicism she now recognised in him swept away the inexplicable joy and wonder of reaching new frontiers and finding a way through unfamiliar territory?

CHAPTER TWO

ONE month of handling the telephone calls and computer data had given Melanie a confidence that prompted excitement rather than trepidation as she rode up in the lift with Rose, her co-worker on this, her first night shift. It was only eight o'clock, but the lamplit streets, the absence of traffic noise, and the hushed, dark building added to a feeling of adventure.

There was little time to savour the moment! The phone demanded attention as she settled into the chair, the caller a doctor from West Australia puzzled over a patient recently returned from China who was now suffering a high fever.

'I've ruled out malaria, which was unlikely anyway, and the salmonella viruses. He was in good health for a couple of weeks after his return, but is now suffering severe abdominal pain as well as the fever.'

While the man detailed his patient's symptoms, Melanie's fingers brought China up on the computer screen and her eyes scanned the rolling lines of information. As different districts offered their own peculiar health hazards, she opened the atlas on her desk to a map of China and asked, 'Where exactly was he?'

'Just a minute, I'll check his file,' came the quick reply, and her fingers hit the 'pause' button to hold the district menu in place.

'He was white-water kayaking in a place called Tiger's Leap Gorge on the Yangtze.'

The information quacked into her ear, and she

sighed. That was a great help! Even with her elementary knowledge of China, she was aware that the Yangtze was one of the longest rivers in the world—it would cross many districts, and pass through two or three different climatic zones.

'Could you hold for a moment?' she said, and concentrated on the map.

Finding the Yangtze, she followed it up towards its source, knowing that the gorge was unlikely to be marked on such an elementary map. Beside her Rose was speaking quietly, and she was vaguely aware that someone else had entered the room, but her mind was on the pale contour lines, working out that a gorge would run through mountains and have steep sides. This meant it should have closer contour marks.

Sichuan Province had mountains and a mass of wiggly lines near the river. She brought it up on the screen, but it offered nothing. Should she persevere with the area or go to arthropod-borne diseases in another file and start from there?

Then her mind seized its own faint clue, following it as swiftly as any computer. Kayaking—water—schistosomiasis—bilharziasis, borne by a little worm that lived in fresh water. Surely this far up the Yangtze would be fresh!

'Have you thought of bilharziasis?' she asked the patient man at the other end of the line as excitement coursed through her. It was like a game, this chase through electronic files to find an elusive clue!

She concentrated now on the screen, delving deeper and deeper into the computer's massive data banks until Schistosoma japonicum revealed itself—a Far Eastern form of the worm that burrowed beneath the skin of its victims, then found its way to the walls of

the intestine and rarely caused any symptoms until
about five or six weeks later when it began producing
eggs.

'An ELISA test will confirm it,' she told the doctor.
'It shows an increase in white blood cells, particularly
eosinophils. A single dose of Praziquantel tablets is
recommended,' she finished, reading the information
triumphantly from the screen.

'Well done!' a deep voice said as she smiled at the
doctor's thanks and dropped the phone back into its
cradle.

Peter Wade was propped against the desk behind
her.

'What made you think of bilharziasis?' he asked,
sounding interested rather than officious, although
contact between them, up until now, had been limited
to formal 'good morning's or 'good afternoon's.

'I knew it was a danger for white-water enthusiasts
on some of the rivers in Africa. Once he said gorge
and kayaking, my brain started to click into gear.'

She smiled at him, still flushed and triumphant with
the heady sense of victory.

He smile back—the old smile she remembered which
sparked in his clear blue eyes and hovered on his lips
like a blessing bestowed on only a rare few.

'I can see why Jan is impressed by her latest recruit,'
he said. 'I've been away more than I've been at home
these last few weeks but I keep hearing your praises
sung whenever I step foot in the office.'

'That's silly,' she muttered, acutely embarrassed by
this tribute. 'I'm only doing the job. She probably
praises everyone who doesn't make a complete hash of
it.'

She squirmed uncomfortably, as ill at ease as a teenager in the headmaster's office.

'Don't argue, Mel—Melanie!' he ordered softly, and his hand reached out and one finger pressed fleetingly against her lips—cool and soft against their heat.

The shrill of the phone broke the moment, and she saw him turn away to speak to Rose as she lifted the receiver and murmured, 'UniversAid, may I help you?'

It was a hospital in Atlantic City, New Jersey, reporting the admission of an Australian couple involved in a car accident. Were they definitely insured with one of the UniversAid-affiliated insurance companies and would the insurance cover their hospital bills?

'Could I have all the details, please?' Melanie asked.

Pulling out a clean file sheet, she jotted down names, insurance details, particulars of the hospital and attending doctor then moved on to injuries sustained.

'The husband has suffered fractures of the tibia and fibula in the right leg, with bruising of the spleen and possibly other internal damage. He's being monitored at the moment. The wife was four months pregnant and has aborted the foetus. She haemorrhaged badly but is now stable, although she's still heavily sedated.'

Pity clutched at Melanie's stomach as she finished her notes. 'If you could give me her name, I'll get back to you in a few minutes,' she said thickly, suprised at how affected she felt by an accident to strangers she would never meet.

'More trouble?' Peter asked, sliding into the chair beside her.

She pushed her sheet of notes across to him, while her fingers typed in the client name and insurance code number.

The details flashed up. Mr and Mrs Allen had a six-week Family Super cover—which was just as well, she thought, remembering the seven-thousand-dollar-a-day charges of some American intensive-care units. She jotted down the details, then turned back to Peter, who was frowing at the form.

'See if we have any details on this fellow either under his name or under the hospital,' he said jabbing his finger at the doctor's name on the new file.

Melanie left the couple's insurance information on the screen, and keyed in the command to open the next file on top of it. While the information search was under way, she watched Peter, amazed to see so clearly the working of his mind in subtle twitches of muscle beneath his cheek and the quick gathering of the skin between his brows.

'You're worried about something?' she prompted as she waited for the machine to respond to her latest request.

'I don't like the thought of that woman on her own over there. Neither of them can provide much support for the other, and she's a prime candidate for post-partum depression without her familiar network of friends and family.'

'Perhaps she has a relative who could fly over to be with her,' Melanie suggested, then pointed to the screen that had finally produced details of the doctor in Atlantic City, including surgery and after-hours phone numbers.

'See if you can get hold of him for me,' he said, 'then phone your contact person at the hospital and assure her about the cover. Ask if the couple's families have been contacted. If they have, then your contact may have some idea of their reaction.'

Dailling through the international code, she could hear Peter's frustrated muttering, and turned to him, an eyebrow raised in interrogation.

'I've been badgering the insurance companies to include cover for a relative to fly to an injured or ill patient,' he explained. 'It would often obviate the need for an expensive medical team to go, when hand-holding is all that's required.'

He sounded so cross she had to smile. He might be punctilious in his approach, but he was accustomed to getting his own way and the insurance companies' refusal to bend to his command was obviously frustrating him.

'Dr Reynolds' office.'

The American-accented voice was so clear, the woman could have been in the next room. Melanie explained who she was and passed on the fact that Peter would like to speak to Dr Reynolds.

'I'm not certain where he is at the moment, but give me your number, dear, and I'll page him and get him to call you "toot sweet!" Dr Wade, was it?'

The cheerful response made Melanie smile, and she carefully repeated the ITD and STD codes.

'He'll get back to you,' she said, the smile still lingering on her lips as she turned to Peter, surprising a frown of such ferocity that she wondered what she'd done wrong.

'Should I have given her your home number?' she quaked, watching as he shook his head, and his features relaxed into a rueful smile.

'No, I'll stay here until we have this sorted out,' he told her, but the *frisson* of alarm the frown had triggerd remained as a shadow behind her relief. Had he come in to check up on her?

Then he explained, as if answering her unspoken query. 'I flew back from Africa three days ago, and I find flying east seems to unbalance my body clock so badly that a normal sleep pattern is impossible for days afterwards. I come in here, rather than tossing and turning in bed.'

She nodded and dialled the hospital, her thoughts turning to the young couple, stranded far from home and suffering not only the pain of physical injuries, but the devastating loss of their unborn child as well.

'What do we do now?' she asked, after she had reassured the hospital accounts section that their patients' accounts would be paid. 'I've only dealt with cases where a family member or the insurance company has contacted us. Do we contact the family?'

'Wait till I've spoken to the attending physician,' Peter replied. 'It might be a good idea if you shift to the next work-space for a while. That way, we can keep the details of this case up on that computer screen without opening half a dozen files on top of it.'

'Will I write it up on the board?' she asked as she straightened up the desk, leaving only the new file on the top of it.

'When we know more, I think,' he replied, standing up from his chair and resting one hand lightly on her shoulder. 'I'll make us all coffee. How do you have it?'

She knew the gesture was a simple way of drawing her attention to his question, yet a warmth she could not understand burnt in the skin beneath his hand.

'Black with sugar,' she murmured, then sighed as he turned to ask Rose the same question, filling her in on the American case, before moving quietly out of the room.

Rose fielded the next call and spoke for a few minutes before calling across to her.

'It's a Mrs Armstrong on line three, Melanie. Her daughter is one of your accident victims in Atlantic City.'

Nerves she hadn't felt before in her telephone conversations dried her mouth, and she had to force herself to shift back to the computer station that held the details then to reach out and press the button that would put the call through to this extension. Was it a side-effect of working nights, this heightened tension she could feel tightening her body?

'We have spoken to the hospital,' she assured the agitated woman. 'They are receiving the very best of care, and will be fully covered for the cost of it.'

'It isn't the money that worries me, it's the baby. They've been married seven years, and always wanted a baby, but finally decided it wasn't meant to be. They put their energy into planning this trip around the States and they'd no sooner made all the arrangements and paid their deposit than Anna fell pregnant.'

There was a pause, then a muffled sound, as if tears were being hasily dispatched.

'She was in such good health, they decided to go ahead with the trip anyway!' Mrs Armstrong finished with a despairing break in her voice that told Melanie more than words. The grandchild had been as eagerly awaited as the child!

Stifling an urge to cry herself, she spoke calmly.

'An accident can happen anywhere, at any time,' she said soothingly. 'They could as easily have been driving to visit you. The most important thing is that they will both be OK, and that they are in good hands.'

There was a mumbled reply, and Melanie continued,

'Providing there's no permanent damage, there can be other babies, Mrs Armstrong. Let's be as positive as we can.'

'But she'll be so upset, all on her own over there, with him injured as well,' came the desperate response, and Melanie knew that no soothing words would cure this woman's despair.

'Dr Wade is in the office now,' she said, knowing that the more information the woman had, the easier it would be for her to cope. 'He's waiting for a phone call from Dr Reynolds in New Orleans who has seen them both.'

'It's too far away!' the woman sobbed, and Melanie wanted to leave the phone and go and sit beside her, an arm around her shoulders, to help her through the long night.

'I know that, but the distance isn't such a problem,' she said with a false heartiness. 'We can sit right here and summon up whatever specialist is required for your daughter and son-in-law, you know. Once Dr Wade has spoken to Dr Reynolds, he can decide if we need to call in more help, and also how long they will have to stay in hospital. It may be that, once they are stable enough to travel, we can bring them home and they can go into hospital here.'

'Can you do that?' the woman asked doubtfully, as if such a solution was beyond the scope of her imagination.

'It might be possible,' Melanie told her cautiously, unwilling to raise too much hope, but determined to give the woman something positive to consider. Winking lights on the phone warned her of two incoming calls.

'I have this number for you on our files, Mrs

Armstrong,' she said, reading out the contact phone number from the computer file to confirm it was still valid. 'I'll call you back as soon as Dr Wade has spoken to Dr Reynolds, and let you know what's happening.'

The hesitancy with which the woman said goodbye told Melanie that she would have liked to keep talking. It was as if the phone connection to UniversAid was a lifeling to hope to which she was clinging, a cord connecting her to the daughter she could not reach and comfort.

Ignoring an impulse to accede to the unspoken request, she ended the call with a final assurance then fielded the first of the incoming calls, shifting to the next chair as she realised it was not connected with the case in Atlantic City.

Peter returned and placed her coffee and saucer of biscuits on the desk beside her, then slipped into the chair she had vacated to take the second call still winking its insistence from the phone.

While she passed on the name of an English-speaking doctor in Bonn to a concerned businessman in Germany, she could hear Peter enquiring about the Allens, asking the questions that would enable him to make decisions for their welfare although they were thousands of miles away.

'Most of the larger hotels can recommend English-speaking doctors,' she told the agitated man at the end of the phone, who was running through the rest of his itinerary and demanding the name and address of a suitable medico at each of his stop-overs.

'I don't wish to discuss my personal business with hotel staff,' he told her angrily.

'Would you like to speak to a doctor here?' she asked, hoping to calm him. Although the medical officers on the staff rarely did shifts in the office, there was always one on call and phone calls could be transferred to him for a long-distance consultation.

She was wondering if Peter would speak to the man, since he was here, when the slight hesitancy between question and answer that typified the overseas connection was broken by an abrupt denial of need.

'I simply want to be prepared in case of an emergency,' the belligerent voice replied, and Melanie wondered if perhaps this man was as uncertain and upset as Mrs Armstrong, clinging to a line stretching from his lonely hotel room, home.

She brought up the cities he'd listed and proceeded to give him the names and phone numbers he wanted, and was relieved when he finally thanked her civilly and said goodbye.

She picked up the coffee and sipped at it gratefully, feeling the sugary sweetness hit her system. Not a medically recommended booster, she knew, but the combination of carbohydrate and caffeine worked wonders on her metabolism, which had begun protesting that it was time for her to sleep.

Beside her, she heard Peter saying thank you to his caller, and turned enquiringly towards him.

'A gynaecologist has examined Mrs Allen, and she's had an ultrasound. There doesn't appear to be any internal damage but she's suffered a massive blood loss and was hypovolemic when brought in.'

'She was lucky they diagnosed it, with the increase in blood volume that occurs in early pregnancy,' Melanie said, shaking her head as her mind followed the woman's progress.

'It appears she was conscious and her first thoughts were for the baby.' He paused and Melanie looked up from the notes she was adding to the businessman's file to find his eyes on her, his face still. 'She'd have known she was miscarrying,' he added quietly. 'Even at four months, the force of the seatbelt cutting across her abdomen could trigger a spontaneous abortion.'

Disconcerted by something she couldn't understand in his voice, she nodded her understanding.

'I suppose we should be glad it isn't worse than that,' Melanie responded, and explained about the longed-for baby.

'We shouldn't be glad or sad,' he told her firmly, the autocratic 'Englishness' back in his voice. 'That's personal involvement, which, as you should know, is not recommended for the medical profession.'

'If we didn't care about people, we'd be engineers or sheet-metal workers,' Melanie told him sharply, angered by his denial of involvement.

'And you don't argue all the time?' One eyebrow rose in a teasing query that made Melanie's heart turn over. There was something about this man that left her feeling curiously defenceless.

'And Mr Allen? What's the word on him?' she asked, ignoring his bait as she forced her mind back to work matters. She hoped she sounded sufficiently detached to satisfy his idea of medical propriety.

'He was suffering abdominal pain, and they considered performing a peritoneal lavage when they anaesthetised him prior to the surgery on his leg, but decided, as he was going to be conscious and in hospital, they could monitor his vital functions closely enough to identify any changes.'

'I suppose if there were signs of internal bleeding they'd have gone ahead with it,' Melanie said, trying to understand what he was telling her. 'Is there some other way they can check on internal damage?'

'CAT scans could identify subcapsular injuries to the liver and spleen if there are any signs that it's necessary.'

'So what do we do next?'

'We, Melanie?' he asked, confusing her completely with a curious cadence in the words.

'UniversAid,' she replied with dignity, refusing to join in some game she did not understand, particularly when his mere presence in the operations-room was causing her to feel an uncharacteristic uncertainty.

'We wait,' he said softly. 'If they're planning an extended visit to the States it may be that they would opt to stay on in hospital over there, until they're well enough to continue their journey. In a case like that, our flying them home could severely disrupt their future plans.'

'But it was a six-week insurance cover, dated from five weeks ago,' Melanie told him.

'You've already checked?' He sounded surprised, but went on explaining in his quiet voice. 'The length of cover always gives us a clue, and we get additional information from the family, if that's available. A set time usually means they have taken holidays from work, and need to be back by a certain day. I suppose we can assume they were on the last leg of their trip, possibly intending to end up in New York for the flight home.'

He was speaking with a calm concentration, but she could see the frown gathering his eyebrows together again, and wondered what was nagging at his mind. As if preoccupied by his own uneasy thoughts, he gathered up her cup, then rose and walked out of the room.

Picking up the Allens' file, she noticed the notes he had added to it and was pleased to see that his writing was decipherable. The phones were quiet, giving her time to walk across and write up the particulars of the two cases on the whiteboard, allotting each a separate case number, and filling in the necessary details with particular care.

Whoever was on duty when the next communication came from Atlantic City, the outline would be there for them, and the reference they would need to access the case in the computer files was clearly visible.

Now she had to transfer the information from the written file to the computer. She moved back to the desk, then remembered Mrs Armstrong. How much of what they knew should she pass on to the anxious mother?

'What would you do, Rose?' she asked as she finished explaining the situation and her promise to phone back.

'Ask Peter,' said Rose promptly.

'But if he hadn't been in tonight, I'd have had to handle it myself,' she argued, unwilling to appear inadequate in front of him.

'But he is here tonight, and as he's already taken on the case I'm sure he'll be the doctor following it through. It's certainly up to him from now on to decide what families are told.'

It made sense, she decided, but that didn't make it any easier to go through to his office and speak to him. It must be the effect of this, her first night shift, that was throwing things out of proportion!

The phones were still silent, so she scribbled Mrs Armstrong's phone number on a message slip and forced herself to stand up and walk across the room.

At the door, she debated ringing Mrs Armstrong and telling her that all was well. They would probably not have any more news until the next day, but the woman's anxiety had been patently obvious, and such blanket reassurances were certain to sound false.

Peering through the glass wall of Peter's office, she could see the back of his dark head as his chair was swung away from the desk, facing towards a low set of bookshelves. It wasn't until she was inside the room that she realised he was asleep, the chair tilted back and his long legs stretched out, heels resting on the bookshelves.

Curiosity drew her forward, until she was close enough to reach out and touch him. Her eyes moved hungrily over his face, taking in the pale lines radiating from his eyes and the grey pallor of tiredness beneath the clear, tight skin.

He was breathing lightly and easily, his well-shaped lips relaxed slightly so that a glimpse of white teeth made him appear to be smiling. Long, dark lashes threw feathery shadows on to his cheeks, matching the straggle of dark hair that had flopped on to his forehead. She resisted an impulse to smooth it back, to press her fingers against the pulse she could see throbbing at his temple.

Get out of here, her mind commanded, but her legs were reluctant to obey. Her heartbeats accelerated, and her fingers ached with the control she was exerting to stop them moving towards him. . .

The sudden buzzing of the phone brought her back to her senses, and, although it was quickly silenced and she guessed that Rose had picked it up in the control-room, she hurried away, deciding to phone Mrs Armstrong and give her an outline of what Peter had learned, and assure her that someone would be in touch if there was any change.

It was the briefest of calls, as the phones had come to life, but she confirmed that the Allens were at the end of their visit and that both families would prefer to have them back at home.

Then all thoughts of individual personalities were banished as she worked methodically through the requests, complaints and explanations of tour leaders, travellers, relatives and overseas insurance agents that were the bulk of the work covered by UniversAid.

'It's only a matter of time before the night-shift phone staff is expanded to three or four,' Rose remarked as they took advantage of a lull in the telephonic demands to eat the sandwiches they'd brought in for 'lunch'.

'Is the business still growing, then?' Melanie asked, uncertain about the history of the company.

'Is it ever!' Rose replied. 'I only do telephones—I've got kids at school and can't be flitting around the world all the time—but in two years I've seen it grow from twenty staff to the forty-seven we have now. That includes the six doctors, of course, who don't work for us full-time but are all rostered to be on call and are also available for repatriation work.'

Was there a limit to how big the service could grow? Melanie wondered, lifting the receiver to her ear again, the fingers of her free hand hovering over the computer keyboard.

'Mel, it's me, Kip,' the voice whispered, and alarm spurted through Melanie as she demanded,

'What are you doing ringing me at——' she checked her watch '—one-thirty in the morning?'

'It's Barry. He called in at about eleven and wanted

to know where you were. He'd obviously been drinking and didn't believe me when I said you were at work.'

'I'm sorry you've had this bother,' Melanie told her, speaking as quietly as she could into the phone in an effort to disguise the fact that this was a personal call. 'Did you get rid of him?'

'No,' Kip muttered softly. 'That's why I'm ringing. I didn't want him to get back into his car and drive anywhere—he could have killed himself——'

'Or someone else,' Melanie interrupted angrily.

'Yes, well. . .' There was another long pause. 'I told him he could stay,' Kip finished. 'In fact, I've finally got him to bed in your room, and I'm ringing to say you'd better crash on the couch when you get home. I thought a stray body in the bed might freak you out after your first night shift.'

'Thanks, Kip,' Melanie said with rueful gratitude. She knew there was nothing else Kip could have done, but Barry was a problem she didn't want to have to handle when he woke up in the morning. Asleep on the couch, she'd make a prime target for his list of imagined grievances or litany of love—the choice depending on his mood!

She was mulling over her own stupidity in befriending Barry on her flight back from Botswana, when Peter Wade walked back into the room. Had he ever arrived at Cynthia's flat drunkenly professing his love? She shook her head. Definitely not a scenario she could envisage, she decided, smiling at her own flighty thoughts.

'I think we'll go over and get the Allens,' he said, as if they had been discussing this only moments earlier. 'I've got a nasty feeling about it, and the sooner we can get there the better.'

'We' as in UniversAid? Melanie wondered. Surely that was what he meant although he was looking at her as if he was waiting for her to respond to some personal invitation.

'I'll get the airline schedules and see what flights depart early in the morning,' Rose responded before Melanie could ask what to do next. 'Have you checked the roster to see who's available?'

'Have I?' Peter responded with a wry shake of his head. 'We seem to have had a rash of incidents lately. I want someone with O and G experience, and Dave's taken that woman back to Hong Kong, Jan's flying in from Switzerland tomorrow, Fred's on holiday, so guess who's left?'

'But you're just back, Peter,' Rose protested, while Melanie read about the other cases he'd mentioned on the board.

'I've been back three days. That's more time than we get on turn-arounds. Get two seats on the first available flight to anywhere in the States,' Peter told her. 'We can take something internal from wherever we arrive. Once I've assessed the situation, I'll call Bill and he can organise the trip home.'

'Easier said than done if you've got to cross the States,' Rose reminded him as she hurried out of the room.

'Your relief comes on at five, that right?' Peter asked, ignoring Rose's words as he turned to Melanie. She nodded.

His face was creased in thought, but the tiredness she'd seen earlier was gone and an air of excitement emanated from him, as if he had picked up the scent of the chase and was burning with an eagerness to get on with it. A glimpse of the adventurer she remembered shone through the polished exterior.

'If we can get on an early flight out of Brisbane, I'll run you home to get your things, or follow you home if your car is here, then we can go straight to the airport.'

'We?'

The word came out like a strangled yelp.

'You and I,' he said patiently. 'We'll go to America and bring the Allens home.'

'But I'm still on trial,' Melanie objected, although her heart was fluttering with a quite unreasonable excitement.

'Believe me, I know that only too well. If I'd had any alternatives, you'd have been the last one I'd have chosen, but as things have turned out, what better way to test your mettle than a field exercise?' he replied, his lips twisting into an indecipherable smile. 'Now, get cracking and print out all the information we have on the case, and while that's happening get on to Mrs Allen's mother and tell her we're almost on our way.'

'It's nearly two a.m.,' she reminded him, and was rewarded with a broad, genuine smile.

'I don't hink she'll mind being woken to be told we're going,' he assured her. 'She might have a special message for the pair of them, and should also be able to suggest the best hospital for them back here. They're from Melbourne, aren't they?'

Melanie gaped at him, unable to believe that this could be happening. She had applied for her US visa on joining the company, as even probationary staff were required to keep this authorisation current, but she had never imagined being called on to use it so soon.

'You might also check the file for Mr Allen's next of

kin and let them know we're off. The office will be in touch with both families and organise things for our arrival back here, once I've assessed the situation over there.'

She could hear the words and see his lips moving, but her mind was not processing the information. All she could think of was Kip saying 'You've always said you'd like a chance to have that part of your life over again'.

'Get cracking, Melly,' he said, and walked away before she could protest at his use of the childish diminutive, or fully comprehend that once again she would be taking a long plane journey with this stranger. And, once again, he did not want her with him!

Would she be able to prove herself on this mission? And could she expunge the memories of her behaviour eight years ago?

She typed in the code number of the Allens' file and keyed in the print command, then lifted the phone to contact Mrs Armstrong, her mind on automatic pilot while the past and the present collided with such force that she found it difficult to think.

CHAPTER THREE

EDUARDO CASEL had been twenty-one, slim, dark and dreamily handsome to the seventeen-year-old Melanie on her first foray away from parental guidance and care. The son of her host family on the student exchange programme, his status as a third-year university student had enhanced his standing in her love-struck eyes, and she had hung on every word he said, openly adoring, swept up in the delightful pain, the exquisite torment, of first love.

She dialled a number and heard Mrs Armstrong express relief, delight and gratitude. The printer by the wall clacked out its information, but Melanie's mind was entangled in the sticky web of the past, as fragments of memory flashed on an inner screen, clear as holiday slides.

Eduardo had been skilful. She had acknowledged that some years ago, when time and maturity had enabled her to look back to her stay in Portugal with understanding and bring the shadows of guilt and horror out into the open. The exercise had been similar to talking about a nightmare in order to reduce its fearsomeness to manageable proportions, and it had helped to bring the past into truer perspective.

Eduardo had not only accepted her adoration, but fed it with subtle touches, brushing past her in the cool corridors of his home, casting meaningful glances at her while they dined, and letting his fingers linger too long in hers as they greeted or parted from each other.

These hidden messages had fired her adolescent body to a frenzy of desire, feeding her rampaging hormones until she'd hungered for him with an aching need that had blotted out her common sense, all thoughts of consequences, and the moral values that were inherent to her upbringing.

The actual consummation of the madness, made more sordid by the fact that it was in a dusty attic directly above the room where his parents slept, had been a painful affront to all her senses, a shattering of the fragile illusion of love. Eduardo's rough force had shocked her and the reality of the physical act of love had left her feeling sick, ashamed and desperately unhappy.

Cessation of noise told her that the printer had stopped, and she hurried across to it and tore off the information, then concentrated on the printed words, checking that all the information they would need was there. The past must be put behind her! This was her opportunity to show Peter Wade that the Melly Ashcroft he had brought home eight years ago was dead and buried, and in her place was Melanie— efficient, calm and capable—a perfect employee for UniversAid!

'And who the hell is that?' the man she was trying to impress demanded a few hours later. He was speaking in a harsh whisper, having drifted silently behind her into her bedroom, clutching the overnight bag she'd dragged out of the hall cupboard.

Melanie's heart quaked. She'd forgotten all about Barry!

'It's a friend of Kip's—staying over. She put him in here because I was on night duty.' She blurted out the first thing that came into her head, hoping the heat she felt as she told the lie was not visible in the shaft of light spearing in from the hall.

Pulling open her underwear drawer, she grabbed at the first sets she could find. No need to take too much when she could wash them out at the hotel. A pair of pyjamas was added to the selection, then a spare pair of jeans, three T-shirts, and an uncrushable skirt.

'Do I have time for a quick shower?' she asked, taking the bag from him and folding in the clothes, adding her running shorts and a pair of joggers.

'Certainly,' Peter told her, his eyes still straying to the figure in the bed. 'I'll make us a cup of tea if that's OK.'

Melanie nodded and pointed him towards the kitchen then hurried into the small bathroom that was sandwiched between her and Kip's bedrooms.

She heard the voices in the kitchen as she emerged, her wet hair clinging damply to her head and her hairdrier and toilet bag clutched in her hand.

'We've no time for hair-drying,' Peter snapped at her, and she spun around to face him, seeing the clear expression of distaste on his face before she caught a glimpse of Barry hovering sheepishly in the kitchen behind him.

'I wasn't intending to dry it,' she told him calmly, although a wave of nausea was sweeping through her body. Getting caught out in a lie is a great way to prove your worthiness as an employee, her conscience needled, as she rammed the dryer and other last minute essentials into her small carry-on bag.

'I'm sorry about last night,' Barry said, carrying her cup of tea through into the living-room and looking at her with the eyes of a mournful spaniel.

Melanie took the cup from him, the familiar exasperation she felt at his refusal to accept friend status biting like acid at her nerve-endings.

'It's Kip you should be apologising to,' she told him curtly, thinking of her friend's tired voice during the one o'clock phone call. She crossed the room to remove her passport from a desk drawer and tuck it safely into her handbag.

'I wouldn't bother keeping up that pretence,' Peter said coolly as he came into the room, obviously anxious to be off. 'Barry has told me about your trip to Africa.'

And made it sound as if we went away together, Melanie thought savagely, feeling far more dismay and anger than was logical. And what business of Peter Wade's was her personal life anyway? She gulped at her tea, feeling it searing down her throat.

'I'm ready, so let's go,' she said, putting down the half-empty cup and picking up the warm but light windproof jacket that accompanied her everywhere she went. She was trying desperately to regain the poise that had won his compliment only hours earlier, but the senseless lie niggled beneath her skin—like a bilharziasis-carrying worm! she thought savagely.

'But I need to talk to you,' Barry bleated.

'There's nothing to talk about, Barry,' she said firmly, then realised how heartless she must sound to someone who hadn't heard her say it a hundred times before.

With a quick good bye flung over her shoulder, she led the way out of the door, her spine stiffening when she heard Peter's taunting, 'Not much of a farewell for your boyfriend.'

'He is not my boyfriend,' she told him through clenched jaws, while he unlocked the car door for her.

'Dropped him after the trip to Africa?' he pursued, holding the door open for her with his usual unnerving courtesy.

'There was no trip to Africa, not the way he makes it sound,' she stormed, furious that the harmony she had felt between them earlier had been shattered by this pointless conversation. 'You've heard Barry's version, but the actual fact of the matter is that we came home on the same flight.'

The urge to slam the door on his needling practically overwhelmed her. Perhaps that was why he'd held it, she thought savagely as he shut it with a gentle click and walked around the front of the car.

'Well, it's none of my business anyway,' he told her calmly as he slid in behind the wheel.

The comment made her want to grind her teeth in fury. Of course it was none of his business, so why bring it up? Why question her in the first place?

'I did warn you that this job is hard on relationships,' he added, as if to stir the embers of her wrath.

She could see his long fingers steady on the wheel — capable hands, she thought, then glanced at his face to see if he'd caught her looking at them. His attention was fixed on the road, his angular profile revealing absolutely nothing.

'I do not have relationships,' she told him, hoping the firmness in her voice would put an end to the confusing conversation.

'Everyone has relationships,' he said pedantically. 'With friends and family, as well as with lovers.'

The last word struck a discordant note in her mind. He'd assumed the 'no-hopers' had been her lovers, she remembered, and she'd done nothing to deny the assumption. Her sheer bloody-mindedness at the time had probably prompted her to exaggerate the closeness of the little band, although the eight young men she'd met up with in the square as Cascais had treated her like a sister.

'I don't have lovers, then,' she said stoutly, trying to repel the new wave of memories with this frank denial.

'Beautiful girl like you, big brown bedroom eyes, hair that holds the morning sun captive in its thick waves—of course you must have lovers. Or are you saying there's no one holding the position at the moment, apart from the luckless Barry?'

Bedroom eyes? For a moment she was tempted to put this increasingly bizarre conversation down to some kind of waking dream occurring in her mind because of the sleepless night, but a quick glance at her interrogator's profile was enought to tell her he was real, and the stern set of his lips suggested this was not the light banter it might have passed for in different circumstances.

It must be another test, she decided—a spot of provocation to see if she would react in an over-emotional way and he could prove her fallible under pressure.

'We're all different, Dr Wade,' she said primly, hoping to turn the conversation back to him. 'And I was taught not to judge other people by myself.'

The car had swept into the car park of a tall block of apartments at St Lucia. On the river, Melanie decided, thinking about the route they had taken from her flat at Toowong.

It slid to a halt in one of the visitors' parking bays, and Peter pulled on the handbrake and turned to her with a teasing smile.

'Sheath your claws, little kitten,' he murmured, his

eyes meeting hers with a strangely rueful gleam in their blueness. 'And call me Peter. Will you come up while I throw a few things together and have a quick shower?'

Melanie nodded, confused by the shift in the atmosphere from cold testiness to warm complicity. Maybe he had decided to make the best of things, she decided. After all, they would be stuck with each other for company for the next few days.

She climbed out of the car and followed him, aware of a certain light-headedness that she put down to lack of sleep.

'I find it's often easier on staff who've been on night shift to take these early international flights. Their bodies are ready to sleep, not all fired up wanting to get on with the day,' he told her as they entered a beautiful foyer, floored in marble, and decorated with tall, healthy plants in brass containers, and low white armchairs.

Was he feeling the same curious detachment as she was, she wondered, that he'd shifted the conversation abruptly back to business?

'As long as I make it to the plane before my body sleeps,' she said as the lift whipped them silently up to the tenth floor.

'I imagine sheer stubborn pride would insist on it,' he responded calmly, making her look quickly into his face to see if she could detect a hidden meaning behind the words.

Eight years ago he'd labelled her the most stubborn, argumentative, wayward specimen of human nature it had ever been his misfortune to meet. She remembered the words as clearly as if he were speaking them now!

He was watching the lift doors open, face blandly still, his mind probably in Atlantic City as the cogs of the operation he had started began turning smoothly through the complicated process of retrieval.

He led her into a carpeted lobby, then unlocked the unit door on the right and ushered her through, waving a hand towards the heavy leather armchairs that were turned side-on to the wide windows.

'Give me ten minutes,' he said, and Melanie drifted across the room, perversely resistant, now she was here, to seeing this place where he lived with Cynthia. Small signs of marital harmony would be too much to handle in her present tired and faintly bemused state, she decided, and focused on the view beyond the wall of glass.

Although the sun had not yet risen, the light of dawn had crept ahead of it, and the scene before her was a muted tapestry of silver, black and grey.

Directly below her, the river flowed, its movement indiscernible, so that it lay like a broad, silver arc — shining mercury spilled across a landscape. Beyond it, the trees on the opposite bank were still darkly shadowed, black guardians of the magic metallic strip. Above them, houses teetered up the steep banks, one-dimensional in the vague light, like geometric shapes stuck on a collage.

Her eyes held the beauty but her mind drifted as purposefully as the unseen movement of the river.

Eight years ago, she'd told Peter Wade she loved him, translating all her fear and confusion into an emotion she craved, transferring her hero-worshipping heart from the betrayer to the saviour. She'd sorted that all out in her mind, too, when she'd relived the episode in her mind much later, and understood the reactions of the teenager she'd been.

But was enough of the past still with her to explain

the ambivalence she felt in Peter's presence? Was what she felt today simply an undiscarded remnant of that torridly overwrought emotion?

'OK, let's check things.'

She spun around, brought abruptly back to the present by the casual words.

He was wearing a dark suit that must be made of the new microfibre, moulding softly to his frame, elegantly correct. Power-dressing! Of course he'd have to wear a suit, she realised—too late—as she glanced now at her own clean but faded jeans and flowered shirt. Staff at hospitals expected their senior consultants to be correctly attired, and reacted to them accordingly. He would command respect without opening his mouth.

'One of our dirvers will meet us at the airport with the equipment case. Jan probably showed it to you. It has things like the Oxylog, catheters, bottles, IV equipment, and some broad-spectrum drugs always packed in it. I've money and credit cards, and you and I both have our passports,' he said oblivious to the new embarrassment that was twisting her stomach.

He patted his pocket and cocked an enquiring eyebrow at her, all business now, as if the prying personal questions had never been asked, and her choice of clothing was of no importance.

Be practical, Melanie, she urged herself, grateful that she'd thrown in that one skirt almost as an afterthought.

'Do we take stretchers?' she asked, remembering the different collapsible models she'd seen in the store cupboard and matching his professionalism with her own stumbling effort.

'I'm hoping we won't need them on this trip. If we do, the airline companies we're likely to fly with on our way home have basic stretchers we can use in emergencies, and all have wheelchairs, so, unless we know we can't get one where we're going, or need the special spinal stretcher, we don't bother to take our own.'

Melanie followed him out of the unit, Cynthia forgotten as she sensed something more behind the words.

'What did Rose mean about it being easier said than done crossing the United States?' she asked as they waited for the lift.

Peter grinned at her, and she felt a flush of warmth course through her tired body.

'Don't miss much, do you?' he said, ushering her through the opening doors, and sending the small capsule slipping downwards again. 'We have a few problems in the United States, flying patients who are dependent on just about anything.'

He watched her as he spoke, and she tried to look intelligent, although the constant togetherness and her dismay over her clothes were tugging at her nerve-endings and disrupting her thought processes.

'For legal reasons, airlines in the States would prefer we use an air ambulance, but the cost is often prohibitive. Litigation is practically a national sport over there, and the airlines are understandably reluctant to carry patients with drips protruding from their bodies, or with lungs relying on a ventilator.'

They were walking back towards his car now, and she moved a little apart and breathed in the fresh morning air.

'If Mrs Allen is on intravenous antibiotics, which is likely after the miscarriage, how do we get around it?' she asked.

'It's a good trip for you to learn the ropes on,' Peter

told her, a certain satisfaction in his tone. 'You'll soon find out what we do if the need arises!'

It was an unsatisfactory answer. *Does he think I won't need to know, if he's going to sack me at the end of the two-month trial?* The thought triggered a miserable little skip in the steady beating of her heart. Then she was back in the car and his body was again assaulting hers with that silent, unseen, seductive blend of past and present.

Perhaps she'd have to walk away herself at the end of the trial! Unless she could get rid of the stray fancies the man provoked, it would be the safest route to take, no matter how much she loved the job.

The airport provided the normal scene of organised chaos, firing Melanie's nerves with excited anticipation. The UniversAid driver had already checked their medical baggage through to Philadelphia, and he handed over the baggage-claim tickets.

'You've been upgraded to first class for the first leg to Honolulu,' he explained, and Melanie cringed. Flying first class for the first time in her life, and she was wearing her oldest, most comfortable jeans!

'Why would the airline do that?' she bleated, shaking her head as she realised how little she knew about the service.

'It's Qantas,' Peter replied, as if that explained everything. 'We fly with them whenever possible because, as our national airline, they are also concerned with the welfare of Australian tourists abroad and will do whatever they can to help us bring them home. We book business class,' he continued, 'and if there are spare seats up front they usually upgrade us. It makes it a bit easier to get the sleep you need to keep going.'

*   *   *

'Sleep well?' Peter's voice pierced the foggy mists of confusion. Melanie looked around. She remembered settling into the wide first-class seat as the plane had taken off from Brisbane, remembered Peter's smile and the way he'd said, 'Well, we're off again, Melly,' making her feel as if she was eighteen again. Everything beyond that was a compete blank.

'You were right about night-duty staff sleeping on the flights,' she said, smiling shyly at her boss while she wondered how ruffled and untidy she looked. 'Have you slept?'

He nodded, a smile playing at the corner of his lips. The smile was reflected in his eyes, and it unsettled her with its. . .intimacy? She had barely settled on this bizarre possibility when it was banished by his next words, all practicality!

'You've time for a wash before they serve lunch. We go through Customs and Immigration at Hawaii, change to an American Airlines flight through to Dallas, then change again for Philadelphia.'

'You sound as casual as if we're taking a bus into town,' Melanie objected, her own bubbling excitement chasing away the shadows of sleep and its attendant confusion as names of places she had only read of dropped from his tongue.

'Oh, I'm excited,' he said, and smiled again, as if he was sharing some very special secret with her.

Her physical reaction to the smile was so extreme, she pulled herself hurriedly out of the seat and stepped over his legs, heading for the washroom as swiftly as her trembling legs would take her. Apart from being her boss, he was a married man! She *must* stop reacting to every smile like a teenager on a first date.

Inside the small cubicle, she splashed water on her

face, scrubbing her hands across it as if the effort could wash away the thoughts that rioted beneath her skull. She brushed her hair back into a semblance of tidiness, wondering at his earlier description. She thought of it as almost fair, the sun-bleached streaks lightening the gentle shade of mouse!

'Hair that holds the morning sun in its thick waves,' he had said!

She brushed her hand over the thickness, and smiled at her reflection. Even if he didn't mean it, a compliment was always welcome.

Between Honolulu and Dallas, Peter told stories of some of the cases they had handled, explaining how much of their work involved the repatriation of elderly people coming out to Australia to visit sons or daughters who had emigrated many years earlier.

'There is often such a great cultural difference between the old home and the new that parents are shocked, and become prime targets for heart attacks or strokes,' he explained.

'That's a dreadful way for something that should be as joyful as a family reunion to end,' Melanie said, unable to hide her dismay.

'A truly dispassionate statement,' Peter teased, but the smile that still hovered round his lips told her he understood how she felt. He expanded on his explanation carefully.

'I think the older generation are impressed by their offspring's obvious success, the big house and shiny new car—things many people, in south-east Asia particularly, would only dream of owning. The disappointment is with their children's lifestyle.'

The statement puzzled Melanie. 'Aren't houses and cars part of that lifestyle?'

'Yes, but it's the things that are missing from it, not what they have, that distress the older generation most. Many of our immigrants drop their reigious observances, and allow their children a freedom unheard of in their native land. The old people see it as a deterioration and express their disappointment, and the young ones can't understand, because materially they have achieved much more than they could ever hope to achieve back home.'

'A no-win situation?' Melanie said as she realised the barriers this would erect within the family.

'Precisely! It leads to arguments and fights that have no resolution. We took an elderly Vietnamese gentleman back to Ho Chi Minh City recently. He had suffered a heart attack, and his doctors suspected he'd had a mild stroke as well, because he simply stopped talking.'

Peter shuffled in his seat as he spoke, his arm brushing against Melanie's hand. Cautiously, she moved it to her lap, shrinking into her own space to keep away from his distracting movements.

'When he refused, or was unable, to talk to his son, the hospital brought in interpreters, hoping that it was all some misunderstanding. He showed no sign of understanding them—or of being able to reply—and it was decided that he was aphasic and that it would be best to take him home.'

'But would he have wanted to go back? Couldn't his family have kept him here?'

'We didn't know, is the answer to your first question, and no, the answer to the second. He was on a visitor's visa; he had to go, legally.'

'Well, that doesn't seem right,' Melanie muttered,

forgetting about Peter's nearness as she fretted about
an old, frail man begin sent away from his family.

'It's the law, Melanie,' he replied, smiling at her
pouting face. 'It was also the correct thing to do. He
was too old to transplant to foreign soil, and his body
knew that, probably before his mind did. We took him
home to a little shack in a rabbit warren of a street,
and he started babbling away to his friends, obviously
enthralling them with all the wonders he had seen, but
so pleased to be home, his happiness shone out of him
like a beacon.'

'But that's a lovely story!' she cried, turning towards
him with her pleasure as transparent as the old man's.

'A lot of them are,' he murmured. His eyes seemed
transfixed on her face, at first mirroring her own smile
with that soft gleam she'd surprised in them once
before, then slowly changing to a wide, blank blueness.
As the accompanying smile faded, and the suggestion
of a frown began, Melanie felt the cold chill of rejection, and turned away, pulling a magazine out of the
seat pocket in front of her with fingers that shook
uncontrollably.

'We should try to get some more sleep,' he said, his
voice now devoid of all emotion. 'We'll have a long
day ahead of us when we eventually reach mainland
America.'

At Dallas they had a two-hour wait for their next
flight, and, after depositing their hand baggage and
Melanie's jacket in a locker, they walked around the
vast terminal, working the stiffness out of their leg
muscles, and trying to orient their bodies to the time
changes.

'You could set out a good jogging track in this place
without leaving air-conditioned comfort,' Melanie

pointed out as they completed their first exploration of the public corridors, breaking the silence that was making her feel uneasy.

'You jog?' he asked, in such a disbelieving tone that Melanie chuckled.

'Is it against the rules?' she teased, pausing in her progress to turn towards him.

'No, it's an excellent way of keeping fit for young people, and physical fitness is essential in this business.' He shook his head, eyes skimming over her rounded hips and full bust. 'You don't seem like the jogging type.'

'Well, imagine how fat I'd be if I didn't jog,' she retorted, made edgy by the unseen chemistry that arced between them with his appraisal. Did he feel it too, or was it only on her side, this uneasiness when they were together, the sense of being a little bit more alive, or alert, or aware, not to mention downright uncomfortable when the conversation veered towards anything personal?

'I can't imagine you fat, either,' he said, shaking his head as if denying some image in his mind. And, as the smile that accompanied the words curled into her heart, Melanie broke up the uneasy hiatus by striding away.

Why should her body react to every smile, every nuance in his speech, as if it imagined he was flirting with her? He was a married man, securely fastened to Cynthia's side if her memories of Cynthia were to be trusted. And she wasn't interested in relationships anyway, she reminded herself, stretching her pace as if danger lurked behind the laggard. Particularly not in the unsatisfactory kind of relationship a married man could offer.

She looked back, and realised he wasn't following.

Now her musing shortened her stride and slowed her feet. Anyway, apart from her own objections to what she considered illicit affairs, it was highly unlikely that he saw her as anything other than the tiresome adolescent he'd once repatriated.

She wheeled into a long arcade of shops, built to tempt the bored transit passenger with bright windows and lavish goods. She must have lost Peter back where they'd paused, but there was another hour before their flight would be called and she was close enough to the departure lounge.

She sauntered along, looking idly into the windows in the hope of spying something special that she could take home to her parents or Kip.

The suit hung on a whip-slim model behind a display of wooden beads. It's knee-length skirt crossed over at the front, and had tiny gathers at the waistline, allowing a certain roominess despite its straight shape. It was a rich tobacco colour, and had a matching, long-sleeved jacket, its straight lines dropping to the model's hips. Beneath it, the clever window-dresser had added a blouse that was a riot of autumn colour—gold, burnt orange, umber and tan—swirling around in an asymmetric pattern.

Mentally, Melanie tried her beige silk blouse under the suit, and nodded in satisfaction, then envisaged the gold T-shirt she had packed, with the skirt, and decided it would be correctly informal.

She ventured inside the shop. Would the price be prohibitive?

'I'm booked on a flight that leaves in an hour,' she told the assistant, who had whipped the suit and blouse off the model in seconds and was ushering her into a booth.

I won't think about the cost, she vowed, when she saw the transformation from scruffy kid to sophisticate. She had her Mastercard and would pay it off if it took her the rest of her life!

'Will it crush?' she asked the assistant, and listened to voluble praise of the miracle fibre used in the suit. 'I'll take it,' she declared, when she could edge in the words.

Refusing to allow her mind to translate the American dollars back to Australian, she asked the woman to pack it for her, and handed over her card, her fingers clammy with excitement.

'Been spending your travel allowance?' Peter asked, when she arrived back at the departure lounge to find him waiting with their bags and her jacket.

'I didn't know we got one,' she replied, smiling up at him as the delight she still felt flowed over to embrace the world.

'You get a little extra to cover odds and ends,' he said, 'although expenses like hotel bills, meals and car hire are usually put on the company credit card.'

Her fascination with the service overcame her personal unease, and she forgot even the new suit as question after question occurred to her.

'Hire cars? Should I have an international licence? And what happens in places where they don't take credit cards? And could I sign a company card? I——'

'Whoa, Neddy!' Peter threw up his hands in surrender, laughing at the eager barrage of questions his few words of explanation had unleashed. 'Let's get back on the plane and I'll do my best to answer all your queries before we arrive in Philadelphia.'

He herded her towards the expandable tunnel leading on to the plane. 'To start with, we usually hire a car and driver. Trying to find your way from hotel to hospital in a strange town after a long flight would be sheer folly. UniversAid try to make their couriers' jobs as easy as possible!'

His head was bent so that his voice came from over her shoulder, and she could feel his breath warm against her cheek.

If you're not interested in an affair with a married man, why did you buy the suit? her mind shouted as the warmth sent shivers down her spine and reduced her knees to sponge-like softness. She stopped in her tracks, then responded mechanically to his shove from behind, shocked that her subconscious could have directed her into such folly!

CHAPTER FOUR

As THE plane lifted back into the sky, Melanie concentrated on the view of Dallas, spread beneath them like a fabulous Lego construction. She was here to learn the ropes, and to assist in the transfer of the Allens back to their home city, not to be mooning after the boss! It was her opportunity to prove how capable she was, and she could hardly do that if she was dissolving into a trembling jelly every time he breathed on her!

'Here's a folder Rose prepared for you before we left.'

Peter's voice interrupted the lecture she was giving herself.

'It has a map of Atlantic City with our hotel, the hospital and the nearest shopping centre marked—all the things Rose considers important!'

Melanie took the plastic folder and opened it quickly, using the movement of her fingers as an excuse not to look at him. The teasing note in his voice was almost too much to bear, as it brought back memories of his patience eight years ago, when he'd tried everything—even teasing—to coax her out of her stubborn sulk.

'You might not believe it after seeing the carrier bag I acquired in Dallas, but I'm not an obsessive shopper,' she told him firmly. If she was proving her worth, she didn't want him thinking her frivolous!

She opened the map and read the little notes pencilled in around the margin before adding, 'But I would like to get something to take home for Kip and my parents, and shopping centres are a good place to see the locals, as distinct from other tourists.'

'I'll see that we sample the best of them,' he promised indulgently.

A slow trickle of something akin to fear started in her blood, cooling her body as it traced through her veins. Jan had told her that staff usually had some time to explore the places they visited, as a two-day turn-around was necessary to ensure that they were fit for the return flight, but she had pictured this exploration as a solo expedition.

How could she handle the silly reactions of her body, if she was constantly in the man's presence? Her ability to maintain the pretence of a calm indifference to him was limited, especially when he was being nice to her!

'I don't know if it's lunch, dinner or breakfast, but we're about to eat again.'

His deep voice broke into her thoughts, and she sighed as he reached across and unlatched her tray from the seat in front of her, his arm resting briefly on her knee in a mimicry of intimacy.

'Anyone would think you hadn't eaten for days,' he remarked a little later as she rested her knife and fork on the tray and poured more soda water in the small plastic tumbler.

'Eating passes the time,' she told him, determined to play the calm, composed international traveller Jan had appointed.

'But it's only one of many pleasurable physical activities to do that,' he said, breaking open his bread roll with his lean fingers, 'although they're not all possible on a plane.'

His voice was soft, yet suggestive, and she fancied

she heard a smile in it. She wanted to look at him, to see if she could read what he felt in his face, to see if she could tell if he was flirting with her.

But he wouldn't do that! He hadn't even wanted to bring her on this trip.

She was well aware that office affairs were possible in any situation, and had seen plenty in her work at hospitals, but Peter Wade did not strike her as a man who would cheat on his wife. For a moment, her concentration on her food lapsed as she followed through her disturbing thoughts.

Could she make that kind of judgement about him? Did she know him well enough? The answer to both questions was no, but. . .

'I'll phone the hospital as soon as we check in and make arrangements for us to see the Allens and the attending doctors this evening if possible.'

She nodded absent-mindedly, her mind still grappling with his behaviour. Surely she would have heard some rumours if he was the kind of man who tried to seduce all the young girls on the staff. Someone would have warned her!

'Once that's taken care of we can rest, and rest includes looking around. It's silly to try and force your body to sleep if it's not ready for it, and best to get into the sleep rythms of this time-zone as soon as possible.'

'Even though we'll be heading back the other way before our bodies have time to adapt?' she asked, deciding it was better to concentrate on her part as the eager young courier than to try to analyse his behaviour and her own erratic responses. 'Perhaps we would be better sleeping during our Australian sleep hours——'

'And partying all night?' he interrupted, with a grin

that would have made her toes curl if she hadn't been being so sensible.

'I suppose it would be a bit hard to expect the American hospital staff to adapt to our time for appointments and such,' she agreed, matching his grin with a wide smile of her own.

The stewardess reached across and removed her tray, hurrying back down the aisle as if they might be approaching an airport, although it was too early for them to have reached Philadelphia.

The 'Fasten Seatbelt' sign blazed as the intercom came to life with a warning to all passengers to return to their seats and fasten their seatbelts as a line of storms was approaching.

The voice had barely died away when the plane plunged downwards with a plummeting, sickening drop that made Melanie regret her hearty meal.

'You OK?' Peter asked, his long, warm hand folding over her fingers, which gripped the armrest so tightly that her knuckles ached.

'It's only a bit of turbulence, Melly,' he added calmly, then let go her hand to slide an arm around her shoulders and draw her close against his chest as the plane lurched and fell again. His free hand prised her fingers loose and then folded around them, drawing them into his lap, while he rubbed the tension away, murmuring soothingly to blot out the cries and gasps of alarm from other passengers and the high, keening wail of a terrified child.

'It'll pull out of it soon,' he assured her as they were thrown against their seatbelts when the plane jolted forward with the unevenness of a car on a badly rutted road. 'These things are built to withstand enormous pressure.'

The cabin tilted, and they seemed to hang, suspended sideways in the air for so long that Melanie heard a thin whimper issue from her lips although she was unaware that she was afraid. Then the shuddering giant straightened itself, and battled on, the fury growing less as it ploughed out of the turbulence.

'You can stop holding your breath now,' Peter whispered in her ear, and she let out the pent-up air in a deep sigh, turning her head slightly. Her parted lips were only inches from his, and her eyes could not avoid the startling blueness of his gaze.

The kiss was inevitable, a celebration of the fact that they were still alive, a mad release of tension that turned from a hearty congratulatory pressing of lips into a thirsting, questing, demanding exploration, reaching deep into Melanie's soul and laying bare all her doubts and denials.

Even as her body responded, moving against his, losing itself in a melting, stirring, joyous release that made her ache with wanting more and more, her mind continued to operate, clattering out disjointed scraps of information and interrogation like an out-of-control machine.

Was it because she had never felt this spark of flame igniting her entire body that none of her friendships with other men had developed into 'relationships'? it asked. She shouldn't be doing this, it reproved. How could he affect her in this way? it demanded, then added the chorus, He's a married man, married man, married man!

'Excuse me, sir!'

Melanie heard the words but could not understand them, then the cough that followed penetrated her brain and she pushed herself away from Peter, turning her flaming face towards the window and peering out as if to find the source of all the turmoil.

'There've been a few minor injuries, and one passenger is in severe pain. You're the only doctor on board and the captain wondered if you would mind having a look at them.'

Peter was out of his seat and following the stewardess down the aisle before Melanie had recovered enough to realise that she might also be useful.

The scene in the back section of the plane was like the aftermath of a disaster as passengers wept, embraced, or cried out, all reacting to the tension in unexpected ways, amid a chaotic jumble of scattered belongings. Cabin staff were attending to those who had suffered minor injuries, and Peter bent over an elderly woman who was leaning forward in an aisle seat, holding her forearm tenderly against her body.

He turned and saw Melanie coming up the aisle and called to her to bring bandages for a sling and swathe from the medicine chest the staff had open on a vacant seat.

'I think there's an anterior dislocation of the head of the humerus. I don't want to try and pop it back in, in case it's due to a fracture,' he told her, moving his fingers around the shoulder girdle of the injured woman. 'Get one of the small pillows from the luggage compartment and put it between her arm and chest then tie a sling, and swathe it to keep the limb immobile. I'll see what the plane carries for pain relief, and be back after I've checked on a child who was burnt by hot tea.'

'I'm Melanie Ashcroft, and I'm a nurse.'

Melanie was pleased when the older woman murmured her name in response. She might be shocked, but while she could still respond to social conventions all was well.

'You heard Dr Wade explain that he thinks you've fractured your collarbone,' she went on, slipping the pillow into place and sliding the material for the sling under the injured arm. 'I know it's painful, but it will hurt less once we get it immobilised.'

She made a pad of a smaller bandage and placed it on the patient's uninjured shoulder to hold the knot of the sling, then folded the material and knotted it to take the weight of the injured arm, with the hand slightly elevated. She tucked the end around Mrs Grant's elbow and pinned it in place, before tying the swathe around her body to immobilise the arm.

She checked the radial pulse and the colour of the fingertips and was reassured that there were no indications of a loss of circulation or feeling.

'Can you find a comfortable position to sit back in?' she asked, and watched the woman ease herself gingerly back in the seat.

'I've some pain-killers in my handbag,' she told Melanie. 'I take them for migraine. Do you think. . .?'

Her voice was weakening, and Melanie knew it was pain and shock. She reached for the handbag and opened it, passing it to the woman who found what she needed with her free hand.

'I'll check with Dr Wade,' Melanie assured her, taking the packet so that Peter could read the composition of the drugs in case the generic names were different.

'I'll tuck this blanket around you, and be right back,' she assured her patient, then hurried down the passage to where Peter was bent over the child.

'They'll be as effective as anything else we could

provide,' Peter told her, squinting at the packet and checking the strength. 'She could take two now, but make a note of what we've done and the time she's taken them for the Airport Medical Service. They will take over when we touch down.'

'Will they land the injured passengers close by or go on to Philadelphia?'

'Fly on, I would think. There are enormous problems involved in diverting a plane.' He smiled at her, adding ruefully, 'It's one of the reasons some companies hate taking our patients—always worried there might be an emergency that will involve them having to land where they're not scheduled to land.'

She smiled back, although her insides were as turbulent as the storm that had tossed the plane around.

'I'll fix Mrs Grant and come back if you need help,' was all she said, and felt proud that she sounded as calm as he did.

The kiss was a reaction, she told herself, moving down the aisle with the tablets and a paper cup filled with water. A reaction she would have to see did not repeat itself. She couldn't fall in love with Peter—he had a wife. What was more, she pointed out to the wayward part of her mind that wanted to argue with this theory, if he was the type of man who cheated on his wife, then he wasn't worth her loving anyway.

'It's all perfectly simple,' she announced, startling Mrs Grant and herself as the words burst out.

'Here,' she told her patient, passing her the tablets and then the little cup. 'I don't suppose you'd have a pen and paper I can use in that handbag?'

The woman nodded, and again Melanie opened it, feeling uneasy as she held it out for Mrs Grant to retrieve what she needed. People's handbags were such personal things!

'I'm writing a note for you to give the medical people at the airport,' she explained. 'It's a safety precaution in case the tablets knock you out and you can't tell them what you've had.'

'So they don't pump me full of something else on top of it, you mean?' the woman asked, and Melanie nodded.

'I'll pin it to the outside of the sling; that way you won't have to worry about losing it,' she explained.

'Well, I must say you're a handy person to have on a plane,' Mrs Grant told her, a trace of colour coming back into her face as the chemicals began to dull her pain.

'It's almost like part of my job,' Melanie told her, smiling broadly as she realised how much she was enjoying working at something that provided such variety, although unexpected variations like the turbulence was something she could live without!

This was definitely the job she wanted to do for as long as possible, she decided. As Kip had said, it was up to her to prove that she was so good, they could not possibly put her off at the end of her trial period.

Calm, composed, unflappable—that was what she had to be.

'Happy about something?'

Peter had joined her in the aisle, his comment wiping the lingering smile off her face.

'I was thinking how much I enjoy this job,' she told him with an underlining nod of her head. 'Is there anyone else who needs attention?'

She'd show him how good she was and ignore all the

stupid distractions that her body and his proximity kept hurling in her path.

'One of the stewardesses was hit by the heavy food trolley and jammed against a wall. Fortunately one of the other cabin staff noticed and secured the trolley before it went charging back down among the passengers.'

'And the stewardess?'

'She's resting in First Class—no obvious damage, but there could be internal problems. I'm going up to see her now; will you come?'

'Of course,' Melanie replied, and followed him along the aisle towards the front of the plane.

The woman was pale and sweating slightly, curled sideways in the wide seat with her knees pulled up as if protecting a painful area.

Explaining that he wanted to examine her, Peter eased her over on to her back, and Melanie pushed pillows under her knees to keep them flexed and ease the tension on the stomach muscles.

'Where's the worst of the pain?' Peter asked, and the girl waved her hand vaguely over her abdomen, but when her gently palpated the left upper quadrant she flinched away and a greyness seeped into the skin of her face.

'See if they carry anti-shock trousers,' he said abruptly, and Melanie turned back towards the medicine chest, only to hear him call after her, 'And get someone to drop this oxygen mask.'

She hurried away, sending a steward back to provide oxygen then hesitating over the contents of the medicine chest. Comprehensive it might be, but anti-shock trousers were not included. She picked up four pieces of sling material and some wide tape and walked back.

'No luck?'

Peter had his patient wrapped up warmly and was holding the oxygen mask firmly over her face. He looked at the bundle of cloth in her hands and raised an eyebrow.

'I did a first-aid course before I went to Africa,' Melanie said, aware of a slightly defensive note in her voice.

'A trained nurse learning first aid?'

He was smiling as he said it and she smiled back.

'It teaches you different things,' she explained. 'One of them was emergency treatment for closed abdominal wounds where there's a suspicion of internal bleeding. You make a bulky pad and tape it snugly in place over the abdomen. I've no idea why, but I thought you might know and brought these in case you want to try it.'

'Pressure, I suppose. I think it's worth a try. I'm too far out of emergency care to remember clearly. Most of my cases are sitting in hospital and all I have to do is keep the equipment running on the way home.'

She smiled at his self-deprecating words, then watched as he bent over his patient and explained what he was going to do.

'You go back to your seat now, Melanie,' he added, 'I'll stay with Abby until we land.'

Feeling suddenly redundant, she shuffled away, slumping back down into her seat and staring blankly out of the window. Of course Peter had to sit with his patient in case she went into shock, or developed other symptoms. But calling her Abby seemed unnecessarily cosy! Was the man a womaniser? If he didn't have a female staff member to flirt with on his trips, did he use his charm on the stewardesses?

That was something else she'd heard about—the bored businessman whiling away a long flight with a little flirtation, wining and dining a pretty member of the cabin staff at his destination.

Surely Peter wasn't like that!

Philadelphia unfolded beneath her and an excitement she could not control eased through her body, banishing the tiredness and disappointment she had been feeling. It was as if she had been transported into another world, and she started in surprise when a stewardess tapped her on the shoulder.

'Dr Wade wondered if you would collect the baggage and wait by the carousels until he can join you. He'll accompany the injured stewardess through to the medical centre, and our staff will take the injured passengers.'

Melanie nodded. She'd seen the big aluminium carrying case that contained their equipment when Peter had opened it for Customs, and been impressed by the documentation he had handed to the official. Every appliance was listed and described and every drug they carried was noted, to be accounted for on their departure.

This might not be a normal repatriation trip, but, as he had said, it was an opportunity for her to prove herself.

The wheels thumped on to solid ground and the passengers let out an involuntary cheer. Melanie put her bag on the spare seat beside her, then reached up into the locker for Peter's bag, slinging its strap over her shoulder as she waited patiently to disembark.

'Good girl!'

She felt his arm across her shoulder and heard his

voice at the same instant as she stood, leaning slightly on the trolley she'd found, guarding their precious equipment.

'Is Abby OK?' she asked, pleased that she sounded almost normal after a journey that seemed to have lasted for days.

'I think she will be,' he told her, then bent over his luggage, searching through it until he found a folder similar to the one he'd handed Melanie on the plane. Out of it he extracted a large sticker with the UniversAid logo emblazoned on it. He stuck this on the big case and steered the trolley towards the exit, his eyes alert for their driver now that they were easily identifiable.

The man who approached them was short, but gave the impression of wiry strength.

'I'm Matt Carson,' he said, stretching out his hand to Peter. 'I'm with Drive-U and will be your main driver while you're here, although you might get one of the others if I'm off duty.'

Melanie responded to the man's warmth and friend-liness with a delighted grin and thrust forward her hand to greet him.

'How far is it to Atlantic City?' she asked, as they emerged into weak late afternoon sunshine and she breathed fresh air for the first time since leaving Brisbane.

'About an hour and a half, depending on the traffic. Pretty quiet this time of the day,' he said, leading the way to a large white limousine parked by the kerb.

'Do we ride around in that thing even when we want to go to the shops?' she asked Peter in an undertone, shocked by the apparent extravagance.

'You'll get used to it,' he replied, smiling at her

egalitarian protest. 'It's the only way to go over here, believe me!'

They watched as Matt loaded their luggage into the boot then Peter opened the rear door of the long vehicle and she slid into an interior that seemed the size of a small living-room.

'Bar there in the middle if you folks want a drink,' Matt told them as he climbed in behind the wheel and set the engine purring.

'I'm disoriented enough without alcohol,' Melanie said in response to Peter's unspoken query.

It's the long trip, she told herself, shutting off her awareness of her companion by looking out of the window. The car slid past suburban streets lined with tall wooden houses, the light traffic flowing smoothly as the day began to draw to a close. She rested her head against the corner cushion and relaxed. They were nearly there!

'I'll drop you off at the hotel and go on to the hospital,' Peter was saying as she came back to consciousness. 'There's nothing to be gained from us both seeing them tonight. You can have a shower and relax for a while. I'll be back in time for us to eat together.'

Was he looking after her because she was new at this business, or was this standard procedure? She wished she knew.

'I'm not that tired,' she protested. 'Why can't we both go to the hospital on our way to the hotel? That way, once we check in we won't have to go out again.'

She must have said the right thing, for his tired face split into a warm smile.

'Are you certain you feel up to it?' he asked. 'It's not standard procedure.' His shoulders moved in a self-derogatory shrug. 'The rule is to get to the hotel and rest before contact, but there's something about this case that's making me feel anxious.'

Melanie felt the camaraderie between them strengthened on this admission and she responded quickly.

'I'm certain I'll rest easier once we've seen them,' she agreed, and Peter leaned forward to tell Matt of their change of plans.

The hospital could have been in any city in Australia, she decided as they swept up the drive to a long, low line of buildings. Well-trimmed flowering shrubs softened the walls, and wide green lawns swept down towards the road.

'You can get the receptionist to call me in the canteen,' Matt told them as they slipped out of the car, Peter pulling on his suit jacket and buttoning one button as they approached the entrance. Melanie tucked her shirt more firmly into her jeans and stood up as tall as she could, hoping she'd pass unnoticed behind Peter.

'Come through this way.'

The soft American accent seemed to lure them forward, and they moved through corridors made more familiar by the distinctive odour that welcomed members of their professions in any part of the world.

'Unfortunately, they're about as far apart as they could be,' their guide explained as they reached the men's surgical ward. 'We have been wheeling Mr Allen over to visit his wife and some of the staff are popping in when they're off duty, but Mrs Allen has been extremely upset, and we haven't really known what to do.'

With her heart beating rapidly now that they were so close to the strangers she thought of as friends, Melanie followed the sister and Peter through to the private room with its windows looking out over the pretty garden. Then Peter was introducing himself, and she was moving forward, to the bedside of a well-built young man with a shock of dark brown hair.

'Could you go and see Anna?' he begged, anxiety providing added strength to his handshake. 'She won't tell me what's wrong, but she's. . .changed, somehow.'

There was bewilderment in the soft brown eyes, and pain as well.

'I'll leave Dr Wade with you and go right now,' she assured him. 'If that's OK with you?' she added to their guide.

'I'll take you over,' the woman said, leading the way back out of the room and down more corridors, then into what was obviously the maternity ward.

What a place to put the poor girl! Melanie thought. The sight of the mothers with their new babies, the sounds of congratulation, the crying of the new-born would all exacerbate her own sense of loss.

'Here's a visitor from Australia for you,' her guide called as she knocked and entered the room without waiting for a response.

'Mum said you'd come,' the pretty blonde cried, reaching out to grasp Melanie's hand and squeezing her fingers until they hurt. 'She rang and said you were on the way, but I didn't dare believe it. I didn't want to hope.'

Melanie sank on to the bed, stroking the thin fingers with her free hand, unable to speak for the big lump in her throat. She forced herself to swallow, then introduced herself.

'And I'm Anna,' the young woman told her, a feverish glitter that was more than excitement evident in her eyes. Melanie's eyes took in the surroundings, noting the drip that was feeding into Anna's arm. Even before she read the chart, she guessed that infection was present, and, as well as nutrients, the drip was providing a continuous infusion of antibiotics. 'When will you take us home?'

'We've only just arrived but Dr Wade will be speaking to your doctor first thing in the morning,' Melanie explained. 'Once he has all the details about you and your husband, he'll decide what happens next.'

'But he will help us get home?'

'I think so.'

'I'm sure so.'

Mealnie spun around at the sound of the deep English voice, and was surprised to see Peter pushing Mr Allen in a wheelchair through the door.

'This is another Peter,' he explained, with a smile.

'But I'm always called Pete,' the young man hastened to assure her. 'So there'll be no confusion on the way home, will there, honey?'

The unfamiliar American endearment had a pleading intensity, as if all he wanted was for his wife to share this mild joke.

Melanie felt Anna's uninterest as if it were a physical presence in the room, and wondered what had gone so desperately wrong between them at a time when they should be leaning on each other for support.

'I thought it best if we discussed the arrangements together,' Peter broke in, as if he too sensed the tension in the air. 'And I've also told Pete this will be the last ride he gets. I want him practising on his crutches as much as possible.

Melanie nodded. The sooner Pete was mobile, the less chance there was of a thrombosis in his leg. With the inactivity of a long flight ahead, the risk was higher.

'Can we leave tomorrow?' Anna's eagerness would have been amusing if the note of desperation hadn't been crystal-clear in her voice.

'Maybe the next day,' Peter explained from the foot of her bed where he was studying her file.

Melanie felt Anna's grip tighten on her hand and saw the tears that gathered in her eyes. She leaned towards her, hoping to hide the other woman's disappointment, passing on messages from her mother and talking inanely about the weather at home and the long flight from Australia.

'Well, we just dropped in to let you know we're here,' Peter said at last. 'We'd better go now and check in at the hotel before they decide we're not coming. Do you want to stay here with Anna, Pete, or will I take you back to your own room?'

'You'd better go,' his wife answered fretfully, and Melanie saw the disappointment on the young man's face.

'Well, we'll all go together, and Melanie and I will be back to see you in the morning,' Peter said, sounding so cool and detached that Melanie wanted to hit him.

Outside the window, darkness was hiding the gardens, and street-lights were beginning to glow. She felt Anna's hand tighten on hers.

'Can you come back and see me after you've settled into your hotel?' she pleaded, and Melanie had opened her mouth to say yes, when Peter interrupted with a quick,

'This is Melanie's first trip with UniversAid and after thirty hours in the air I think she'll be ready to fall into bed as soon as she's eaten.'

There was something fussily pedantic in his tone,

and Melanie felt herself stiffening. Who was he to decide what she did or didn't do? Training and protocol forbade arguing in front of patients, so she squeezed Anna's hand then bent to kiss her flushed cheek.

'I'll be back as soon as I can,' she whispered to her, and followed Peter and his charge towards the door, glaring at his back to give vent to some of her anger.

'She needs someone with her,' she told him as they strode together down the corridor after settling Pete back into his bed.

'She also needs someone who will be capable of supporting her all the way home, which you won't be if you overdo things tonight,' he told her sharply.

'I'd forgotten how bossy you were,' Melanie muttered, quickening her pace to keep up with his long strides.

'Had you?' he said, casting a glance over his shoulder at her. 'Well, I haven't forgotten how impossible you become when you're overtired. Nothing much has changed, eh, Melly?'

She couldn't tell if he was teasing her, or if the unfamiliar inflection in his voice was reproof.

'I'm not tired,' she muttered ungraciously, then realised that arguing over something utterly pointless undoubtedly indicated exhaustion. But she couldn't let it rest, and, as they came to a halt beside the reception desk, she added with a childish pout, 'And don't call me Melly!' then remembered that she'd intended to be cool, composed and capable.

She could have cried with frustration!

CHAPTER FIVE

THEY were booked into a suite at Bally's Grand Hotel, a place that seemed to Melanie, as she walked through the foyer, to be a huge poker-machine palace.

'Why a suite?' she asked suspiciously as they rode up to their rooms.

'Because we need space. It's possible this journey will have to be done in stages,' Peter explained, impatience straining his voice. 'Contrary to what you might believe, a thirty-hour plane trip is not the ideal convalescence for seriousy injured people.'

'So what do we do?' she asked as they were shown into a lavish sitting-room by the bellboy.

'I don't know, and won't know until I've spoken to the doctors who are caring for them.'

'Some doctors!' she muttered belligerently, ignoring the comfortable furnishings in the room. 'Fancy putting the woman in the maternity section were she's surrounded by reminders of her own loss.'

'It's standard procedure,' he replied with infuriating calm. 'You can hardly expect the consultant gynaecologist to be trailing all over a hospital that size to visit one extra patient.'

'Oh, no! We wouldn't want to upset a doctor, now would we?' she bit back at him as something she could not control forced her to bait him.

'Why not?' he said. 'You never mind doing it!'

The words were so quietly spoken that she might almost have imagined them, but they killed the impulse to fight as effectively as a bucket of water quenched a small fire.

'Your room is through that door,' he added, waving his hand towards the right. 'Maybe a shower will improve your temper.'

A shower wasn't likely to wash away her concern about Anna Allen, but she picked up her belongings and trudged through into a large bedroom complete with two queen-size beds, and a private bathroom opening off it.

This constant bickering with the boss was hardly the way to prove her composure and competence, she reminded herself, shaking out her new suit and hanging it up in the small wardrobe. Vowing to keep her opinions to herself in future, she pulled clean clothes out of her bag and walked through into the bathroom.

Steaming hot water and plenty of soap washed away grime and tetchiness, so that she emerged tired but definitely more relaxed. She shrugged into the thick towelling robe supplied by the hotel and was rubbing her hair dry when she heard Peter's voice.

'Do you want to dress and go down to the dining-room for a meal, or shall we order something to eat up here?'

Walking into the bedroom, she saw his head poked around the door, his bare shoulders, tanned and wide, also visible. Again the word 'intimate' flickered in her mind.

'I'd much rather eat up here,' she said quickly. 'Then I can fall into bed straight after the meal.' The word 'bed' now jolted her, and she added quickly, 'I am tired!' and hoped this admission would serve as an apology for her pre-shower behaviour.

'I'd never have guessed,' he replied with the same

curious smile that had startled her earlier. 'What would you fancy for dinner?'

'Something light,' she said quickly, covering her confusion with words. 'Maybe a hamburger would be the appropriate choice.' She smiled back, but all he did was nod, and disappear like a genie withdrawing into his bottle.

The situation of a man and a woman travelling together was disturbingly domestic, she decided, combing the tangles out of her hair. As she leaned towards the mirror, she noticed how the front of the bathrobe gaped, revealing too much of her full, thrusting breasts.

This is business, she reminded herself, deciding to put on her clean jeans and a T-shirt. There were enough problems in her mind without adding the ridiculous image of the two of them together in matching bathrobes!

He was wearing a pair of navy blue casual trousers and a paler knit shirt that clung to his spare frame like a second skin, defining his pecs and deltoids, not strongly developed as a result of weight-lifting, but firm and hard as if they were put to regular use in more practical pursuits.

'Have you seen the Atlantic yet?'

'The Atlantic Ocean?' She shook her head as if to clear it, realising she had completely forgotten that they were in a foreign country with new sights to see, new streets to explore.

'It's right out there through the windows,' he added, putting a casual arm around her shoulder and drawing her towards the heavily curtained side of the room. Thrusting aside the drapery and sliding open the glass door, he guided her through, his arm dropping away, but his body still so close behind her that she fancied she could feel him breathing.

'It's like a picutre of the place in a travel brochure,' she whispered as her eyes took in the lamplit boardwalk stretching north and south away from the hotel. Beyond that, a cloud-veiled moon cast pale shadows on the moving ocean, whose might, unrecognisable in the restless, silvered sheen of the water, was heard in the dull thunder of the waves tumbling on the shore.

'I'd forgotten we were here,' she added, trying to explain her feelings yet not wanting to break the spell of harmony that had settled on them both.

'It's a good thing to be preoccupied with your patients,' he told her, moving to stand beside her, his hands outstretched to grasp the rail. 'But not to the exclusion of all else,' he continued, 'and especially not at the expense of your own health and well-being.'

He's reminding me that it's a business trip, she realised. Teaching me things I'll need to know if I'm travelling alone!

She shook away a contrary sadness. They were sharing this adventure as co-workers, nothing else, and the sooner she got that through her thick skull the better, she chided herself, turning her back determinedly on the suggestive moonlight-on-water scene and walking back into the brightly lit sitting-room.

'You were right about Anna being in the wrong place at that hospital,' Peter said as they sat down to tackle the enormous hamburgers that Room Service had provided. 'It's always hard on miscarriage patients to be in the O and G ward, but it is where they'll get the best specialist care.'

Melanie nodded, accepting his words as a truce.

'There's something wrong between Anna and Pete,'

she said, pleased to be back on a professional topic.
'The air fairly crackled with static when you wheeled
Pete in.'

'And I thought. . .'

Again he spoke so softly that she wondered if she'd
heard the words, but a quick glance at his face revealed
nothing more than a wry grin.

'I did wonder,' he said now, ignoring the half-
finished sentence. 'Pete seemed overly anxious for a
man about to go home.'

He picked up a long potato chip in his fingers and
Melanie watched as he raised it absent-mindedly to his
lips and bit into it with strong white teeth. His lips were
soft, a contrast to the hardness, and she found herself
licking her own lips, gone suddenly dry.

'Any suggestions?'

The question brought her back to earth.

'Maybe all they need is time together, time to talk
and sit in silence, to hold hands and share a physical
comforting,' Melanie offered shyly.

'Which they won't get if they go straight home.' He
spoke with such emphasis that Melanie wondered if he
knew something she didn't know, but his face had a
shuttered look that closed her out, and she knew she
must learn not to question every statement he made,
or argue with every decree.

Finally, he pushed his plate back and looked at her
across the table.

'They won't be able to cope without help for a
while,' he told her, 'which means they'll have to go to
one or other of their parents' homes. Their friends will
pop in to hear about the holiday, and commiserate
about the accident, and time alone will be the last thing
they'll get.'

'But we can't do anything about that,' Melanie argued, forgetting her decision to remain passive. 'They won't be our responsibility then.'

'That doesn't sound like the young woman who wanted to spend the night holding Anna's hand,' he mocked, and all her resolutions flew out the window.

'I'm only trying to remain detached,' she told him haughtily, 'as ordered by my boss! Maybe the solution is to put them in hospital when they get home, until they can manage on their own!'

'The hospital here isn't helping heal whatever rift exists, so why should an Australian hospital?'

The well-being that the hot shower and hearty food had engendered began to drain away. Was this part of her work experience, this needling at her to argue both sides of the case?

'Well?' he demanded.

'Well, what?' she replied crossly. 'I don't see what we can do! Unless we. . .'

She paused, twirling her fork in her fingers, while she ran through the skeleton of an idea in her head, searching for the objections he was sure to make.

'Unless?' he prompted.

She looked up to see his eyes on her face, an eagerness there that she couldn't quite understand.

'Could we bring them here for a day or two before we go? The rooms have two beds so he wouldn't constantly be crashing his cast into her, but they would have time together and we could look after them.'

She saw the smile spread across his face and the gleam of excitement in his eyes.

'You did grow up into a sensible young woman, Melly Ashcroft,' he said, his voice warm with praise. 'And we might make a courier out of you yet! You've got to learn to think on the run. Often we arrive at a place after a horrific journey and find the situation is totally different from our expectations. A courier must be able to adapt, to change plans, routes, medication, whatever!'

The pleasure of his praise swept through her, banishing all other thoughts.

'Is that what we'll do?' she asked, her eyes sparkling with delight that she'd guessed correctly, yet as she watched his face she saw his smile fade and the controlled, mask-like expression slip back into place.

'If you can handle sharing the other bedroom with me,' he said, his voice devoid of all emotion.

Opening her mouth to protest, she remembered his words about thinking things through, and closed it quickly.

The couple would need care. Anna especially would have to be checked during the night. If she remained on the drip, it would have to be monitored. It would be impossible to dump them in a room and have to tiptoe around the hotel corridors at night in order to reach them.

'Worked it out?' She looked up to see Peter's eyes fixed on her face, a slight tightening of his lips making him look grim.

'I think so,' she told him, then remembered her suspicions about his behaviour towards her earlier. 'But surely I could sleep here in the sitting-room.'

She waved a hand towards the small couch.

'There are two extremely large beds in each bedroom, Melanie,' he reminded her. 'And all we'll be doing there is getting enough sleep to make sure we can take the Allens safely home.'

He made it sound as if *she* were the one not to be

trusted, she thought resentfully, then remembered her behaviour in the past and felt the blush sweep upwards.

'Speaking of sleep has made me realise how much I need some,' she mumbled, standing up and heading towards the door of her room. 'What time will we be leaving for the hospital in the morning?'

'We won't be,' he told her. 'You'll stay here and rest while I go over and meet Dr Reynolds. I'll find out what I can, and be back by ten o'clock. The arrangements we make from there on will depend on what he has to say.'

Stifling the urge to demand that she go with him, she nodded her agreement, then said goodnight and departed. Anna would hardly expect her to be visiting at eight o'clock in the morning, and the thought of a good night's sleep was infinitely tempting.

Melanie woke to a sense of loss, a name falling from her lips in the half-conscious state that preceded complete awareness.

In her dream, she'd lain with Peter, his muscled arm heavy across her shoulders, protecting a sleep that had been deepened by a strange satisfaction. Her body stirred, remembering, and she was struck by a peculiar sense of shame and bewilderment.

As her recollections of the dream grew clearer, she twisted uncomfortably. Adolescent boys had sexy dreams; she knew that from her studies. But women?

None of her friends had ever mentioned it, she thought, rubbing her hands over her body as if to satisfy the longings that still twitched beneath her skin.

She sat up, looking around the still dark room, trying to orient her mind and body. The little travelling alarm by the bed told her it was seven o'clock, local time, but she knew her restless body would not allow more sleep.

Slipping out of bed, she crossed to the window and pushed back the curtain, shivering at the cold greyness of the ocean that splashed on to the beach far out beyond the board-walk. Beneath her, joggers and walkers dotted the boards.

She'd go for a run!

Dressing quickly, she pulled on the light windproof jacket over her T-shirt and shorts, laced up her shoes, and left her room through the door that led directly into the hallway.

She found the lobby deserted except for the bellboys, although she could hear music and muted voices from the area beyond the entrance, where gambling tables operated all night. Anxious to breathe fresh air, she headed past the banks of poker machines and out into the cold, crisp morning.

She stretched against the raised edge of a garden bed, then crossed the road, falling in behind two male joggers who chatted quietly as they ran. Their pace was perfect for a warm-up run, she decided, peeling off her jacket and tying it around her waist as her arms and legs began to loosen with the exercise.

Ten minutes later, she pulled out from behind her pacemakers, and stepped up her pace, running easily and breathing deeply. It was exhilarating and a sense of well-being stole over her, banishing the silly stirrings of her body.

Peter Wade was giving her every opportunity to prove herself capable of doing a good job. It was still a probationary period, and she was constantly under review, her behaviour monitored and her decisions checked.

His rare lapses from guide and mentor into something more—friendly?—were not the advances of a man who wanted a bit of fun outside his marriage, but another part of the same test. What kind of courier would she make if she fell into bed with every attractive man she met along the way?

If she'd been more mature, like the people they usually employed, the problem might not have arisen, she decided, running automatically, oblivious of her surroundings as her mind cast around for solutions that would explain Peter's behaviour.

That must be it, she told herself, then accelerated, as if to flee the answers she had found. Her feet pounded on the grey boards, and her chest rose and fell as she breathed in the oxygen she needed to feed her straining muscles.

Now the scene opened up before her and her eyes photographed impressions as she passed. The hotels that had lined the street further back had given way to houses, two or three-storeyed wooden structures, some painted bright colours, others weathered to a grey that matched the dirty ocean.

She turned, determined to take some time later in the day to explore what lay beyond the famous walkway. Now she needed exercise, needed the adrenalin rush her efforts would provide, and the physical exhaustion at the end of it.

There was a sharp rap on the interior door as she slipped back into her room from the hall. Peter must have heard her return, and wanted to give her some last-minute instructions.

She opened it to him, surprising a look of repressed anger on his face.

'Please leave a note if you're going out,' he said stiffly, his eyes sliding over her sweat-sheened arms and down legs that looked longer in the brief, wide-legged running shorts.

'I didn't realise you'd look in on me before you left,' she said, shivering slightly as her body started to cool.

'You might have known I'd want to check,' he snapped, backing away from the door.

Bemused by his behaviour, she remained where she was, watching as he gathered up some papers he must have been studying over breakfast, and shoved them into a slim leather folder. She wished she could see his face, which was bent away from her, although she knew how hard it was to read his mood in that stern visage.

When he finally looked up at her, his mood was not hidden after all, for a frown had drawn his black brows together and slammed his lips closed as tightly as a steel trap.

'Get yourself showered before you catch cold in that skimpy outfit, and I'm not certain that running alone is sensible, particularly in a foreign country,' he said coldly.

He made it sound as if they were in the wilds of Afghanistan!

'There were probably two hundred other people out there running or walking,' she told him sweetly, 'but if you'd like to accompany me tomorrow I'd be happy to have your delightful company.'

She smiled at his scowling face and waggled her fingers in a little wave of farewell. It was all part of the test, she reminded herself as she shut the door with exaggerated caution although her instinct prompted her to slam it in his face. It was a test she intended to pass with flying colours!

The phone rang as she emerged from the shower.

'I'm sending Matt back to the hotel,' Peter's voice informed her, dispensing with polite preliminaries. 'Have your breakfast then hop over here; the problem you mentioned is worse than we feared and I'll need your persuasive tongue.'

Was he being sarcastic?

'Should I meet you somewhere first or go straight to Mrs Allen's room?'

'Straight to her room would be best. I'll see you in an hour.'

The disconnecting click told her the call was over. Business was business. She dressed quickly, deciding to wear the skirt she had brought from Brisbane with a striped T-shirt that matched it perfectly. A little make-up covered the shadows of tiredness that lingered under her eyes, and a few hearty strokes with the hairbrush brought the shine back to her bright hair.

'Efficient, composed and capable,' she told her reflected self, then gathered up her handbag and jacket and left the room.

'Breakfast is being served through here, ma'am,' a smiling bellboy told her in response to her enquiry. He led the way through a wide passage lined with poker machines, and into a long room with scattered tables made private by screens of potted plants. Voices and laughter echoed round the space as Melanie slipped into a chair at a vacant table.

'Coffee?'

A waitress had appeared in front of her with a steaming pot of fresh brew that smelt so delicious, she had to have it, although at home she would have chosen tea.

Ordering breakfast was harder! The menu offered an enormous choice for someone used to cereal and toast, and even after she had decided what to have she had more choices to make. It appeared that American breakfast eggs came in a multitude of ways!

Was the Allens' problem the result of the accident—or could the problem have been partially to blame for the accident? Arguments in cars could lead to less concentration on road and traffic conditions.

Her thoughts detracted from the delicious breakfast as she prepared to face whatever might lie ahead. And why Peter would think that she'd be of help in a marital crisis situation she did not know, she decided, finishing a second cup of coffee. He was the one who was married!

It's part of the job, Melanie, she reminded herself as she left the room and hurried out to the lobby to find Matt.

'I don't want to see Pete at all!' Anna informed her, defiance written all over her pretty face as Melanie came quietly into the room.

'Well, we can't take you home, in that case,' Melanie told her briskly. 'We do a double deal or nothing.'

She felt mean as she watched the fight die out of the anxious eyes, to be replaced by despair.

'I don't mean to sound harsh,' Melanie assured her, hurrying to perch on the edge of the bed and take her hand, 'but you still need a doctor in attendance if we're to fly you home. Dr Wade and I can't possibly split up to take you and Pete on separate planes.'

Ignoring the pout that had appeared as she explained, she hurried on.

'Has Dr Wade explained that we'd like to get you out of here and into the hotel for the night? We're trying to break the trip into stages to make it easier for you.'

'He said something about it, but I don't want to share a room with Pete.'

Hearing this ungrateful reponse, Melanie felt like slapping her patient. There was an obvious solution: she and Anna could share one room while the two Peters had the other.

Anna had begun to list her husband's shortcomings, but Melanie ignored her, trying to decide what would be better for Pete and Anna before blurting out this idea.

'Have these things always bothered you?' she asked, remembering that the couple had been married for years.

'Yes! No-o-o! I don't know! Maybe being away with no one but him for so long made it all worse.'

'Maybe you were overtired with the travelling and your pregnancy. Maybe petty grievances became exaggerated on the trip. Tell me where you've been.'

It was a wise move, for Anna brightened immediately and spoke of the beginning of their holiday with such remembered joy that Melanie knew the dissatisfaction with Pete had not been present throughout the holiday. Slowly, she led her through the places they had visited, the things they had seen, hearing the love the two of them had shared in the memories of this recent past. Then Anna's voice changed as she told of New York. They had spent a week there prior to driving south to the Atlantic coast where disaster had overtaken them.

'What happened in New York, Anna?' she asked gently, recapturing the fluttering hand that had slithered from her grasp. 'Talking about it might help.'

The silence dragged on for so long, she thought she might have failed, then suddenly the story came tumbling out.

'We'd been to the theatre one night and were walking back to our hotel when these young kids grabbed hold of a man in front of us and started pushing him around.'

'Oh, heavens!' Melanie responded faintly, assuming the poor woman had seen a murder committed and would have the haunting memory of it with her forever.

'I wanted to run away, find a policeman or get help or vanish—anything!—but would Pete come with me?' The anger was raising the pitch of her voice, forcing the words through the remembered tension. 'He had to help!' she wailed. 'He handed me his suit jacket and rushed in there to get himself killed, forgetting all about me and the baby.'

Now she was crying in earnest, racking sobs interspersed with little whimpers of distress and helpless sniffles. Melanie put an arm around her shoulders and drew her close, patting at her shoulder and murmuring soothing nothings.

'It was probably an automatic response for him to get involved. No one likes to see a person being attacked. I would think a man's natural impulse would be to help.'

'But he could have been killed,' Anna sobbed, and Melanie knew that everything would be all right if only she could get the two of them back together again.

If Anna's despair had been because she herself might have been killed, then the marriage could well have been beyond repair. Anna felt aggrieved that he'd deserted her, but her real terror had been for him, and somehow the thought of life without Pete remained with her still, curdling her thoughts about him and her feelings towards him.

'Have you told him how worried you were at the time?' she asked, and felt the girl nod against her chest.

'I told him how selfish his actions were,' she mumbled, 'and all he did was argue that he had to help. Then I said, See if I care if you get yourself killed, and after that things got worse and worse then the bus turned out of the lane and hit us and I lost the baby and there's nothing left for me. Not even Pete.'

'You've been through too much emotional strain as well as the physical injury and shock,' Melanie told her. 'Maybe you'll feel differently once you get home, so that has to be our first priority.'

Her feeling that the Allens needed time together was stronger than ever, and she wondered how Peter was getting on with his piece of the problem.

'Dr Wade is determined that you both move to the hotel as soon as he can get your release organised. Once there, you can have a proper rest before we leave. We're trying to arrange a direct flight to Los Angeles to cut down on travelling time. We'll rest again overnight in an airport hotel before tackling the last leg home.'

'As long as I don't have to be in with Pete,' the girl reminded her with a mulish look on her face.

Poor Peter, Melanie thought, remembering her own equally fractious stubbornness when he'd been trying to help her. Then the great idea was born! Thinking of

Peter and their journey together had given her the clue she needed.

Summoning a suitably coy expression to her face, she turned to Anna, beginning hesitantly.

'Well, if you really couldn't bear to share with him, I suppose we could swap, but it's very awkward, you see. . .'

The sentence stumbled so convincingly that she knew she had caught Anna's attention.

'It's like this. . .' Again she paused, hoping the shame she felt at the lie was causing a becoming blush. 'You see, Peter—that's Dr Wade—and I are just married——' she had slipped an African ring from one hand to the other as she'd thought of the idea '—and we were supposed to be on our honeymoon when this trip came up, and we've been on planes for what seems like days and days, and last night I was so tired. . .'

Again she let her voice trail off, but the stiffening of Anna's shoulders told her she'd broken through the self-pity that had been blocking her thoughts.

Then the blush that she had practically forced into place turned to a burning chagrin as she felt a hand settle on her shoulder and knew immediately that Peter was in the room behind her.

At what stage of her story had he slipped silently into the act? There was no time to wonder, although she could feel her body beginning to tremble beneath his touch. Anna was speaking, her words rushing out as she turned from the assured to the assurer.

'Well, I suppose Pete and I can put up with a night together for a good cause,' she conceded with the kind of roguish smile people bestowed on newly-weds. 'It must have been dreadful to have your honeymoon disrupted this way. Why, Pete and I——'

She stopped abruptly, but the thought must have continued in her mind, for a sweet smile spread across her face and the defensive control softened before their eyes.

'When do we leave?' she asked Peter, while Melanie squirmed under his firm grip, wishing to distance herself from his touch and the insidious messages of his body.

'I should have you all signed out in an hour,' he promised her. 'Melanie can take the car and collect your personal belongings that are being held at the hotel where you'd been staying.'

'It will be good to get into some of my own clothes,' Anna told him with a beaming smile. 'And to be able to get around without the drip-stand.'

'We might have to keep the drip for a while,' Peter warned her. 'I haven't seen your specialist yet, which means I don't know if he'll insist on intravenous antibiotics, or agree to change you on to oral medication.'

'But I'm feeling much better,' Anna argued, then the corners of her mouth drooped and she added a pitiful, 'Physically, anyway!'

'The pain of loss takes longer,' Peter said quietly, then bent and whispered to Melanie, 'Would you please wait outside for a few minutes?'

It was such a formal request that she knew she was in trouble. Telling Anna that she and Peter were married had been stupid, but she'd been unable to think of any other excuse to get the couple into the same room.

The few minutes stretched to fifteen, and she wondered what Peter was finding to talk about, while her own agitation grew and grew, fed by the imaginary conversations with him that she was practising in her mind.

By the time he emerged, pulling the door closed behind him, she was so overwrought that she met the expected reproof with an excuse before he had time to speak.

'You told the same lie to get us into that hotel in Lisbon. I know they need to be together, and it was the first thing that came into my head.' She glared at him as she spoke, daring him to argue.

'It's OK Melly,' he replied, not smiling, but not frowning either. 'Now, here's the address of the Allens' hotel, a note from Pete authorising you to collect their things, and a signed traveller's cheque to settle their account. Matt will take you there, then back to the hotel, where you'd better shift your gear into my bedroom if you want your story to stick.'

I must look like a flashing neon sign, Melanie thought as the heat swept up into her face again. Calm yourself, she ordered hastily, then lifted her eyes to meet Peter's for the first time since they'd met in the hospital room.

'Do you want me to come back here when I've done that, to help with the transfers?' If he could pretend nothing had happened and concentrate on business, then so could she!

'I think not,' he said. 'Although you could go through their cases and send Matt back to the hospital with clothes for each of them.'

Melanie nodded, pleased to see that he was looking and sounding satisfied with the arrangements.

Then he reached out and touched her again, deliberately, with one finger under her chin, tilting it up towards him so that her eyes could not avoid his. Her body filled with fire.

'It's going to mean you won't have much time for shopping, sightseeing and exploring, bringing the Allens out of hospital like this. One of us will have to be with them all the time, you know, and the other should be resting or sleeping. I'm sorry to spoil your trip this way.'

'As if I care about that,' she said stoutly. 'We're here to do a job, aren't we? Not to be tripping about the neighbourhood.'

'You *have* grown up,' he said, leaning towards her to murmur the words in a peculiarly husky undertone, while his eyes held hers with an intensity that made her shiver. 'Grown up in many different ways.'

Then he bent as if to drop a kiss on her parted lips and she found herself holding her breath as she waited, but he jerked upright suddenly, and his hand fell away, brushing against her neck and skimming oh, so lightly against one taut breast.

CHAPTER SIX

MELANIE turned and fled. It was sexual harassment, that was what it was! And in a hospital corridor of all places.

She found Matt in the hospital lobby and gave him the name of the Allens' hotel while her mind juggled with a dozen different concerns. Anna's problem won, and she wondered if sharing a bedroom for a day and a night would help her and Pete sort out their problem.

On the other hand, her and Peter's sharing a bedroom was likely to exacerbate her own confusion, as the tug of physical attraction she already felt for him was likely to be strengthened by the close proximity.

'What is this place?' she demanded of Matt as he pulled into the drive of a huge, ornate, painted palace.

'It's the Taj Mahal, ma'am,' he told her, his voice apologetic as if he, a local, felt some collective responsibility for the ostentatious décor.

'It's certainly different,' Melanie told him as she slid out of the car with Pete's cheque and letter of authority. 'I should only be a few minutes.'

The Taj might look like something out of a movie set, but inside the calm American efficiency she had found at the hospital made light of her task. With a vague feeling of distaste at opening someone else's luggage, she found underwear, baggy shorts, shirt and a warm jacket for Pete and a skirt, blouse and cardigan for Anna. She folded these into a small bag, and put it into the car as the heavy cases were loaded into the boot. Matt dropped her and the cases back at the Grand, leaving her with one of the helpful bellboys, while he headed back to the hospital with the small bag of clothes.

Her bed had been made up while she was away, and her room was spotless. It took her a few minutes to gather up her belongings and transfer them to Peter's room, although her hand shook slightly as she hung her suit in the wardrobe beside his neat business shirts.

It's a hotel room like any other, she told herself crossly as the jittery feeling spread through her body. And with separate beds, each the size of a football field, there'll be no accidental intimate moments!

In Lisbon they'd shared a small double bed, fully clothed, but together because he hadn't trusted her not to flee if left on her own. She'd turned to him, half asleep, and, clinging to his shoulders, had sobbed out all the doubts and anguish of the past months in a senseless litany of shame and despair.

He'd held her against his chest, stroking her painfully thin shoulders and murmuring soft, meaningless words into her hair until the racking sobs subsided, and she'd cuddled, like a child exhausted by a tantrum, against him.

When the embrace had changed she could not remember, knowing only that it had. One moment she had been a child and the next an awareness of him as a man had sung through her veins like a wild, tumultuous chorus of desire, firing the nerve-endings that Eduardo had coaxed into sensitivity, and setting her body trembling with a need she had not fully comprehended.

By some osmosis beyond rational explanation, his body had felt and recognised the signals hers was transmitting, and in her mind the carer had become a lover and she had moved against him, unconsciously using her body to tempt his further towards a culmination she had only once experienced and still barely understood.

Here, with her hand on his shirt, and the male smell of him in her nostrils, she remembered the desire that had flared between them, the hot, panting breaths, the twisting, seeking hands, the softness of her body against his hardness, and the silken feel of skin sliding against skin as the barrier of their clothes had disappeared as if by magic.

Hot, slick kisses had pressed against her lips, her throat, her shoulder, and finally her breast, torturing her to an agony of wanting, as she'd twisted in his arms begging for him to relieve the pain, to take away the hunger—to love her, love her, love her!

Had it been the sound of her voice, or the articulation of her need, that had frozen his body so suddenly that she could still remember feeling the heat leave it? He'd turned his back on her, pulling at his clothes, and had climbed from the bed like an old man.

'I have just betrayed everything I believe in,' he had said in a voice so filled with pain that she had cried for him, although he had thought the tears were for herself, had read them as the selfish tears of a spoiled brat who had not been given what she wanted—begged for, in fact!

The jangling summons of the phone brought her back to the present. No wonder he hadn't wanted her working in his company—or accompanying him on this trip! And if she was thinking his behaviour verged on sexual harassment, there must be stronger words for her own provocation eight years ago.

'Could you meet us in the lobby?' Peter asked

quietly, unaware of the turbulent memories his business shirt had dredged up.

Pete was on crutches, the weight of his broken leg supported on a metal frame protruding from the bottom of the cast. Beside him, Anna looked interestingly pale, and alarmingly fragile, as she perched on the arm of one of the big leather chairs that dotted the lobby.

'You should be in a wheelchair,' Melanie told her as she waited with the pair while Peter completed check-in formalities for them.

'I didn't want to be wheeled into a hotel,' she explained. 'I'll put up with it at the airport, but not here.'

'You've only got to get from here to the lift, and then from the lift to our room,' Pete reassured her, although his eyes were anxious as they rested on her white face.

'And you got rid of the drip,' Melanie remarked, wanting to keep the light conversation going.

'Not quite,' Anna told her, raising her left arm so that Melanie could see the IV lock on the catheter in her arm. 'I'll be plugged in again when we get upstairs,' she explained. 'Dr Wade has the solution and antibiotics in his kit.'

Peter walked towards them and Melanie reached out to help Anna up, and took her arm as they walked to the lift.

'Please make use of this sitting-room,' Peter told them as they entered the suite. 'You've been cooped up long enough in the hospital and probably won't want to spend all day in your bedroom.'

He pushed open the door into their bedroom as he

was speaking, and smiled his approval when he saw their cases neatly stacked on the low luggage bench.

'Have a rest for a while, then later you can sort out what you'll need on the journey home, remembering that we'll be stopping for another night in Los Angeles. If you can reduce what you want with you to the small carry-on bags, we'll check the heavy luggage right through to Melbourne.'

Anna nodded, and Melanie wondered if she was the organiser for the couple. She led Pete into the bedroom.

'We'll give you some time to settle in while Melanie and I check up on what we'll need on the flights.' Peter closed the door on the two of them then signalled to Melanie to follow him through into the other bedroom.

'Does she still need IV medication?' Melanie asked, her anxiety about her patient overcoming all other considerations.

'Not really,' Peter replied, 'but she's been on IV fluids since the accident, and as she's still got some bleeding following the miscarriage I thought it best to keep the IV catheter in place. It's only a few days since the accident and major fluid imbalances could still occur.'

'As they would in abdominal surgery?' Melanie asked, thinking through the implications of his words.

'Exactly!'

'So how will you know and what will you do?'

Making rational medical decisions that would have to be carried out on a lengthy plane journey seemed unreal to her.

'I'm going to hook Anna up to a drip whenever we get a chance. Bear in mind that the airlines here won't transport a patient on a drip, and you'll understand that the stop-over in Los Angeles is for more than a good night's sleep.'

'Hook her up overnight, then plug the catheter until we reach the next stop-over.' Melanie shook her head in wonder at the simplicity of the solution. 'What will you give her?'

'She was on whole blood, then lactated Ringer's solution for acute blood loss replacement, but I think we could switch to a slow infusion of five per cent dextrose solution. At 125 ml an hour a 10-gtt-a-millilitre tube will supply the litre in eight hours. If we start now, she can have a night without the drip tubes hooked up, and should be able to sleep better. The dextrose solution should keep her plasma volume stable, and as she's eating normally we shouldn't have a problem with an electrolyte imbalance or a lack of nutrition.'

Melanie nodded, mentally listing the signs of fluid excess or depletion she must watch for when she checked her patient while Peter opened the big case they'd brought with them and pulled out the equipment they would need.

'These bits join up to make a drip-stand,' he told her, handing her some slim metal rods.

And he expects me to know precisely how, she thought, trying to banish the feeling that the accidental touch of his fingers had ignited in her skin.

It was surprisingly easy, she discovered, although she had the advantage of knowing what the end result would look like.

'Do you think Pete's OK?' she asked, as much to break the silence as for any medical reason.

'I think he's fine. They did a scan and could see no internal damage. Anxiety and fear can often produce surprisingly realistic symptoms. I think he was blaming himself for the accident although the police have assured him he couldn't have avoided it.

'Poor man!' Melanie said quietly, setting a sealed IV kit beside the stand. 'He's lost his unborn child as well. I sometimes think the grief of the father-to-be gets forgotten in these tragedies.'

'Little miss soft-heart,' Peter teased as he gathered up the gear they had assembled and headed out of the room to find his patient and hook her up to the drip.

It turned into an enjoyable day as they relaxed in front of the television, marvelling at the choice available to the local viewers and recognising many of the programmes from home. Pete and Anna joined them for lunch, withdrawing to their room for a rest afterwards before joining them again later in the afternoon.

'This is the life, eh, Anna?' Pete remarked as they sat around the table enjoying an unorthodox feast ordered through Room Service. They had each chosen one main meal and one sweet off the menu, and were sharing the dishes in order to try more of what the hotel kitchens had to offer.

It was evidently the opening that Peter had been waiting for.

'So you didn't stay in a hotel like the Taj Mahal every night of your trip?' he asked.

'No way,' Anna told him. 'More often than not it was a youth hostel. We'd saved the Taj for last,' she said, the sadness engendered by the abrupt end to their holiday clear in her voice.

'And then we only had half a night there,' Pete added. 'We arrived late, then left early the next morning to explore the surrounding area, intending to return by lunchtime to really enjoy the hotel facilities.'

'You might come back one day,' Melanie suggested, while Peter diverted Anna with a question about places they had visited on their trip.

The conversation took off, with the pair vying to provide the best insights and the funniest travel stories, the words tumbling so naturally from their lips that before long they were turning to each other for confirmation and smiling at each other as they shared the special memories.

'Early night for all,' Peter said finally, when he detached the drip from Anna's arm at eight o'clock. 'I've arranged wake-up calls at seven, in case we all sleep in. If you wake during the night and need anything at all, press 2 on your bedside phone to make our phone ring. One of us will be in to help you immediately.'

'How much time will we have in the morning?' Melanie asked, not knowing what arrangements Peter had made for the trip home.

'We'll have breakfast at eight and leave by nine. We're driving up to JFK Airport at New York and will fly out from there on Qantas direct to Los Angeles. Overnight accommodation has been arranged at the airport Sheraton, in a suite like this with direct phone contact between our bedrooms.'

'You go to a lot of trouble to make it easy for us,' Pete said, a huskiness in his voice that made Anna turn and take his hand while she nodded her agreement.

Melanie blinked back a tear. They would be all right now, she was certain, but her own reaction worried her. She'd seen people in love before today! So why was their shared feeling causing her to feel misty-eyed?

Maybe it was related to the queasy feeling that had surged through her when Peter had said 'our bedrooms', as if the charade was going to accompany them home.

'Is there anything you need, anything you'd like me to get for you?' she asked Anna while Peter helped Pete through to their bedroom.

'No, thanks,' Anna replied, a slight flush of excitement still colouring her pale lips and shining in her eyes. 'We might be crocks at the moment, but I'm sure we'll manage between us.'

Melanie turned away, but heard Peter speak to Anna as he left the room telling her to keep an eye on Pete and make sure he didn't try to get around without at least one crutch.

'And he'll need some help getting undressed and bathed tonight—and dressed in the morning,' he added, then closed the door, trusting Anna's instincts to take over the role of carer.

'Do you think they'll manage?' Melanie asked doubtfully, following him through to their bedroom. Was Anna ready to do much to help?

'I think so!' Peter replied, flopping down on to one of the beds and stretching his arms above his head, lying spread-eagled and seemingly relaxed against the rich red brocade of the bedspread. 'They'll certainly do better than they were doing in the hospital, even if they have to yell at each other to clear the air. All their feelings were stifled in that artificial world, and their physical injuries made matters worse.'

Melanie nodded, uncomfortably aware that she was hovering in the room, uncertain what to do next, and discomfited by Peter's carefree attitude.

'Well, are you going to stand there all night? Would you like to have a shower and go to bed? Or, if you'd rather, I could get Matt to take you on a tour of

Atlantic City by night. I know the shopping malls will still be open if you want to spend some money.'

She remembered how we excited she'd felt at the thought of seeing the city with Peter. Somehow, the prospect of undertaking her exploratory tour with Matt, nice though he was, lacked appeal.

'I think I'll opt for a long, hot shower and then bed,' she said, and picked up her small bag to find her toilet articles and the skimpy pyjamas she'd thrown in when she'd packed, knowing that the hotels would all be heated beyond her comfort level.

Thankful that the hotel provided towelling robes, she hurried into the bathroom. He was gone when she returned to the bedroom, but the light shone from the adjoining room and she noticed that he had shifted the medical case from the bedroom floor. He must be sorting out what they would need on the trip home, she decided, thankful that she had the room to herself.

Leaving the robe on the end of the bed, she slipped beween the sheets, and felt the tiredness she'd been holding at bay steal through her body. The book she'd intended reading remained unopened, and she turned off her bedside lamp and was asleep within seconds.

Peter shook her awake, his hand warm on the bare skin of her shoulder, his voice deep and still husky with sleep.

'Time to move, Melanie,' he said as she struggled back to consciousness. 'Shower's free.'

Prising her eyes open, she sat up in the bed and pushed her hair back from her face.

Peter had turned away, and was buttoning the grey striped shirt that hung out over his dark trousers. His feet were bare, making him seem strangely defenceless.

They were nice feet, long and white, with the boniness she always noticed in his hands. Vulnerable feet, somehow!

'Up now!' the feet's owner said firmly, glancing quickly over his shoulder at her somnolent form. 'I've let you sleep an extra half an hour and Anna may need some help or moral support before she's ready to face breakfast.'

His words shamed her, and she shot out of bed and into the bathroom, pausing only to lift the robe from the foot of the bed and drape it round her shoulders. Not that there was any call for modesty! Apart from his occasional lapses, which she still imagined might be part of some testing process, Peter treated her like a fellow professional—entirely sexless!

'And I'm not disappointed,' she told her mirror self aloud as she stepped under the steaming water.

The bedroom was empty when she returned, and she pulled out her new suit. She was going to New York for the first time, and even if that visit would be a drive through or around the city to the international airport she intended to dress for the day.

Packing the bright blouse that she'd bought with the suit, she pulled out her own gold T-shirt and pulled it on with the skirt. It looked great, she decided, setting the jacket aside to complete the outfit later and packing her belongings swiftly.

Slipping moisturiser and lipstick into her handbag, and checking that her passport and wallet were handy, she set her belongings neatly on the end of her bed, ready to pick up when they were ready to leave. Peter's things were in a similar pile on his bed. Compulsively neat or simply experienced in quick getaways? she wondered.

'Breakfast is here!'

His call reminded her that this was another working day, and she hurried through to the sitting-room to find Anna and Pete already seated at the table. Their clean clothes and relaxed, smiling faces told her that they were managing to look after each other, and had found the love that shock had masked.

'Good morning, you two,' she said, smiling at their contagious well-being. 'Are you ready for your ordeal by flight?'

'It won't be such an ordeal,' Pete told her, his hand reaching out to cover Anna's where it lay on the table. 'More an adventure! Imagine the challenge of pushing your way through airport queues with this,' he added, tapping his cast.

'And every minute in the plane will be bringing us closer to home,' Anna told her.

The smile might be fixed firmly in place but there was a transparency about Anna's skin that worried Melanie. She was pleased when the couple finished their meal and went back into their bedroom to pack, refusing her offer of help.

'Do you think Anna's fit enough for this?' she asked as soon as the door closed behind them.

'Not really.'

Peter's reply surprised her but she waited for him to enlarge on it, knowing now his habit of pausing as if sorting out the most precise words to convey his thoughts.

'But I don't think she was going to get any better in hospital the way things were between them.'

'So if you had your way you'd pop her back in until she's stronger, now that they've sorted out the emotional hassles.'

He smiled at her and her silly heart flipped over.

'We've no time to be debating options, and we don't know how much the thought of going home—right now—contributed to the reconciliation. We have to make our decisions and see them through, but always be prepared for the worst.'

'And what worst should we be prepared for?' Melanie asked, her mind now firmly focused on the professional aspect of the journey ahead of them.

'The worst scenario would be a deep-vein thrombosis in Pete's case, and a haemorrhage in Anna's. Now let's get the medical case unlocked and see what we'll need for either of those possible emergencies, then re-pack them into the smaller case to carry with us on the plane.'

'Interesting case when you consider we've got to carry an anticoagulant for one patient and a coagulant for the other. Should Pete be on a low-dose heparin to prevent clotting? It will be hard for him to move about much in the plane and it's a long flight.'

Melanie stacked absorbent pads into the carry-on case as she spoke, letting Peter go through the drugs they carried to decide what would be needed.

'I spoke to the doctor who's been treating him, and he feels certain he's not at risk. He's a young, fit, healthy man with no predisposition to thromboembolic disease. If you think how long they used to keep patients immobile after surgery, the risk factor for Pete is extremely low.'

'And what of Anna?'

'We'll carry Premarin as a 25mg intravenous injection for an emergency, I'd like you to speak to her before we leave and warn her, without frightening her if possible, that it's a possibility but not something to panic about.'

Peter looked up at her as he spoke, impressing on Melanie the gravity of the situation with a set face and concerned blue eyes. For the first time she realised that UniversAid personnel would often have to weigh up risks and consequences as they took decisions for the people whose well-being was in their hands.

'You'll have to accompany her to the bathroom on the trip, so you'll be able to keep an eye on things,' he continued in the same serious tone. 'As long as she understands to speak up if she feels any discomfort or if there are any changes in her blood loss we should be all right. It's the people who don't want to make a fuss who cause most problems. They are anxious to get home, and because they don't want any hitches they tend to hide symptoms we should know about, often with disastrous results.'

The words were a warning, and Melanie made a silent vow to win the confidence of the people she would travel with, and to impress on them the importance of talking about how they felt—all the time if necessary!

'We're packed and ready to leave,' Pete announced, wandering into the room as Peter finished transferring the drugs he would want to the small case.

'I'll have a quick word with Anna,' she told him, and slipped into the second bedroom where Anna rested on the edge of the bed.

'Are you OK?' she asked, and was rewarded with a warm smile.

'Everything's fine,' she said, 'but I still feel so tired. I'm wondering if there might be something else wrong with me.'

'You've lost a lot of blood, and had physical bruises and injuries to contend with as well as worry over Pete and the loss of your baby. It will take a long while for you to pick up, and you've got to make sure you give yourself the time to do it.'

'I can do that once I get home. I gave up my job before we left, although Pete only took accumulated holidays. I'd thought. . .'

'I know,' Melanie told her, hurrying to put an arm around her shoulders and draw her close. 'You'll have another baby, Anna, I know you will but it's important to make sure you're strong and well before you conceive again.'

Sitting down beside her, Melanie explained as carefully as she could about the possibility of haemorrhage, assuring her that it could be treated but it was important not to ignore any early warning signs.

She felt Anna shiver, then the woman's body straightened, and Melanie knew that she would be all right. There was a determined, fighting spirit beneath the young woman's fragility.

With all the precautions taken, the trip was uneventful. They were met at JFK Airport by attendants from the medical centre, who provided wheelchair transport to the two protesting patients and facilitated their transfer to the plane.

'No upgrades, but extra seats,' Peter explained to Melanie when she saw the arrangements that had been made to accomodate Pete's cast. The four of them took up two rows of three seats, with the back removed from one to enable him to rest his foot on the seat in front.

'By sitting in the middle seat, you can shift your foot

to the floor in front of the aisle seat when you get cramped with it straight out in front,' Peter explained as he pushed Pete's crutches under the seat, and propped his leg on a cushion.

Anna took the window-seat and clung to Pete's hand, the excitement and trepidation that warred within her evident in her flushed face and over-bright eyes. Peter and Melanie settled in front of them, one on either side of the cast, a positioning that pleased Melanie, as she did not want to be distracted by the masculinity that her boss's body seem unconsciously to exude.

'So far so good,' Peter remarked, adjusting his seatbelt as the plane taxied towards take-off. 'It's your shift now,' he added, then closed his eyes and appeared to go straight to sleep.

And I might as well have been wearing my old jeans, for all he noticed, Melanie thought, then shuddered at the implications behind that thought. She looked across at his relaxed figure, slumped in the wide seat.

Had he been up to their charges during the night? she wondered, pulling a book out of her handbag to keep her mind off the man and his behaviour. She would be the carer for the patients on this section of their homeward journey. Looking around, she located the bathrooms only a few yards in front of them, then turned and checked through the gap above Pete's foot that her patients were belted in.

Anna's head rested on Pete's shoulder, and she, like Peter, seemed to have drifted off to sleep. Pete nodded and smiled, and she turned back, peering out of the window beyond Peter's profile at the distorted glimpses of the huge city the rising plane had to offer.

So that's New York, she thought, but did not regret not having had time for sightseeing. She was only beginning to learn the intricacies and challenges of this job she had taken on, and was content to concentrate on it to the exclusion of all else.

Well, not quite all else, she admitted silently, stealing a glance at the man who slept only two feet away from her.

Maybe it was a mistake to get too involved in this job. If this silly infatuation she seemed to feel for Peter didn't go away, could she continue to work for UniversAid? Would her own irrational reaction to this man she barely knew mean that she'd have to be the one to make the decision? Would she have to say no, when and if a permanent position was offered in another few weeks?

It was a question that stayed with her through the night in Los Angeles, exaggerated by the fact that sleep would not come, and she was achingly aware of the quiet breathing in the bed beside hers, and of the soft prowling in the night as he checked on their charges.

At times it seemed as if invisible threads joined her body to his, so that she knew every breath he took, every movement he made.

He is not for you, her brain kept telling her, but the messages failed to reach her nerve-endings, which fired continuously, responding to his presence with an errant will of their own.

Could she continue to work with him? The question hovered in her mind as she played her part of the perfect carer all the long, weary way home.

CHAPTER SEVEN

'WELL, how do you feel after your first mission?' Peter asked as they took their seats on the domestic flight in Melbourne. In two hours they would be back in Brisbane, and Melanie was thinking of a hot bath and her own bed when Peter broke the easy silence that had settled between them.

'Tired,' she told him. Not to mention unsettled, cranky and depressed, she could have added but didn't, saying instead, 'I can't seem to feel any particular satisfaction at getting them safely home. I should be glad but. . .'

'You'll feel the satisfaction later,' he assured her. 'Leaving our clients, even with friends and family to support them, is always a bit of a wrench, both personally and professionally.'

'I suppose that's how I feel,' Melanie responded, glad to talk about the safer aspect of her underlying sense of loss. 'It's as if I've abandoned my patients and lost two good friends at the same time.'

She felt him shift in the comfortable airline seat, and even in her exhausted state her body reacted to his movement, traitorously wanting to slide sideways so that her shoulder could brush, accidentally, against his, and feel his warmth. Folding her arms across her chest to avoid contact with him, she stared out of the window, concentrating on what he was saying in order to blot out her own confusion.

For nearly a week Peter had been by her side, and

although he had shown nothing more than comradely interest in her—apart from one tension-filled kiss that didn't count and a few fleeting instances of flirtatiousness!—the thought of parting from him when they arrived home was filling her with an irrational dismay.

'It's a peculiarly close relationship,' he went on, 'this one that develops between couriers and patients. You are together twenty-four hours a day for however long it takes to get the patient home—and in some cases, where the patient is extremely fragile, or the rescue situation remote, this could take up to a fortnight.'

Had he felt like this about her? Had he been reluctant to leave her when they'd finally arrived on the Gold Coast, in spite of her wayward behaviour?

She couldn't ask! Better to keep to the strictly professional aspect of their relationship and hope that their paths wouldn't cross too often at that!

'In another few days,' he added, speaking quietly and calmly as if he sensed her disorientation and wanted to help her through the maze, 'it will be eaier to look back and put it into perspective as a job well done.'

'I hope so,' she told him, aware that she should make some contribution to this conversation, while her mind devised ways she could avoid seeing him at the office. Permanent night duty might be one answer.

'You will,' he assured her, turning to smile at her glum face and pat her gently on the shoulder—a distinctly fatherly as opposed to lover-like gesture! 'You're tired now, and probably jet-lagged as well. After a trip like this, you're due three days off. Phone Jan in a day or two for your new roster hours. She'll also make a time for a debriefing.'

'Debriefing? You make it sound as if it has been a military operation.'

'It's akin to one, Melanie,' he said seriously. 'Although that's just a fancy name we use for sitting down with one of the senior staff and running through the whole scenario. It helps by identifying hitches that can be ironed out in future repatriations and isolating good ideas to be incorporated into future plans.'

'But surely you can do that. You were in charge; all I did was tag along and do as I was told,' she said aloud, aware that she sounded grouchy. She wanted to avoid him, not spend cosy hours in Jan's office reliving their journey together!

Again he smiled, irritating her with his imperturbable good humour in the face of her crankiness.

'We'll each remember different things,' he explained. 'And you'll find it works in your favour as well, because talking it through puts the whole operation into perspective, and Anna and Pete will become nice people you've helped, not friends and patients to be constantly worrying about. We usually conclude with a medical report from the doctor here in Australia on their current state of health, and that ties up the loose ends and closes the case satisfactorily.'

Does it, Dr Wade? she asked silently, turning away from him to look down at the dark green of the tree-clad mountains as they followed the curving ridge of the Great Divide back towards home.

Brisbane spread beneath them, the red roofs like 'Welcome Home' banners strung out especially for her. Her heart lifted and she smiled as she turned to Peter to point out the high, curving arc of the Gateway Bridge spanning the river as it widened on its journey to Moreton Bay.

'Coming home is always special,' he said, smiling back at her, his blue eyes full of warm complicity.

'Is it home for you now?' she asked, as a hunger for more knowledge of this man stirred dangerously within her.

'It has been for a long time, Melanie,' he replied, still holding her gaze, as if his eyes were trying to convey something that his lips could not say.

Home for him and Cynthia! That's what he's saying, she thought, but even that depressing conclusion could not kill the dangerous sense of rapport that his smile had established between them.

The plane touched down, engines roaring as it decelerated across the tarmac. It was impossible to speak—even if there had been words to say. It's just a job that brings people close. He's your boss, and he's married! she reminded herself, watching him stretch his long legs and shrug the stiffness out of his broad shoulders.

They waited until the intial rush for the doors had eased, then Peter stood up and pulled their bags out of the overhead lockers. Slinging them both across his shoulder, he reached down to take her arm, steadying her as she clambered awkwardly out of her seat.

'You've done well, Melanie,' he said quietly, his eyes again holding hers as if to emphasise his words.

Discomfited by his praise, and his closeness, she pushed ahead of him down the aisle. So she *was* being tested all the time they were away! The confirmation of her own suspicions irritated her, although common sense should have told her this would be the case. How else would they know she could be trusted to carry out operations on her own?

'I've got to collect the medical baggage, but then I'll drop you home,' he explained as they walked down the tunnel towards the arrival lounge.

'I can get a cab,' she protested, not wanting to spend any more time with him while she was tired, confused and vulnerable.

'It's on my way, Melly,' he said reverting to the irritating, childish diminutive of her name as he invariably did when she was arguing with him.

'Hi, Melanie!' another voice called, and she looked around the cluster of people waiting in the lounge, to see Barry's beaming face.

'We rang your office to find out when you'd be home. Kip's working so she asked me to meet you,' he explained, greeting Peter like a long-lost friend and bouncing around the two returning travellers like a large and friendly dog.

'Here's Melanie's bag!' Peter handed him the small bag, and turned to Melanie. 'Ring Jan for your duty hours and I'll see you in a few days.'

Then he was gone, striding through the crowd, his shoulders weaving as he avoided the dawdlers, the back of his head as uncommunicative as a fence post.

'Is this all your luggage? The car's out here.'

At least Barry didn't need any responses! He was happy to talk, and rarely waited for an answer to a question before offering a comment or asking something else.

'Thank you for coming,' she said at last as the car headed towards home. The words were not as warm as she'd intended, but that was tiredness. She was so immensely grateful he had come that even the possible repercussions of a renewed interest in her would be worth suffering, as it had saved her from the final effort of pretence with Peter.

* * *

'Can I see you in my office, Melanie?' Jan called from
the door of the operations room.

It was Wednesday, and close to the end of her shift,
on this, her fourth day back at work. She'd been
allocated the early morning time-slot that began at five
and finished at midday. The timing had pleased her, as
it meant she did not have to see Peter when she came
in, and could leave with the other girls on the shift,
hiding among them as she walked past his office.

Now she was summoned to Jan's office! It must be
for the debriefing he had mentioned the day they
returned, and her unruly heart would be put to the
test.

He wasn't in the room when she entered and she was
steeling herself for his arrival when Jan's words brought
her thoughts to an abrupt halt.

'I know you're not long returned from a trip, but
you're the only woman we've got at the moment who
knows Africa.'

'You want me to go to Africa?' Melanie echoed,
then added, 'Who with?' as a suspicious and ungram-
matical afterthought.

'It would be on your own. Do you think you could
manage? It's a routine hand-holding job, a young
woman in eastern Botswana as a volunteer who's had a
bit of a breakdown—depression, not coping with the
conditions, the climate, the people, and who knows
what else? The volunteer organisation has asked us to
bring her back.'

'Who is she with?' Melanie asked as her mind
scooted ahead to the girl who had failed to adapt and
enjoy what should have been a great adventure, the
girl who was so miserable, so far from home.

'The same group you worked for,' Jan replied.

'That's why I thought you'd like to go. At least you'll be dealing with people over there that you've met before, and you'll know the set-up.'

'I'd love it,' Melanie told her, excited by the prospect of seeing her friends again. 'As long as you think I'll be able to handle it.'

'I'm certain you will. We'll organise the flights from here before you leave, and the organisation has undertaken to look after her until you arrive.'

'There's a flight each Thursday from Sydney to Harare, which is the closest international airport,' Melanie told her. 'Would it be possible to fly in and pick her up then fly out on the same day if they brought her that far?'

'I'll see what we can arrange with the organisation and talk to Bill about flights,' Jan said. 'You'd better see Peter for malaria prophylaxis in case you have to stay over, and speak to him about what sedatives you might need if she's overwrought.'

The moment has come, Melanie thought, steeling herself to face him with an efficient professionalism.

'He's in his office at the moment,' Jan added. 'You pop in and sort out the drugs while I get Bill busy on the flights and speak to the Volunteer Association about possible meeting places. If that flight still goes Thursdays you may have to leave here tonight and stay overnight in Sydney.'

Melanie forced herself to leave Jan's office with a semblance of enthusiasm. The prospect of going to Africa *must* outweigh the disadvantage of spending a few minutes with Peter!

He looked up at her, unsmiling, as she entered, and echoed Jan's question.

'Do you think you can manage?'

'I'm certain I can,' she responded, matching her mood to his with a businesslike crispness.

His eyelids dropped, shuttering his gaze, and he pushed a notepad uneasily about on his desk, bumping it against bottles of drugs before eventually focusing on the notes he had written on it.

'No doubt you're aware that falsiparum malaria is resistant to chloroquine in East Africa?'

Melanie nodded.

'As volunteers, we used chloroquine and Maloprim in combination—one tablet of Maloprim on Wednesdays and one of 300 mg of chloroquine on Sundays,' she explained.

'Starting the chloroquine a week before you left?'

Melanie nodded again, wondering what the difficulty was.

'You may not need anything, but in case you have to stay over you'll have to take precautions. All the usual treatments begin early, but you could take a low-dose doxycycline, which is often used for short-term stays in resistant areas. One 100mg capsule of Doryx each day with plenty of water,' he explained, lifting some capsules out of one of the bottles, dropping them into a glass vial and labelling it as he spoke.

'But if I'm going to turn around and come back on the same flight, it won't be necessary, surely? The plane arrives and departs in broad daylight, and I might not have to leave the air terminal. The danger lies in being outside between dusk and dawn.'

'You should still be prepared for anything,' he said sternly, and she bit back another futile argument.

She knew doxycycline was one of the tetracyclines, and they invariably gave her thrush, but that wasn't something she was about to discuss with Peter Wade.

Perhaps she could wait until she knew when they were coming back before taking the first tablet.

'Take one before you land, just in case,' he ordered, as if reading her rebellious mind. 'Who knows what will happen when you arrive? And, if your plans are disrupted, there's no guarantee you won't forget later. And if you stay, one every day, you understand?'

Yes, sir! she wanted to snap in response to his dictatorial tones, but she bit her tongue and contented herself with a nod as he moved on to antidepressant drugs she would be carrying for her patient.

'I'll give you Sinequan. It's a mild antidepressant effective on a wide range of psychoneurotic disorders including anxiety neurosis, which is probably this woman's problem.'

He was delving into a medical chest as he spoke, as if unwilling to look at her, or uninterested in anything more than the prescribing of a suitable drug.

'Wouldn't she have been receiving treatment already?' Melanie asked. 'It's not the end of the earth, and they do have hospitals and doctors in the larger towns.'

His head came up abruptly and he gazed across at her, as if perplexed by her statement.

'If she has been treated and has been on any of the monoamine oxidase inhibitors, then she'll have to continue to use them, as MAOI therapy must be discontinued at least a fortnight before using other drugs. I'll put a pharmaceutical reference book in the medical kit. You can check on any drug she's been prescribed and find any contra-indications or precautions. And don't hesitate to contact me if you're in any doubt.'

He paused, but she sensed that he hadn't finished.

'It's a one-person job, Melanie, but I must admit I'm not happy about you taking it.'

He doesn't trust me, she thought as despair lanced through her.

'I know many of the people who work for the organisation over there, and I've nursed in a psychiatric ward. I know a little of the language, and I should think I was the perfect choice.' She argued automatically, determined to hang on to this opportunity to prove her worth. 'As Jan said, it's a simple hand-holding job that needs a woman.'

It was his turn to nod, and as he looked up again his eyes scanned her face, as clear and unreadable as a summer sky.

'If she's deeply depressed, she could be suicidal, although the only report we've received to date hasn't indicated any attempts. Make sure you keep the drugs with you at all times. The case is small enough to fit into your hand luggage, and the vials could go into your handbag if you stay over and have to leave the hotel.'

She watched the frown twitch his eyebrows together and her mind slipped from the job ahead of her as she restrained an impulse to reach out and smooth the frown-lines away.

'You do understand,' he said sharply, and she reached out and picked up the tablets he had bottled instead.

'I won't let them out of my sight,' she assured him, and rose, knowing that to stay any longer would be courting more heartache.

'See Jan for flight arrangements and then go home and get organised. I'm still trying to contact the supervisor in Botswana and if I get any further details I'll let you know on the way to the airport.'

The last words halted her escape.

'I can drive myself to the airport and leave my car in the long-term car park.'

She forced out the words, although her heart was behaving most erratically as she wondered, with stupid hope, why he would choose to drive her.

'I'll take you out,' he said flatly. 'The girl is from Brisbane so you'll be bringing her back to here. One of the doctors will have to meet you anyway, to check out the patient before we hand her over to her family. Whoever meets you can drive you home.'

And that's that, she thought as her heartbeats decelerated in the light of this prosaic statement. She walked back to Jan's office, determined not to let her reactions to Peter affect the pleasure she felt in the prospect of going back to Africa.

'We've made two return bookings,' Jan told her as she came back into the room. 'One is for a same-day return, if we can organise the patient to be brought to the airport. The alternative is for a flight back via South Africa three days later. If that doesn't suit you, when the time comes, it would be worth waiting in Harare for the direct flight next week.'

'I hope I remember all this,' Melanie said, clutching her head theatrically as Jan poured out the information.

'You will, but it's all written down if you do need to confirm anything, and as you'll be phoning us every day, you can always call for extra help or ask Bill to reorganise your travel arrangements.'

Jan passed her a card with UniversAid's toll-free

number emblazoned on it, plus the time-differences between East Africa and Brisbane clearly marked.

'Now, about your patient,' she continued. 'Her name is Robyn Ryan, and she's a twenty-one-year-old student who has been away three months.'

'So the problem probably began soon after she arrived, and they've been coaxing her along thinking it was homesickness.'

'That's the most likely scenario,' Jan agreed, pushing a file across the desk. 'Here are copies of her application forms and the details of her interviews by the selection panel, her medical report from that time, and her references. It might give you some background that will be useful in getting her to talk—even if it's only about her family. Anything that takes her mind off the sense of failure she must feel will help.'

Melanie picked up the file and leafed through it.

'Now, if you've no more questions, I suggest you go home and pack what you'll need. You're booked on tomorrow morning's six-thirty flight to Sydney, and Peter has volunteered to be the one to see you off.' She smiled, as if relieved it wasn't to be her job!

'He'll call for you at five, and will have the tickets, credit cards, tentative hotel reservations and, hopefully, a proper medical report on Robyn from Botswana. OK?'

Jan's confidence in her radiated from her cheerful, smiling face, and Melanie smiled back. She had travelled alone often enough for it to hold no terrors, and she was certain she could handle her 'patient'. The only doubt was the farewell party, if you could call one person a party!

It's only a half-hour drive from my place to the airport, she told herself reassuringly as she drove back to her flat. I can manage that long in his company without falling to pieces.

Five o'clock in the morning was not a good time for resistance, Melanie decided as they drove through the deserted city towards the airport. Her body, still heavy with sleep, had reacted with a sensuous longing to snuggle up to him, to rub and press against him in the way cats did 'against the legs of those they favoured.

Her head, distracted by the effort of control, took refuge in a stolid silence. She was a courier, being dispatched on another mission, and she must act appropriately.

'Excited about going back to Africa?'

Had he asked the question to break the silence? she wondered. He certainly didn't appear to be interested in her answer, for he stared ahead, watching the traffic-free road with all the concentration of a Grand Prix driver on a dangerous circuit.

'As I'll probably be flying in and straight back out, there's not a lot to get excited about,' she told him, intending to match his disinterest with her own casual approach. Then the thought of going back to the warmth and colour, the vibrancy that seemed to light the air of Africa, triggered a tingling thrill.

'I suppose even someone in transit at the airport can walk outside and smell the place,' she added, smiling irrepressibly at the thought. 'Yes, I am excited!'

'You really enjoyed your time there?'

She had heard the amazement in people's voices before, but the utter astonishment in Peter's widened her smile.

'I loved it,' she said simply, 'the bits I saw of Central and East Africa. The people are friendly, and kind.

Gentle giants, someone once called them, and that's how I saw them.'

'Some of those same gentle giants are the children and grandchildren of the most feared warrior races on earth,' he objected, turning to look at her now with a teasing glint in his eyes.

'Every country on earth has had tribal wars and conflict between old and new settlers, going back as far as history records, and beyond.'

He was negotiating the roundabout that gave access to the airport drive, so did not reply, but the look he shot in her direction as they settled on to the wide, straight road had an indefinable, questioning quality as if something had surprised him. She thought over her words then shrugged the thought away.

He dropped her at the entrance then drove off to park the car while she queued for check-in and seat allocation. It was a relief to be away from him, she decided, but knew it wasn't true when she kept glancing around, eager to see him again before she left.

He caught up with her at the entrance to the departure lounge, and, taking her arm, led her to a quiet spot by the wide glass wall that provided a view out over the tarmac.

'I haven't been able to speak to the doctor who saw Robyn,' he said in a confidential undertone that sizzled into her ears like a secret message of some kind. 'I did speak to someone at the hospital where she was treated, but the story I got there was unsatisfactory.'

Melanie tried to look intelligent, although her hormones were stirring wildly, sparking flames that licked along her nerves as she felt his breath on her lips and savoured his maleness in her nostrils.

'I'll make sure someone from the organisation meets

you at the airport, whether the girl is with them or not. That way, you'll know immediately what's happening. If there's any change in status I'll get a message to you on the plane.'

Melanie was startled out of her preoccupation for an instant. Surely a simple operation like this did not need this level of military precision!

'The return tickets are in the travel wallet, there are everyday drugs like aspirin in the small medical bag, and the pharmaceutical guide is also in there.'

He was rattling off instructions like a robot, but there was nothing robotic about the messages his body was sending her. It had swayed closer as he spoke, so that only a thin layer of air separated them.

'You must ring as soon as you arrive and again before you leave. If you have to stay over, call every night. We need to know what's happening.'

She nodded, unable to speak. She knew all this, so why was he repeating it, drumming it in as if she were an imbecile?

Her head kept up a silent protest, as much to distract her attention from the agony of her body as for any other reason. The space between them was not the insulation she needed. A brick wall might have served the purpose, but three inches of air, zinging with electrical impulses, magnified her desire to lean against him, to ease her heavy, tingling breasts against his chest, and feel the hardness of his thighs against the aching centre of her femininity.

'And don't take any risks,' he was saying sternly when she dragged her mind back to his lecture. 'If the situation develops into anything you feel you can't handle, call for help. The volunteer organisation, the

local hospital, the police, call anyone. Don't try to
tough it out on your own, understand?'

She nodded again, upset that he sounded so angry
with her. It was as if he'd suddenly decided she was
incapable.

The thought acted on her aroused body as effectively
as a cold shower, and the fire she'd been battling
against sputtered and fizzed, dying beneath his vocal
irritation.

Yet his body still sent a different message, subtle but
strong. It cast a reel of silken thread around her,
holding her where she stood while it sang it's silent
need.

He's married! You're imagining things! If he liked
you, would he be speaking to you in this way? The
thought whirled around her head.

Half heard, his precise instructions continued, but
she was lost in the muddied waters of desire once more,
and battling against her own resurgent hunger.

'They've called my flight,' she blurted out, desperate
to escape yet unable to move.

'Yes, you've got to go,' he echoed hoarsely, yet
made no attempt to stand aside, or to release her from
the bondage of his sexuality. 'I don't want you to go,'
he said, when the silence straining between them had
reached snapping-point.

'I'm quite capable of flying to Africa and bringing
back a young woman who's depressed,' she said curtly,
and stepped backwards, unable to bear, for another
instant, the unspoken messages that battered her body.

Her heel caught against the window-frame, and she
tilted sideways as her leg gave way, but whether she
would have fallen remained a mystery, for his hands
reached out and seized her shoulders, pulling her across

the space that had been so ineffective a barrier, and holding her hard against him.

'Are you OK?' he asked after too long a moment, his voice soft and rasping, as if he had been running and was finding it hard to get enough breath to speak clearly.

'I'm fine. It was a silly stumble,' she said quickly, raising her hands from his shoulders and patting at her hair in an effort to distract his eyes from her flushed face. 'That's the final call; I've got to go.'

She stepped sideways this time, but his arms followed her, his hands still gripping tightly to her shoulders.

He's going to kiss me! she thought, her heartbeats accelerating wildly.

But the hands did not pull her forward, giving her instead a little shake.

'You've got to go,' he echoed, looking at her with the question in his eyes that she'd seen earlier, the question she couldn't understand. 'Remember to ring when you arrive,' he added, smiling determinedly at her puzzled face, his eyes clear and unreadable once again.

With his hands still touching her body, he turned her and pushed her gently towards the departure gate, and the smiling stewardesses who waited patiently for her to join the flight.

It probably looked like a lovers' farewell, she thought dismally, acknowledging their smiles with a wan effort of her own. A little last minute tête-à-tête, then a quick—or not so quick!—embrace.

Would they believe it if I told them it was strictly business? she wondered as she reached her seat and settled into it for the flight to Sydney.

Probably not!

Had her body believed it was strictly business?

Definitely not!

Her mind cantered around in circles as the plane taxied and thrust upwards into the blueness, asking and answering questions that had no relevance.

Hormones notwithstanding, her relationship with Peter *was* a business one—and that was how it had to remain.

CHAPTER EIGHT

AFRICA was as bright and beautiful as she remembered it, she decided as the plane circled above Harare. The dark green leaves of the tulip trees hid the bright orange flowers she knew were there and contrasted with the soft mauve of jacarandas in full bloom. Massive figs, poincianas and eucalypts reminded her of home, but the traffic jostling on the narrow strip of bitumen between the red dirt on the suburban roads told a different story as overladen buses veered around the constant flow of pedestrians. Bougainvillaea provided a riot of colour against the wide green lawns around the embassies and beautiful private gardens, and swimming-pools lay like blue jewels beneath the brightly burning sun.

Her heart lifted as the plane dropped from the sky.

This was what she loved about travel—the rising tide of half-fearful expectation of what might lie head, the continual challenge of journeying into unknown territory, of taking that first small step towards unimaginable pleasure and delights.

Could anything else compete with it? she wondered, as if to reassure herself that her ambitions were still in place.

Sex might, came a craven whisper from the part of her mind she'd shut down when she'd left Brisbane. Not just any sex, it hurried to assure her, but a satisfying sexual relationship with someone you really loved, a giving and taking of pleasure that was in itself as much a voyage into the unknown as this one was.

The wheels thudded into the ground, and her thoughts came to an abrupt end.

For most of the journey, she'd managed to put Peter and his bizarre behaviour firmly out of her mind, repeating cautions to herself until she had forced her brain and, hopefully, her body to accept them. And now she was thinking not of love but of sex! All right, she'd added love to the thought, but sex had come first.

The plane slowed and stopped, and the scramble to collect belongings began. She sat until the queue had diminished to a few families waking tired children and gathering up toys. Diplomats, most likely, she decided as she shouldered her small bag and headed down the aisle, wondering if she'd be back on the plane in a few short hours.

'Melanie, it is very good to see you!' The rich, velvety voice called to her above the heads of the crowd as she came through the customs exit.

Ambrose had been her supervisor during her stay in Botswana, and she flung her arms around his ample figure and hugged him tightly, then looked around to see if he'd had brought her 'patient'.

'I have spoken to your boss back in Australia,' Ambrose told her quickly, reading the question in her searching eyes. 'I have explained to him the circumstances and confirmed your booking at the hotel.'

He led the way towards the exit, and as the doors slid open Melanie felt the blast of aromatic heat that to her was the essence of Africa.

'So I'm not going back on today's plane?'

She breathed deeply, as if to rejuvenate all the cells of her body with the hot mysterious air.

'No!'

Ambrose bent to unlock the door of a battered old car, holding it open for her while she slid into the stifling interior.

'There's a problem?' she asked, as he settled in beside her.

'You might say that,' he answered cautiously, avoiding her eyes by concentrating on the road.

I'd forgotten that it takes patience to get the full story over here, she thought, while her mind scouted around for the most direct yet acceptable approach.

'Are you Robyn's supervisor?'

There was a short, sharp nod of confirmation.

'And is she here in Harare?'

Another nod.

'Is she well enough to travel?'

Again the dark head bobbed, though less decisively. It was time for a different kind of question.

'Where is she at the moment?' she asked, and watched his face to see if she could detect any changes in the placid mask.

'She's at the hotel.'

There was a pause long enough to be called an awkward silence, but Melanie had decided she'd asked enough. Finally, as the car turned into the wide main road and approached the large luxury hotel where she would be staying, he added the words he had not wanted to say.

'She doesn't want to go home, Melanie,' he told her, then clamped his lips closed again.

And you could hardly drag her kicking and screaming to the airport, Melanie realised, feeling a pang of

sympathy for her old friend as she recognised the social
and moral issues that had made his task impossible.

'I've got a booking home via South Africa, leaving
here Sunday,' she told him. 'Perhaps by then I'll have
persuaded her it's the sensible thing to do—even if I
have to promise her she can come back again some
other time.'

The fleeting look of horror on Ambrose's face was
enough to make her wonder what Miss Robyn Ryan
had been up to during her short time in Africa. If she
was in a depressed state, suicide was the most likely
medical emergency. Had she attempted it and persuaded them to cover it up? The volunteer organis-
ations had an obligation to report any illness affecting
their workers at least to the headquarters in the volunteers' home country. It was then up to the home base
to decide if the information should be passed on to
families.

'There is a nurse from an agency with Robyn,'
Ambrose told her formally as he accompanied her up
the steps and into the hotel. 'We have arranged for her
to stay as long as you are here, to help you in caring
for her.'

Melanie felt anxiety surge through her body. There
was something more serious than a mild depression
caused by homesickness wrong with Robyn if the
organisation had arranged for a nurse to stay with her.

She glanced at Ambrose as she waited for the clerk
to process her arrival, but the lugubrious expression on
his face told her there was nothing more to be learnt
from him.

'Will I see you again while I'm here?' she asked,
hoping to win a smile. 'Perhaps you and Sylvie would

like to come in and have dinner with me one night. To-morrow?'

In her own ears the question sounded like a plea, and she knew she was asking for his continuous support as she realised how alone she was going to be in the situation that lay ahead—except for the nurse from the agency, of course!

'I will ring you this evening,' was all the reply she was going to get. He put out his hand to shake a brief farewell. 'The nurse has my number if there is anything I can do,' he added, then turned and walked away, leaving her to follow the bellboy towards the lifts, and up to the suite booked by UniversAid before she'd left Australia.

Robyn Ryan was sitting in the small room that divided the two bedrooms. It was beautifully furnished with bright woven curtains that suggested native hand-crafts, ornately carved furniture, and a huge platter of gourds and fruit arranged as a centrepiece on a small dining table by the wall. Her prospective patient was watching an old American comedy show on television with an intensity it did not deserve.

In the other armchair, a nurse with the fine features of the Indians who had come to Africa as labourers generations earlier was watching her patient and the programme with equal concern.

'I'm Melanie Ashcroft,' she said brightly, stepping into the tableau with a quaking heart.

Her fellow professional rose to shake hands with her, but Robyn's attention remained riveted on the television screen. Assuming that the girl hadn't heard her, Melanie moved across to tap her on the shoulder and say, 'Hi,' in what she hoped was a confident and friendly tone.

Robyn remained immobile, ignoring the newcomer with a concentration that frightened Melanie.

'I'm Priti Kavansh,' the nurse said, covering the awkward silence with her own introduction. 'And this is Robyn.'

Still the girl ignored them and Melanie felt her discomfort growing although she hid it behind a bland unconcern.

'Which is my bedroom?' she asked, looking around the room so that the question was not directed at anyone in particular.

'It's through here,' Priti responded, opening the door that led off one side of the small room. 'There is a shower off it if you need to freshen up after your long flight.'

At least she's trying to ease the situation, Melanie thought, and rewarded her with a warm smile.

'I'll take you up on that. I feel like a grubby six-year-old after a particularly rough day at school.'

Priti smiled, but Robyn's attention hadn't wavered from the screen. Then, as Melanie moved to close the door behind her, she heard her say in a soft but determined voice, 'I am not going home!'

Well, that's nothing if not definite, she thought as she dragged off her travel-stained clothes and dug in her bag for clean ones. I suppose I should be grateful she's speaking to me at all!

As she stepped under the shower, she remembered Peter's instructions. 'Ring as soon as you arrive', he'd ordered. Well, she'd arrived, but apart from the fact that she wouldn't be returning on the same flight, which Ambrose had already told him, there was nothing else to report.

She'd ring this evening, when she had more idea of

what was going on in Robyn's mind, and maybe some slight clue as to how she could handle the situation.

Hot water streamed over her body, washing away the lethargy that long flights imposed. She shampooed her hair and was rinsing off the bubbles when the phone rang.

Would Priti answer it?

She turned off the water and listened, but the shrill summons continued. Pulling a thick towel around her body, she hurried through to the bedroom and picked up the extension by the bed.

'You were told to ring when you arrived,' Peter's furious voice spat into her ear.

'Ambrose had already advised you that I won't be on the return flight, and as our patient has refused to speak to me and I haven't had time to hear or see any medical reports it seemed pointless.'

She hoped she sounded calmer than she felt as irritation at his attitude and a devastating excitement at hearing his voice warred within her.

'You should have rung anyway, if only to let us know you arrived safely,' he said, his voice softer now, coming through the wires like a husky whisper that tingled across the nerve-endings in her skin. 'Do you have my home number?'

She shook her head, bemused by the question, then realised he couldn't see her response and replied with a doubtful, 'No'.

'Here it is.' He gave the list of numbers with a crisp edge to his voice, asking her to repeat what she had written, before adding a curt, 'Phone me later at home. I need to know what's happening over there.'

She heard the click that disconnected him and felt a

shadow of guilt. Had he been waiting at the office for her to call?

She checked her watch. It was only three hours since the plane had landed. Eleven in the evening at home. Perhaps he'd had other couriers checking in, which would explain why he was in the office so late.

Whatever the reason for his impatient call, it was a reminder that she was here to work. She dressed quickly and went through to join the other two women.

'Do you think we could have a talk about what you would like to do?' she asked Robyn, wondering if anything would distract her fixed attention from the television screen.

I've got three days before we have to leave; should I push this now? she wondered, thinking ruefully how excited she'd been by the 'challenge' of this job!

Priti stood up and indicated her chair, then slipped through the door that must lead to the second bedroom. Melanie sat down and focused on the show, recognising it as one she had seen as a child. She waited until an advertisement for a particularly impressive bicycle came on, and spoke again.

'Is there anything special you'd like to do this afternoon, Robyn? Have a wander round the shops, perhaps, or go to the native market?'

Did she imagine the movement or had the girl actually shuddered?

'It seems a boring way to spend a lovely day, cooped up inside watching television,' she added, and this time was rewarded with a response.

'I like it,' Robyn told her, her eyes never leaving the screen although the advertisement had changed to one extolling a particular brand of fertilizer for legume crops and was less than riveting.

So Melanie sat.

She'll have to go to the bathroom eventually, and I can talk to Priti then, she decided. Maybe if I have some background I'll be able to decide how to handle her.

The afternoon dragged on, and Priti returned, pulling up another chair, so the three of them sat in silence broken only by American-accented voices and canned laughter.

'Is there an especially good dining-room in the hotel, Robyn,' she asked as dusk darkened the room, 'or should we go out to eat? I've only driven past this place before. It was too expensive for me to visit when I was over here as a volunteer.'

She dangled the informtion in front of the girl, hoping it might stir her interest if the question about food was ignored, but the silence continued.

Melanie was pleased that Priti had declined to answer for Robyn, although words were obviously burning on her lips. She sat on, determined not to appear to give in to the stubborn silence, but her mind whirled as it sought for something that might open a chink in Robyn's armour of uninterest.

She was wondering how to organise a television malfunction, when her patient rose without a word and walked through to the bedroom.

'Has she been like this since you met her?' she whispered to Priti.

'Just the same,' the other nurse sighed. 'The doctor at Mahalapye gave her tablets, and at first, Ambrose said, she talked about things she had done and seen during her stay. Then they got back here to Harare, in the traffic and noise, and she became very upset, saying, "Take me to a hotel, take me to a hotel," all the time.'

'Ambrose would have loved that!' Melanie said with a grin that won a similar response from Priti. 'So he brought her here?'

'Yes, and phoned the agency to arrange a nurse to stay with her. It was only yesterday, but I can't get her to talk or to go outside. She sits here and watches the television all the time, even through the night, as if she's afraid to sleep. We've had meals sent up, and she's eating well. It will be costing your company a great deal in a place like this!'

Concern darkened her beautiful eyes, and Melanie hastened to reassure her.

'The company won't complain about that—as long as I get her safely home. If she refuses to travel, I'm not certain what I can do.'

She wondered about getting help from the embassy, and cursed her own inexperience. She was supposed to be able to think on her feet, to come up with alternatives until she found something that would work. If she wanted to prove she was the best apprentice UniversAid had ever had, she would have to find a way through the problem.

'I think we'll start by turning off the television,' she announced as she heard the toilet flush and realised that Robyn would be back with them shortly.

Robyn came back into the room, her eyes going automatically to the blank screen. She walked across to turn it back on, but Melanie stepped in front of her.

'I thought we might leave it off for a while,' she said quietly. 'It will give us all a chance to talk, to get to know each other. Television is the most unsociable of all mankind's inventions.'

'I don't have to talk to you,' Robyn muttered, pushing Melanie aside to reach the television switch.

'I think you do.' Melanie swung back into her path, and looked her straight in the eye. 'UniversAid is paying the bill here, Robyn, and as I represent them I think I should have some rights. I'm not turning it off for good,' she added calmly as a flush of anger rose in the other woman's pale cheeks, 'just for ten minutes while we talk about possible plans.'

There was a split-second between her realisation that there was more wrong with Robyn than mild depression and the forceful shove that sent her reeling back into the television set, knocking it off its stand with a shattering explosion of glass and the sparking sound of electricity suddenly let loose.

Priti flicked the switch at the wall then rushed towards her as she lay awkwardly across the broken set, but Melanie waved her urgently away, towards the door through which Robyn had disappeared.

'See where Robyn's gone. If she leaves the hotel, ask one of the staff to go with you and follow her if you can. With two of you, one can stop and ring here to let me know what's happening.'

Priti ignored her frantic waving and reached out to steady her as she stood up. 'She'll be in the bedroom,' the nurse asssured her. 'I'll check for you, but that's where she'll be. She won't go out! Whatever it is that's worrying her is tied up with the outside world. It's as if she's found this little hole and crawled into it for safety.'

Melanie listened carefully, thinking through what Priti was saying. It made sense, particularly as Robyn's agitation had increased when Ambrose had driven into the city.

She had known enough about her condition to ask him to get her to a hotel. Was it agoraphobia?

'And the television is shutting out the things she doesn't want to think about, even here, in the safety of the hotel?' she said slowly.

Priti nodded. 'I think so.'

'Then we'd better get another one, I suppose,' Melanie said, looking down at the shattered mess with a rueful grin.

It was then that she felt a hot, wet stickiness running down her arm and on to her fingers. She twisted around to see the gash down the back of her triceps. Long, but not deep, she decided, and hurried into the bedroom for a towel to staunch the flow before she spread blood all over the hotel suite.

'I'll check on Robyn then come back and bind it for you,' Priti told her, pushing her into a sitting position on the bed.

And what am I supposed to do? Ring Peter and admit I can't handle the situation? Melanie lifted the receiver, then put it down. Pride made her determined to find a solution. She had time on her side. Somehow she had to get through to Robyn, to convince her that she was a friend, here to help her out of the dark maze her mind had fashioned for her.

She looked up as Priti came back into the room with wadding and plaster. She must have her own emergency kit, Melanie thought, then turned to her as a fellow professional.

'Have you any ideas about how I should handle this?'

'I haven't much experience with psychiatric problems, but perhaps a specialist?'

'Do you know one you could recommend?'

'I know a man who is considered highly at the hospital where I worked, but. . .'

Priti's voice trailed away.

'But what, Priti?' Melanie asked, unable to understand this sudden reversion to silence.

'He is a native and I don't know how much of Robyn's problem is to do with black people, and how much with people in general.'

The words, blurted out with embarrassment, made Melanie think, but there were obvious discrepancies in this concern.

'But she doesn't get agitated by your presence, and Ambrose drove her back to the city——'

'Maybe she knew Ambrose before whatever happened that triggered this.'

Melanie shook her head, tiredness creeping through her bones as she realised the futility of their guessing game.

'We could keep this up for days,' she admitted. 'What we need is an expert.'

Should she ring the office back in Brisbane and ask if they had anyone to suggest? You're on your own, Melanie, she reminded herself. If the office wasn't there at the end of the telephone line, what would you do?

'I'll ring the embassy first,' she told Priti, answering her own question, 'and see if they can recommend a psychiatrist. Maybe they know of a white woman who practises here,' she added with a grin. 'Or, better still, a woman like yourself. I obviously aggravate Robyn far more than you do.'

She reached for the phone and was soon talking to an English-speaking psychiatrist from Brussels, wife of a businessman in the city, who ran a small clinic on the outskirts of Harare, and also served most of the ex-patriot population when their isolation drove them towards neuroses.

'I'll come over in an hour,' she assured a grateful Melanie, agreeing to stay and have dinner with them in the hope that Robyn might be more forthcoming in a social atmosphere.

'You said Robyn had been treated by a doctor in Mahalapye. Did Ambrose give you a medical report from him?' she asked after she had explained the position to Priti.

'Robyn had it, but threw it away at some stage, as far as we can make out. She is on——' Priti fished in her pocket and produced a small bottle of tablets '—Nortab, 25mg three times a day. It's nortriptyline,' she added, reading from the label. 'Do you know it?'

'No, but I'll look it up in a moment. Does she object to taking them?'

Priti shook her head. 'I give her one with meals, and so far she hasn't objected. Ambrose said they were to ease the depression, but they seem to agitate her.'

'So it could be the tablets causing the problems.'

It was a medical problem beyond her capabilities, she decided, and was thankful she'd called for help.

Elise Charpentier was a petite blonde with sparkling blue eyes. She brought with her an aura of calm confidence that worked on Melanie's tattered nerves like a soothing balm.

Another television had been delivered to the sitting-room, and Robyn was persuaded to join them, greeting Elise with a sullen nod.

'Shall we order dinner to be brought up, or would

you like to go down to the dining-room?' Melanie asked her, hoping to get some response.

'Perhaps we should eat here,' Elise suggested, her eyes on her new patient, taking in the untidy hair and the dull eyes. 'Is there a room-service menu?'

It was the first positive response Melanie had seen Robyn make, for she grabbed the patterned card that held the menu, and studied it with a greedy intensity. As the phone rang again, Melanie left them to it, and walked through to her bedroom to answer it.

Peter's temper hadn't improved.

Quietly Melanie explained what was happening, pointing out to him her intention to ring him as soon as Elise had spent time with Robyn and suggested possible courses of action.

'Has she been on medication?' he barked into the phone, and Melanie told him what had been prescribed.

'I haven't had time to check on it in the book yet,' she said feebly, feeling that somehow she was failing in this major test.

'I can tell you it's a drug that's commonly used for mild depressive states. The difficulty with it and other MAOIs is that if the patient is misdiagnosed, which can easily happen, and the depression is a phase of something more complicated, it can trigger latent schizophrenia or manic depression.'

'Oh, great!' Melanie said bitterly. 'That's more believable than the original diagnosis.' She rubbed at her bandaged arm. 'So what do we do?'

'Leave it to the psychiatrist. You did the right thing getting on to her immediately. Give her my number and get her to ring me when she's come to some conclusion, or, better still, ask her to ring me from the hotel before she leaves. That way I can talk to you both.'

Melanie checked her watch.

'It's two a.m. at home, Peter,' she objected. 'There's nothing you can do that can't wait till morning. Why don't you get some sleep?'

'You've been up as long as I have,' he reminded her. 'Just ring me, Melanie!'

It was an unmistakable order!

'I will,' she promised, then was devastated when he mumbled,

'I shouldn't have let you go!' into the phone before he hung up.

He doesn't think I can cope. The thought hammered in her head, making her more determined than ever to bring Robyn home safely.

Three hours later she was wondering if commitment was worth the pain.

Priti had handed Robyn her tablet at the beginning of the meal, generating a tension in Melanie that she found hard to dispel. Was Elise watching her patient as warily? She had certainly looked at the tablets and nodded her understanding of the prescription. Had the idea of the drug triggering some latent problem occurred to her? She wished she'd had an opportunity to speak to Elise alone, but had not wanted to interrupt the doctor's tentative forays into friendship with Robyn.

The four of them had enjoyed a delicious dinner, with all but Robyn entering into the pretense that it was a normal social occasion. Elise entertained them with stories about her travels through Central Africa, and Melanie contributed snippets of her adventures in Botswana. Priti had asked questions about Australia, and they had relaxed back into their chairs, sipping at their coffee, when the explosion occurred.

Robyn had pushed aside her coffee-cup with an abrupt movement that rattled the china and risen to her feet. She looked around, and her eyes seemed to register the replacement television set. She strode towards it.

Priti shrugged her shoulders as if to say, Well, we managed to keep it off for a while, and Elise put her hand on Melanie's arm as she murmured, 'Let's see what she does.'

It was hardly what they had expected, for the woman seized the largest gourd from the platter that had been placed on the television set while they used the table for dinner, and swung it viciously downwards smashing through the screen with a demonic force that terrified the onlookers.

Then she whirled around, once, twice, three times, like a discus-thrower gathering momentum and the shapely object flew through the air towards the table.

'Ring hotel security,' Melanie managed to gasp as she leapt to her feet to shield Elise. She pushed Priti, who had also risen, towards the door, then the missile hit her head and the world went black.

She came to under the table, her head resting on Elise's knee, while the decorative arrangement was reduced to a litter of broken pieces around their feet.

'Stay still, we're fairly safe here,' Elise whispered. 'She's getting her fun throwing things. I don't think she's at all homicidal.'

'That's a comfort,' Melanie retorted, feeling the tender lump on the side of her forehead. 'I'm glad those things dry out to such light shells.'

'I've a sedative injection with me that I'll give her if

Priti manages to get enough help to hold her, then we'll have to admit her to hospital and see if we can stabilise her. You certainly won't get an airline to take you home while she's in this state.'

A book fluttered towards them, followed by the large menu. She was running out of things to throw! What would she decide to do next?

'Do you think the drugs were a trigger?' Melanie stilled her fear with the whispered question as a cushion joined the flying objects.

'I'd say almost certainly,' Elise whispered back, then sighed. 'It's a problem because residual effects of the drugs she's been on will react against many of the controlled drugs we could give her now. It will have to be done carefully and in a controlled situation. You understand that?'

Melanie nodded, and at that moment the door from her bedroom began to open, and Elise clutched at her arm and pointed at the main entrance and the other bedroom door. They were also opening cautiously.

'Can I talk to you for a moment, Robyn?' Priti asked, wisely using the door as a shield as another cushion flew through the air towards her.

She must have signalled to the security people, for two women and a man slipped into the room and moved purposefully towards the distraught traveller.

The scream she gave as they took hold of her arms curdled Melanie's blood and made all the hairs on the back of her neck prickle to attention. Forgetting her aching head, she crawled out from under the table and helped Elise to her feet.

'Priti, would you call an ambulance, please?' Elise asked quietly, ignoring the screams that ricocheted around the room like an unearthly siren. She walked across to collect the small briefcase she'd brought with her, and with steady fingers and an apparent lack of concern filled a small syringe and moved towards the girl who twisted desperately in the grip of her captors.

'This will make you feel better, Robyn,' she said calmly, her slightly accented English mellowing the words. 'We'll take you to hospital and look after you there.'

Melanie looked away, unable to bear the sight of Robyn's face, contorted in a rictus of fear. There was nothing else that they could do, she knew that, but a sense of failure descended on her like a black cloud.

The drug worked quickly. One minute the helpers held a fighting machine of superhuman strength, and the next a limp, almost comatose patient, who was helped tenderly to a chair and eased into it as the pity all of them felt went out to her in gentle kindness.

'Can I go to the hospital with her?' Melanie asked.

'Only if you want that head of yours X-rayed,' Elise replied, reaching out to feel the tender spot above Melanie's temple. 'I don't think it's necessary, but I would prescribe a good night's sleep and an easy day tomorrow.'

'But Robyn is my responsibility,' she objected, and was rewarded with a smile.

'Not now, she isn't,' Elise told her. 'She's my patient. I will go to the hospital and admit her, then speak with colleagues about her case. As with any patient in such a fragile state, I will not allow visitors for a few days.'

'But——'

'No buts, Melanie,' Elise told her as the ambulance attendants arrived with an extremely worried hotel manager. 'You go to bed, and I will ring you in the morning. Give me your boss's phone number and I will

156   UNRULY HEART

also ring him and tell him what is happening. I think
Priti should stay with you for the night, in case you
suffer a delayed reaction to the bump on your head.
OK?'

Melanie smiled and nodded. Suddenly she was
pleased to be told what to do. Her own brain had
stopped working, but whether from tiredness or overload she couldn't decide!

CHAPTER NINE

THEY came home on the direct flight to Sydney a week later, Robyn so heavily drugged that she slept every time she sat down. Melanie woke her for meals, and her heart went out to the docile woman who was now pathetically grateful for Melanie's assistance.

Unable to remember her stay at the hotel, she had accepted Melanie as a friend sent to bring her home, and she'd turned to her with a dependency that filled Melanie with a deep sadness.

As the plane circled above the blue-grey waters of Botany Bay, waiting for landing instructions, one of the stewards slipped into the vacant seat beside the two women.

'There's a message for you to stay on the plane. Someone from the Airport Medical Service will be coming on board and will help you through Customs and transfer you to your domestic flight.'

Melanie felt a surge of relief. She had been worrying about her ability to prop Robyn up for the time it would take to get through immigration procedure.

'Thanks,' she murmured to the man, who nodded understandingly and left as the plane touched down.

She watched the other passengers troop off, glad that she would be leaving on her own. In spite of the week in Harare, the black eye she'd developed as a result of the flying missile attack was now an interesting rainbow of yellow, dull green and purple. Not the sort of face to be showing in public! she decided, then she stood up and spun around at the sound of her name.

Or was it at the sound of his voice?

Peter was belting up the aisle towards her, his long strides betraying anxiety, his face pale and drawn.

'I didn't expect you to be the medical help that was coming on board,' she cried as tears of relief poured down her cheeks.

'Melly!' he groaned, and his arms came round her, holding her close against his chest and he ran his hands over her body as if to assure himself that she was all there. 'Oh, Melly!' he muttered again, his lips pressed against her hair and his arms tightening into bands of steel that cut into her flesh and squeezed the air from her lungs.

Dazed, yet delighted by this unorthodox reception, she snuggled against him, drawing a strength from his warmth while her head whirled with a million questions and her body began to flicker with desire.

A stewardess trying to get past brought them both back to the present, and Peter turned her, still in his arms, to allow the intruder to pass. Then one hand left her back and reached up to lift her chin, and he cursed under his breath when he saw her face, then brushed the tears from her cheeks with long fingers that trembled against her skin.

'I should never have let you go,' he said, his lips a thin white line in his grim face. 'Never, you hear?' he added, shaking her as if to emphasise the point as his fingers brushed against her bandaged arm.

'Customs are waiting for you,' the stewardess called from the back of the plane, and Melanie sat back down in her seat and shook Robyn awake.

'We're nearly home,' she said, and all the joy of

Peter's presence was lost as she realised the words had no meaning for the girl. She looked up at Peter with all the aching doubt vivid in her eyes.

'She'll understand when the effect of the drugs wears off,' Peter said briskly, reading her thoughts as clearly as if they were written on a blackboard.

'But what if she's always on a dosage that dulls her to this extent?' she asked as the tears started to seep down her cheeks again, but whether because of concern for Robyn or disappointment that his manner towards her had changed she did not know.

'Get your bags, Melanie, and go on through Customs,' was Peter's abrupt response, the words cool enough to jolt Melanie out of the moment of pity. 'Will you recognise her luggage?'

'It's a brown backpack,' Melanie responded automatically to the businesslike tone that was such a contrast to his earlier warmth. Was he regretting the emotion-charged reunion? Was he angered by his momentary loss of control?

'Good! You get hold of it and put it through with your own carry-on bag, and I'll bring Robyn.'

The words jolted into her head. This is work, that's what he's saying, Melanie thought sadly as she walked through to the emptying customs hall. But why had he rushed to her and held her so tightly?

It wasn't as if she'd been in any danger. Once Robyn had been admitted to hospital, she'd had a pleasant week in Harare, but the excitement she'd expected to feel had been tempered by a longing to get home. It had been more like a holiday than work, although she had spent a lot of time with her patient after Elise had stabilised her.

And it wasn't as if he hadn't known she was safe!

She had rung the office every morning, as instructed, speaking to Jan or one of the telephone operators. Added to which, he had phoned her himself most evenings, to hear about her latest visit to the hospital and check on her patient's progress.

She collected the brown backpack and carted it over to a waiting customs officer, explaining the situation as she dropped her own small bag beside it.

She'd begun to look forward to Peter's phone calls, had collected snippets of information to pass on to him—to keep him talking longer. It was simply that he was a link with home, she'd repeatedly assured herself, ignoring the skipping beat of her heart whenever the phone had rung.

And Peter?

She turned to watch him come into the hall, supporting Robyn with a strong arm around her waist. Robyn was chatting to him, as alert as Melanie had seen her, but instead of feeling pleased she was aggravated by their closeness.

He's not for you, she told herself as the customs inspector rifled through the gear in Robyn's bag.

But the phone calls hadn't been entirely necessary, her heart argued, setting up a rhythmic tattoo as the pair drew nearer. And something in the way he had lingered, prolonging the conversation, had suggested more than the caring concern of an employer.

'All set?' the source of all her problems asked cheerfully as a small motorised buggy with a medical sign emblazoned on its side drews up beside them.

'You're clear here,' the customs officer announced, and Peter seated Robyn gently in the buggy while the driver dropped the two bags in the back and waved an arm for Melanie to climb into the back seat beside her patient.

'I'm taking you across to the domestic terminal,' he announced as he manoeuvred the silent vehicle out of the hall and on to the tarmac, where maintenance vehicles ran around under the wings of the huge jets like chickens at the feet of squat hens.

'Beats the bus,' Melanie told him, peering around with interest to keep her mind off the conundrum that was Peter.

'You take Robyn up to departure lounge fifteen,' he told her as they disembarked from their unorthodox transport. 'I'll check her bag in and get our seat allocation, then come on up and join you.'

There was a tentative smile on his lips, but his eyes held a gravity that frightened her. In fact, he looked— uncertain? She looked again. Well, maybe 'confused' was a better word. For a fleeting moment she thought he looked almost as confused as she felt, but what he had to be confused about she couldn't fathom.

Unless he, too, felt the electricity that permeated the air between them, the impulses as charged as lightning bolts that sent *frissons* of fear along her nerve-paths!

She grasped Robyn's arm and led her away, chatting cheerfully as she guided the girl through the crowds. This was no time to be worrying about things she could not understand—least of all *frissons* of anything. The word must have bobbed into her head from the book she'd been reading on the plane trip home!

She concentrated on her charge. It was the first time Robyn had been faced with a large crowd of people since she'd left hospital, as special arrangements had been made to seat them early on the plane from

Harare. Would she react in spite of the drugs that were depressing the action of her central nervous system?

Melanie could feel a building tension in the tightening muscles of the arm she held. She spoke reassuringly, but was immensely relieved when a member of the ground crew came forward to meet them as they reached the departure lounge.

'You can go straight on board,' the smiling woman said. 'They've rung through from the front desk to ask me to look out for you and see you seated up the front.'

'Spoilt, that's what we are, Robyn,' she said gaily, hurrying her past the waiting crowd in the wake of the stewardess.

She felt the relaxation in the girl as soon as they were safely on board, and made a mental note to tell Peter that they should wait until everyone was off before leaving the plane in Brisbane.

'Everything OK?' he asked, sliding into the seat beside her a little later, with the same anomalous smile she'd seen earlier hovering on his lips.

Maybe it was more anticipatory than puzzled!

Her body was not confused by smiles. Its welcome leapt in her blood, so tantalisingly alive, she was certain he must be able to feel the bubbling intoxication.

'Thanks to you,' she murmured as calmly as her catching breath would allow. 'I thought for a moment the crowd waiting to board might upset her, but the stewardess whisked us straight through.'

If he wanted businesslike, then that was what he'd get, although the effort to appear composed was overwhelming!

'And we'll disembark last in Brisbane,' he said, anticipating her warning.

Think about your patient, the remaining scrap of
sanity in Melanie's head prompted. Robyn had closed
her eyes again, and Melanie slid a finger around her
wrist and felt her pulse, pleased to feel the steady
rhythm.

The activity in the cabin had ceased as passengers
strapped themselves into seats, and the plane began to
roll forward. They sat in silence while the stewardess
repeated the safety instructions, and the massive
engines roared as they lifted the plane off the ground.
Robyn, unfazed by what was happening, slid sideways
in her seat, and drifted off to sleep once again.

'You did an excellent job in every way,' Peter told
her when the noise died down and the aircraft levelled
out at its flying height. The special warmth she thought
she had heard over the phone deepened his voice, and
his closeness radiated heat into her skin.

'I came close to panicking,' she admitted, embarrassed by his praise, 'and would have been lost if I
hadn't found Elise.'

'But you reached out for help and you found it. No
one could have handled it better.'

The words sent a shiver of delight through her body
and she turned to him impulsively, her hand reaching
out to grip his arm.

'Does this mean I've passed all the tests? Does it
mean you'll take me on permanently?'

The muscle tensed beneath her hand, and he looked
into her face. The warmth and softness she fancied she
had seen in his eyes and heard in his voice disappeared.

'Does the job mean so much to you, Melly?' he
asked gravely, and the shock of the question stopped
her breath in her throat.

He was going to fail her!

'Of course it does!' she told him as despair mustered a courage she'd forgotten she had. 'It combines the two things I love more than anything—travel and work. It gives me a sense of achievement, being able to help people, even over the phone, when they are feeling desperate. It's a wonderful job and I've worked hard at it, and I can't think of one decent reason for you to turn me down!'

She glared her defiance at him, but his only reply was a tense frown and a quiet, 'Can't you, Melly?' uttered with such gravity that she could find no answer.

She battled against the tears that were burning behind her eyes, and turned to look past Robyn and out of the window, until the stewardess leaned towards them offering tea or coffee.

'I'll have a coffee, please,' she said, the words tumbling out as she bit back an angry denunciation of his behaviour, his perfidy—his calling her 'Melly'!

'Your two-month trial has a few days to go yet. Before deciding, I'd like——' He stopped suddenly, as if fearing he would say too much, then the stewardess was passing down their coffee and the moment was lost.

Melanie felt her stomach clench into a tight ball, but she forced herself to reach out for her cup with steady hands. The way she felt in Peter's presence was hardly conducive to good employer-employee relations anyway, she told herself, sipping at the bitter brew. She would probably have turned the job down even if he had deigned to make it permanent.

But disappointment as bitter as the coffee churned inside her, and a sense of injustice flared alongside it, fuelling her sense of outrage.

She thought of the channels open to her to fight for

her right to be employed, and was engaged in an imaginary conversation with the equal opportunities commissioner, when his hand brushed against her arm, and her blood began to sizzle in her veins.

She couldn't fight Peter!

'I was saying,' he began tentatively, looking anywhere but at her although his body was still bombarding hers with unspoken messages, 'that I'd like an opportunity to speak privately with you before that decision is made, Melanie.'

His voice was so correctly, formally *English* that it chilled her, even while the beautiful cadence of it sent shivers of delight tingling to the very tips of her toes.

What do you mean? she wanted to ask, but something told her she might not like the answer.

He was still studying the interior of the plane as if inspecting it for flaws, so she ignored the statement, and lost herself in chaotic thoughts.

Something also told her that she hadn't imagined the warmth in his voice over the phone each night, nor mistaken the ardour of his greeting. Could it be that Peter was every bit as attracted to her as she was to him? For, in spite of her lack of experience in such matters, she was certain that the sensory darts and pinpricks that stirred her blood to flame whenever he touched her must be reacting on him to some degree. Such electricity couldn't all be a one-way current, surely!

But what could he offer?

She almost laughed aloud. Laughed, because what she really wanted to do was cry.

Was he going to ask her to be his mistress? Was that it?

If that was what he wanted to discuss, she could

understand his reluctance to have her on the staff, she realised bitterly. It would be far too awkward for him, conducting an affair in full view of his employees!

Disappointment quenched the stupid licks of flame and dimmed her hope. It was as if her knight in shining armour had turned to face her, and she'd found him — rusty! Tarnished by his own weakness and duplicity.

'I'll drive you home when we've handed Robyn over to her family,' he said at last, his voice a hoarse croak, as if her thoughts had cut him back down to something small and uncertain. 'Maybe we can talk then if you're not too tired. I don't seem able to explain—to talk to you properly—in public like this!'

Melanie banished the instant rush of pity his words, and the pathetic tone in which they were issued, provoked. Men played on women's sympathies to get what they wanted. It was the oldest ploy in the book.

Ignoring his offer, she turned her face away from him and her mind back to her rehearsal of her conversation with the equal opportunities commissioner, strengthening her case with a defiant bravado that hid an aching heart.

Then Brisbane spread beneath them, and she began to wonder if she could slip away while he was speaking to Robyn's family, and take a taxi home.

'Robyn's booked into a private clinic here in Brisbane,' her nemesis said calmly, reverting to his business persona with an ease that exasperated her. 'They are sending a car and a trained nurse to the airport to take Robyn and her family back to the clinic together.'

'It's a shame she can't go straight home, but I can understand their taking precautions.' She remembered the violence of the woman's attack and shuddered, although her hand, as she shook Robyn awake, was gentle and her heart prayed for her charge's recovery.

The crowd of people greeting passengers had thinned by the time they disembarked. A woman in her fifties rushed towards them and folded Robyn in her arms, leading her towards a bank of chairs, while the man with her walked awkwardly beside the pair, his arms held out as if to shield them both.

Beyond them, as she followed, Melanie saw Kip's beaming smile, and realised with a sinking heart that Barry was with her.

'So the boyfriend that isn't has materialised again.'

The harsh words slapped against her, jolting her to a standstill so that his body cannoned into hers.

'Well, at least it saves me driving you home and making a fool of myself,' he muttered into her ear, then turned away and strode over to speak to the nurse who stood watching the family reunion with a broad smile.

'Do you have any baggage? Do you have to sign off or anything, or can we take you straight home?'

Kip's words flew like bullets from her lips, and Melanie wondered, as she kissed them both warmly, what had happened to cause such excitement. It wasn't just her return home, that was certain!

'You've been coming and going, and we've barely seen you, but something so unbelievable has happened, Mel,' Kip blurted out as they packed into her small car, Melanie taking the back seat as Barry walked around to the driver's side.

Melanie looked at her friend in surprise. Kip's enthusiasm for causes and concerns was well known to her, but this was something special. She glowed and bubbled, and even looked as if she'd lost some weight. There was a curious difference about her.

'You'd better tell me,' she said drily, thinking that she could use some good news given the ominous statements her boss had been throwing at her lately.

'Can't you guess?' Kip demanded, twisting around to face her as Barry pulled up to pay the parking charge.

'I've been travelling all day, Kip,' Melanie excused herself. 'It's hardly conducive to rational thought, nor a good preparation for Twenty Questions.'

'It's Barry and me!' Kip announced triumphantly, and Melanie saw the flush rising in Barry's neck. 'We're in love, aren't we?'

She tugged his arm and he nodded a silent corroboration of her news, while he concentrated on easing the car into the flow of traffic. Once this was negotiated he flicked a rather shamefaced smile over his shoulder at Melanie, as if confirming what Kip had said and apologising to her at the same time.

'But that's lovely!' Melanie exclaimed, realising that an appropriate reaction was expected of her. 'I'm really pleased for you both,' she added, although her heart was filled with sadness and her body felt heavy with pain.

She did not envy Kip her happiness, and Barry was a worthy suitor for her. It was partly because Barry was a pleasant chap that she herself had been unable to get rid of him, not wanting to hurt his feelings with a harsh finality.

'It started the night he came over—before you went to the States,' Kip was explaining, and Melanie sat half-listening while part of her mind pointed out that it meant she would be on her own now, another friend paired off! 'We talked and talked, and something sparked between us.'

'That's great!' Melanie said feebly, knowing the enthusiasm she expressed in the two words was too lukewarm to be acceptable. Or was Kip too much in love to notice?

'With you being away so much, I was wondering if you'd mind if Barry moved into the flat.'

Kip's words underlined Melanie's images of loneliness.

'We'd keep your room for you and you can still use it as a base, but once you're appointed to permanent staff you'll be travelling more and more.'

Which is what I thought I wanted, Melanie told herself, wondering why the idea lacked all appeal at the moment.

Was it because she no longer believed the permanent job would be hers, or because she was tired, or because. . .?

Kip's voice rattled on, but Melanie was lost in her own tangled thoughts. Could it be that she was jealous of Kip's happiness? Was it possible that love and marriage might suddenly be a more appealing dream for the future than work and travel?

Her heart turned over and she bent forward in her seat, shivering slightly as the dreadful doubts assailed her. She wrapped her arms around her suddenly cold body, and watched the river through the delicate tracery of jacaranda boughs and flowers, the colours taking her back to Africa, where life had seemed much less complicated and Peter's voice over the phone each night had planted a tiny seed of hope in her heart.

It had withered now, that seed. He hadn't even said goodbye to her when she'd left the airport, engrossing

himself in a conversation with the nurse, as if he were
the one who had brought Robyn home.

She had slept for most of her three days off, but felt
little benefit from it as she rode up in the lift with one
of the telephone staff on her return to work. As she
watched Julie slide the metal plate into the slot that
would allow the lift to stop on their floor, she realised
she had lost the excitement of her ambitions.

Two months ago, her sights had been set on the day
she would receive her own plate and be able to send
the lift skyward. It had become the symbol of success
to her, but now she wondered if she would ever be
given one—or if she would ever use it, if she was.

Jan called to her as she walked towards the control-
room, and she turned back, pleased that she didn't
have to walk past Peter's office just yet.

'Would you like to use Peter's office to do your
written report on the trip?' Jan asked. 'He's away at
the moment, and you'll find it quieter than the control
room. Here's a report from the doctor who is treating
Robyn at the moment. I think you'll find it interesting.

Melanie picked up the sheaf of papers Jan pushed
across the desk, praying that the prognosis would be
better than she'd allowed herself to hope.

'You'll see he hasn't diagnosed schizophrenia,
although onset during adolescence and early adulthood
is common and being in an isolated situation could
trigger a latent disorder. He's hoping it was an isolated
incident of an affective disorder and is doing a full
range of tests to try to rule out the common medical
illnesses that can present as psychiatric disorders.
There are metabolic and endocrine disorders, cardio-
vascular causes like lupus and also severe systemic

infections that could cause mental instability.' Jan added quietly, 'So don't despair yet! Add this preliminary paper to your report, and we should have another file from the doctor before the debriefing.'

'It's a dreadful thing to say, I suppose, but I do hope they find a nice treatable disease.'

'So do I,' Jan told her. 'Schizophrenia is not something you'd wish on your worst enemy.'

Her gaze swept over the fading bruises on Melanie's face, and concern darkened her eyes.

'Are you certain you feel fit enough to come back to work?' she probed. 'You still look very tired. Drained, almost!'

'Thanks!' Melanie said. 'That's all I need!'

The edge of bitterness in the words shocked even herself. Jan didn't deserve that.

'I'm sorry,' she added, with a wry shake of her head. 'Nothing seems to be going right at the moment, but that's no reason for me to take out my bad temper on you.'

'That's OK,' Jan assured her. 'But I hope you're not feeling out of sorts over some imagined failure in Zimbabwe. I don't know one of our couriers who would have handled that situation any better. I'm extremely proud of my protégée, although I died a thousand deaths when I realised the volatile situation I'd plunged you into.'

'You weren't to know that Robyn's condition was likely to deteriorate so badly.'

'No,' Jan agreed, 'but, believe me, there was no way I could convince Peter of that. If there'd been less complicated travel arrangements, I think he'd have been over there the next day, especially after we heard you'd been injured.'

Jan spoke in such a prosaic way, she made his concern sound normal, but her eyes, still scanning Melanie's face, seemed to be looking for clues.

'I wasn't badly injured,' Melanie protested. 'More colour than pain!' She rubbed the side of her face ruefully, while she battled against an impulse to ask Jan where Peter had gone. 'I'd better get on with the report,' she said, moving back from Jan's desk.

'Then take some more time off if you'd like it,' Jan told her, but Melanie shook her head. To be in the small flat while Barry and Kip billed and cooed at each other was more than she could bear.

Peter's office was too full of him! She ran her hand over the soft leather of his chair, imagining the imprint of his body on the hide, and the hairs on her arms stood on end with an electrifying pleasure.

She breathed deeply, drawing in the musky maleness that hung in the air like a fine veil, a faint trace of a lemony polish mingling with leather, and paper, and a vaguely familiar smell that must be the aftershave he wore.

The desk was bare, except for a large, old-fashioned leather blotter and a leather box that held pens and pencils. The computer terminal looked out of place on the polished surface, beside the accessories of another age. She slid into his chair, leaned back and sighed.

At least there was no picture of Cynthia on the desk! Or was it in a leather folder that matched the desk set—one he could pick up and take with him when he travelled?

For a moment she wished she'd looked around more carefully on her brief visit to his home. Maybe there she'd have found some clue to the persona of the man who was her boss, some idea of his private life.

Get to work, she ordered her reluctant self, reaching out to switch on the computer, and thinking of the report she must tap into its memory.

She settled back in, but the spark of excitement that had filled her first two months was missing, and duty hours on the phone dragged by with a slowness that devastated her.

Office gossip told her that Peter was in Nepal, preparing to bring back a trekker who had been injured in a rock-fall. The young man had to be stabilised before he could travel, which meant it could be a week or more before they returned.

Each time she lifted the phone, her heart leaped into her mouth, then sank back into her boots when she realised it wasn't him on the other end of the line.

I don't want to speak to him, she continually reminded herself, but the reminders had little effect on the reactions of her body when the phone rang, or on the pain that crawled along her nerves when she heard his name mentioned.

CHAPTER TEN

PUTTING on a bright face at home became increasingly difficult, although Melanie was aware that Barry and Kip barely noticed her existence. Should she find somewhere else to live? Or would she leave Brisbane when she left UniversAid?

Then Mario arrived, blowing back into her life at the end of a day at work like the hot wind she'd experienced in Portugal. The leader of her band of 'no-hopers', he had returned to university to complete his degree soon after she'd departed, and was gaining a reputation in Europe as an innovator in sports medicine.

'I had no time to write,' he explained as they walked beside the river together, catching up on the last eight years that their rare letters had barely touched. 'It came up suddenly, this opportunity to travel to the World University Games in Brisbane.'

He accented both syllables of the last word equally, and the peculiar pronunciation made her smile.

'That is the place the angry doctor took you back to, so long ago,' he continued, 'and from there you travelled to your parents' home. I remembered, you see, Melanie!'

He looked so pleased with his cleverness, she had to laugh, although mention of the 'angry doctor' prodded the bruise she carried in her heart.

'So I say *sim* and come to Brisbane and I telephone

to your home and your parents tell me you live here already.'

His brown eyes glowed with pleasure, and his smile of delight at his own cleverness made Melanie stop and hug him, clinging to his wiry frame as she'd clung eight years ago. Then she'd fled from Eduardo's persistence, getting as far as the local square before realising that she was alone in a foreign country, and that her only security was back in a house that held both fear and shame.

'You are happy now that you have grown up?' Mario asked her, his arms still holding her loosely as he looked into her eyes.

'I suppose so!' she said lightly. 'I've got a fantastic job and——'

'And someone to love?'

'Love's not important!' she said, gaily brave as she denied her aching heart. 'Not at the moment, anyway.'

His face grew serious as his eyes scanned her face.

'I think for some people maybe not,' Mario replied, with a very European shrug of his shoulders. 'But for you, Melanie, maybe it is! After all, it was love you went searching for when you became tangled up with Eduardo.'

'Do you know so much about love now, Mario?' she teased, hoping to steer him off a subject she had no wish to pursue.

'I do, Melanie,' he said seriously, steering her off the path by the river and down to the bank, where he pulled her down to sit by the water's edge. 'See!'

He pulled a slim wallet from his pocket and opened it to show a picture of a beautiful, laughing girl.

'This is Juanita,' he said simply, the love glowing in

his dark eyes and almost oozing out of the pores of his skin.

Melanie felt its strength like the radiant heat of a fire, and smiled at her old protector.

'I am thrilled for you!'

He nodded, as if accepting only what was his due.

'In four months, we have our first baby,' he told her proudly, and Melanie's love life—or lack of it—was forgotten as they talked of the future, and the lives of the others who had made up their little band.

They walked slowly on towards the shopping centre, stopping to eat at a small Italian restaurant, then meandering back to the flat, hand in hand, like children who were reluctant to part.

'Where are you staying?' Melanie asked, when they reached the shadows of the trees that sheltered the small block of flats.

'We have rooms in one of the university colleges,' he explained. 'I can get a taxi back to there.'

'I'd drive you, but we had that wine with dinner,' she explained apologetically. 'Anyway, come in and have a cup of coffee before you go.'

Kip and Barry were watching television, but they looked up as the pair came in, and were soon caught up in conversation with Mario asking question after question about Portugal, Spain, and then Europe in general.

'You see,' Kip explained to Melanie as they made another pot of coffee, 'Barry and I have been talking about taking a year off and travelling after we're married. Meeting your friend makes it all sound real and exciting.'

Melanie smiled and nodded. She was tired, and

ready for bed. She'd see Mario again while he was here! Surely their questions would keep.

She rejoined the others with a false smile in place, but Mario, who had looked after her so well once before, was not fooled.

'I am keeping you up!' he protested. 'Even long ago you could not adjust to our late hours in Portugal.'

'If you mean eating dinner at ten o'clock at night, I certainly could not,' she told him.

'I will go,' he said, but the other two begged him to stay.

'We'll drive you back when we've had this cup of coffee,' Barry promised.

'Or you could stay here, if you don't mind sleeping on the couch,' Kip added. 'It's quite comfortable.'

Mario looked enquiringly at Melanie, who nodded, and yawned for the third time in five minutes.

'If you're coming back to dinner tomorrow night,' she told him, 'you could stay the night, drop me at work in the morning, and take my car back to the university. That way you've got transport to get back here.'

Everyone seemed pleased with the arrangements, so she said goodnight and left them talking.

'There was a phone call for you earlier,' Kip remembered to tell her as she ducked from the bathroom to her bedroom a little later. 'Someone from work, but he said it wasn't important.'

It couldn't have been another courier job, or they'd have kept trying to contact me, she decided as she fell wearily into bed. Whatever it was could wait till morning.

* * *

Mario handled her little car well, adapting easily to driving on the 'wrong' side of the road. He pulled into a space outside UniversAid's offices, and slipped out to open the car door for her and walk her up the stairs.

'I will see you tonight!' he said, bending to kiss both her cheeks and then raising her hand to his lips before running lightly back down the steps.

'Very touching!'

The deep voice ground out the words as she came into the shadowy darkness of the foyer. She didn't need to wait for her eyes to adjust to the dimmer light to know who had watched the theatrical farewell.

'So you're back,' she said baldly, although her heart was pounding so loudly he must surely be able to hear it, and her breath fluttered erratically in her lungs like a moth trying to escape from a box.

'Just in time to realise how wrong a supposedly sensible man can be in his judgements.' The words were as cold and hard as stones, and every bit as painful as they hit against her. 'Sheer common sense kept telling me I was wrong, but would I listen?' he added, with such cosmic scorn that she felt like punching him.

The lift door slid open, and she hesitated, unwilling to enter such a confined space with him.

'Scared?' he challenged.

'Why should I be?' She gathered up her courage and stepped inside. Now that he was back, her future would be decided one way or the other, but, whether she wanted the job or not, she was determined to fight for her right to be offered it. And fighting began by not backing down!

She watched his profile surreptitiously as he slid the plate into the control, seeing the faint white lines fanning out beside his eyes, and the deep crease that strain had pressed into his cheek.

I'm sure Cynthia doesn't look after him properly, she thought. Why else would he seem so tired and defeated?

The urge to fight slid away, and in its place was a burning desire to reach out and touch him, to hold him in her arms and knead away his fatigue, her fingers light with love.

'Are you going to appoint me to permanent staff?' she demanded abruptly, horror at her thoughts making the words sound more belligerent than she'd intended.

'I suppose I am,' he replied, staring straight ahead at the lift doors as it slid silently upwards.

'Well, don't sound too delighted about it!' Melanie said sharply. 'You either think I'll be a good employee or you don't.' Weeks of frustration fuelled the rage now sizzling within her.

'Oh, I think you'll be a good employee, Melanie,' he said, turning half towards her so that she could see a smile twisting his lips in a way that hurt her.

'But there's a "but", isn't there? Some reservation, like a hangover, hovering in your mind.'

Her voice had risen and the doors had slid open, but the stab of pain the smile had caused had been the final slosh of petrol on the embers of her anger, which burst forth now like the shower of sparks from a firecracker.

'And it's all based on a prejudgement you made eight years ago, before you even met me. Mario and his friends were bad, you decided, "no-hopers", in fact, and it followed I must be bad as well, to be with them. You didn't wonder why I ran away from the Casels' house. You didn't ask if I had a reason. You simply picked me up with a distasteful look on your proper

English face, as if I were something nasty washed up by the tide, and carted me off, issuing orders every step of the way!'

He must have touched the controls again, she realised, for the lift doors had closed, but her anger was not shut off as easily.

'I asked you when I started if you'd hold my past against me. I didn't want to start the job if it meant you were going to put me off after two months.'

'I've told you you can have the damn job!'

He was slumped against the corner of the lift now, his eyes turned up towards heaven as if exasperated once again by behaviour that could only be labelled childish. But Melanie was beyond rational thought as words she hadn't ever wanted to utter burst from her lips.

'I don't want your damn job,' she fumed. 'I don't want to have to keep coming to work, and seeing you, and knowing you're still judging me all the time. I don't want it any more! I can't handle it any more!'

And then, all passion spent, she began to cry, letting go of all the pent-up emotion in a rain of tears she could not control.

'Don't cry, Melly,' he whispered, his hands moving towards her, then hesitating, held at bay only inches from her shoulders. 'Please don't cry,' he begged again in a strangled undertone.

Then the hands descended and he drew her close, leading her out of the lift and into a room she had never seen before. He leaned back on the desk and drew her hard against his body so that she rested between his legs, and felt the security that only seemed to come from being in his arms.

'Is it too late to ask you about Portugal?' he whispered against her hair, and she shook her head, denying the telling, not the question.

'I'd like to know,' he added in a voice that seemed to hold as many tears as she had shed. 'I need to know,' he amended, pushing her back from him so that he could look down into her face.

His skin was pale, and the lines of tiredness seemed deeper than they had been earlier. His eyes held an expression of such kindness, it made her want to cry again, then they crinkled at the corners and he said with a rueful smile, 'Consider making me listen as a kind of penance for my neglect back then.'

His hands rested lightly on her shoulders, while his knees still held her captive.

Would it help to tell it all? she wondered, then knew that maybe it would.

'It's a tacky little story, in hindsight,' she said bravely, holding his gaze as she tried to read his reaction.

'It can't be any worse than I've imagined,' he muttered, leaning forward to brush an apologetic kiss across her forehead.

With halting words, she repeated the full story for the first time, telling him all the little details that had been kept hidden in her heart, freeing all the bewilderment and humiliation she had felt as she finally exorcised the ghost that was Eduardo.

'And the "no-hopers"?' he asked, when she had finished.

'Found me in the square,' she said, smiling now, as a lightness she hadn't felt for a long time invaded her being. 'They'd decided to take a term off university studies and explore their country. They scooped me up and took me along with them. They looked after me better than they would have their own sister, Peter, and insisted I keep in touch with my parents. It wasn't their fault I got sick!'

'So you kept telling me,' he said, smiling at her again in a way that made her want to fling herself back into his arms. 'I owe you, and them, an apology.'

The hands that rested on her shoulders trembled slightly, as if he too felt the magnetic force pulling them together.

I can't fall back into his arms! she warned herself, then, emboldened by the relaxation in the tension between them, she turned her thoughts back to the conversation and said cheekily, 'Well, you can apologise to one of them. Mario is here with the Portuguese team at the World University Games!'

'I thought I recognised him. Followed you halfway around the world, has he?'

The words had a crispness that told her they were back to playing games.

'As a friend!' she emphasised. 'In fact, I think he might have looked me up to tell me all about his beautiful wife and soon-to-be-born baby.'

'And it upset you, that he's got a wife?'

Had he heard the panic in her voice that the word 'wife' always caused her? It had certainly brought her back down to earth with a thud. Little tête-à-têtes like this, with Peter, were definitely off-limits.

'No, I'm delighted,' she said abruptly. 'Now I'd better get to work before Jan sends out a search party. Where are we, anyway?'

'We're at work, Melly. At the place where, not so many minutes ago, you were telling me you didn't want to be! I'll ring through to Jan and tell her you're with me.'

He half turned to pick up the receiver, but his knees still pressed against her thighs and she lacked the will to move away, because her body was convinced it had come home to rest at last. She heard the murmur of his voice, taking in the musical quality of it rather than the words.

Would Jan wonder what she was doing with Peter? Wonder where they were?

'Now, tell me why you don't want to work here,' he prompted softly when he turned back towards her, his blue eyes shining with a tenderness that made her insides dissolve into a shaking jelly.

She shook her head, caught in a net of emotion from which she could see no escape.

'Could it be something to do with an attraction between us?' he asked, the question jolting her head back so that she stared, speechless, into his clear eyes.

'Did you think I didn't feel it, Melly?' he asked. 'Don't you know it has nearly driven me mad? Do you wonder I don't want you working here, when every time I catch a glimpse of you, or smell you perfume after you've walked from a room, I am so distracted from my work I can't think straight?'

A tiny shudder of joy rang through her as she heard the confession, but it was a joy tempered with sadness. Knowing he was attracted to her was hardly enough to wipe away all the other obstacles.

'At first I thought it must be the tail-end of an over-developed sense of responsibility I'd felt for you for a long time,' he continued, and the seriousness in his voice made her look carefully at him again, but his face told her nothing. 'Then I realised it was more than that when I felt like killing that fellow who was asleep in your bed.'

The quiet vehemence of the statement shocked her, especially when she saw the tendon twitching in his clenched jaw and read the remnants of the anger he had felt.

'Now and then. . .' He paused, then seemed to gather strength. 'Occasionally, I imagined that you might have felt something towards me, but every time. . .'

She held her breath, willing him to continue, to say the words she wanted to hear even if a culmination of their feelings would prove impossible.

'Damn it, Melly,' he muttered, pulling her close against him again as if unable to look into her eyes any longer. 'Wherever I went, I kept tripping over your young men! I knew it could never be, and yet. . .'

'And yet?' she whispered, her lips against the warm skin at the base of his neck, where a pulse beat an erratic tattoo in time with her own over-anxious heart.

'And yet what I felt for you continued to grow, until it consumed every fibre of my being. Does that make you want to laugh?' he asked harshly, his hands biting into her shoulders with such force that they were causing pain. 'It was as if I was following a destiny beyond my control—right from the time I came back to Brisbane like a migrating bird, to the place where I'd first met the jolting loss of not having you by my side, knowing I would probably never see you, and determined not to look for you, but here in case fate ever decreed that it was meant to be!'

Was he saying he'd felt something more than lust for her that night in Portugal? Was he saying that the cold, despairing anger had been his protection against what he saw as an irrational appeal, the forbidden attraction between doctor and patient?

'You thought I was a spoilt, self-indulgent little brat,' she objected, remembering the many times he'd labelled her that way.

'And I tried to make myself believe it,' he assured her, 'however much my instinct told me there was more to you than that.'

The doubt in him embarrassed her, and her eyes dropped to study the patterned carpet on the floor, her mind too confused to argue with him.

'Then I'm sitting in my own office, resigned to a life where work is more important than a permanent relationship, more or less at peace with the world, and you walk into view, your hair so much more golden than I'd remembered, your smile so much more beautiful, your body so infinitely desirable I wanted to reach out and pull you into my arms, to hold you close like this, and feel your heart beating against mine.'

The words had stopped making sense, but some subliminal message held Melanie still.

'Then all the glowing excitement faded from your face, and I knew you didn't want to see me. I felt betrayed. My stupid dream splintered into a thousand fragments and I almost hated you. How could I stand to see you round the office every day, to be reminded of my own stupidity in keeping such a fantasy alive?'

'But you had Cynthia,' Melanie bleated, hoping that speech might bring her back to reality from a dream in which she seemed to float, a dream of love, unmentioned yet, but surely getting closer with every syllable he uttered.

'Cynthia and I agreed to go our seperate ways after I returned to London eight years ago,' he said quietly.

'You didn't tell me! You led me to believe she was here!'

Melanie twisted indignantly out of his grasp, needing to see his face, to try to read what lay behind this extraordinary confession.

'It was a protective reflex, Melly,' he confessed, the strange twisted smile hovering again on his lips.

She waited for more, but there was nothing, just her and Peter, locked in a strangely non-sexual clasp, his face portraying a shadowy reluctance that looked almost like fear.

'Is that all?' she demanded, when the shadows spread across her like a heat-deadening cloud and coldness began to seep into her bones.

'It's enough stupidity for one working morning, surely,' he said, self-mockery back in his strengthening voice, as he pushed her away from him and stood up, looking over her head towards the lift foyer. 'Enough to explain why I was reluctant to have you working here! Travelling with you nearly drove me demented with the effort of keeping my hands off you. Then you went off on your own to Africa, and that was worse, because I couldn't sleep for worrying what might happen to you. Then there was Barry! Can't you understand what seeing you with other men does to me, Melanie Ashcroft, or is all your compassion reserved for your patients?'

'I meant is that all you're going to say about your feelings for me?' she asked in a tight little voice that barely hid the quaking of her heart.

'What else do you want?' he roared, all restraint gone as he flung his hands in mute appeal towards the heavens. 'Blood? I tell you I love you to distraction and you say "is that all"!'

'You didn't actually say you loved me,' she pointed

out, the words fluttering on her breath as she held a growing delight and excitement only barely in check.

'Didn't say I loved you?' he thundered, glaring down at her. 'What else is this whole sordid confession, this great blurting out of an idiocy that has hampered my life for the past eight years?'

He paused for a moment, but it was only to take a breath, because the tirade continued to rain down on her head.

'And how do you think I felt when every time I tried to say it earlier your boyfriend would appear and carry you away from me? I love you, Melly,' he raged in a very unloverlike voice, but the words held the music of the angels to Melanie's ears.

'Then maybe you should kiss me,' she said hopefully, tilting her face up towards him with a prim little smile hovering on her lips.

He groaned and pulled her close again, pressing his lips to hers with such burning hunger that she was shaken by the magnitude of the power she'd unleashed. This was not just a kiss that sealed a love long blooming, but a triumphant taking and giving, a passionate pledge of such fierce possession, her body quivered with the might of it.

As his lips slid away to press against her still bruised temple, she dragged air into her lungs, trying to steady the pounding of her heart, and the tumultuous beating of her pulses.

'I love you, love you, love you, Melly,' he repeated as his lips tracked back towards her mouth, already parted to drink in the taste of him, to capture again the spirit of the conquest they both had made at last.

Alison Roberts was born in New Zealand, and says, 'I lived in London and Washington DC as a child, and began my working career as a primary school teacher. A lifelong interest in medicine was fostered by my doctor and nurse parents, flat-sharing with doctors and physiotherapists on leaving home, and marriage to a house surgeon who is now a consultant cardiologist. I have also worked as a cardiology technician and research assistant. My husband's medical career took us to Glasgow for two years, which was an ideal place to start my writing career. I now live in Christchurch, New Zealand, with my husband, daughter and various pets.'

**Look out for RIVALS IN PRACTICE
by Alison Roberts,
coming May 2002, in Medical Romance™**

RIVALS IN PRACTICE

When a storm throws a rural New Zealand town into
chaos, Dr Jennifer Tremaine's professional prowess is
put under pressure! She's relieved to see surgeon
Andrew Stephenson step into the fray. She hasn't
seen him since medical school – but now beneath
the familiar rivalry stirs a new sensation...

**Alison has now written over 15 books for Medical
Romance™. She's especially popular for her exciting
emergency stories set Down Under!**

MUM'S THE WORD

by

Alison Roberts

CHAPTER ONE

SARAH KENDALL was spoiling for a fight.

She knew exactly who her target was and her long legs took the stairs effortlessly two at a time. She was unaware of the heavy disc of her stethoscope, bouncing painfully against her collarbone. The fury which had so far propelled her almost at a run through the busy corridors of Christchurch Central Hospital, across the carefully landscaped buffer zone and into the new, purpose-built, office block of hospital management had not abated even slightly. Although aware that it might be detrimental to her cause, Sarah didn't pause to allow herself time to calm down.

Management had a lot to answer for. The pain caused by the implementation of new health reforms had touched everyone in the medical arena, but this time they weren't going to get away with it. Dr Sarah Kendall was simply not going to let it happen. The angry shove she bestowed on the heavy fire-stop doors was enough to make them swing several times, before closing again.

The wide, carpeted corridor in which she now found herself was obviously enemy territory. Devoid of the normal hospital obstacle course of people, trolleys and equipment, the freedom of movement and the quiet was unnerving. It reeked of power—and control. This was management, all

5

right, Sarah noted scathingly. They were simply on another planet as far as what a hospital was really about.

The secretary who emerged rapidly from her office received what Sarah hoped was a polite nod but her query about an appointment was ignored. Sarah's pace slowed only as she approached the door with a brass plate that read MR P. B. HENDERSON, CHIEF EXECUTIVE OFFICER. Paul Henderson, the new face in senior management. He was rumoured to be sympathetic to the needs of both doctors and patients. Sarah Kendall was in just the mood to test the rumour.

Sarah rapped briskly on the door and opened it, without waiting for a reply. She really didn't care if he was in the middle of a meeting. The way she was feeling right now she was quite prepared to take on any number of management personnel. But Mr P. B. Henderson was alone. Clearly startled by Sarah's abrupt entrance, he remained seated at the massive oak desk which dominated the office, a pen poised in his hand. Sarah pushed the door shut behind her with her foot.

'I will not allow you to take that child away from her mother.' Sarah was pleased that her tone didn't betray the fact that she, too, was startled.

Sarah had expected a grim-faced adversary, grey-haired and pushing retirement, with a pin-striped suit and an attitude to match. Paul Henderson was far too young. Yes, there was a cluster of grey hairs at his temples but the luxurious black waves were far too tousled. He could do with a haircut. His dark eyes were far too blue, and as for his clothing—rolled-up shirtsleeves and a loosened collar and tie!

The impression took only seconds but Sarah had still received no response. Perhaps his attitude was the only thing left to match her expectations. She took a step further into the office.

'Alice Forster, Ward 23. Thanks to you, she is about to be forcibly removed from her mother's care and I am not going to let that happen.'

'And you are?' The upward movement of Paul Henderson's eyebrows was the only acknowledgement of Sarah's vehement tone. He appeared unruffled, remaining seated at his desk with his pen still poised.

'Sarah Kendall. *Dr* Kendall,' Sarah added with some emphasis. 'Senior registrar, Ward 23. Alice Forster is my patient, *Mr* Henderson.' Again Sarah placed emphasis on the title, this time due to the anger she had no intention of suppressing.

'Would you like to take a seat, *Dr* Kendall?' Paul Henderson's repetition of Sarah's emphasis was just enough to let her know that it had annoyed him. She also noted with startling clarity how the lines at the corners of his eyes deepened as they narrowed slightly.

'I won't, thanks.' Sarah didn't want to relinquish her height advantage. Even seated she could see that Paul Henderson was a large man. His sheer masculinity was distracting and served to push Sarah's anger up a notch. She brandished a rather crumpled sheet of paper, produced from the pocket of her white coat.

'This is a directive from your office, Mr

Henderson. It states that the hospital intends to up-
hold the court's ruling in the case of Alice Forster
and—'

The interruption was smooth. 'I believe that directive was addressed to the consultant this child
was admitted under. Dr Martin Lynch?'

'Alice Forster has been under my care since she
was first diagnosed with acute lymphoblastic leukaemia nearly twelve months ago. I am much more
intimately acquainted with the wider ramifications
of this case than is Dr Lynch. In any case, he agrees
with me.'

'That's not the impression I get.' The tone was
still controlled. Smug, Sarah decided. No, more
than that. Arrogant.

'Dr Lynch agrees with me in principle—as anybody with even a remote interest in humanitarian
issues would. He is not, however, willing to take a
stand and defy a management directive.'

'Which you are.'

'Obviously.' Sarah met his direct stare. Not only
arrogant, she decided, but also patronising. Typical
management, after all. She felt a flash of relief when
he broke their eye contact, but as his gaze flicked
down and then up again she saw the beginnings of
a smile and remembered what she was wearing.

While a great hit with the children on the ward,
her Bart Simpson sweatshirt, jeans and the large,
yellow, sun-shaped badge on her white coat which
said HI, I'M DOCTOR SARAH were not exactly appropriate in the present circumstances. The feeling
of being patronised intensified and Sarah leaned
forward over the large desk, speaking more quietly.

'I am not only prepared to defy management. I will, if necessary, create adverse publicity for this hospital by defying the court's ruling that this child be removed from her mother's custody.'

'The issue is not the removal of the child from her mother.' Paul Henderson's hint of a smile vanished and his gaze returned to meet Sarah's hostile glare. 'It is about the granting of a father's rights of access to his terminally ill daughter and his contribution to her welfare.'

Sarah's voice rose sharply. 'Alice's welfare can only be served by remaining with her mother in a safe environment and receiving the medical care essential to her well-being.'

'Her medical care is going to be provided by her father. As I understand it, he has hired private medical staff at some considerable expense. He—'

Sarah interrupted angrily, her words tumbling over each other. 'This child has been cared for twenty-four hours a day by her mother from the moment she became ill. Alice was only five when that happened. She had just started school and she charmed everyone she met. She had curly blonde hair, big blue eyes and a smile that never quit. We all fell in love with her and were just as happy as her mother when she went into her first remission.' Sarah straightened, her lips pressed firmly together.

Paul Henderson was silent. He fiddled slowly with the pen he still held but his eyes were fixed on Sarah's face. Sarah stared at his hands as the long fingers toyed with the pen. Surgeon's hands, Sarah noted abstractedly—or maybe a musician's. After the briefest silence she turned and walked slowly towards the large window of the office. She stared, unseeing, at the magnificent view it framed.

'It didn't last, of course. I've lost count of the number of times they've been back. They've both suffered through countless painful and unpleasant experiences. Chemotherapy, infections, blood tests, bone-marrow biopsies. But Alice managed to keep smiling. We all hoped against hope that the bone-marrow transplant would succeed even though it wasn't a perfect match. The graft versus host disease put an end to that hope. The steroids needed to control that have swollen Alice's face until you can hardly recognise her. She has bleeding into her gut and joints.

'We can control the pain but she can't move very much. She had already lost all her hair from the chemotherapy.' Sarah's voice dropped almost to a whisper. 'The smile is still the same. But it doesn't appear very often now and it only appears for one person. And that's her mother.'

Sarah whirled from her position at the window. Her tone became harsh. 'Her father's, Simon Forster's, interests are purely his own. He's in local politics, wants to move into the national arena and this looks like good P.R.' Sarah strode back to the desk. 'For the sake of publicity he intends to haul a dying child away from the only person important to her into the care of total strangers—'

'He's hardly a stranger. He's the child's father. We have no business judging his motives.' Paul's tone was finally angry. He stood up as he spoke. Sarah found her gaze travelling up—and up. At well over six feet Paul Henderson towered over her, but Sarah wasn't about to let herself be intimidated.

'Simon Forster walked out on Isobel Forster when Alice was less than two years old. You're talking about a man who has refused any contact or—'

'Or been refused any contact, perhaps?'

Sarah talked over the interruption. 'Or any financial support for her or her mother, even when Alice became ill.' Sarah snorted incredulously. 'You're talking about a man who even refused to allow himself to be tested as a possible bone-marrow donor when his daughter's illness became critical!'

Paul Henderson walked around the side of his desk. 'I admit it's a tragic story. And one that you have portrayed with admirable eloquence. Unfortunately it has nothing to do with the present situation.'

'How can you say that?' Sarah was so incredulous her voice squeaked.

'This is a hospital, Dr Kendall, in case you've forgotten. We are concerned with a patient's medical condition and care. We do not have the luxury of making decisions or interfering with social issues, marriage guidance or custodial disputes. This is up to other authorities.'

Paul Henderson raised his hand sharply to pre-empt Sarah's interruption. 'As I understand the situation, there is nothing more we can do for the child that cannot be effectively managed outside the hospital. Many would argue that the terminal stage of anybody's illness is preferably managed in a non-medical environment. If the parents choose such a course we have to support it where possible. We cannot afford to keep beds open purely on moral or social grounds—particularly in direct opposition to the ruling of a family court which has presumably considered *both* sides of this story.'

Sarah's brown eyes flashed. 'Of course—it all comes down to money, doesn't it, Mr Henderson?' She took a step closer to Paul. 'Well, let me tell you, there are people lying in those beds—not accounting sheets. Perhaps if you actually took some notice of that you might do a better job at management of a hospital.'

Paul closed the gap between them. 'Perhaps you should try being a doctor instead of a social worker, Sarah Kendall. For your information there's a little more involved in management than counting pennies.'

With only a matter of inches between them, they glared at each other. Sarah's beeper sounded but she ignored the intrusion. She tossed back her hair with an angry shake of her head.

'And, for your information, Mr Henderson, there's a little more to being a doctor than counting pills!'

Sarah turned on her heel and stormed out of the office, her beeper punctuating the silence behind her. Still seething, she made her way rapidly down the stairs. She should have known better than to expect a change of heart from management. Angry as she still was, Sarah was also acutely aware of another emotion, threatening to override her anger. She recognised it just as her beeper sounded for the third time.

Exhilaration. That's what it was. The sparks that had flown in the office of Mr P. B. Henderson were still with her. There was something about that man—quite apart from his blatant physical attributes. Or perhaps it was simply the atmosphere. Perhaps Sarah was just more aggressive than she had ever realised. She rarely became embroiled in heated discussion let alone all-out verbal battles. Sarah couldn't help a wry grin to herself as she entered the main hospital wing and made her way to the nearest telephone. Perhaps she should indulge herself a little more often.

Paul Henderson shook his head in amazement. He remained in his office, staring down from his window, long after the figure of Sarah Kendall had been swallowed by the main hospital wing. That had to have been the most extraordinary encounter he had ever had. Just who the hell was Sarah Kendall—apart from being, without doubt, the most attractive woman he had ever seen?

'Feisty little thing,' he murmured, and chuckled out loud at the thought of how she would respond to the description. How old was she? In those clothes she could pass for a teenager. The tightly fitting jeans had advertised a coltish length and slimness to those legs, but even that ridiculous, shapeless sweatshirt had failed to hide the curves of a mature woman. And that hair! Bathed in the sunlight from the window, it had seemed to be sprayed with golden glitter and so straight it rippled like silk when she shook her head. She could do with a haircut, though, Paul mused. The soft fringe was so long it almost got caught in those magnificent eyelashes. Any longer and it might hide those extraordinary brown eyes...

With some difficulty Paul Henderson cleared his mind of the overwhelming impressions with which Sarah Kendall had left him. His anger was gone and he recognised that it had been born of embarrassment—embarrassment that he'd had no knowledge of the background issues of this case and hadn't made any effort to find out. He prided himself on seeing both sides of an issue, but it hadn't occurred to him that in this case one of the sides had its own sides that both deserved consideration. Never mind that he was snowed under with fending off a strike by the cleaners, that the papers were about to publish damning figures about current waiting lists for surgery and that the extension to the emergency department had mysteriously doubled in cost since the estimates. It was no excuse to lose sight of what a hospital was really about.

Wasn't that exactly what he had told himself he could and would do when he took this position? With his background he was one of the few who would be able to see both sides of every dispute, be able to mediate and create a co-operation between medical and management staff which could become a shining example to the rest of the nation. If this was an indication of his success so far then Dr Sarah Kendall was absolutely right. He was losing sight of what hospital beds were really about. And it wasn't good enough. He pressed the button on his intercom.

'Sally? Get Martin Lynch on the phone for me, please.'

The persistent beeping of Sarah's pager had been a call from the emergency department. Sarah found herself listening to a brief summary of a case referred urgently to hospital by a GP—a six-year-old girl who had become progressively more unwell since yesterday and now looked like a case of meningococcal meningitis. Sarah moved quickly towards Emergency. Six years old. The same age as Alice Forster. Sarah bit her lip. If she was going to do her job properly she would just have to forget about Alice for the moment.

Was Paul henderson right? Was she too emotionally involved with her patients and did that make her function less effectively in her primary role as a physician? It was an issue that needed some thought but now was not the appropriate time. Or place.

The emergency department registrar showed Sarah to the cubicle where a small girl lay curled up miserably on a bed. Her eyes were screwed shut. Sarah smiled at the very anxious-looking parents and laid a hand on the child's forehead.

'Hi, Charlotte. My name is Sarah and I'm a doctor. I'd like to have a look at you and see if we can't make you feel a bit better.'

The feverish feel of the child's skin was expected after the telephone call but the registrar hadn't mentioned the faint rash around Charlotte's eyes. It was an unusual rash, like tiny blood spots under the skin. Sarah touched it gently. A possible sign of meningitis, it could also be caused by a transient rise in venous pressure after an event such as vomiting.

'When did she start vomiting?' Sarah directed the question at the child's mother.

'Last night. Just once. But she's been sick several times this morning. It makes her cry—she says it hurts her head.'

'Did you notice anything about the way she vomited?'

'Well, yes. It was different than last time—but that was ages ago. She's normally very well.'

'How was it different?'

'Kind of, well—it went a long way.'

Sarah nodded. Projectile vomiting was another prominent feature of meningitis. She leaned closer to Charlotte.

'Does the light hurt your eyes, sweetheart?'

Charlotte nodded slightly but then whimpered in pain.

'Your head still hurts a lot too, doesn't it?'

Sarah received no response. The child turned her face away into the pillow. Sarah glanced up at the emergency department registrar, Matt Warnock.

'Kernig's sign?'

'Positive.'

'OK. I'll just check that.'

With plenty of encouragement, and help from a nurse, Sarah turned Charlotte gently but firmly onto her back. Placing her hand under the back of the child's head, Sarah attempted to flex Charlotte's neck. The girl's whole trunk lifted from the bed and she began to cry miserably. Gently Sarah replaced her head on the pillow. She completed her examination as quickly as possible, checking Charlotte's abdomen, listening to her chest and looking at the rest of her skin. She found nothing to change her initial impression and moved to the end of the bed to speak to the parents.

'It seems quite likely that Charlotte is suffering from meningococcal meningitis. We'll admit her immediately and I'll do a lumbar puncture as soon as we get her up to the ward. Along with the blood tests, which have been taken here, that will let us know exactly what bug we're dealing with, but we'll start intravenous antibiotic treatment straight away. We don't need to wait for the results.'

Charlotte's mother spoke in a broken whisper. 'People die from meningitis.'

'It's a serious illness,' agreed Sarah, 'and sometimes it progresses too quickly to be managed, but Charlotte's already been ill for twenty-four hours and her condition is not too serious yet. Antibiotics are extremely effective with this disease. I'm confident we'll get on top of things pretty quickly. Would you both like to come up to the ward with her?'

Charlotte's mother nodded. She turned to her husband. 'Could you dash home and get Charlotte's nightie and some of her toys? Don't forget Boo-Boo!' She looked at Sarah apologetically. 'That's her favourite bear. She never sleeps without him.' Her voice wobbled and tears looked imminent.

Sarah stood back to make room for Charlotte's bed to pass. She touched the child's cheek. 'I'll see you upstairs in a few minutes, sweetheart. Mummy's going to come with you, OK?'

Sarah reached for the telephone as they left but motioned for Charlotte's father to wait.

'Do you have other children?' She pushed the buttons on the phone as she spoke.

'Yes—two. Her brother's at school and we left the younger one with a neighbour.'

'Right. We may need— Excuse me.' Sarah turned her attention to the phone. 'Angela? I've got a six-year-old, Charlotte Newman, on her way up. Probable meningococcal meningitis. Could you set up for a lumbar puncture, please?' She listened for a few seconds, nodding. 'That's right. Benzylpenicillin, IV. We'll start as soon as we've completed the puncture. I'll be there in five minutes.'

Hanging up the phone, Sarah turned back to Mr Newman. 'We should get the results of the tests within a few hours, and if we're correct in the diagnosis it would be advisable for all family members to have a prophylactic course of antibiotics— just to protect you all from catching a disease you've been in close contact with. I'll ring your GP as soon as we have the results and arrange things if you can get in touch with your clinic later.' She smiled. 'I'd better let you go and collect Boo-Boo. I'm sure Charlotte will be keen to see him.'

The paediatric department was like no other in the hospital. It was a melting pot of specialties, with the paediatricians working with or alongside consultants from virtually every area. Parents were en-

couraged to stay with their children where possible
and formal visiting hours held little authority. With
the number of nursing staff, visiting teachers, physio and occupational therapists, as well as doctors,
the traffic of adults was constant. But it was the
children, of course, who held centre stage.

Paediatrics was probably the busiest, definitely
the brightest and frequently the noisiest department
in the hospital. The specialty was demanding, difficult, exhausting, heart-breaking and enormously
rewarding. It was an area either loved or hated. The
ones who hated it moved rapidly into other depart-
ments. Sarah Kendall had stayed.

The twin wards 22 and 23 were spacious and
brightly decorated, the atmosphere relaxed and
friendly. Sarah walked past a huge mural of
Maurice Sendak's ''Wild Things'', having their
rumpus on the walls of Ward 23, as she made her
way towards the treatment room. As she passed the
central desk area Angela Grant, the nurse manager,
looked up from the paperwork she was sorting with
one hand. The other was balancing a wailing six-
month-old baby on her hip.

'They're almost ready for you, Sarah. How did
you go in the lion's den?'

'Things got a bit heated. I'm not sure I did much
good.'

'What's Paul Henderson like?'

Sarah smiled without amusement. 'Tall, dark,
handsome and—bureaucratic. Bottom line is that
we can't afford to keep beds open on social grounds
and custody disputes are none of our business.'

Angela groaned. 'Typical management, then?'

Sarah shrugged. 'I'm not sure I'd call him typical.' She glanced up as a red light came on over a
door near the central desk. 'They're ready for me.
I'll catch you later.'

'No, I'll catch you.' Angela grinned. 'Guess
who's pulled out his IV line again?'

It was Sarah's turn to groan. 'Not Anthony
again?' She stooped to cover her shoes with surgical bootees and to don a gown, before entering
the treatment room. She was quite happy to postpone for as long as possible the prospect of dealing
with the hyperactive three-year-old boy they were
treating for pneumonia.

Charlotte Newman lay in the same position in
which Sarah had last seen her. Two nurses were
busy, one talking to Charlotte, the other making
preparations for the procedure. Like the nurses,
Charlotte's mother wore a gown and mask but
Sarah could see the fear in her eyes.

'Why don't you sit over here, Mrs Newman?
That way you can hold Charlotte's hand.' Sarah
smiled at the girl, reaching for a mask and bent to
her eye level, before tying it on.

'This won't take long, darling. I'm going to give
you an injection in your back. It won't hurt much
because I've got special medicine to make it go
numb. It's very important because it's going to help
us find out what bugs are making you sick and then
we're going to give you some more medicine to
bop them all off. OK?'

Rewarded with the smallest hint of a smile, Sarah
stroked the girl's cheek. 'I think you're a real cham-

pion, Charlotte. I'll bet your mum's really proud of you.'

Sarah nodded to Judith, the senior nurse, waiting to assist her and then turned to the basin to scrub up. She cast her eye over the adjacent trolley as she did so.

'What gauge needle have you got there, Judith?'

'Twenty.'

'Right. Have you checked that the stylet fits the needle barrel?'

'Not yet.'

'OK, I'll do that.' Sarah took the towel that Judith held with a pair of forceps. She dried her hands and then put on the surgical gloves.

'You prep her while I go over this.' Sarah began to check the instruments and drugs on the trolley.

Once she was ready both nurses held Charlotte in position, lying on her left side. Her back was bright orange from the disinfectant and a sterile drape exposed only her lower spine.

Sarah counted and then carefully introduced the needle into the space between the third and fourth lumbar vertebrae. Having infiltrated the area with local anaesthetic, she changed to the needle and stylet. She angled the needle slightly as she advanced slowly, withdrawing the stylet frequently to check for the emergence of cerebrospinal fluid.

The staff kept up a running commentary of encouragement for both Charlotte and her mother, but Sarah fell silent as she felt the decrease in resistance to the needle that indicated she was in the correct position. When she withdrew the stylet completely, however, the clear fluid dripped only reluctantly.

Sarah held her breath as she rotated the barrel of
the needle, without altering its position. The drips
came more readily and Sarah breathed a sigh of
relief as she collected the sample into the required
three serial tubes. She replaced the stylet and then
withdrew the whole system from the child's back.
She pressed a sterile swab to the puncture site and
leaned over her patient.

'You know something, Charlotte? I was right.
You are a real champion.'

The insertion of the IV line was completed with
minimal trauma and Sarah was delighted when the
first dose of antibiotics had been administered. For
the moment the invasive procedures were over. She
looked at Judith.

'Have you got a single room available?'

Judith nodded and Sarah smiled at Mrs Newman.
'There's a bed in the room for you as well. We'll
get Charlotte comfortable and we can keep the
room dark for the moment. Judith here will be keeping a close eye on her and I'll be in and out quite
often.' She turned to the nurse.

'We'll need half-hourly neurological observations. Response to command, hand grip on both
sides, movement of feet, pupillary reflexes—the
usual line-up. Blood pressure and heart rate, of
course, and I want plasma and urine electrolytes
monitored carefully. Fluids need to be restricted at
present as well.'

Sarah left them to transfer her young patient to
her room and stopped back at the central desk to
write up her admission notes. She would have to
come back later to fill in details missing from the

admission history. Right now both mother and child needed a rest.

Angela appeared, still carrying the baby who now bestowed a beaming smile on Sarah. Sarah smiled back but felt a familiar wrench. Six-month-old baby Jack was waiting for surgery to start the reconstructive process on a seriously cleft lip and palate. His smile was split in the middle right up to his nose. The plate he had worn over his gums and palate for months in preparation for the surgery had wires which extended out over both cheeks.

The surgery was booked for early the following week. Jack was in for the day for assessment to check that he was fit for an anaesthetic and to have blood tests. He was also to be seen by an ENT surgeon due to the repeated ear infections to which he was prone because of the deformity.

Sarah smiled again. 'You're going to look like a completely different baby next week, Jack. Isn't that great?'

Angela sat the baby on the desk beside Sarah. 'How did your puncture go?'

'Brilliantly. She's a great kid.' Sarah moved the test tubes beside her out of the baby's reach. 'Can you get these off to the lab straight away?'

'Of course. Have you seen Anthony yet?'

'No.' Sarah twirled her chair and scooted across to the trolley that housed patient notes. 'I want to check this morning's lab results. I think he can go onto oral therapy now.'

'They haven't been filed yet.' Angela riffled through an in-basket of result forms. 'His temperature was normal this morning.'

'Good. He'll be much happier when he's mobile.'

'Ah, but will we?'

Sarah grinned. 'You'll cope.' Standing, Sarah stretched her back. 'Why is it so quiet in here at the moment? Not that I'm complaining!'

'It's 2 p.m.,' Angela pointed out. 'Rest time.'

From 1 till 2:30 p.m. the ward assumed a mantle of peace that staff tried hard to enforce. It was the only time of day that visitors were not welcome and staff visits were kept to emergencies only.

'I suppose Alice is asleep?' Sarah queried.

Angela nodded. 'So's Isobel. I just checked on them.'

'I'll leave visiting till later, then.' Sarah sighed. 'I wish I had some good news to give them.' She glanced away. 'What's Michael doing out of bed?'

Angela echoed Sarah's sigh. 'He's really down today.'

Sarah eyed the boy, sitting slouched in a wheelchair at the far end of the corridor. Ten years old, Michael was having a difficult time, coming to terms with the amputation of his leg following a car accident. Convinced he would never play his beloved football again, he had withdrawn into angry, uncooperative behaviour. A stump infection had delayed his discharge and Michael refused to be encouraged by anyone.

'Right. It's time we did something about this.' Grinning at Angela, Sarah reached up to a high shelf and produced a black plastic skull cap complete with large round ears. She jammed it on her head and walked purposely towards Michael.

Dropping to her haunches beside the boy in the wheelchair, Sarah eyed the quiet expanse of floor in front of them.

'I'll bet you can't go faster than me down to the end of the corridor even if I just walk.'

'Course I can.' Michael's tone was disinterested but Sarah noted that both hands inched towards the top of his wheels.

'Bet you can't!'

'Can too. Even if you run.'

'I'm not going to run.'

Michael eyed her suspiciously. 'Promise?'

'Of course.' Sarah tucked her hair behind her ears. 'Running inside is not ladylike. Are you on, then?'

'I guess.'

'Right. Ready? Go!' Sarah started slowly but rapidly increased her pace to try and keep up. She broke into a run as they passed the central desk but Michael was way ahead of her. He braked hard as he reached the last door and turned swiftly. Sarah slowed to a walk again but not quickly enough.

'Cheat!' The delighted crow echoed down the corridor. 'You ran! I saw you!'

'Yeah. I guess I'm not so ladylike.' Catching Angela's eye, she saw the smile as well as a disapproving head shake. The grin on Michael's face was so good to see that Sarah ignored the silent remonstration of her breach of rest time. She grinned at Michael. 'Want to go again?'

'Sure.'

They turned to assume starting positions but Sarah's smile faded as she saw the group of people advancing on them. All men, all well dressed. All heading for Alice Forster's room. It spelled trouble.

'I'm sorry, Michael. I'll have to do this later.'

Michael shrugged, his smile gone. Sarah leaned close to his ear.

'Next time I'm going to run as fast as I can and I'll beat the wheels off you.' She caught the flicker of a grin as she moved after the men. She saw that Isobel Forster had emerged from her daughter's room and had closed the door protectively behind her. As Sarah passed the lifts the doors opened. Paul Henderson and Martin Lynch appeared beside her. Sarah was moving at a rapid pace but Paul Henderson's long strides overtook her in no time.

'Let me handle this, Dr Kendall.'

'No way,' Sarah snarled. 'I know what they're here for.'

Paul caught Sarah's arm and forced her to a halt. 'I'm quite aware of why they're here and I'm asking you to let me handle what is essentially a management concern.'

Sarah jerked her arm free but she could still feel the pressure of his fingers. She noticed the transformation effected by the neatly knotted tie, recently combed hair and the tweed jacket now worn by the manager. He would fit right in with all the other sharks now gathering.

'You want me to stand back so you can help them destroy the only quality left in a child's life.' Sarah deliberately kept her voice down but Paul's words were even quieter.

'No. I'm asking you to stand back because they may be less than impressed, being ordered about by someone wearing a Bart Simpson sweatshirt and Mickey Mouse ears!'

Sarah gasped. She had completely forgotten her headgear. She snatched it off but found she could only follow in the wake of the two new arrivals. She joined the edge of the group now gathered in front of Alice's room as introductions were finishing between Simon Forster, his solicitors and the hospital representatives.

'I'm sorry, gentlemen,' Paul Henderson informed the group. 'We've had to change our plans. Alice Forster's condition has deteriorated to the point where we are unable to discharge her.'

Sarah's eyes widened with alarm. Why had she not been informed? Catching Isobel's eye, she realised that Alice's mother was just as surprised as she was. What was going on?

'That was not the case when we spoke this morning, Mr Henderson.' The solicitor's tone was wary.

'Medical conditions such as this are subject to rapid change. A review was called for early this afternoon and it is the opinion of the paediatric consultants involved that the child should not be moved. Is that correct, Dr Lynch?'

Martin Lynch nodded. The older man caught Sarah's astonished gaze and his look warned her to remain silent.

Paul spoke more firmly. 'Management is going to back this decision and is quite prepared to take the case back to court if necessary.'

Sarah caught Isobel's eye again and they exchanged another look of astonishment.

'That is exactly what will be necessary,' the so-

licitor said crisply. His associates nodded their
agreement. 'I can assure you the resultant publicity
will not be welcomed by the hospital, Mr
Henderson. It will also be expensive.'

Paul Henderson stepped closer to the speaker. He
looked down at the younger man. 'I doubt very
much that the publicity will be welcomed by your
client either.'

'Simon Forster is a father who is simply desperate for a last chance to be with his child. He has
been unable to overcome the obstructions placed in
his way. The court has already demonstrated its
sympathy to his cause.'

Paul lowered his voice. 'They may be less sympathetic when they learn that Simon Forster has
made no effort up till now to be with his child and,
in fact, refused to allow himself to be tested as a
possible bone-marrow donor, which was his daughter's only hope of a cure to this disease.'

The look that Simon Forster received from his
legal advisors suggested that no mention had been
made of these facts. Paul stepped back to stand beside Isobel Forster.

Sarah was stunned. She was quite sure that Alice
Forster's condition had not changed. She watched
as Simon Forster and his legal representatives retreated. Martin Lynch excused himself and Isobel
returned to her daughter's room. Left alone with
Paul Henderson, Sarah felt awkward.

'What made you change your mind?'

'Perhaps management isn't quite as unfeelingly
bureaucratic as you'd like to believe, Dr Kendall.'

'Perhaps it's more a case of the squeaky door getting some oil,' Sarah responded.

'Are you suggesting that I should not have responded to your intervention?' The hint of the smile Sarah had glimpsed that morning was now much more developed. 'Would you like to argue your way into changing the situation again?'

Sarah grinned reluctantly. 'No, thanks. What I meant was perhaps you just need enlightenment on other cases as well.'

'Are you offering?'

Sarah looked up to meet an intense gaze. They were standing close together. Almost as close as they had been that morning. The sparks were no longer flying but there was a heat Sarah felt very tempted to stir up.

'What do you mean?'

'Have dinner with me. Let loose a few more of your views on management. I'll see if I can defend my side of the war zone.'

Sarah tossed back her hair. 'That's a challenge I'll have to accept. I can only see that as my duty as a doctor.'

Paul Henderson smiled again. 'I'll ring you later. Right now I think you have a patient waiting. It looks serious.'

Sarah looked around to see Michael, glowering at her from his wheelchair. She hid a smile.

'You're right. It is serious. You'll have to excuse me.' Sarah raised her Mickey Mouse ears in farewell, before settling them firmly back onto her head.

'OK, Michael. There is absolutely no way you're going to beat me this time.'

CHAPTER TWO

IT WAS an afternoon for triumphs. Large and small.

Flushed with the success of beating Sarah three times in a row, Michael had even greeted his physiotherapist, Cheryl, with a smile when the increase in activity signalled the end of the ward's rest period.

Cheryl caught Sarah's eye in surprised acknowledgement of the boy's mood change. Sarah grinned in response and then crouched beside Michael.

'We haven't finished this contest yet,' she warned. Her gaze flicked up to meet Cheryl's again. 'What is it today, Cheryl? Crutches?'

'Sure is.' Cheryl's cheerful tone belied the struggle she was having, working with Michael. Up till now he had refused point blank to even attempt walking, and Sarah knew that the last effort on the part of the long-suffering physio had resulted in the crutches being hurled across the room. His artificial leg was already being made but Michael's attitude made its immediate usefulness questionable.

'Right.' Sarah nodded. 'That's great. Can you bring up a pair my size tomorrow as well?'

Cheryl nodded, bemused. Sarah gave Michael a stern look.

'That's going to be tomorrow's race, kid. You and me. On crutches. Same time, same place.'

Sarah rose smoothly and waved, without giving Michael any time for a response. 'See you then.'

The visit to Alice Forster's room was a time of quiet celebration between mother and doctor, a release from the stress of the last few days, which had escalated ever since they had learned of Simon Forster's legal bid to gain custody of his daughter. Alice was still asleep. Sarah bent and kissed the puffy cheek of the tiny girl and automatically checked her subcutaneous infusion line, running her finger gently down the tubing. It was a pump system that allowed Alice to control the amount of pain relief she received. So far, it was working well.

Isobel watched quietly from her position at the window and Sarah moved to give her a hug. Over the many traumatic admissions the two women had become good friends and Sarah shared the heartbreak of this current and probably final time they had together.

She looked at the young mother with concern. 'You look all in, Isobel. You should take a break while Alice is asleep. One of the nurses could stay with her.'

'I need to be here when she wakes up,' Isobel replied quietly. 'I don't want her to ever open her eyes and not see that I'm here with her.'

Sarah hugged her again. 'And that's exactly where you're going to be. You're safe now.'

'Thanks to you. What did you say to that manager to make them change their minds?'

Sarah grinned a little shamefacedly. 'Quite a few things.' her grin faded. 'I didn't think he had listened but I was wrong—thank goodness.'

Isobel sighed. 'It would have been nice to take her home one last time. But after this I couldn't cope—not without your support and knowing we're in a place we're safe.'

Sarah glanced around the small room. 'It looks like a home to me.'

The walls had been covered with posters and pictures drawn by Alice's classmates. Cards from friends and colourful mobiles hung from strings across the room. A television set and VCR stood in a corner, a stack of her favourite movies and recordings of shows beside it. The entertainment was often a vital distraction in the long hours of a sleepless night.

A borrowed trolley was covered in books and games, stuffed toys and dolls sat in heaps on the floor and the end of Alice's bed and a procession of plastic ducks covered the entire window-sill. Ducks were a huge favourite with Alice. A treasured soft yellow velvet one was tucked in its usual spot in the crook of her right elbow. *The Story of Ping* was lying face down on her bed, still open at the point at which she had fallen asleep. Sarah smiled. She had read that one to Alice herself on several occasions.

'Oh, I forgot to give you something this morning.' Sarah fished in her white coat pocket and carefully unfolded a piece of glossy paper. 'It's a fantastic picture of a duckling. I found it in a medical journal, of all places. I was reading it at breakfast.'

'She'll love it.' Isobel smiled her thanks.

'Have you seen any ducks today?' The window of Alice's room overlooked the river. A large armchair was positioned so that many hours could be comfortably spent with Alice in her mother's arms, watching the activity near and on the water.

'No. I've been too worried to— What on earth is that awful noise?'

Sarah's eyes widened in horror. 'Somebody's certainly having a good wobbly.'

The crescendo of shrieks was appalling.

'Good grief!' Isobel cast an anxious glance at Alice who stirred slightly.

Sarah thought of Charlotte Newman, trying to rest in her darkened room. This was not going to help.

Excusing herself, Sarah marched purposefully towards the dreadful noise. She knew it was Anthony even before she entered the playroom and found the large three-year-old hurling toys and screaming. His mother was in tears, pleading with Anthony to 'be a good boy and swallow your medicine'. A grim-faced Judith stood beside her, holding a medicine glass.

Sarah couldn't help grinning at Judith. 'Not much wrong with his lungs now, is there?'

Judith spoke through clenched teeth. 'I believe it was your idea he went onto oral therapy?'

'Yeah.' Sarah rolled her eyes and took the glass of pink liquid from Judith. 'Get Mum out of here for a minute, Jude. I'll see what I can do.'

Left alone, Sarah ignored the boy and his tantrum. Instead, she ran to a stuffed bear which Anthony had been beating against the table, before discarding it with force.

'Oh, no!' she said in tones of horror. 'Poor

teddy!' Sarah threw herself onto her knees, cradling
the bear, aware that Anthony was watching her. His
volume had increased, if anything, on finding he
was being ignored.

'Have you got a broken arm? Leg? Is it your
ear?' Sarah focused her attention on the bear. 'I
have just what you need, teddy.'

The packet of jellybeans that came out of her
pocket signalled an abrupt end to Anthony's
screams. He moved closer.

'First you have to take your medicine,' Sarah told
the bear firmly. She held the small plastic container
against the toy's mouth and pretended to tip. 'Well
done! What colour jellybean would you like? Red?
Green? Ah, a blue one.'

'Red.'

Sarah turned her head quizzically. 'Oh, would
you like a red jellybean, Anthony?' She feigned
surprise. 'You have to swallow the medicine first,
like teddy did. Can you do that?'

After hesitating briefly, Anthony nodded. As
Sarah dispensed the red jellybean she held up the
empty container and grinned triumphantly at the
window of the playroom where both Anthony's
mother and Judith were watching. The boy's mother
rushed back to her son with relief.

Judith caught Sarah's eye. 'Expect a beep in
about six hours when he needs his next dose.'

'Hmm. He looks almost well enough for discharge, don't you think?'

'Absolutely.' Judith chuckled. 'Martin Lynch is
down in the office. Have a chat to him about it. He
was looking for you.'

Sarah bit her lip. 'He probably wants to discuss the little scene I had with management this morning.'

'Could be.' Judith gave her an unsympathetic shove. 'Go and get it over with—and don't forget about Anthony.'

'As if I could.'

Sarah found her consultant in the staff kitchen. She followed his example and made herself a cup of coffee. Realising she had missed lunch, she also raided the biscuit tin. 'You seem to have made quite an impression on Paul Henderson.' The older man's tone was amused.

'Oh?' Sarah concentrated on stirring her coffee. She noted the thump and increase in her heart rate at the mention of his name. A vivid image of him, towering over her in his office, sprang to mind and Sarah felt the heat of a blush prickle the back of her neck. 'I'm surprised he changed his mind about Alice.'

'I'm not.' Martin Lynch smiled at his senior registrar. 'But I'll say no more about that.' He shook his head gently. 'I'm going to miss having you around, Sarah. Have you decided what you're going to do next month when your run with us finishes?'

'No.' Sarah swallowed the last piece of her biscuit. 'There's an opening in Neonatal Intensive Care but I'm not sure I want to go back there. It's pretty draining stuff. I'm filling in there with some nights on call at the moment and even that's a bit much.'

Martin Lynch nodded. 'Working with children

and babies is emotionally difficult. And you do tend to get too involved, Sarah. It's not good for you.'

'And not good for my patients?'

'I didn't say that. You're a superb doctor, Sarah. The best registrar I've ever had. But what sort of life have you got for yourself? The way you get so involved here it makes me wonder whether you have any personal life at all.'

'It's terrific,' Sarah assured him. 'Every chance I get I'm working on my research papers for you and those fascinating case reports you keep wanting me to write up and submit to the journals.'

Martin laughed. 'Don't forget the presentation you're doing for Friday's lunchtime meeting.' He sobered quickly. 'Is it that bad, Sarah?'

Sarah sighed. 'I'm beginning to wonder.'

'Maybe you should take a few weeks off at the end of this run—have a think about what direction you want to go in. I'll do whatever I can to help you when you do decide. My offer of part-time work at my private clinic is still open, you know.'

'Thanks, Martin.' Sarah rinsed her cup and then smiled. 'I'll need a few weeks just to finish all the paperwork you've given me.'

Martin frowned. 'That reminds me, I've given Angela a large stack of results that need tabling for the paper on the effects of low-dose medication on preventing recurrence of febrile seizures. I'd really like to get it away this month. Would you like me to take over the writing?'

'And lose first authorship? No way.' Sarah shook back her hair. 'I'll manage.'

They walked out of the kitchen together. Sarah

had passed on the decision of whether to discharge Anthony by the time they reached the office. Angela waved a result form at Sarah.

'First bloods back on Charlotte Newman. Looks like you were right, Sarah.'

'What about?' enquired Martin.

'Case of meningococcal meningitis,' Sarah informed him. 'I'm just going to review her now.'

'I'll come with you.' The consultant turned to Angela. 'Can you restrain young Anthony, please? I'll examine him with a view to discharge in a few minutes.'

Sarah caught Angela's expression and smiled. Another good outcome likely. All things considered, it had really been quite an extraordinary day.

When her beeper later heralded a call from Paul Henderson, confirming their dinner arrangement, Sarah had to take a deep breath and remind herself that the day was not yet over.

Only a year ago the muted decor and peaceful solitude of the small, high-rise apartment had seemed a haven. Now it was little short of being oppressive. Sarah dropped her large canvas shoulder-bag onto the oversized cream sofa as she hurried past. Several journals, pens, a floppy disk and the sheaf of lab results that needed tabling slid out to land on the pale pink carpet. Sarah ignored them.

Stepping out of the shower a few minutes later, Sarah wrapped a towel around her hair and by-passed the pile of clothes on the floor. Then she sighed, turned and scooped up the pile, depositing it firmly in the laundry basket. Catching sight of her sweatshirt, Sarah shook her head. Bart Simpson clothing and a Mickey Mouse hat. Well, that was an impression she had every intention of blotting out.

Easing on the sheer black tights that completed a set of sensuous lingerie, Sarah was aware of the knot of excitement centred a little lower than her stomach—excitement that Sarah Kendall had not associated with a man for many years. Her career had always been her priority. Was it just because she was feeling dissatisfied with the direction her life was taking that she was feeling this way now? Or was it just that she had finally met a man whose attractions she couldn't resist?

'It's purely an intellectual attraction,' she told herself as she chose the most sophisticated dress she could find in her wardrobe. Slipping on the sleek-fitting, black short-sleeved dress, Sarah was delighted to find it was still a perfect fit. Goodness knows how long it was since she had last worn it. She added a string of tiny pearls to follow the curve of the rounded neckline.

Armed with a hair-dryer, Sarah swept her over-long fringe out of her eyes and turned the ends of her hair under so that it hung just above her shoulders and swung in a smooth curtain when she moved her head. Hurriedly, she redid her make-up, put in some pearl stud earrings and eased her feet into the black high-heeled court shoes. At five feet-six she had no need of the extra height and no doubt her arches would not be thanking her later, but Sarah was determined to present an ultimately feminine image.

Simply tactics, she reasoned. It was Paul, after all, who had described their opposing views as a war zone. After this morning he was hardly likely to expect sophistication. Throwing his expectations off balance could only be to her advantage. In fact, it was surprising that he hadn't suggested meeting at the Pizza Hut or McDonald's instead of the up-market French restaurant they had agreed on. Sarah grabbed a light evening jacket and bag and quickly locked up her apartment. Another advantage might be to arrive at the restaurant a few minutes early.

Sarah did arrive early at the restaurant but not as early as Paul. He got to his feet lazily as the waiter showed Sarah to the quiet corner table, his dinner jacket and immaculate grooming as appropriate to the elegant setting as her own attire. But Paul Henderson had gone one better. As the musky scent of his aftershave greeted Sarah's appreciative nostrils she realised she had completely forgotten to apply any perfume. She cursed inwardly even as she smilingly accepted the proffered glass of champagne.

'How did you know I liked champagne, Mr Henderson?'

'I didn't.' He cocked an eyebrow. 'I thought you might like something to argue about—to break the ice, as it were.' The smile was teasing. 'Ordering something, without letting you have your say, seemed like an ideal way to accomplish it. *Dr Kendall*,' Paul added, the emphasis on her title tempered by what Sarah now realised was a rather charming smile.

'You can call me Sarah,' she offered, returning the smile. 'Actually, I love champagne.'

Paul raised his glass in a toast and Sarah drew in a long breath as the crystal clinked musically. Ice might be more appropriate than anything to break it with, she thought with dismay. The room must be over-heated. That was a far more acceptable reason for the increased heart rate and flushed skin Sarah was experiencing than the effect of a man she had met only hours previously.

'It's rather warm in here, don't you think?'

'Just right for me.'

The steady gaze of the dark blue eyes made Sarah uncomfortably suspicious that Paul knew exactly how she was feeling—and the real reason why. She shook back her hair.

'I'm surprised. Isn't being cold-blooded a prerequisite for a position in management? I would expect you to be more affected by heat.'

'We thrive on it.' Paul leaned across the table. 'In fact, we need a certain amount to even get moving. We lie about in our offices, just hoping that some hot-blooded medico is going to come storming in and generate enough heat to stimulate some action.'

Sarah laughed. Her contagious gurgle was enough to make heads turn at a neighbouring table, smiling in response to the sound.

'I suppose I ought to apologise.'

'Please don't.' Paul drew the champagne bottle from its nest of ice in the silver bucket. 'It's not often that an incredibly attractive and incredibly angry woman bursts into my office and rants at me on someone else's behalf.'

Sarah held up her glass as he spoke and Paul put the neck of the bottle to its rim. The glass shook slightly and Paul's other hand closed over Sarah's to hold it steady. The hiss of escaping bubbles was not masked by Paul's soft words.

'It could be the most exciting thing that's ever happened to me.'

The glass was full but Paul did not release either her hand or her gaze. Sarah swallowed hard.

'I wasn't going to.'

'Burst in?'

'No—apologise.'

Paul's laughter broke the increasing tension the touch of their hands had evoked. Sarah concentrated hard not to spill her wine as he finally released her hand.

'The end justifies the means, I take it?' His smile was again teasing.

'In this case, absolutely.'

Paul looked around as the three-piece band started some unobtrusive, romantic background music.

'Do you dance, Dr Kendall?'

'Not often, Mr Henderson. Do you?'

'Almost never.' He held her gaze. 'Shall we?'

'Why not?'

Sarah found she could think of several reasons the instant Paul Henderson's hands touched her body. The air around them seemed alive with a sexual tension she found frightening. She had only just met the man, for heaven's sake, but her feelings were so powerful she felt she would betray them if she relaxed even slightly. They moved awkwardly, out of time to the music, and both seemed relieved to break off and return to their table where they spent several minutes in silence, studying and making selections from the menu.

The silence continued. And grew. By the time their entrées were served it was decidedly uncomfortable. Sarah found it unbearable but couldn't think of a way to break it. Paul seemed nervous. Even though she knew virtually nothing about the man, sitting opposite her, Sarah sensed that his nerves were completely out of character. They both ignored the food on the table. Sarah was reaching down beside her chair for her evening bag, on the point of excusing herself to visit the rest-room, when Paul suddenly cleared his throat.

'Do you believe in love at first sight, Sarah Kendall?'

Sarah dropped the bag. 'No,' she responded quickly. Then her eyes met the intense stare directed at her. She felt drawn into the gaze as though by a magnetic force. She was enveloped in it, captured by its intensity and the answering response she felt to it. Her voice was now a whisper. 'That is, I never thought…' The whisper faded.

'I would have said no as well—' Paul filled the silence quickly '—yesterday. Now I'm not so sure.' He frowned slightly. 'I'm not talking about sexual attraction, here, Sarah—however powerful I recognise that can be. I'm talking about something more…' He searched for the word he wanted. 'More profound.' Paul leaned across the small table again. 'I find you profoundly disturbing, Dr Sarah Kendall.'

Sarah laughed nervously. 'Gee, thanks,' she quipped. Then she sobered. She knew it had been a struggle for Paul to say what he had. To reveal his feelings on such a personal level. Suddenly she was in a position of power over a man she had met only that morning—one she had seen only as a powerful adversary. The power she had now been handed was on a different level, certainly, but it was no less real and its significance was frightening.

'I don't claim to be intuitive,' Paul said quietly, 'and I don't think I'm entirely egotistical, but it seems to me there's something a little unusual happening here. Either what I'm feeling is being simply reflected back at me or there's a possibility that you're experiencing something similar.' His look held an apology. 'Perhaps I'm making a fool of myself. You can tell me if I am. I can take it.' His mouth curved into a half-smile. 'It's another prerequisite of being a manager.'

This was crazy, Sarah thought. She was caught in an emotional tidal wave which reason told her was simply not possible. Yet it was happening, and part of her had no desire to fight it. A large part of her.

'You're not making a fool of yourself, Paul,' she finally answered a little shakily. 'But it's too fast— too big. It's frightening. We don't even know each other.'

'Sarah Margaret Kendall, age thirty-three. Majored in education and child psychology, gaining a double degree with distinction before entering

medical school, from which graduation was also
with distinction. Reports from all specialties worked
in are outstanding, particularly Paediatrics, the current run in which is due to expire next month.

'The only reservation held by consultants is that
Sarah Kendall is inclined to become too emotionally involved with her case-load. She is highly recommended for a consultancy position if applied for
but the impression given is that she may wish to
proceed in another direction. Sarah Kendall is, for
some inexplicable reason, single, lives alone and is
quite probably the most beautiful woman on earth.'

Sarah grinned. 'You didn't get that last bit off
my file.' She sat back, feeling the tension ease a
little. 'OK. Fair's fair. Where do I get the file on
you?'

Paul's smile was calculating. 'Perhaps I should
retain a certain air of mystery. It might make me
more attractive.'

'I wouldn't worry about that,' Sarah muttered
darkly.

'Suits me.' The smile became almost smug.
'What is it you'd like to know?'

Sarah's query was prevented by the arrival of an
unhappy-looking waiter.

'There is something wrong with your soup? Sir?
Madam?'

Sarah and Paul looked at each other guiltily.
They had completely forgotten their entrées.

'I'm sorry,' Paul said smoothly. 'There is nothing
wrong with the soup. We were—ah—distracted.'
He caught Sarah's eye again and they both suppressed smiles.

'I understand, sir.' The waiter's eyebrows moved fractionally. 'Would you like some more soup or shall I serve your main course?'

'The main course, thank you,' Paul responded. 'I don't think either of us really needs an entrée, do we, Sarah?'

The double meaning may have been lost on the waiter but Sarah understood only too well. She swallowed hard. The birth of their relationship had been fiery. It had already escalated into what, for Sarah, was unknown territory. Should she simply allow it to happen? And what would happen? A tumultuous ending perhaps with scars on both sides? Or was the bridled passion something that could grow and eclipse the shadows of the unknown? That possibility was too important to compromise.

'No,' Sarah agreed quietly. 'We don't need an entrée.'

CHAPTER THREE

THE outpatient visit had been more for the mother's benefit than the child's.

Having dispensed explanations and reassurance over the period of what had become a lengthy visit, Sarah had to force herself to concentrate on her task. The odd but very pleasurable tingle that announced her mind was slipping back to last night's dinner—or, rather, what had happened afterwards—simply had to be overruled.

'I've checked Chelsea over very carefully, Mrs Ross,' Sarah announced. 'There's no evidence of any physical abnormality or developmental problems. Basically, she's a very healthy little girl. The fact that she's had febrile convulsions doesn't necessarily mean that she's epileptic.'

'But she's had two!' Mrs Ross said for the third time. 'And one of them was that horrible long one. It went on for hours! I was so sure she was going to die!'

'Prolonged seizures are very distressing. Even the twenty minutes or so that Chelsea suffered can seem much longer. Most of them are, however, a child's first febrile convulsion, as it was in Chelsea's case. The risk of recurrence of prolonged episodes is very low, about one to four per cent. They are far more likely to last only thirty seconds

46

to a few minutes as Chelsea's recent convulsion did.'

Mrs Ross wasn't convinced and shook her head in disbelief. Sarah sighed inwardly.

'Chelsea hasn't suffered more than one convulsion during each period she has been running a high temperature. She was admitted to hospital after her first seizure and the investigations were very thorough. We have, in fact, just completed a study that suggests low-dose medication has no effect on the possible recurrence of seizures. When you move to higher doses you get into problems with side-effects. You have no family history of epilepsy and there is no evidence of any abnormal development. I don't feel there is an indication at present that Chelsea should be on long-term, continuous medication.

'As I said, we'll give you some diazepam suppositories which can be used in the unlikely event that Chelsea has another seizure lasting more than five minutes. Are you sure you understand what I told you about their administration?'

Mrs Ross nodded. She looked a little happier at being reminded of the emergency medication.

'If that should happen then certainly we would look at continuous medication, but in the meantime you can take measures to help prevent this happening again, Mrs Ross.' Sarah spoke encouragingly. 'If you have any suspicion that Chelsea is running a fever then take her temperature. If it's up at all give her some paracetamol, remove any warm clothing and sponge her down with a damp cloth. Don't use cold water or fans, though, because that will make her shiver and actually raise her temperature. It's not a guarantee to prevent recurrence but it can certainly help.'

Sarah glanced over at the toddler who was happily sifting through the basket of toys in the corner of the examination room. She knew there was a waiting room full of people outside and she was desperate for a cup of coffee after this, her third case of the clinic.

'We'll review Chelsea in three months, Mrs Ross, unless there's a problem, of course. Your GP can contact us at any time.' Sarah stood up, signalling an end to the interview. She handed over the prescription she had written, whilst talking. 'I'm confident you won't need to use this but having it available should certainly help your peace of mind.'

The outpatients' senior nurse came in as Mrs Ross left with her daughter. She handed Sarah a cup of coffee.

'You've got two minutes till I send in the next one,' she warned. 'Let's hope they're not all as anxious as Mrs Ross!'

Two minutes. Sarah closed her eyes and blissfully let her mind escape back in time. What an amazing evening! That second dance they'd had before their main course had been served... Suddenly their bodies had melded together as one fluid unit with not a hint of the earlier stilted movement. The main course had arrived, and had been ignored. The chef had been the one to enquire what was wrong at that point. Both too inebriated with emotion to be embarrassed, Paul and Sarah had paid the bill and escaped the restaurant.

Whose idea had it been that they went back to her apartment? Sarah couldn't remember. The pleasurable tingle became almost pain as Sarah relived the next part of the evening. If their bodies had melded together on the dance floor so well, it had been a pale shadow of the union of their lovemaking.

'Oh, God!' Sarah groaned, feeling herself blush furiously. 'On a first date, too!'

Never in her life had she allowed things to happen at such an extraordinary pace but, then, she had never in her life felt this way about anyone else. It had seemed so wrong but at the same time so absolutely right. It had only been during the drowsy peace of spent passion that Sarah had realised she still knew nothing about this man. And she hadn't had the chance to talk then.

Paul's departure from her bed and her apartment had been distressingly abrupt. His reasoning that he couldn't turn up at work in his dinner jacket hadn't really excused his haste, but his final lengthy kiss and whispered words had.

'I may have only met you for the first time this morning, Sarah Kendall, but I feel like I've known you in my heart for a very long time.'

The kiss had stifled any reply but Sarah could only have agreed. It had to be some sort of magic and, as such, Sarah suspected it could vanish as quickly as it had appeared. Even if it did, she could never regret having experienced it. It was more than falling in love. It was—

It was young Lawrence West, a child who was failing to thrive and suffered from recurrent respi-

ratory infections. He was going to need comprehensive examination and investigation for the possibility of cystic fibrosis. Sarah could only hope that
her consultant was moving his share of the patient
load through at a faster pace, otherwise they would
have no hope of finishing this clinic by lunchtime.

In fact, it was one o'clock by the time Sarah
headed in the direction of Ward 23. She had a date
with another young boy and a pair of crutches,
which she had no intention of missing for anybody.

Well, almost anybody. Seeing Paul striding towards her in the busy main floor corridor, Sarah's
step faltered and her skin flushed with confusion.
How could they act normally after last night? What
if he thought that was a typical first date on her
part? Confusion was replaced by embarrassment
and Sarah concluded that attack had to be the best
form of defence.

'So, you did make it in eventually.'

'What do you mean?' Paul came to a halt, standing very close to her. Sarah didn't move back.

'I went up to your office at 8 a.m. I was dropping
in Alice Forster's notes. You said you wanted to
look at them in case of legal repercussions?'

Paul nodded. 'I got them. Thanks.'

'Well, your secretary tells me you're never in
before nine.'

He nodded again. 'Is that a problem?'

Sarah laughed. 'Not at all. Nice work if you can
get it!'

'Too right.' Paul leaned even closer. 'I think I'm
going to have to kiss you. Right now.'

'No way!' Sarah took a step back and glanced

nervously over her shoulder. 'I have to go. I have a very important appointment.'

'What are you doing tonight?'

Sarah's pulse rate zoomed up as she caught the look of desire in those amazingly blue eyes. It corresponded with a distinct thump in the region of her lower abdomen. She knew what she'd like to be doing tonight.

'I'm on call,' she said sadly. 'Neonatal Intensive Care. I'll be here all night.'

Paul smiled at her tone. 'Never mind,' he consoled her. 'There'll be another time.'

'You bet,' Sarah said. 'And not just for what you're thinking about, Paul Henderson. I still know absolutely nothing about you.'

Paul's eyebrows lifted suggestively but Sarah ignored the innuendo and began to move away.

'And what's more, I haven't even begun to give you my views on hospital management.'

Paul's smile was decidedly smug, Sarah thought. Once again he had the upper hand. Why was it that Sarah felt he was so completely in control of this situation? That he was creating the magic that had her caught so completely in its spell?

Angela waved at Sarah as she hurried through the ward.

'I was just going to beep you. Michael's been waiting there for ten minutes. He won't even sit down. Here...' Angela reached into the store cupboard and produced the adult-sized pair of crutches. 'And try not to make too much noise, please. It is rest time.'

Sarah grinned. She knew Angela was just as thrilled as she was at the breakthrough with Michael. They were, however, much quieter today. Sarah tucked one leg up behind her and hopped beside the boy who made a valiant effort, despite tiring halfway down the corridor. She deliberately made her own effort even more awkward.

'You cheated again,' he accused her. 'You let me win.'

'You deserved to,' Sarah told him. 'It was much harder work for you.' She gave him a hug. 'Well done, Michael. I'm proud of you.'

He looked mollified. 'I'll get faster,' he stated. 'I just need more practice.'

'Absolutely,' Sarah agreed. 'But have lots of rests too, though. Same time tomorrow?'

'Yeah, I guess.'

Alice wasn't asleep this afternoon. She lay in her mother's arms, the blue shadowing under her eyes indicating a bad spell. Sarah kissed her gently.

'Seen any ducks today, darling?'

Alice nodded slowly. 'Six,' she whispered. 'But no ducklings yet.'

'Maybe tomorrow.' Sarah smiled. She caught Isobel's eye. They both knew it was the wrong time of year for ducklings but it was too hard not to allow Alice some hope of a fervent wish. Isobel's eyes were also heavily shadowed.

'Bad night?' Sarah queried unnecessarily. At Isobel's nod she pressed her lips together thoughtfully. 'We might need to increase the morphine dose in the infusion and make it continuous,' she said quietly, stroking the bald head of the child in Isobel's arms. 'Where is it hurting, sweetheart? Is it your legs again?'

'It was my tummy,' Alice said, 'but it's better now.' She closed her eyes, easing her head back onto her mother's shoulder.

Sarah waited until Alice was asleep, before discussing the potential bowel and bladder problems her young patient might be facing due to her degree of debility and the pain relief she needed. They both agreed that any invasive procedures had to be avoided unless the problems became unbearable. Sarah charted a very mild laxative when she returned to the ward office. Her familiar sadness at the Forsters' situation was increased, if anything, today by the personal happiness that had burst into her own life.

It was because of Alice Forster that this has happened, she realised suddenly. Would it be too much to expect a little of the magic to rub off on her?

The stress of the neonatal intensive care unit was particularly noticeable that evening—so many tiny scraps of humanity, fighting the odds for survival, a few disbelieving parents, keeping a late vigil by the incubators. Sarah hated to see the impossibly small babies on life support systems, attached by so many wires and tubes to the ventilators and monitoring systems. She recognised that she felt it too keenly. While she knew her performance was still better than average in this area she also knew that it wasn't a place she wanted to be in the long term.

What did she want long term? Sarah loved her

work with children, loved the interaction with their families. But it wasn't enough. With each discharge she felt a loss, a termination of her care which seemed unsatisfying. If she was lucky she might see them again in an outpatient clinic but more often than not they simply vanished from her life. There were plenty more to take their place, of course, but the overall effect was draining. Sarah knew she gave too much. She made repeated efforts to keep her involvement purely professional, but then an Alice Forster or a Michael came along and she was lost again.

There was the research as well, and Sarah loved the academic side to her job. There was immense satisfaction to be gained by collecting, analysing and forming conclusions about data that might be of direct benefit to others. Even the writing was satisfying when she finally found the time to do it. Writing a textbook was another attractive possibility, but on its own it would still be not enough.

Sarah Kendall was searching for a focus in her life. It was what made her reaction to meeting Paul Henderson so frightening. The thought that she may have found something which she had unknowingly been searching for wasn't something she was ready to admit, even to herself, because she couldn't know whether it was to be trusted. To know that it was so central to her life and then to lose it would be far worse than not knowing.

She could admit to sexual attraction, the passion she had never known she was capable of. She could admit to being in love. That was reasonable even given the short time frame. What wasn't reasonable was to suggest that it could be the core of her future happiness and satisfaction with life. That was simply too dangerous to be reasonable.

The nagging feeling that the significance of this new relationship was too great added an underlying stress level that her evening's work only increased. When her beeper went again shortly after 9 p.m. Sarah felt bone weary and her tone was dispirited when she punched the buttons for the telephone number her pager displayed. It was not a number she recognised.

'Sarah Kendall.'

'I love you, Sarah.'

It was the last thing Sarah had expected to hear, and her weariness evaporated instantly. Excitement took its place.

'Hello, Paul. Where are you?' The call had been internal.

'In my office. We had an emergency meeting thanks to this threatened strike by the cleaners. Can I buy you a coffee?'

'Actually, I'd love some fresh air. I'll meet you in the courtyard in front of your block.'

The crisp night air was refreshing but any chill Sarah experienced was negated by the warmth of Paul's body as he took her in his arms. His lips met hers with a gentle greeting that quickly spiralled into a reminder of last night's passion. Sarah responded avidly to the silken caress of his tongue and lips, needing no encouragement to press the length of her body against his. Paul's desire was obvious but Sarah knew it couldn't be any greater than her own. It took a supreme effort to push herself away.

'This isn't the place for this, Paul.'

His grin was wicked. 'Come up to my office, then.'

'I'm on call,' Sarah reminded him. Not that the idea wasn't tempting. She stepped further away from Paul to try and distract herself, moving to sit on a bench set amongst the shrubbery. 'Come and talk to me instead.'

Paul sat willingly beside her and took hold of her hand.

'So, how's it going, Dr Kendall?'

'Awful,' Sarah replied despondently. 'We just had a premature delivery of twins. We had to ventilate both of them due to severe respiratory distress syndrome. The anaesthetist took care of one but I had to do the other. It's a procedure I really hate.'

'Endotracheal or nasotracheal intubation?'

'Nasotracheal. They looked like they might need ventilation for quite a while.'

'What gestation?'

'Twenty-eight weeks—but they were really tiny. Eleven hundred and nine hundred grams.'

'Still, survival is more directly linked to maturity than weight, isn't it? What were their five-minute Apgar scores like?' Paul stopped suddenly. 'Why are you staring at me like that, Sarah?'

'You're a manager, Paul Henderson.' Sarah spoke very slowly. 'Why do I feel like I'm talking to another doctor?'

Paul smiled. He looked, Sarah thought, as though he were about to pull a rabbit from a hat.

'I was a general surgeon in my previous life,' he admitted. 'Smallish hospital. I had a few emergency Caesareans to handle.'

Sarah kept staring. 'Just how previous was this life?'

'I've been in management for three years now. I've done the odd locum, just to keep my hand in. I miss the patient contact.'

Sarah let her breath out in a silent whistle. If anything, this admission underlined the fact that she knew nothing about this man. What on earth would send a surgeon into the management camp? A career disaster of some kind? Being struck off? No, he couldn't have been struck off if he'd been doing locums. Disturbed, Sarah withdrew her hand from Paul's.

'What made you go into management?'

'Various things,' Paul replied. He seemed suddenly preoccupied.

'Don't be evasive,' Sarah said, more sharply than she'd intended. 'I need to know what your motivation was. It just seems such an extraordinary thing to do.'

Paul rubbed his chin with his hand. 'OK. I was working in a small hospital. I could see the problems with the health system the way it was—we all could. Waiting lists increasing, operating time being cut, good staff leaving in droves to enter the private system or go overseas. I could see the need for reform, I could see what management was trying to achieve and I could see only too clearly the huge gap in comprehension and communication between management and medical staff. I thought there had to be a way to bridge the gap. I thought I could do it. When the opportunity came up for a management position I took it.'

Sarah nodded. So far it seemed a plausible motivation. Admirable, even.

'I was a great success,' Paul continued with a modest smile. 'We stayed within budget, cut waiting lists and improved standards of patient care and working conditions. After some initial hiccups relations between management and medical staff improved dramatically.'

'You proved your point, then,' Sarah said, 'so why didn't you go back to practising medicine? You said you missed the patient contact.'

'I was head-hunted. If it worked in a small hospital, why not try it on a much larger scale? Besides...' He grinned at Sarah. 'What medical position would allow me to roll in at 9 a.m., have weekends off and no call?'

'You're not at home now,' Sarah reminded him. She glanced at Paul curiously. 'Is it working on a larger scale, then?'

Paul shrugged. 'No. Not yet. The system is too fragmented. There's too much antagonism and resistance to change. And I'm getting bogged down with things like this cleaners' dispute.'

'What's the problem?'

'We have a small pool of permanent staff who put in a lot of overtime. It would be far more cost effective to employ more people on a standard rate of pay. It would also improve the service. Amongst other changes to working conditions the union won't agree to its members losing the overtime bonuses. I can see both sides of the issue but I can't allow it to jeopardise the efficient running of the hospital and it seems so far away from the medical issues I'd rather be involved in.' He caught Sarah's hand again. 'Then someone like you bursts into my office and I suddenly realise how far away I am from real hands-on medicine.'

'You sound unhappy with your job.'

'I am. I know I haven't been here long but I feel caught in no man's land between each side in a war zone. I'm failing both sides and can't see a way to bring them closer. I'm frustrated, I guess. I'm not sure this is the direction I want my career to take. I'm forty years old now, Sarah. I feel I ought to know which way I'm going by now and be happy with it.'

'I know the feeing,' Sarah murmured. She squeezed the hand holding hers. So many questions were now tumbling through her head. She had made a start in understanding Paul but there was so much more she wanted to know. While his explanation of his career change was plausible Sarah instinctively felt there was more to it. As she framed her next query, however, her beeper sounded.

'Damn,' she muttered. 'Just when I'm finally finding out something about you.' She unclipped her pager.

'There's always next time.' Paul smiled. 'That will be your turn to rave on. What are you doing tomorrow night?'

'It's my mother's birthday. Family party,' Sarah said apologetically. 'What about the weekend?'

'I'm tied up, I'm afraid.' Paul also looked apologetic.

'The whole weekend?' Sarah's eyes widened with surprise.

'Afraid so.'

Sarah glanced at her pager as it beeped again. 'That's the emergency department,' she said quickly. 'I'll have to run.'

And run she did. It wasn't far from the courtyard but it gave Sarah time to wonder at what now seemed like evasiveness on Paul's part. The whole weekend? He hadn't even offered any sort of explanation. He was hiding something, Sarah concluded, just like he'd hidden the fact he was a doctor. Man of mystery, indeed. Just how much could she trust him?

He rang her three times during the next day, but trying to see each other proved to be an exercise in frustration. Paul was caught all morning in further meetings with the cleaners' union. Lunch was out. Sarah had managed to finalise her presentation for the paediatricians' meeting between calls last night. Now she had to deliver it. Sarah missed the planned coffee together mid-afternoon due to the admission of three-year-old Amy Turner who was suffering what appeared to be a severe dose of measles. It had upset ward routine. The case needed to be isolated, immunisation details checked on other patients and the worry discussed that the epidemic being experienced up north was making an appearance in the South Island. Sarah rang Paul's office just after five to find he'd already left for the day.

'Nice for some,' she muttered darkly. She realised that, among many other things, she had absolutely no idea where Paul lived or what his home telephone number was. Still, a little breathing space over the weekend was probably a very good thing. She might even be able to view recent events in a more objective light.

'It has to be a man!' The delighted repetition by her older sister, Helen, grated on Sarah.

'Nonsense. Why can't I just look happy to be having an evening at home? It is Mum's birthday after all.' Sarah bent to scratch the ears of an elderly golden retriever, who waved his tail gently in appreciation.

'It's more than that.' Helen peered closely at her sister. 'You look like...' She paused to consider, her lips pursed. 'You look like a woman who's recently had a very good—' She whispered the last of her sentence into Sarah's ear.

Sarah looked shocked. 'Helen!' She glanced at the door as her nine-year-old niece, Holly, bounded into the room, flanked by two more retrievers. 'Shh!' she warned Helen.

'Well, it's about time—that's all I can say.' Helen reached for a box of matches. 'Holly, do you want to help me light the candles?'

Sarah paused in the doorway of the dining room while the cake was being carried triumphantly to the table. She gazed at her parents with great affection. Her father, Jack, was a country GP, a large, gentle man who took his job and position in the small rural community very seriously. Her mother,

Evelyn, was also a large woman, her size matched by her cheerful and enthusiastic personality. Evelyn had also trained as a doctor but had given up her career without apparent regret to raise her three children.

The eldest, John, lived in Australia. Helen had become a solo mother when Holly's father had walked out on them shortly after her birth. Now that Sarah had also left home Evelyn devoted her considerable energies to her beloved dogs. She bred and trained retrievers, often travelling to show them or to compete in obedience or agility trials.

Sarah joined in the singing, kissed her mother, declined the cake and with some difficulty moved the rumps of two dogs to allow room for her to sit on the huge old sofa. Watching her mother open and exclaim over her gifts with Holly's enthusiastic input, Sarah relaxed and soaked in the atmosphere. She loved this place.

The rambling country house was never quite tidy, always smelled of dogs and was one of the happiest places Sarah knew. It was a home in every sense of the word, and Sarah missed belonging here the way she used to. She would always feel at home and be welcomed here but it wasn't the same any more. It wasn't enough.

Her sterile apartment only accentuated what she was missing but even a house in the country wouldn't be a solution. It was the whole package Sarah craved. Home—and family. And career, she reminded herself. Perhaps her mother's example had put her off even looking up till now. She had loved her career too much to even consider its sacrifice, despite her mother's declaration that motherhood was the ultimate career.

It certainly wasn't that she was missing interaction with children. Quite apart from her work, Sarah was almost a second mother to Holly and had shared as much as possible of her upbringing so far. She welcomed the girl now with a big hug as Holly came over to share the sofa. Carrying dishes away from the table, Helen paused to smile at their embrace.

'Tick, tick,' she said cheerfully to Sarah.

'What?'

'It's your biological clock. I can hear it from here!'

Sarah groaned and disentangled herself from the squash of child and dogs to help clear the table. Children were certainly part of the nebulous package she wanted her future to contain. Children, a dog or two, of course, and...a husband. Helen might declare that they were entirely superfluous but her bitterness belied her conviction. Sarah had observed her struggles as a single mother and knew it wasn't an option she would choose either. Thank goodness she had been practical enough to unearth some protection from the depths of her bathroom cupboard the other night.

The hour's drive back to the city later that evening gave Sarah too much time to think. She had spent considerable energy recently, wondering where her career was heading. Now her desires seemed to be crystallising with an entirely new priority. Was it the frustration with pressures at work? An overload of emotional involvement with cases that either ended in tragedy or vanished from her life? Or was it because up until now a vital piece of the jigsaw had been missing?

Was Paul Henderson the missing piece?

The Saturday morning ward round went quickly. Alice Forster had rallied, her pain well controlled again. Isobel took her out in a wheelchair to feed the ducks and get some sunshine. Michael was practising hard with his crutches but Sarah wasn't quite ready to discharge him.

'Maybe on Monday,' she promised. 'I've got one more challenge for you first.'

Charlotte Newman was well on the way to recovery, her temperature normal for the first time. Another forty-eight hours and she could also go home.

All in all, it was a satisfying morning and Sarah decided she would spend the rest of the day working on her paper. She had nothing better to do unfortunately. Feeling disturbed at the sudden dip in the emotional roller coaster the last few days had provided, Sarah stopped in the main foyer of the hospital on her way out. A chocolate bar from the vending machine was definitely called for.

It was while she was searching for some coins in her wallet that Sarah became aware of the boy sitting in the waiting area on the other side of the foyer. Although she could only see the back of his dark head, something about him alerted Sarah that he was doing something he knew he shouldn't.

Intrigued, she fished her chocolate bar out of the dispensing hatch and moved towards the boy. He reminded her of Michael. Perhaps it was just the fact that he was sitting alone. Or maybe it was the slump of the skinny shoulders. She still couldn't see what he was doing. Breaking off a piece of chocolate, Sarah bit into it and edged closer. Then she smiled.

The boy was carefully and very furtively ripping a page out of one of the magazines left for people in the waiting area. He had it mostly covered with his hand as he slowly removed it, glancing around frequently to check whether he was being observed. He hadn't noticed Sarah, approaching from behind. Once removed, he quickly folded and refolded the picture, but not before Sarah had glimpsed it—a police officer, holding his dog. The huge German shepherd was smiling more than his handler, Sarah thought. She moved closer to the boy.

'Hi, there,' she said cheerfully. 'You're not lost, are you?'

The boy jumped guiltily and stuffed the picture into his pocket. He shot a quick glance at Sarah but she ignored his action.

'Would you like a piece of chocolate?'

The look she now received told Sarah that no one was stupid enough to talk to, let alone accept a gift from, a stranger. Sarah was struck by her second glimpse of the child's eyes. A very dark blue. He reminded her strongly of someone but she wasn't so sure it was Michael any more.

'My name's Sarah,' she offered, sitting beside him. She wasn't happy, leaving him to wait on his own. The boy's shoulders hunched a little further and Sarah received no reply. She tried again.

'What's your name?'

'Daniel.'

But it wasn't the boy who spoke. At the now familiar tingle the voice caused, Sarah looked up, startled. She looked up at the tall figure of Paul Henderson, at the dark eyes now observing her very carefully. And suddenly, appallingly, she knew who this child reminded her so strongly of. He was a junior version of the man standing in front of her.

'His name's Daniel,' Paul said. 'He's my son.'

Sarah's mouth dropped open. She scrambled to her feet. She could feel the blood drain from her face. Of course. It all made sense. She'd known he'd been hiding something. She'd known there was reason to doubt whether she could give her trust as easily as she had given her body to this man. She clenched her fists.

'I can see what ties up your weekends,' Sarah said tightly. 'It's an important family time.'

'Yes, it is,' Paul agreed evenly. 'We're going fishing this afternoon.'

'I'm sure you'll catch something,' Sarah said flatly. Her horror was being overtaken by anger— an anger even greater than that which had first propelled her into Paul Henderson's orbit. She lowered her voice to an acid whisper. 'I'm sure you can hook anything you fancy.'

Sarah turned and fled as fast as dignity in a public place would allow, but not fast enough. Paul caught her arm and pulled her to a halt beside the vending machine.

'Just what did you mean by that remark?' His voice was quiet. Dangerously quiet.

Sarah jerked her arm free, rubbing it with unnecessary vigour.

'You must think I'm really stupid, Paul. Either that or you're so full of yourself it didn't occur to you to think it might matter.' She kept rubbing her arm. It had hurt, but not that much. 'I understand now why it was so urgent for you to get home the other night. Management meetings don't usually go through to breakfast, do they?' Sarah laughed incredulously. 'How long did you think it would take for me to find out, Paul?'

'I was going to tell you—'

'Like hell you were!' Sarah snarled. She ignored the startled look from a man who was approaching the vending machine. The stranger changed his mind and walked away rapidly.

'It was a good line, Paul. "Do you believe in love at first sight?"' Sarah's mimicking was sarcastic. 'Do you often use it, Paul? Does it always work that quickly when you fancy a bit on the side?'

The anger flashed in Paul's eyes. 'You surprise me, Dr Kendall. Perhaps you're not the person I thought you were.'

'Obviously not,' Sarah agreed venomously. 'You don't know me at all, Paul Henderson.'

'And you don't know me.' The clipped tone was a warning.

'I don't think I want to,' Sarah said slowly. She glanced over at Daniel who was watching them, his face expressionless. Sarah turned away. It felt as if time was suddenly in slow motion.

'Your son is waiting for you. Goodbye, Paul.'

CHAPTER FOUR

THERE wasn't much satisfaction to be gained by saying 'I told you so' to herself, but Sarah said it anyway.

How right she had been to suspect that Paul was hiding something. How naïve was it possible to be at the age of thirty-three? He was forty years old. No woman in her right mind would bother denying how good-looking he was, an ex-surgeon who now had a job in senior management with, she imagined, an executive salary to boot. Of course he would be married. And what woman could be married to Paul Henderson, without wanting to produce a junior Paul or Paula? Probably a couple of each, Sarah told herself bitterly.

How right she had also been not to allow herself to give in to the idea that his significance in her future might be paramount. Missing piece of the jigsaw, indeed. Huh! Perhaps Helen was right, after all, in her assertion that men were simply not worth the trouble.

Why could she find absolutely no satisfaction in proving herself so right? It was as though a door she had been undecided about trying had now been slammed and locked in her face, thereby removing the choice she had wanted the chance to make. Well, so be it, then. She had a wonderful career and more children than she could cope with. She would simply have to make the best of it. She just wished her traitorous body would co-operate and stop preventing sleep by the painfully vivid memories of the sensations those skilled hands could arouse...

It was amazing how constructive anger could be when channelled in the right direction. The paper on the use of low-dose medication to prevent recurrences of febrile seizures fell into place and was written with remarkable speed and cohesion. Sarah knew her conclusions, which contradicted recent reports from other groups, would spark some controversy but she also knew that they were soundly based.

It was to be hoped that they might spur other research teams to expand their own investigations, thereby improving knowledge on dosages and regimes that would provide the most effective therapy. Delivering the paper to Martin Lynch's secretary on Monday morning to be typed up, Sarah then swung her attention towards her patients. There was no medical problem that could be thrown at her at present that she couldn't handle. The more the merrier.

There was certainly more but none were particularly merry. Two more cases of measles had been admitted over the weekend. The case she had admitted on Friday afternoon was causing concern and had been seen due to severe conjunctivitis and emergent bronchitis the previous day. The complication of pneumonia was a real danger with measles and antibiotics had been started. Sarah was even more concerned when told that Amy Turner had been difficult to wake that morning.

Post-infectious encephalomyelitis was a very serious complication of measles and carried a high mortality rate of ten per cent. The toddler was Sarah's first port of call.

Amy's pulse rate was slow and her breathing slightly irregular, but what was more alarming were the unequal pupil sizes and abnormal reflexes on one side. Sarah called in Martin Lynch immediately. After his examination he called the paediatric intensive care specialist and they arranged an urgent CT scan to check for raised intracranial pressure. They also arranged transfer of the child to the intensive care unit.

Sarah spent time with Amy's parents, trying to be both honest about the possibilities but optimistic that this would be a case where the progression would halt and a swift recovery would follow. She watched as her patient and the parents set off towards the radiology department with the two consultant specialists in attendance. There was nothing more she could do for Amy now other than to keep her fingers crossed.

Sarah's attention to detail when checking the other two measles cases was even more than usually meticulous so it was mid-morning before she could look in on Alice Forster. The girl was still in her bed.

'She says she doesn't want to get up today.' Isobel Forster looked worried. A Walt Disney video was playing but Alice seemed uninterested.

'What's up, sweetheart?' Sarah let her hand rest on the small forehead briefly. 'Does something hurt?'

Alice shook her head a little. 'Not really.'

'I think we might take your temperature again.' Sarah smiled.

'It was normal this morning,' Isobel informed her.

Sarah was lifting the stethoscope from around her neck. 'I'm in super-doctor mode today. Let's just check everything. You don't mind, do you, darling?'

Rewarded by a now rare smile, Sarah put her earpieces in place and asked Alice to take a big breath.

'And again, sweetheart.'

This time Alice coughed as she exhaled and Sarah caught her expression.

'Does it hurt you to cough, Alice?'

'Just a bit.'

'Has she been coughing much?' Sarah directed the question at Isobel who shook her head.

'Maybe once or twice in the night.'

'OK.' Sarah clicked on a small torch. 'Let's have a look at that throat. Say Ah-h!'

On the face of it there didn't seem anything significantly different about Alice, but Sarah's instincts told her something was brewing. The temperature was raised but only fractionally, the cough was dry and there were no worrying sounds in her lungs, no redness in either her throat or ears. It was the child's dullness that bothered Sarah.

'Keep an eye on her and call me if you're worried,' she told Isobel. 'I'll ask Angela to increase her observations and I'll pop back when I can.'

As she was due to see Charlotte Newman for a

discharge examination Sarah poked her head only briefly into Michael's room.

'Hope you've been practising hard, Michael. I've got something special lined up for you today.'

Michael grinned and waved a crutch at her, narrowing missing Judith who was straightening his bed. She tried to look cross but didn't quite manage it.

Sarah spent the rest of the morning in Theatre, watching the repair of baby Jack's cleft lip and palate. The surgeon carefully marked points on the baby's face with a pen.

'Stand over here, Sarah. You'll get a better view. I'm putting these landmarks on to make sure we end up getting things as symmetrical as possible. It's easy to lose sight of where things need to go once we've opened everything up.'

He began to inject local anaesthetic into the baby's lips. 'This reduces the bleeding,' he explained to Sarah. 'It also builds up the tissues so they're easier to cut.'

Sarah watched in fascination throughout the two-and-a-half-hour operation and was admiring of the finished result. The surgeon stood back but shook his head.

'I can always find something I think I could have improved on.' He stripped off his gloves. 'He'll look a lot worse in a month's time. The scar tissue contracts and looks terrible but it eases off again. In three or four months we'll have a much better idea of the result.'

'It looks wonderful,' Sarah assured him. 'I'm really impressed.'

'I'm really hungry.' The surgeon grinned. 'That was a long haul. How about some lunch?'

Sarah glanced at the clock on the wall. It was just after 1 p.m. 'I'd love to,' she said apologetically, 'but I can't. I've got a patient waiting.'

A hurried trip back to her car allowed Sarah to collect a large paper bag that was sitting on her passenger seat. Then she made her way to Ward 23.

A few minutes later, carrying the adult-sized crutches under one arm and the paper bag under the other, Sarah took Michael down in the lift, through the busy main foyer and out into the courtyard area between the main hospital wing and the administration wing. A few staff members were enjoying some sunshine during their lunch break, dotted about the seating provided in the area. Sarah pointed to an unoccupied seat on one side of the courtyard area.

'That's your goal,' she told Michael.

'What?' Michael's eyes narrowed suspiciously.

'And that's mine.' Sarah indicated another bench seat on the other side of the paved area. It happened to be the seat on which she had sat with Paul Henderson the night she'd been on call and had found out about what he'd called his 'previous life'. Well, that little episode now belonged to her own 'previous life', Sarah thought bitterly. Past history. Brief and best forgotten. She turned over the paper bag and tipped out the light plastic soccer ball it contained. Michael's jaw dropped. He began to turn away.

'Wait a sec,' Sarah ordered. She adjusted her crutches, standing on one leg, then balanced on one crutch and swung the other carefully to contact the light ball. It skated over the paving and she hopped after it.

'Ready?' she called. Turning, Sarah hit the ball back towards Michael. It rolled to a stop in front of him. With an expression of having to humour an idiot, Michael shifted his balance, lifted his crutch and tapped the ball without enthusiasm. It rolled only a few inches.

'Come on, Michael,' Sarah shouted. 'Boot it!'

Michael hopped forward a step, settled his balance and took a healthier swipe at the ball. It flew up in the air, bounced and rolled well past Sarah.

'Yes!' she yelled. She turned and hopped after it but suddenly Michael was there as well. He must have put in a lot of practice over the weekend because his speed and balance had improved enormously. Sarah tried to hit the ball but Michael's crutch made first contact. He kept it under control, dribbling it along in front of him until he reached the bench.

'Goal,' he shouted. 'I win!'

'Hang on a minute,' Sarah protested. 'What happened to half-time?'

They spent a happy ten minutes, playing, until Sarah could see Michael was tiring. She put the ball under her own bench for the first time and then sat down on it.

'OK, you win. Three goals to one.'

Michael hopped over, the signs of tiredness gone.

'I thought you were tired,' Sarah said.

Michael grinned. 'I thought you needed a goal.' He sat down beside Sarah.

'Cheat!' Sarah told him affectionately. She put her arm around the boy's shoulders. 'You can go home tomorrow, Michael. I'll miss you.'

Michael glanced up shyly. 'I'll miss you, too.'

'You can keep the ball,' Sarah told him. 'When you get used to your new leg give me a ring and we'll have another game.'

Michael looked dubious and then a familiar sullen expression began to appear. Sarah gave him a feather-light punch on his arm.

'Hey! You've gone from not walking to playing soccer in the space of a few days. Your attitude is the only thing that could hold you back from now on, Michael. I know you can do anything you want. You know that too, don't you?' Sarah leaned down to look sternly at the boy beside her. 'Don't you?' she repeated.

'I guess.'

'Yeah, I guess too.' Sarah smiled. 'And I guess I better get back to work.' She stood up, extending a hand to Michael. As she straightened her gaze swept up the administration block. Right up to the fourth floor. Framed against the window of his office stood Paul Henderson. She was too far away to read his expression but it was clearly him and he had obviously been watching her. For how long? Sarah wondered, cursing her body yet again for the painful signals it was sending. Taking a deep breath, she tore her gaze away from the window and shook back her hair.

'Come on, Michael,' she said firmly. 'It's time to go.'

*   *   *

Martin Lynch's firm was on take for Paediatrics the next day, meaning frequent trips for Sarah to the emergency department which had to be managed on top of her normal ward and outpatient duties. Her first case, a nasty dose of croup, was admitted for observation. While the baby's breathing sounds were marked and continuous and the pulse rate high there was no indication of significant airway obstruction. The parents were confident of the history of the illness so there was no question of an inhaled foreign body, smoke or chemicals involved. An allergic reaction was also unlikely.

The cause was most probably viral and could well resolve rapidly but Sarah wanted the insurance of having intensive care and intubation facilities available should the situation deteriorate. Even with this degree of difficulty in breathing, the illness was terrifying to both parents and child and Sarah dispensed reassurance in large doses.

She accompanied the family up to the ward and took the opportunity to look in on Alice. Her temperature had returned to normal and she seemed brighter but Isobel told Sarah she had been coughing more during the night. Still uneasy, Sarah checked her carefully again and left instructions for the increased observations to continue.

The busy day was exactly what she needed. Her anger at both Paul and herself had receded but had been replaced by an acute sense of disillusionment. It required quite an effort to remain outwardly as cheerful and optimistic as normal but Sarah was confident she was managing. Saying goodbye to Michael nudged her spirits down further and she was glad of the call to Emergency that came shortly after.

'A two-year-old boy, Jamie Wilson,' the registrar informed Sarah. 'He collapsed while walking with his mother a short time ago. Apparently only unconscious for a few seconds and no seizure activity noted. He'd appeared normal since but she brought him in because she's worried. Heart rate is 52 beats a minutes and irregular. Blood pressure is 98 over 60 and the respiration rate is twenty a minute.' He showed her the ECG strip he was holding.

'It's an abnormally slow rate with complete heart block,' Sarah confirmed. 'There's the odd premature ventricular beat as well. Has he had any diagnosis made of congenital heart disease?'

'Not according to his mother.'

Sarah examined the child and they took another ECG trace. She questioned the mother carefully but could discover nothing very helpful. Jamie had been looked after by his grandmother earlier in the day. Sarah sent Mrs Wilson to ring her mother. 'Check whether he had any falls and knocked his head or chest. Or he may have eaten something odd. Get her to check the bathroom cabinet for any drugs in the house.'

Sarah ordered a chest X-ray and blood work-up, booked an echocardiogram and called in a cardiologist. The boy's heart rate was still far too slow and his level of consciousness was dropping. She also contacted the intensive care unit.

Mrs Wilson rushed back into the room at the same time as the cardiology registrar arrived.

'My mother went to check around the house—

that's why I took so long. She says the bottle of tablets on her bedside table is empty. She doesn't know how many there were—'

'What tablets were they?' Matt interrupted.

'They were for her heart—digoxin?'

Sarah and the cardiology registrar nodded. 'How long since he took them?' he asked.

'It's only an hour since I collected him but he was with her for about three hours. She doesn't know when he went into her room exactly but he did go looking for the cat about halfway through the visit.'

'We're too late for ipecac,' Sarah commented. She looked down at the little boy who was now unconscious. 'Is it still worth doing a gastric lavage?'

'Has he eaten anything since that time?'

Mrs Wilson shook her head. 'We were going home for tea—that's when he fainted.'

'It's worth doing,' the cardiology registrar told Sarah. 'We don't know how many tablets he took and he may still have quite a lot undigested.'

Matt Warnock nodded. 'Can I leave you to it, Sarah? We've got a serious MVA on the way in.'

Sarah was already busy with her preparations. 'Of course, Matt.' She turned to the nurse. 'Make sure it's a cuffed endotracheal tube,' she ordered.

'I'll get a lignocaine drip set up,' the cardiology registrar told her. 'And we'd better have an emergency pacemaker tray ready. I don't want to see that heart rate drop much further. We'll need some more bloods, too. We'll have to monitor serum potassium and digoxin levels carefully.'

Sarah donned a plastic apron and gloves. Tilting the boy's head back, Sarah gently inserted the cuffed endotracheal tube to protect his airway. Then she quickly measured the distance between his chin and umbilicus, marking the distance on the orogastric tube before inserting it.

'I'll have the syringe, thanks.' Sarah aspirated the stomach contents carefully with the syringe and then connected rubber tubing and a funnel to the orogastric tube.

'Have you warmed the saline?'

The nurse nodded. Sarah watched as she cut the bag and poured the saline into the funnel Sarah was holding.

'Whoa! That's enough.' Sarah lowered the funnel. 'Put that basin a bit further over here.' Splashed with the liquid now able to empty through the tubing, Sarah was glad of the large apron. She repeated the cycle several more times, before removing the tubing.

The IV line was in place, blood samples taken and drip started by the time Sarah had removed her apron and gloves.

'I'll get him up to ICU,' the cardiology registrar told her. 'They're ready for us. They've got the digoxin specific antibodies in already. Hopefully we'll get him back to you before too long.'

The emergency department was chaotic with the arrival of victims from a multiple MVA as Sarah left. She decided to walk the long way around the outside of the building to get back to the ward. A few minutes' peace and quiet and some fresh air were just what she needed.

Following the river-bank, which led to the car park behind the administration block, Sarah paused for a moment to watch the ducks and think about Alice. When a tiny movement in the grass caught her eye she ignored it initially. Then she looked again.

'I don't believe it!' she whispered aloud. Dropping to a crouch, Sarah peered into the grass. The movement of the blades progressed and Sarah leaned forward onto her knees.

The voice came from behind her. 'Sarah, what on earth are you doing? Are you all right?'

'Shh!' Sarah commanded. She watched intently, still on her knees. When she saw the renewed quivering in the grass ahead of her she cupped both hands and lunged carefully.

'Yes!'

'What in God's name are you up to, Sarah Kendall?' Paul demanded.

Sarah stood up slowly, her cupped hands held against her chest. Her eyes shining, she slowly lifted her thumbs.

Paul stepped closer. His head almost brushed hers as he looked down. Nestled into the cup of Sarah's palms was a tiny duckling—a ball of yellow and black fluff, with bright black eyes and a miniature beak that now opened to emit a series of worried peeps.

'I don't believe it,' Paul whispered. 'It's completely the wrong time of year for ducklings.'

'I don't believe it either,' Sarah said softly.

Paul looked around, scouting the grass and

nearby river. 'I can't see any more. And there's no sign of the mother. It's weird.'

'It's a miracle,' Sarah breathed.

'What on earth are you going to do with it? It won't survive if you let it go.'

'I've got no intention of letting it go,' Sarah said calmly. She looked at Paul for the first time. 'It's Alice Forster's greatest wish to see a duckling before she dies. We didn't think there was any hope of it happening at this time of year. I even rang all the farms where I knew people to see if I could get hold of one.' Sarah had to blink back the sudden moisture in her eyes. 'And now she's not only going to see one but she can touch it—keep it with her in her room.' Sarah bent her head and a tear she couldn't block dropped onto the duckling's head.

Paul extended a finger and gently swept the drop of moisture from the soft fluff. Then he cupped his hands over Sarah's and enclosed the duckling again.

'You're the most amazing person I've ever met, Sarah Kendall.'

The words and tone caressed her, and when Sarah met his eyes she felt the huge weight she had been carrying for the last few days begin to melt away. But his next words halted the process.

'I'm just sorry you have such a low opinion of me.'

Sarah stiffened. 'What did you expect, Paul? That I would be happy to share you?'

'No. I wasn't sure.' Paul sighed. 'As you said yourself, things happened too fast and they were

too big. I wanted just a little more time. I know
having a dependent child is enough to put some
women off. I've been there before.'

'Not to mention a dependent wife,' Sarah
snapped. 'Or was that going to wait just a little
longer as well?'

'No, I wasn't going to mention her,' Paul said
quietly. 'And it's an ex-wife, despite your obvious
assumptions. Catherine walked out on me when
Daniel was fourteen months old. We haven't seen
her since. And I haven't wanted to. She's past history and I'd prefer her to stay that way. The birth
of my son was the only good thing to come from
what was obviously a huge mistake—an error of
judgment that I was hardly likely to want to discuss
with a woman I had just fallen in love with.'

Sarah's eyes widened. *Had.* He had used the past
tense. Even his tone suggested that it was just another part of his 'past history'. She felt a sharp pain
knife through her body. 'I—I'm sorry, Paul. I didn't
think—'

'No. You didn't.' Paul looked away. He slid his
hands into his pockets. 'What you did think was
that I could lie about my feelings simply to entice
a partner for an extramarital affair. I find that in-
sulting. And very disappointing. You didn't trust
me.'

Sarah swallowed hard. He was right and she
couldn't think of a thing to say in her own defence.
The silence that fell was an abyss which Sarah felt
in danger of falling into.

'Paul?' Sarah queried in a small voice.

'Yes?' The blue eyes were carefully blank, as though a shield had been erected.

'Could I—could I borrow your handkerchief, please? This duckling's done something a bit yucky in my hand.'

Paul closed his eyes briefly and then his lips twitched. He pulled the white silk triangle that decorated the top pocket of his jacket and shook it out. Silently he handed it to Sarah.

'Thank you.' Sarah gently transferred the duckling into the handkerchief and then carefully tucked it into her white coat pocket. She bent to wipe her hand on the grass. When she looked up Paul was gone. She straightened, watching his back as he strode towards the car park with his hands back in his pockets.

Was it just the excitement that explained the flushed cheeks and sparkling eyes? Sarah watched as Alice reverently touched the duckling, sitting on her bed.

'Is he mine, Sarah?'

'He's all yours, darling.'

'Can I keep him?' The joy in the child's voice brought a huge lump to Sarah's throat. She was aware that Isobel was crying silently.

'Of course you can, sweetheart. For as long as you want.' Sarah sat on the edge of the bed. 'My mum knows all about raising ducklings and she'll tell me what we need to feed him. When he's too big to live in your bed he can go on her duck pond.'

'He'll never be too big,' Alice whispered breathlessly. 'He can swim in that big washing bowl we use for my bath.' She stopped suddenly, coughing.

Sarah frowned and reached for her stethoscope. 'Let me have a listen to your back, Alice.' She helped her sit forward and pulled up her pyjama jacket gently. 'You decide on a name for that little fluffball while I check you out.'

A few minutes later Sarah caught Isobel's eye. 'Her temperature's up and I can hear a few crackles. We'll start some antibiotics, I think.'

Isobel's eyes flashed with alarm. 'Bronchitis?' she queried quietly.

'Could be.' Sarah folded her stethoscope. Her instincts told her it was more likely to be pneumonia but she didn't want to put her fear into words. Both women knew what that would mean.

'I know what I'm going to call him.'

'What's that, darling?' Sarah returned Alice's happy smile.

'Ping.'

Following her mother's instructions, Sarah arrived at the hospital the next morning armed with tinned cat food, wholemeal bread and a pair of tweezers. She had to walk through a line of picketing cleaners to get to the main entrance and the obvious escalation of the problem made her think of Paul. She had taken the crumpled and stained handkerchief home to wash. She knew she could use it as an excuse to see Paul again, but would he even want to see her?

The confused jumble of her thoughts had led to a sleepless night. She blamed herself and then became angry at Paul again. Why should he have expected such complete trust so instantly? Wasn't that pure arrogance on his part? She didn't even know him.

But you reciprocated, she told herself. You agreed that you didn't need the 'entrée'. You matched his passion physically. If she hadn't been prepared to trust him how could she have done that? It put the encounter on a purely physical level, which disgusted her. OK, she admitted, she had trusted him—or had wanted to trust him. But who wouldn't have made the same assumption she'd made when confronted by his son? Was that so hard for him to understand?

Sarah wanted desperately to put things right, but Paul had walked away from her. Would her pride allow her to crawl back and beg for forgiveness? At the moment the answer was no, but the white silk handkerchief could wait. A symbol of potential resolution. A flag of surrender maybe, Sarah thought with a crooked grin.

Ping ate his breakfast enthusiastically and Sarah made herself late for her paediatric outpatient clinic, by staying to watch the duckling's first swim in the large enamel basin. Isobel followed her out as she left.

'She's worse, isn't she, Sarah?'

Sarah nodded. The chest X-ray had confirmed her fears that pneumonia was setting in. 'We're doing all we can, Isobel. You know that, don't you?'

Isobel nodded. Her voice caught. 'I've never seen her this happy, though. You, finding that duckling. It was…it's…'

'Magic,' Sarah said firmly. 'That's what it is.' She gave Isobel a quick hug. 'Enjoy it as much as you can—both of you—and call me if you need me.'

The call came even before the clinic was finished. Sarah called Martin Lynch in as well. He examined Alice gently. The child was feverish and very drowsy. The consultant's look as he finished his examination told Sarah all she needed to know. Isobel had also caught his expression and she turned away suddenly towards the window, wrapping her arms tightly around herself.

Sarah placed an arm around her shoulders. 'I'll come back as soon as I can. We'll see this through together.'

The calls to other patients were an unwelcome distraction through that long afternoon. When she was called to the intensive care unit she found Jamie Wilson's potassium and digoxin levels were falling and he was back in a normal heart rhythm and rate. Sarah made the necessary arrangements to have him transferred to the ward. He would need continued monitoring and treatment for at least a week until his digoxin levels were under the toxic range.

Normally she would have been thrilled with the rapid recovery her other young transfer to the unit had made. Amy Turner was out of danger and also ready to move back to the ward, but even the delight of all the parents involved failed to lift Sarah's spirits. Her responses were automatic, the focus of her thoughts too narrow to allow emotional involvement with these cases. It was a relief when her shift ended and there were no more calls to interrupt the vigil she was sharing with Isobel.

Alice's level of consciousness slipped further, and as darkness fell her breathing became quieter. Dangerously quiet. Still she held on and at one point roused enough to ask for Ping. Isobel lifted the duckling from the small box he was in beside her pillow and cupped Alice's hand around him. It was a struggle for her to keep her eyes open but she managed a smile.

'I love you, Mummy.'

'And I love you, darling.' Isobel's cheek was laid gently against her daughter's, the tiny body cradled in her arms. Sarah perched on the side of the bed, one hand stroking Alice's head gently, the other on Isobel's shoulder.

It seemed an eternity and yet it seemed no time at all until Alice's laboured attempts to breathe finally ceased. Still they remained there, the three of them, physically connected, though now only two suffered any pain.

The pain was unbearable. Sarah finally left Isobel to have some time alone with her daughter for the last time. Unseeing, she stumbled outside and collapsed on a bench in the courtyard. The familiarity of that particular bench didn't even register. She buried her face in her hands and her whole body shook uncontrollably but silently. No tears would come—the pain was too intense.

Sarah was unaware that anybody had come until she felt arms, drawing her close. She had no need to uncover her face to know to whom they belonged. She felt the warmth and comfort available and buried her face against the hard chest.

'Alice just died,' she whispered brokenly.

Then the tears came, racking sobs that would have embarrassed her if she'd been aware of making them. Eventually the soothing words and stroking movements of the hands that held her permeated her misery. She struggled to control herself and gratefully accepted the handkerchief Paul produced.

'That's two you owe me,' he told her seriously.

Sarah laughed through her tears and Paul drew her against his chest again.

'I intend to collect the debt.' He stroked Sarah's hair back where the strands had caught on her damp face. 'I'm sorry, Sarah. I'm sorry that Alice has died and I'm sorry I gave you a hard time.' He brushed a tear from her cheek with his thumb. 'I expected too much too soon. I know that.' Bending his head, he placed his lips against her hair. 'It was only because I wanted to give you that much myself. Can you understand that?'

Sarah blew her nose inelegantly and then nodded.

'And can you trust me?'

Sarah raised her eyes and met the plea in Paul's. 'Yes,' she breathed. 'I'm sorry, too, Paul. I knew I could trust you. I just wouldn't let myself believe it.'

'Well, now you can,' Paul said firmly. 'Now I'm taking you home—and I'm staying. You can't be alone tonight.'

'But what about Daniel?'

'Our housekeeper lives in the same apartment block. She knew I might be late tonight with this meeting with the cleaners' union. She'll be happy to stay overnight. I'll just need to get back in time to see Daniel for breakfast and take him to school. Is that all right with you?'

'Oh, yes.' Sarah sighed. 'Yes, please.'

CHAPTER FIVE

'THIS is a first for me,' Sarah whispered. She held tightly to the hand of her companion.

'I hope it's the last,' Paul said solemnly.

'I'm not sure I can cope.' Sarah took a deep breath. 'What if I break down and make a spectacle of myself?'

'Nobody can make a spectacle of themselves, crying at a child's funeral,' Paul told her softly. He squeezed her hand. 'Amazingly enough, I've still got plenty of hankies.'

Sarah smiled guiltily. She still hadn't returned the two he'd already loaned her.

They sat quietly, holding hands and waiting as the tiny old chapel in the grounds of the hospital filled to overflowing with Alice's friends, her mother's family and the many staff who had been touched by Alice Forster's short life. Alice's father was noticeable only by his absence, much to Sarah's relief.

The service was simple—and very moving. Sarah cried openly as did everybody there, including the minister. When Sarah looked up to see the tears on Paul's cheek she used the crumpled, borrowed handkerchief to wipe them away. Their eyes met and the sadness they shared added yet another link in the chain that was binding them together. Still holding hands, they later walked beside the river.

'What happened to the duckling?' Paul queried.

'I took him out to my parents,' Sarah replied. 'He's doing fine. Mum's got a real knack with young creatures. He can go and live on their duck pond when he's older.' She sighed and then smiled wistfully. 'I guess a little bit of the magic did rub off on Alice after all.'

'What's that?'

Sarah just smiled again. 'Thanks for coming today, Paul.'

'She touched my life, too, you know.' Paul drew Sarah into his arms. 'Do you realise it was Alice who was responsible for us meeting?'

Sarah nodded and then lifted her head up. Paul kissed her softly.

'Would you come and have dinner with me tonight?' he asked.

'What about Daniel?'

'I meant with us. At our apartment.'

Sarah hesitated. 'I don't think Daniel's too keen on me. He wouldn't even say anything the morning I met him.'

Paul sighed heavily. 'Daniel's very wary of women. Any that he's cared about have abandoned him. First his mother and then a nanny he got very attached to. He keeps his distance now.' Paul kissed Sarah again. 'But it's only a matter of time. He's very like me and I know he'll love you when he gets to know you. How could he help it?'

Sarah basked in the warmth of the look she received but then her brow creased.

'I think it might be a bit threatening to invade

his home just yet. Why don't we meet on neutral territory?'

Paul nodded. 'I forgot you majored in child psychology. What do you suggest?'

'Something fun. Why don't we go out to Orana Park on Saturday? I'll borrow my niece and dilute the atmosphere a bit more.'

Paul grinned. 'Great. God, I hope you'll like him.'

'If he's just like you, how could I help it?'

The pain of losing Alice had affected Sarah's work that week. The flow of admissions, outpatients and emergencies kept up but Sarah found it quite easy to keep a professional distance. One nine-year-old boy who bravely battled through a severe asthma attack nearly broke through the self-erected barrier but the room to which he was admitted had been that of Alice Forster. Now stripped bare of the personal furnishings and decorations, it felt to Sarah as though the room had also died. She kept her visits to a professional minimum. She would be glad when this run ended in a couple of weeks. It was time for a break and maybe a complete change.

Alice Forster seemed to have been quite symbolic, Sarah mused. She had been admitted for the first time during Sarah's first week on the ward and now this chapter in her life felt like it was coming to a close. Alice had also been the catalyst for something Sarah now knew would form the next chapter.

The impression of the child's importance in her life was heightened on Friday afternoon when Sarah found Isobel Forster, waiting to see her. The two women embraced fondly and then Sarah stepped back to search her friend's face.

'How are you, Isobel? I've been thinking about you all the time.'

'I'm taking things one day at a time,' Isobel responded. 'I'm OK, I guess.'

'The service was very special.' Sarah smiled. 'She was a much-loved little girl.'

Isobel nodded. 'How's Ping?'

'Doing very well. Growing fast by all accounts.'

'I'll never forget you, doing that for Alice,' Isobel said quietly. 'It made the end the happiest time she had in here. I really just wanted to thank you—but words are so inadequate.'

Sarah smiled gently. 'You don't need to thank me. I loved Alice too. I'll never forget her.'

'There's something I want you to have.' Isobel fished in her shoulder-bag. She drew out the yellow velvet duck and pressed it into Sarah's hands. 'Keep it,' she begged. 'I hope one day you have a little girl of your own. Maybe the duck will remind you of Alice sometimes and the memory will make you treasure your own child even more.'

Sarah was still holding the soft yellow duck when she left the ward for the day an hour later. She wondered again at the amazing bond she had witnessed so often between mothers and their children. Sometimes it had evoked a feeling akin to jealousy in her. Would she ever be able to give and receive the kind of unconditional love the bond represented?

At present, her future contained the possibility of

a stepchild. While she knew that bond could never be quite the same, it could still be very rewarding. But what if Daniel refused to accept her in his life? Would that be enough to destroy what she and Paul had found in each other? Sarah felt very nervous about their planned excursion the next day.

Her nervousness increased when they met at the entrance to the safari park on Saturday afternoon. Daniel refused to make eye contact when introduced and he ignored Holly's greeting. Holly rolled her eyes at Sarah. They all remained silent as they purchased their tickets.

'Where to first?' Paul studied the map he held. 'We've got thirty minutes until the lion feeding. Shall we take a guided tour or go walking?'

'What would you like to see, Daniel?' Sarah made an effort to sound casual.

'Dunno.' The tone was sullen and Holly made another face at Sarah.

'I want a ride on the train,' Holly announced. 'We'll have to be quick—it's about to go.'

'Come on, then.' Paul set off and they all followed, climbing on board the trailer being pulled by a tractor. Paul sat down first and Sarah moved to sit beside him but somehow Daniel got there first. He made eye contact with Sarah then and his look was triumphant. Sarah repressed a smile at the unsubtle hint and sat behind them with Holly at her side. Separated, and with the commentary of the guide making conversation impossible, Sarah tried to relax. She had hoped that the two children might hit it off and make things easier but so far the outgoing Holly was clearly unimpressed by Daniel's reserve.

Things got worse at the lion feeding. Daniel refused to handle the lumps of raw meat they were offered. Holly took two, threw them down the tube and peered after them to see the lions snatch and devour the food. Then, her fingers covered in blood, she raised her hands and wiggled her fingers in Daniel's face.

'Beware the ghost of doom!' she intoned in a hollow voice.

'Get lost,' Daniel replied. He stepped back to stand close to Paul.

Sarah caught Paul's eye. He rolled his eyes in a good imitation of Holly's earlier reaction but he looked worried at the same time. She pointed Holly in the direction of a water trough. 'Wash off the ghost of doom,' she ordered. 'We'll go and see the tigers and then find some afternoon tea.'

They set off, the adults setting a brisk pace. Holly kept up with them but Daniel lagged behind a little, radiating disapproval.

'He's a bit of a nerd, isn't he?' Holly whispered loudly to Sarah.

'Shh! Give him a chance,' Sarah responded quietly. 'Why don't you try talking without us around?'

'OK.' Holly slackened her pace to allow Daniel to catch up.

'At least she's not shy,' Paul commented. Walking side by side, their hands brushed together as Paul moved closer to talk. Sarah resisted the impulse to hold hands. That certainly wouldn't improve the ambience of the outing.

'I'm sorry this is so difficult,' Paul apologised.

'I didn't expect it to be easy,' Sarah assured him. 'Don't worry. I don't give up that easily.'

The children were still behind them by several paces but Holly's voice carried clearly. 'She's not my mother—she's my aunt. I haven't got a father.'

'Well, I haven't got a mother.' Sarah listened keenly as she heard Daniel begin to talk for the first time. 'I don't want one either.'

Sarah tried to catch Paul's eye but he'd closed them, his expression a silent groan.

'Well, I don't want a father,' Holly announced. 'So there! My mum says they're surflous.'

'Superfluous.' Sarah couldn't help providing the correction.

'What's that?' Daniel's query was a suspicious growl.

'Um. More than what you really need.'

'See?' Holly's tone was triumphant. 'Sarah thinks so too.'

'Hey, wait on! I never said that!' Sarah looked over her shoulder to frown at her niece but Holly's cheeky grin warned her that the conversation wasn't finished.

'Your dad is Sarah's boyfriend,' Holly informed Daniel.

'He is not!'

'Course he is, stupid. Why do you think they're going out together?' She lowered her voice. 'They'll probably get married.'

Paul's stifled groan carried only to Sarah's ears. She didn't dare look at him.

'They will not.' Daniel was ready for a fight. 'My dad's never going to get married again. He says there's two of us to get married to and he doesn't believe there's anybody that special in the whole world.'

Sarah was sure she could feel the heat of his glare directed at the back of her head. Holly, however, wasn't impressed.

'Well, my mum says she bets anything that this is *it*. She said if he's managed to hold her interest for more than five minutes he must be something amazing. And she said it's about time and something about a clock.'

'A clock?' Paul's despairing look had given way to frank amusement. He dropped back to wait for Holly. 'What did your mum say to you about a clock?'

'I'm not sure,' Holly confessed. 'She was talking to Gran, not me.'

'You shouldn't have been eavesdropping,' Sarah admonished. 'And you certainly shouldn't be repeating what you heard.'

'You told me to talk to him,' Holly told her aunt accusingly. 'It was the most interesting thing I could think of.'

'Can we go home now, Dad?' Daniel glared at his father.

'Soon.' Paul sighed. Then he flashed a grin at Sarah, before turning back to Holly. 'So, what did your gran say after that bit about the clock?'

'Paul!' Sarah was horrified, but they both ignored her.

'Gran said that anyone that puts that sort of sparkle in Sarah's eye is OK by her and she was going to keep her fingers crossed.'

'That was an unmitigated disaster!'

'Oh, I don't know. I really like Holly. Are you all so outspoken in your family?'

Sarah rested her head on Paul's shoulder. They had found a secluded bench on the river-bank and for once their lunch breaks had coincided.

'And I thought taking Holly might help,' Sarah said with a sigh. 'It couldn't have been worse, could it?'

'Nope.' Paul sounded remarkably cheerful. 'But you don't give up easily, remember?'

'I'll think of something,' Sarah promised. 'Hey, I'm not on call tonight. Any chance of you getting away?'

'I'll talk to Mrs Henry.'

'Is she your housekeeper?'

'Yes. She's a widow and seems glad of the extra cash. Daniel doesn't like it but he's having to get used to it, what with all the out-of-hours meetings the cleaners' dispute has caused.'

'Was Daniel the real reason you went into management?'

Paul nodded. 'I found I didn't really know my son. There he was, about to start school, and his upbringing had been left to a series of live-in nannies and housekeepers. His behaviour was deteriorating and I suddenly realised I had a very lonely and unhappy little boy on my hands. I had to change something pretty drastically and the long hours at work and on call seemed an obvious place to start. I did think I could do a good job in management but it was the hardest thing I've ever done—leaving surgery.'

'Has it helped Daniel?'

'Oh, yes. We're much closer. He's still not as happy as I'd like him to be, though.'

'And neither are you.'

'I'm much happier than I was a couple of weeks ago.' Paul bent to plant a series of kisses on Sarah's face and lips. 'God, I'll make sure Mrs Henry is available tonight. I'm having severe withdrawal symptoms.'

'Good.' Sarah scrambled to her feet after a quick glance at her watch. 'I'd hate to think I was suffering alone.'

As they walked back to the main entrance together Sarah suddenly chuckled.

'What's so funny?'

'That I got so angry, thinking you were having an affair with me. It *is* like having an affair— snatching bits of time together. Only it's not your wife we have to worry about. It's your son.'

'I'm sorry things are complicated,' Paul said slowly, 'but I can't apologise for having Daniel. Until I met you he was the only person in the world that I would have sacrificed everything for. Now he's just got to accept that I'm not prepared to sacrifice my relationship with you.'

'It'll work out,' Sarah promised. 'It has to. I just need to find a key, that's all.' She paused thoughtfully as their paths diverged. 'Does Daniel want to be a policeman when he grows up?'

'Good grief, I don't think so. What on earth makes you ask?'

'It's just that when I saw him that first time he was…uh…looking at a picture in a magazine. A police handler and his dog. It looked as though it might be significant.'

Paul laughed. 'It was the dog, not the policeman.' His smile vanished. 'Daniel has a passion for dogs. He's begged for one for years but there's just no way I can accommodate it. Not with our lifestyle.'

'That's great!' Sarah enthused.

'Sorry?' Paul was clearly bewildered.

'You've just given me the key, I think. Keep Saturday free. I'll pick you both up as soon as I finish my ward round.'

Sarah's excitement about her plan and the sheer joy that last night's few hours together had given her had to be shelved the next day as she faced a hectic time on take. The firm's houseman had to cope with most of the ward duties as Sarah found herself unable to get away from the emergency department.

Her first case was a very distressed six-year-old, David Hill, having his first severe asthma attack. He was unable to use the peak flow monitor, but with the help of his mother and a nurse Sarah was able to attach a blood-pressure cuff and measure the major swing in blood pressure caused by massive respiratory effort against constricted airways. The airway obstruction was severe. She started the nebuliser treatment another staff member had prepared while she had been making her brief examination.

'We'll use compressed oxygen, not air,' Sarah reminded the junior houseman. 'We'll get an IV line in and start steroids as soon as we've completed this nebuliser.' She looked again at her young patient with concern. 'If there's no real improvement then I'll do an arterial stab to check blood gases and we'll repeat the nebuliser.'

Leaving the other staff to supervise David, Sarah went to see a twelve-year-old girl, Bonnie, who was waiting next door. Her mother looked very relieved to see Sarah.

'Bonnie's had this terrible headache for two days,' she explained. 'She fainted yesterday and we went to the GP. He said to go home and give her some paracetamol, but it was no better this morning and the doctor said to bring her straight in here. He said it could possibly be meningitis.'

Sarah examined the girl carefully. She was certainly very sick and had a stiff neck but there were no other indications of meningitis.

'Bonnie's obviously very unwell,' she told the mother. 'I can't say for sure what's wrong but certainly with her symptoms the possibility of meningitis has to be considered. She has some of the symptoms, like a stiff neck, but her pain is unusual in that it's quite localised to one side. Other signs I might expect are not there but there's only one way to be sure and that's to do a lumbar puncture. Have you heard of that, Bonnie?'

The girl shook her head miserably. Sarah explained the procedure and then went back to check on David while the nursing staff set up. Not too happy with his progress, she ordered a trolley and preparations for inserting an IV line and doing an arterial puncture. She smiled grimly at the emergency department registrar, Matt, who stopped her as she was heading back to Bonnie.

'We've got a very sick baby just come in. Severe gastroenteritis and looks pretty dehydrated.'

'I've got a lumbar puncture to do now.' Sarah frowned. 'Can you get an IV in and do an arterial stab on David Hill for me? I'll get to the baby in five minutes. What cubicle?'

'Four.' The registrar vanished behind David's curtain.

Sarah had Bonnie sitting up and leaning forward to perform the lumbar puncture. The procedure was over quickly and Sarah then inserted an IV cannula and arranged for the girl's admission.

'We'll know the results within a few hours,' she told them. 'In the meantime, we'll start some antibiotics and get you comfortable up in the ward, Bonnie.'

The baby was another girl, Paige, and she was also very ill. Fourteen months old, she had had vomiting and diarrhoea for several days, was running a high fever and looked terrible. Her eyes were quite sunken, her skin had lost much of its elasticity and felt cold and clammy. Her level of consciousness was still good, however, and she hadn't suffered any convulsions.

'We're going to need to replace the fluids Paige has lost,' Sarah explained to the distraught young parents. 'We'll have to admit her and keep a close eye on her for a day or two.'

Sarah weighed the baby and found she was nine kilograms. She smiled at the parents. 'That makes my job easier. I won't need a calculator.'

'Why's that?' Paige's father relaxed visibly at Sarah's smile.

'With the condition Paige is in we assume that she's lost eight to ten per cent of body weight so that is the amount we need to replace.' Sarah put on gloves and swabbed the baby's scalp. 'I'm going to put a tiny tube into a vein here so we can put the fluids through it.'

Paige's wails as the nurse restrained her made Sarah's job easier, distending the veins on her scalp, but it made it much more distressing for the mother. Sarah smiled sympathetically and then turned her attention to slipping the needle into the vein.

'It's twice as hard to have things done to your children as it is to have it done to yourself, isn't it? There, that's got it.' Sarah reached for a syringe and clipped it onto the end of the needle. 'I'm going to take a blood sample first and then we'll tape it down and attach the infusion.' She gave the baby back to her mother and nodded at the nurse.

'Make up 800 mils half-strength isotonic saline.' Sarah turned back to Paige's parents. 'We're going to admit Paige now and I'll be watching her very carefully for the next few hours. When we've replaced the fluids she's lost then we'll start another infusion at a slower rate to maintain her levels.'

Even when she finally made it up to the ward, having missed the lunchtime Paediatric meeting and presentation, Sarah found her time taken up completely by her new admissions.

David was improving slowly, but he still needed continuous nebuliser treatment as well as IV medication. Bonnie's mother was much happier, having professional help to care for her sick daughter, but Paige was concerning Sarah. Her electrolyte deficits meant frequent adjustments to the rate and strength of her infusion, and Sarah didn't feel confident that things were under control until she finally left the hospital at ten p.m.

In contrast, the atmosphere in the ward on Saturday morning was controlled and positive, and Sarah found all her new admissions improved. David was down to a nebuliser treatment at three- to four-hourly intervals, Paige was ready to be offered an oral feed and Bonnie's test results had ruled out meningitis. It now seemed likely that she was suffering from mycoplasma pneumonia, which would still mean observation for several days and a lengthy course of antibiotics. After a whirlwind catch-up on all her other patients Sarah was happy to leave the hospital.

The effects of the positive morning were still with her when she drove over to collect Paul and Daniel. She wasn't going to let the child's unresponsiveness undermine her optimism. Sarah refused to tell them where they were going until she turned into the long, tree-lined driveway of her parents' property. Having primed her mother, Sarah was pleased to see the whole family contingent of eight retrievers waiting to greet them. Her mother had even embellished the plan by coming out, holding a tiny representative of the latest litter. Sarah saw Daniel smile for the first time when Evelyn handed him the puppy.

'Look after this chap for me, Daniel. I'd better get this mob under control.'

At the sharp whistle the dogs abandoned their enthusiastic inspection of Paul and milled around Evelyn. 'Sit!' she ordered.

Sarah saw the look of awe on Daniel's face as all eight dogs sat and gazed adoringly at their mistress. She was amused to find the expression mirrored exactly on Paul's face.

'Don't get out of line around here,' she warned him. 'It's not worth it.'

'I've got every intention of behaving myself,' Paul replied. He grinned at Sarah's father. 'How come Sarah hasn't turned out to be the model of obedience?'

'It's beyond me.' Jack laughed. 'Come and have a beer before lunch.'

Evelyn and Daniel vanished into the puppies' quarters. They still hadn't appeared thirty minutes later after Paul had finished his first beer, admired Ping's progress and had begun an animated conversation with Jack about the perspective a rural GP had of the current health system. Sarah decided the bacon and egg pie her mother had made was in dire need of coming out of the oven. Evelyn and Daniel appeared briefly at that point, wolfed down some lunch and vanished again. Daniel shot a grin at his father as he left.

'Evelyn's going to show me the obedience and

agility stuff she does. She says it's really easy to train a dog.'

Sarah felt a wrench at the child's grin and happy tone. God, he was so like his father. Paul gave her a thumbs-up sign. 'You were right,' he told her.

'What about?'

'Your mum's certainly got a knack with young creatures. I don't think I've ever seen him this happy.'

'This is the perfect place for kids.' Jack pushed his chair back. 'We don't get enough of them around here now. Plenty of dogs, though,' he added thoughtfully. 'And I guess there's not that much difference. Same need for constant feeding, same level of noise, same dirt being tracked through the house…'

Sarah laughed. 'At least we didn't shed hair!' She nudged Paul. 'Are you going to stop eating? I want to show you all my childhood haunts.'

It was getting dark by the time they drove back to the city. They stopped and had fish and chips for dinner at a country pub. Daniel didn't stop talking and the conversation was all about the dogs.

'It's quite hard to teach them scent-retrieving,' he explained to his father. 'What you do is carry around a hanky or something and make sure it's covered with your smell—'

Paul looked suspiciously at Sarah. 'Is *that* what you're doing with my hankies?'

If Daniel was disturbed by the look that passed between the adults he didn't show it. 'Then you have other hankies that don't have your scent on them. You have to use tongs or something to spread them around.'

Paul's and Sarah's gazes caught again and held. There was no need to speak. The wonderful afternoon they'd all had and the bubbly child now sitting with them was all the encouragement they could have hoped for.

'When the dog picks up the right one you have to praise it heaps. If it goes for the wrong one you just ignore it and put it back.'

Paul smiled at his son. 'Your dinner's getting cold, mate.'

Daniel looked embarrassed. 'I guess I'm talking too much. Sorry.'

'Don't be.' Sarah's lips curved into a gentle smile. 'I'm glad you had a good time, Daniel.'

'I did. Thanks.' Daniel looked away but then his eyes turned on his father. The pleading look in his eyes reminded Sarah of the retrievers they'd left behind. 'I wish I could have a dog, Dad.'

'Wishes come true occasionally,' Paul said thoughtfully. 'All you need is a bit of magic.'

'Yeah.' Daniel's face fell into familiar lines again. 'There's not much of that around, though, is there?'

'Oh, I don't know about that,' Sarah murmured. 'I've noticed a bit here and there.'

CHAPTER SIX

THE magic was about all right.

The sense of family they had achieved on Saturday was enough for both Paul and Sarah to feel confident that their own wish could come true. It was a week of frequent meetings, joyous love-making and excited plans.

'We'll get Daniel a dog!'

'Maybe two,' Sarah agreed.

'A house in the country!'

'Absolutely. How about a new job for you?'

'Terrific idea. But what about you?' Paul looked serious suddenly. 'I don't expect you to give up a promising career because of me and Daniel.'

'I'm not even sure what I want to do yet,' Sarah said. 'I'm seriously considering taking Martin Lynch up on his offer of part-time work in his private practice. I'd like the long- term follow-up that would give me on patients. General practice would be good for that as well. Dad will have to retire some time. And I'd have time to try other things. I'd like to write a book.'

'What sort of book?' Paul looked intrigued.

'Maybe a sort of practical paediatric guide for parents. What to worry about and what *not* to worry about. Maybe a bit of psychology thrown in as well.'

'You might need some first-hand experience,' Paul warned.

'I've got plenty of experience,' protested Sarah.

'Not as a parent,' Paul grinned wickedly. 'But that can be arranged. Come here.'

'No way! I'm not following in my sister's path. I intend to have a husband first.'

'That can also be arranged,' Paul promised. He kissed Sarah's neck, his hand lightly brushing her breast on a downward path.

'Mmm. Well, in that case...'

During her last week on her paediatric run Sarah seemed to be busier than ever. The joy she had found in her relationship with Paul spilled over into her professional life and nobody could fail to notice the change. Martin Lynch was delighted for his registrar.

'I knew he'd been impressed with you,' he said with a smile. 'I just didn't realise how much.'

Angela was astounded. She admired the huge diamond solitaire on Sarah's finger. 'I thought you said he was an unmitigated bureaucrat who didn't listen to anything you said.'

'I did say he was tall, dark and handsome as well.' Sarah twisted the ring on her finger.

Paul had dragged her away after her outpatient clinic the day before. They had trailed around numerous jewellery stores, with Sarah protesting all the way.

'We can't do this yet, Paul. Daniel's not ready.'

'We don't have to set a date,' Paul had argued.

'I just want some visible evidence that this is really happening. That you feel the same way I do.'

Sarah had met his intense gaze and had smiled gently. Then her smile had stretched to a grin. 'You haven't proposed yet.'

'Haven't I?' Paul looked horrified. To the amusement of the jewellery store manager, two assistants and several other customers, he dropped to one knee in front of the counter.

'Sarah Kendall, will you do me the honour of becoming my wife? I love you,' he added hastily.

Sarah's gurgle of laughter had the whole shop smiling. 'Of course I will. Please get up off the floor.'

The onlookers clapped as Paul scrambled to his feet. 'Right. Let's get on with finding this ring.'

The presence of the ring on her finger was a constant, though unnecessary, reminder to Sarah of how happy she felt. She was enjoying her ward round. Bonnie was finally ready for discharge and a much happier girl than when she'd been admitted with suspected meningitis the previous week.

'You'll need to stay on the antibiotics for another two weeks,' Sarah told her, 'but your chest sounds great and the X-ray we did this morning looks fine. We'll see you in the outpatient clinic when you've finished the course of pills.'

Not that she would be seeing her, Sarah realised with a pang. She wouldn't have any contact with these patients again and she still hadn't made any arrangements about what she was going to do. She touched the diamond on her finger as though it were a talisman. The future might be unknown but it would be shared, and that was enough to dispel any qualms.

Her visit to David Hill was also a happy one, despite the upper respiratory tract infection which had complicated the control of his asthma and delayed his recovery.

'You haven't had any dip in your morning peak flow rate for three days,' she congratulated him. 'We can take out the IV line now. We'll go back to your normal inhaler treatment and a course of pills. We'll keep you in for another day or two but then you can go home. Oh, look at this.' Sarah fished in her pocket. 'What do you think of this new inhaler holder?'

'Cool!' David's eyes lit up.

Sarah handed over the bright yellow plastic container in the shape of Bart Simpson's head. 'You can get a glow-in-the-dark Casper or Spiderman as well,' Sarah told him. 'And they're going to bring out Tweety Bird and Daffy Duck shortly.'

David looked at the sweatshirt Sarah was wearing again. 'I like Bart Simpson. Thanks, Dr Sarah.'

Sarah refused to be dismayed when she saw Angela's grim expression on her return to the office, but the nurses's words curtailed her optimism.

'We've got a re-admission coming in.'

'It's not Michael, is it?' The last report Sarah had had from the physiotherapist was that Michael was doing well—the fitting and adjustment of the artificial leg was progressing rapidly.

'No, not Michael. Worse.'

'Let me guess. Anthony?'

Angela nodded. 'His GP's referred him back. Another dose of pneumonia.'

'Probably the same one,' Sarah growled. 'I wonder just how successful his mother was at keeping up his medication.'

'IV treatment again, I suppose,' Angela said with a sigh.

'And for longer this time, I expect.' Sarah nodded. 'Call me when he gets here. We'll have to check for any underlying immunological problems as well.' She grinned ruefully. 'Lots of blood tests. Oh, excuse me, I want a word with Cheryl.'

She caught up with the physio. 'How's Michael?'

'Great,' Cheryl responded. 'He's coming in for an appointment this afternoon in the department. Why don't you come and see him?'

Sarah found them in the gymnasium later that day. Michael was walking between two bars, but only holding one. Wearing jeans and track shoes he looked like any other ten-year-old boy.

'Wow!' Sarah exclaimed. 'Which leg was it again?'

Michael's grin told her that was exactly what he wanted to hear. 'Watch this, Sarah!' Michael let go of the bar and walked unaided. His gait was a little stiff but his balance looked good.

'Where's the soccer ball?' Sarah smiled.

'I need a bit more practice first,' Michael admitted, 'but the kids at school are going to let me play when I'm ready.'

Sarah hugged him hard. 'I'm really proud of you, Michael. I'll bet you're proud of yourself, too.'

His grin was shy. 'Yeah, I guess.'

Anthony's re-admission was not quite as traumatic as Angela had feared. The little boy was sick enough not to put up too much of a physical struggle as Sarah took the blood tests and inserted an IV cannula. His hand looked like Fort Knox by the time she'd finished. The needle was covered with an upturned plastic container attached to the splint and stuck down with strong tape before the bandaging began.

'He'll never get that out,' she declared confidently. She watched the X-ray technician leave and wondered if she looked that harassed herself. While the physical struggle had been manageable the noise level had been exhausting. Sarah was very glad to escape herself.

It was unfortunate that Sarah decided to clear her in-basket at that point. Instead of recovering from her encounter with Anthony, she experienced a real slump in her mood. The blood tests were back on a little girl she had seen in her outpatient clinic the day before.

Two-year-old Natasha had been referred because of an apparent susceptibility to infection. While the illnesses had been minor their frequency had been causing concern and there was a suspicion of anaemia. Sarah's misgivings had been aroused on hearing that the child had suffered a nose-bleed recently, and her suspicions were now confirmed. Natasha was suffering from acute lymphoblastic leukaemia. Another Alice Forster, Sarah thought miserably. I couldn't go through that again. Ever.

Paul noticed her quietness when he met her after work. Sarah explained.

'She may do very well,' he encouraged her. 'The majority do these days.'

'There's still the trauma of the tests and treatments, though,' Sarah replied. 'And the agonising worry hanging over her parents for years.'

'It's the worst part of being a parent,' Paul agreed. 'Even when your child is perfectly healthy, like Daniel, there's always that fear that something might happen.'

They walked in silence to the car park.

'It doesn't happen very often, though. Your perspective gets skewed in a job like yours.'

Sarah nodded. 'It's time I took a break.'

'Do you feel up to tonight?'

She nodded again. 'I'll have to be back here by ten. I've agreed to cover for the neonatal unit. They still haven't filled their registrar position. They're putting a bit of pressure on me to give it serious consideration.' Sarah sighed. 'I hope I get some sleep but right now I'm more worried about this dinner tonight. Do you really think it's a good idea to tell Daniel yet?'

Paul waved as Sarah got into her car. 'I don't want to wait. I think he'll be thrilled when we tell him about our plans. Especially if he gets to have a dog.'

'I don't want a bloody dog!'

Daniel's language was no shock to Sarah but the anguished expression on his face certainly was. He looked from his father to Sarah and back again. The food on the table was ignored.

'You said we didn't need anybody else,' he accused Paul. 'You said we were a team.' His voice held the hint of tears.

'We *are* a team, Daniel,' Paul assured him gently. 'A great team. But Sarah could be part of the team.'

'Why?' Daniel struggled harder against the tears. 'Why do you want her?'

'I love Sarah, Daniel,' Paul said quietly.

'You said you loved me!' Sobs now punctuated the shouted words and Paul held out his arms to his son.

'I do love you, Daniel. More than anything.'

The small boy ignored the offered embrace. 'Not more than *her*!'

Silently Paul went to put his arms around his son but Daniel struggled free. He ran from the room and a door slammed loudly in the hall.

Paul started to move after him but stopped. 'I'll give him some time to calm down. Then we'll be able to talk.' He looked at Sarah who still sat at the table, staring down at her hands. 'I guess the house in the country wasn't enough.'

Sarah shook her head in agreement.

'Even the dog wasn't. I was sure that would swing it.'

Sarah looked up finally. 'This isn't going to work, Paul.'

Paul frowned. 'I thought you didn't give up easily.'

'This is different.'

'Why?' The tone was demanding. Sarah could see that the stress caused by Daniel's response to the news of their engagement had upset Paul deeply. This wasn't the best time to discuss any-thing.

'Why?' Paul repeated, the word almost a bark.

Sarah took a deep breath. 'Daniel's bond with you is the only security he's ever had. He's not confident enough to share that.'

'Well, he'll have to learn.' Paul sounded angry suddenly. 'It's something he'll just have to accept.'

'You can't force someone to accept something emotional,' Sarah said quietly. 'It's not in your power to control it.'

'He just needs some time.'

'No. It's too deeply rooted for that.' Sarah shook her head.

'He doesn't have to accept it, then. But he'll have to learn to live with it. I'm not giving you up, Sarah.'

'It wouldn't work, Paul.' Sarah had been twisting the ring on her finger. Now she eased it off. 'I'm not going to jeopardise the relationship you have with your son. You would only resent me for it. Maybe not immediately but one day you would, and it would be enough to undermine what we have together and eventually to destroy it.' She placed the ring carefully beside her plate and stood up.

Paul looked at the ring and then his gaze burned into Sarah's eyes. 'So you're prepared to throw our relationship away on the say-so of an eight-year-old boy?'

'He's not just a boy, Paul. He's your son.' Sarah picked up her bag. 'And I'd rather throw it away than watch it being destroyed piece by piece.'

'This doesn't say much about the strength of the love you claim to have for me,' Paul said bitterly.

'Perhaps it says more than you think.' Sarah's voice was flat. The pain growing within her was too great to acknowledge.

'Well, if it's that easy for you to throw away, perhaps I don't want it. Why don't you just leave? Go on!' Paul turned his back and began to clear the table. The dishes clashed as he gathered them together angrily.

Sarah opened her mouth but no words came out. She wanted to run to Paul, to put her arms around him and erase the angry exchange. But the muffled sob she heard from behind the closed door in the hall made her pause. Paul walked into the kitchen and out of sight. The situation was impossible and any attempt to rectify it at this point would probably only make things worse. Sarah turned and stumbled from the apartment.

If only they had waited. They could have waited to tell Daniel about their engagement. More importantly, they could have waited to discuss his reaction to it. How could they possibly have been rational in the aftermath of the emotional scene and with the knowledge that a small boy was sobbing his heart out in the room next door? She shouldn't have been so quick with her negative prognosis either, Sarah thought miserably.

She parked her car behind the administration block of the hospital and rubbed her finger where the ring had been. Her natural optimism had declined with the stress of treating Anthony and had

hit bottom on learning of Natasha Ward's leukaemia. It hadn't had a chance to surface again, before
being faced with Daniel's anguish.

Why did it seem so easy for the sparks to ignite
between Paul and herself? For the anger to take
over and disguise the love so effectively? I suppose
it's the flip side of passion, Sarah admitted. Just like
the flip side of the joy of parenting is the worry
about a sick child. She headed towards her office
to collect her white coat and hoped she wouldn't
be faced with too many examples of that type of
anguish tonight.

The neonatal intensive care unit was almost full
that night but the situation was controlled and stable
when Sarah arrived. She was early and there were
no new admissions on the way so she sat at the
central desk, reviewing the notes. It was a distraction from her own misery and would allow her to
be prepared if any complications arose.

Sarah glanced up sharply as an apnoea alarm
sounded but the passing nurse merely flicked the
tiny baby's toes. The reminder to start breathing
again was effective and Sarah turned back to the
notes with a sigh. She needed more of a distraction
than this was providing. When her beeper sounded
she reached towards the phone with relief.

It was Paul. 'Sarah, I'm sorry. I can't believe I
told you to go. It's the last thing I want.'

Sarah glanced around the unit. The staff were all
preoccupied but she lowered her voice anyway.
'It's the last thing I want, too, Paul.'

'I was upset. I couldn't believe Daniel would be
so anti.'

'How is Daniel?'

Paul sighed heavily. 'We've had a long talk. I tried to reassure him. Tried to explain that my loving you didn't mean I loved him any less. I also tried to explain that not having you in my life would make me very unhappy and that wouldn't help my relationship with him.'

'How did he react to that?'

'He was pretty quiet. I guess he needs a bit of time to adjust to the idea. He's asked me to read him a bedtime story. He's done that for himself for a long time now so I think he's still upset.'

Sarah's beeper sounded. 'I'd better answer that,' she said apologetically. 'Can I call you back?'

'I'd really like that.' The warmth of the response flowed through Sarah as she replaced the handpiece and immediately lifted it again to dial the number on her pager. In response to that call Sarah hurried down to Emergency. A ten-day-old baby had been rushed in, after being found not breathing and blue in his bassinet. Resuscitation attempts had been successful and Sarah found no evidence of any abnormality when she carefully examined the baby.

'Has he been unwell at all in the last few days?'

The baby's mother was pale. She shook her head.

'Is this your first baby?'

The young woman nodded. She held tightly to her husband's hand and it was he who answered Sarah's queries about the pregnancy and delivery. All had been normal.

'What position was he sleeping in?'

'On his back. We knew about not letting him

sleep on his stomach and not having a sheepskin. We thought we were doing all the right things.'

'I'm sure you were,' Sarah assured them. 'We can't explain why this happens in a lot of cases.'

'If we hadn't checked on him…' The mother's voice was a terrified whisper.

'It's very lucky that you did.' Sarah wrapped the baby back in its shawl and placed him in his mother's arms. 'We'll keep George in tonight and monitor his breathing. We'll be able to check him more thoroughly tomorrow as well.'

'What about after that?' George's father spoke up again. 'Wendy was nervous enough as a new mother before this. We'll never get any sleep now.'

'We can discuss the use of an apnoea monitor at home if necessary,' Sarah told him. 'They can be a hassle and cause stress with false alarms, but in view of this attack you might be happier to use one, at least for the next few months.'

'Will it stop it happening again?' George's mother looked hopeful.

'It doesn't prevent a baby from having an episode of not breathing,' Sarah said carefully. 'What it does do is give you a warning so that you can respond.' She smiled at the parents. 'You responded very well in this case and George seems fine. Let's get you up to the ward. The nursing staff can show you the monitors and discuss it with you again.'

Sarah tried to ring Paul back, having seen George up to the ward, but there was no answer. Puzzled, she let the phone ring and ring.

'It must be a good book,' she decided finally, replacing the receiver. Heading back to the neonatal unit, Sarah realised she'd left her stethoscope in Emergency. Her beeper sounded as soon as she'd retraced her path.

'Sarah?'

'Paul. What's wrong?' She had recognised the voice, but only just. He sounded terrible. 'What's happened?' Sarah cried.

'It's Daniel.' Paul seemed to be catching his breath. 'He's run away.'

'What?' Sarah was shocked. 'Are you sure?'

'I went to read him a story and he wasn't in his room. I've checked the building, and Mrs Henry's and the garage.' There was a moment's heavy silence. 'I've just called the police.'

'Oh, God,' Sarah breathed.

Beside the wall phone Sarah was using was the desk on which stood a radio transmitter. It was the contact point between the department and the ambulance service. It warned the department of incoming casualties and their status, and also allowed medical advice to be given to paramedics, attending an accident scene. It crackled into life as Sarah clutched the phone. A senior nurse depressed the button on the microphone.

'Emergency here, Ambulance Three.'

'We're attending a hit-and-run accident, involving a boy approximately eight to ten years old. Serious head injury, unconscious. Please advise on airway control.'

Sarah covered the mouthpiece of the telephone. 'What street is it in?' she asked urgently. The nurse looked up at her sharply but passed the microphone to the registrar on duty, Matt Warnock.

'Please,' Sarah begged. 'What street?'

'Sarah?' She could hear a frantic note in Paul's voice. 'Sarah? Are you still there?'

'Hang on, Paul.' Sarah covered the phone again. Matt paused in his queries about the child's vital signs. 'Worcester Street,' he told her tersely.

'Paul? Are you anywhere near Worcester Street?'

'It's just around the corner. What—?'

'There's an ambulance attending an accident,' Sarah said carefully. 'It probably isn't Daniel, but—'

There was nothing more she could say. Sarah could hear the thump of the dropped handpiece as it swung against the wall. A few seconds later came the tone of a disconnected call. Sarah hung up at her end and tuned in to the instructions the registrar was issuing.

'Do you have an oral airway in place?'

'Affirmative.'

'Ventilate by mask. Have you got IV access?'

'Working on it now.'

'Make sure it's wide bore. Use one third normal saline. Let half a litre run in fast. Put on a cervical collar and use a spinal board. What's your ETA?'

'About ten minutes.'

Sarah closed her eyes. Don't let it be Daniel, she begged silently.

But she knew.

She knew it couldn't be anyone else.

CHAPTER SEVEN

IT WAS the longest ten minutes of Sarah Kendall's life.

The identity of the young hit-and-run victim had been confirmed when Paul arrived at the accident scene just as they were transferring Daniel to the ambulance. Matt took one look at Sarah's face and contacted another paediatric registrar on duty to arrange cover for the neonatal unit. He contacted the neurosurgical registrar on take, an anaesthetist and the X-ray department. The high status number and the triple 8 code given by the paramedic staff had been a priority signal to get the appropriate specialists and equipment to Emergency.

'We need a portable unit in Emergency and have the CT scan staff on standby,' he ordered. 'We've got a young accident victim on the way in with multiple injuries, including a compound, depressed skull fracture.'

Sarah shuddered. It had been Paul who'd examined Daniel in the ambulance and made the diagnosis of the head injury. Sarah had never felt so afraid in her life. Would Daniel even make it to the hospital? If he survived, was he going to have terrible brain damage? She knew Paul would blame himself. What if he also blamed their relationship— or her?

Sarah watched as the staff prepared the resusci-

tation room, IV, X-ray and cardiac monitoring
equipment. She could do nothing to help. It was
almost surreal, this waiting period. Medical staff
from the various specialties were gathering as the
wail of the siren was heard in the distance. Her own
fears had to be forgotten. Right now it was only
Daniel who mattered.

She ran with Matt and the triage nurse to help
lift out the stretcher as the ambulance doors swung
open. Then reality hit as she saw the small head
swathed in a blood-soaked dressing, the airway dis-
torting the mouth and the paramedic holding the
ambu-bag. She looked at the end of the stretcher
where the portable cardiac monitor showed an erratic trace and then to the other end where the bag
of IV fluid was being held aloft by a white-faced
Paul. The moment seemed suspended in time and
then suddenly Sarah found it easy to forget about
herself totally as controlled chaos broke out.

They took the stretcher at a run to the resuscitation room. Four people arranged themselves instantly on either side.

'On the count of three. One, two...'

They lifted the small body, gently transferring it
onto the bed with the least possible movement to
the head and neck. Sarah could only stand and
watch as the team of medical staff went to work.
The anaesthetist took over the airway, suctioning
out secretions. The neurosurgical registrar checked
pupils and reflexes, calling to Daniel to try and get
a response. Daniel's clothes were being cut away
by a nurse. Another was replacing ECG leads and
taking blood pressure. Matt was inserting a second

IV line. It seemed as if everyone was talking at once.

'Any CSF leaking from the nose or ears?'

'Fifty percent oxygen.'

'We need bloods for CBC, electrolytes, amylase...'

'Do an arterial puncture for blood gas...'

'Type and crossmatch. We need units here now—he's losing a lot of blood. Start some haemaccel, stat—'

Sarah pressed herself further into the corner as the staff moved rapidly. She watched in horror as the dressing from Daniel's head was removed and fresh blood covered the gloved hands of the neurosurgical registrar, gently examining him. She had to move again as the bulky X-ray machine was pushed in. The orders still flowed.

'Skull, cervical spine, chest and pelvis shots.' The X-ray technicians joined the throng of staff.

'He's bleeding from somewhere else. This scalp wound isn't enough for that drop.'

'Has he got a gag reflex?'

'Yes. Pass me that nasogastric tube.'

'Four broken ribs, right side.'

'What's the blood pressure?'

'What's the Glasgow coma scale score?'

Sarah found the sounds blurring. She could still hear people calling to Daniel, trying to elicit some sort of response.

'No eye opening—pupils dilated.'

'No verbal response.'

'Minimal flexion to pain. GCS score of five.

We'll intubate now.' The anaesthetist's orders took priority for the moment.

'I don't want any additional anaesthesia if we can avoid it or we could push him into refractory shock. He's deeply enough unconscious. Give me some spray local for his throat and we'll go for a crash intubation.'

'We've got a haemothorax here, thanks to these broken ribs,' Matt advised.

'That explains the extra blood loss, then. We'll do an intercostal drain as soon as we've got him ventilated. Somebody booked a CT scan?'

'Blood pressure's dropping—unreadable,' a nurse warned.

'Tachycardia!' Someone else advised. 'No, ventricular fibrillation.'

'He's arresting!'

The X-ray staff and several others backed away as the activity became frantic. Sarah knew she shouldn't really be there. She was only a spectator. But she wasn't watching alone. Her hand had lost all feeling due to the vice-like grip in which it was being held. She wasn't sure who turned away first as the CPR began on Daniel but she clung to Paul and held him, hoping somehow to drive away the horror of what was happening. She felt the man in her arms cringe as they heard the discharge of the defibrillator.

'Sinus rhythm.'

The sigh of relief was collective but it was several seconds before Sarah and Paul turned back to the scene. Gradually, the staff completed their urgent investigations and the ventilation procedures were finished. A more controlled atmosphere descended and Matt finally left Daniel's side and came over to Paul.

His smile acknowledged the grim situation. 'We're over the first hurdle.' He tried to sound encouraging. 'He's stable for the moment.' He glanced back at Daniel, frowning. 'He's got severe bruising on his right leg but no fractures. The broken ribs caused a haemothorax—we've drained a good half-litre of blood from his chest and shouldn't need to treat that any further. Pelvis is OK and no sign of abdominal haemorrhage. The most serious injury is obviously the skull fractures and we're going to take him up for a CT head now.'

'Fractures?' Sarah had not picked up that there was more than one.

'He's got the depressed, compound fracture on top and another fracture at the base,' Matt told her. 'That one doesn't look too serious but I expect he'll have a couple of pretty black eyes. Anyway, the scan will tell us a bit more so let's get this show on the road.'

Paul nodded grimly. Sarah kept a tight hold of his hand as they trailed after the bed and attendant staff. They had both been in this situation many times but never on the receiving end. The change in perspective was total. And terrifying. Despite her own knowledge and experience, Sarah felt helpless, totally dependent on the professional staff around them. If she felt like this, she could only imagine what Paul was going through. Being able to interpret the test results and understand the language and procedures didn't make it any easier. In some ways it made the situation worse.

The CT scan was performed quickly. Sarah watched silently as Daniel's tiny form disappeared into the circular opening of the huge machine. She watched Paul's face as his eyes, darker than she had ever seen them, were riveted to the screens, displaying the images. His voice, as he discussed what they were seeing with the radiologist and surgeon, was hoarse with strain.

'Dual fractures. I'm more concerned with this compound one.'

'We've got some cerebral contusion and haematoma here…and here.'

'Doesn't look too extensive.'

'It's well away from the motor complex. That should reduce the risk of seizures.'

'We'll still need a loading dose of anticonvulsants prior to surgery.'

'When will you operate?'

'Immediately. I want to relieve those haematomas and elevate the depressed fracture. We'll have to repair the dura as well but it doesn't look too bad.' The surgeon laid his hand on Paul's shoulder. 'We'll start antistaphylococcal antibiotics immediately. We should be in Theatre within an hour. It's looking pretty manageable from where I'm standing at present.'

Sarah and Paul stayed with Daniel until he was taken to Theatre. Suddenly, after all the intensive activity and all the people around them, they were left alone.

'Let's get some fresh air,' Sarah suggested.

Paul shook his head. They were in the theatre reception area. Paul's request to observe the surgery had been gently but firmly refused by the surgeon, much to Sarah's relief. He was a parent right now, not a surgeon—ex or otherwise. The theatre was no place for him to be. She took his hand and led him to the theatre staff's common room, deserted at present thanks to their emergency and a Caesarean in the adjoining theatre.

'Sit down,' she ordered. 'I'll make us some coffee.' She went to hand Paul a mug of the steaming liquid but he had his face buried in his hands.

'This is all my fault,' Paul groaned. 'I'll never forgive myself if...if...' His voice faded. The end of the thought was unbearable.

Sarah put both mugs down on the table and sat beside Paul. 'I'm to blame just as much as you are, Paul.'

'Don't be ridiculous.' Paul's chair was pushed back with a harsh scrape. He jerked to his feet and began to pace around the small room. 'I was the one who pushed it. I insisted on our engagement. I was determined to tell Daniel about it. I had to have what *I* wanted so badly. Never mind my son.'

'You've done everything you could for Daniel,' Sarah stated firmly. 'For God's sake, Paul, you've brought him up entirely by yourself. You've thrown away a career you loved just so you could be there to take him to school in the mornings, read to him at night, spend the weekends with him. You've given him all the love and security he could need.'

'Not enough.' Paul's voice was agonised. 'You said yourself he wasn't secure enough to share my love. No wonder he felt he wasn't important any more. That he had to run away to try and show me how much he mattered. How could I have been so bloody selfish?'

'Don't make it an evil thing that we fell in love, Paul.' Sarah struggled against tears. The stress of their situation was being made so much worse by watching the man she loved, tearing himself to pieces. 'Please!'

Paul stopped pacing. He threw himself back into his chair. 'I'm not,' he said brokenly. 'It's just— I'm torn apart, Sarah. I love my son but I didn't love him enough. I should have known how he felt. I wasn't prepared to give you up for his sake, even temporarily. And now, if he…' Paul drew in a long shuddering breath. 'If he doesn't make it how can we live with the fact that it was our relationship that was responsible? I'm in a totally no-win situation here, Sarah, and it's killing me.'

'Would you rather I wasn't here?' Sarah spoke quietly, ignoring the tears that escaped and rolled down her cheeks.

'No. God, no.' Paul reached out and took Sarah's hand in both of his. 'You're the only lifeline I've got right now. Don't leave me.'

Sarah's lips trembled. 'I'm not going to leave, Paul. Not unless you want me to.'

'If anybody's to blame it's the driver of that car!' Paul's voice rose in anger. 'Did you know he stopped and then took off? The bastard!' Paul let go of Sarah's hand and his fist crashed onto the table. 'How could anybody do that? To a child…' He stared, unseeing, at the spilled coffee. 'Thank

God there was a witness. If the ambulance hadn't got there so fast...'

'Did they get a licence number?'

'No. Male driver. A late model Japanese car of some description. Black.'

'No wonder Daniel didn't see it.'

'He wasn't looking.' Paul rubbed his forehead with his palm. 'He was too upset to think about looking.'

'Mr Henderson?'

Sarah and Paul both jumped and then froze. Sarah found she couldn't breathe as she waited for the nurse to speak. How long had they been in here? It seemed too soon for news. How could it be anything but bad?

'Daniel's in Recovery now. Would you like to come and see him?'

The small boy looked peacefully asleep. The dressings to his head were a pristine contrast to the blood-soaked dressing they had last seen. Sarah listened quietly as the surgeon explained the situation to Paul.

'Very straightforward. We elevated and debrided the bone fragments and repaired the dural lacerations. Minimal extradural and subdural haematomas which we've cleaned up. We'll continue the prophylactic anticonvulsants. We've got an ICP monitor inserted.' The surgeon pointed to a probe, coming through the bandaging on Daniel's head. Sarah looked at the monitor reading as she heard the surgeon discussing the dosage of steroids and diuretics he was planning. A rise in intracranial pressure would signify what Daniel was now most at risk of—the development of acute brain swelling.

'We've got arterial and Swan-Ganz catheters in,' the surgeon continued. 'I want to keep a close eye on pressures and cardiac output for the moment. We'll keep hyperventilation going and monitor respiratory function, and he's got a urinary catheter in place. We need to keep an accurate fluid balance and watch renal function. These lines here...' he touched the plastic ports attached to another catheter in Daniel's arm '...are for serial blood sampling. That one's for IV drug administration and for fluids, which are at two thirds maintenance at present.'

Paul nodded.

'Any questions?' He looked at Paul and then raised an eyebrow at Sarah. 'No? We'll make a move to ICU, then. I'll see you shortly.' The surgeon made a final check of Daniel's pupil reaction. 'We'll reduce the sedation tomorrow but I can't say when he'll regain consciousness. So far he's doing as well as we could hope for.'

It was in the early hours of the morning before Daniel was settled in the intensive care unit. A comfortable armchair was placed alongside his bed for Paul. Sarah felt suddenly out of place.

'Do you want me to stay?'

Paul's face held only the hint of a smile as he looked at her. The lines around his eyes were deeply etched, the shadows beneath them mirrored by the dark roughness of his unshaven beard. He looked exhausted and desperately unhappy. Sarah touched the roughness of his cheek.

'You're going to need a razor and a change of clothes. I'll go and get them for you.'

'Thanks.' Paul caught her hand and pressed it against his cheek for a moment. The gesture conveyed all Sarah needed to know.

'Have you got your key?'

Paul shook his head. 'I didn't stop to lock up.'

Sarah nodded. 'I'll fix it. Is there anything special of Daniel's you'd like me to bring? For when he wakes up?'

Paul's eyes thanked her for her optimism. He sighed heavily. 'I can't think. Oh, wait. There's a book he always reads—an encyclopaedia of dogs— and there's an old toy, a kind of dog thing with black spots. He's had it since he was a baby.' Paul's voice had a harsh edge to it. 'One of the only things his mother ever gave him. God knows why he kept it.' He pressed his lips together and shut his eyes, as though blotting out a memory or perhaps the present situation.

'I'll find it,' Sarah promised. 'I'll be back as soon as I can.'

'You should get some sleep,' Paul said heavily. 'There's no rush. We're not going anywhere.'

Sarah did manage a couple of hours of troubled sleep just before dawn. Daniel was stable and Paul was by his side. It was a vigil Sarah was unable to share completely, either in time or emotionally. She was, however, not in good shape when she arrived for duty on Ward 23.

'What on earth's the matter?' Angela and Judith fussed around Sarah. If they noticed the fact that her engagement ring was now missing they said nothing. Sarah was still explaining the situation, somewhat tearfully, when Martin Lynch entered the office.

'I read about the accident,' he told Sarah. 'It's front-page news. You shouldn't be here.'

'I need to do something,' Sarah protested. 'The waiting is so hard.'

'You're in no condition to treat anybody.' Martin Lynch gripped Sarah's shoulder. 'You need some food and some rest and to be there when they need you.' He smiled at her kindly. 'They're your family-to-be.'

Angela and Judith made noises of agreement. 'Everything's under control here,' Angela assured Sarah. 'Even Anthony's IV line is still in.'

Sarah smiled lopsidedly. 'I knew he wouldn't get that one out.'

'Go,' Martin Lynch ordered. 'There's only a few days of your run left and I'll see it covered. We don't want to see you back here unless you're handing out wedding invitations.'

If only they knew, Sarah thought miserably as she left the ward, how unlikely that now was. Paul had said he was in a no-win situation. She felt that she was also in it—even deeper. If Daniel survived and Paul broke off their relationship at least he would have his son. Sarah would have no one.

That's not entirely true, she reminded herself. Starting her car, she found herself heading out of the city. She still had her family and right now that was where she needed to be. She rang Paul as soon as she got there. The situation was unchanged.

'I've still got your key. I'll get another change of clothes for you and come in this evening. Ring me if there's any news.'

'Get some sleep, Sarah. One of us needs to.'

'I will. I'll watch Daniel tonight so you can get some, too.'

There was a silence. Sarah could feel the despair at the other end of the line. 'Paul?'

'Yes.'

'Don't give up. On anything.'

Not giving up was also the message Sarah's parents gave her repeatedly. Her mother's optimism, good food and care for her well-being was enhanced by her father's practical advice and encouragement. Sarah felt rested and greatly cheered by the time she arrived back at the hospital. She found Paul reading to Daniel from the encyclopaedia of dogs.

'''Road exercise on a lead is important for all dogs,''' she heard. '''It is essential to harden the pads of the feet, strengthen the toes and keep the nails short.'''. Paul stopped and looked up as Sarah approached. He smiled ruefully.

'I ran out of things to talk about. I doubt if he can even hear me, anyway.'

They both looked at the unconscious child. The bruising around his eyes had darkened dramatically, giving him a racoon-like mask. The rings were made all the more dramatic by the contrast they made with the white bandaging and his pale skin.

The rhythmic click and hiss of the ventilator and the bleeps of various monitors filled the silence.

'You don't know that,' Sarah said. 'Even if he can't respond, some part of his brain might be aware of your presence and the sound of your voice.'

'That's what I keep telling myself.' Paul sighed.

'Has he shown any signs of waking up?'

'There's some spontaneous respiration,' Paul told her. 'That's about all. Cardiac function is stable. They've taken out the Swan-Ganz line.'

'That's a start.' Sarah looked at all the other lines still attached to Daniel. There was a fair way to go.

Paul followed her gaze. Then he took hold of her hand. 'I'm glad you're here, Sarah.'

'So am I.' Sarah looked at Paul with concern. He obviously hadn't used the razor she'd brought him. If he'd changed his shirt that wasn't apparent either. The rolled-up sleeves and sweat stains made him look even more exhausted. 'You need to have a shower and shave,' she told him firmly. 'And to get into some clean clothes.'

'No. I can't leave him.'

'It's only for ten minutes, Paul. You'll be a lot more use to him if you're feeling better. I'll be here.'

Eventually Sarah persuaded him and he did look refreshed when he returned. He refused to go out for food, however, so Sarah collected dinner on a tray from the cafeteria and carried it back. He also refused to sleep, despite Sarah being there to watch Daniel, but exhaustion finally took its toll and Paul fell asleep in the armchair. Sarah covered him with a blanket and sat on another chair close to the bed.

Nursing staff came and went unobtrusively. They changed Daniel's position and checked his skin condition, suctioned the airway and checked the respirator tubing connections. One nurse came to put artificial tears in his eyes, another to take blood and urine samples. Recordings of measurements and observations were added to frequently. But Sarah felt mostly alone. She watched the monitors, watched Paul sleeping and watched Daniel's still face. She took hold of one of the boy's hands and just sat, quietly holding it, not speaking or moving.

Sarah became aware of the warmth of the small hand and felt it gradually flow into herself. At some point during the lonely vigil Sarah became acutely aware of the love she now felt for this child—not just because he was a part of the man she loved so deeply but just because he was Daniel. A small boy who had been betrayed by his mother and was lonely for the love he should have had from her. A child, like his father, who was passionate about the things important to him and desperately sensitive and vulnerable.

Sarah wanted more than anything to enfold this child, to make everything all right and to let him know how much she loved him. She wondered at her own intense reaction. This must be how mothers feel, she thought, and she felt a slow tear trickle down her cheek.

Paul slept for several hours but couldn't be persuaded to leave Daniel for fresh air or breakfast. By dinnertime that day, however, he was ready for a

break. Sarah was worried about his emotional state.
They were in a kind of limbo that could only be
broken when Daniel regained consciousness. So far
he had shown no signs of doing so. A repeat CT
scan that day had been promising. All his vital signs
were stable and he was being successfully weaned
from the ventilator. His breathing had been stable
enough to take him off the machine for long per-
iods, leaving him to breathe through the endotracheal tube.

When the coma showed signs of further lightening they would then remove the tube to let him
breathe unassisted. There was even some response
to painful stimuli, such as eyebrow pinching, but
still he wouldn't wake up.

Throughout another long night and day they held
on. The media interest in the story continued. The
hunt for the driver of the car escalated. Paul was
interviewed by the police. The driver had been
aware of the accident and it was possible he had
returned to observe the aftermath. Had Paul noticed
anything? There had been onlookers but he had
been aware of no one but his son. Now his only
concern was for Daniel's welfare. He couldn't help.

He refused interviews with the media who now
listed Daniel's condition as serious but stable and
concentrated their attention on the police operation
to narrow and trace the make of car involved.
Cards, flowers and gifts from well-wishers poured
into the hospital. Most had to be stored away from
Daniel's area in the intensive care unit.

Paul became more easily persuaded to leave his
son's bedside for short intervals. By the evening of

the fourth day Sarah was seriously worried. Despite the strength Paul showed and shared with her, she sensed in him a desperation that seemed close to breaking point.

She watched him pick at a meal in the cafeteria and then they walked by the river. Sarah noticed how often his eyes flicked down to the pager she was still carrying, despite having finished her hospital duties. He expected, and at the same time dreaded, a summons. Still, they talked. Not about Daniel. The long hours they were sharing together had provided an opportunity to really talk—about themselves.

They discussed their families, their childhoods and schooling, their dreams. Sarah felt she finally knew this man she had fallen in love with, and the knowledge only served to increase that love. The only thing they didn't discuss was marriage. Underlying much of what Paul said was the commitment he felt to his son and the priority he now gave their relationship. Sarah was too afraid to find out how she now fitted in.

Another topic they avoided was Daniel's mother, Catherine. Although curious, Sarah was quite content to wait until Paul felt ready to tell her about his ex-wife. It would not be that evening, however. When Sarah's pager sounded they both looked at each other in alarm. Hand in hand, they ran back towards the hospital, taking the stairs rather than waiting for a lift. When they saw the two police officers outside the doors to the intensive care unit they both slowed and then stopped, paralysed by a mutual fear.

Had the intensive police operation to find the hit-and-run driver now become a homicide inquiry?

CHAPTER EIGHT

'HE'S been arrested.'

'Who?' Paul seemed bewildered and Sarah knew the stress and exhaustion were taking a greater toll on him than she had feared.

'The hit-and-run driver,' the police office explained. 'He came forward finally. We thought you'd like to know.'

'Not really.' Paul began to walk towards the ICU doors. 'I've got my only child lying in a coma. That's the only thing I'm interested in.'

The police officers looked embarrassed. 'He was a teenager,' one said to Sarah. 'He panicked. Apparently, he returned to the scene shortly afterwards but saw that help had already arrived. He's very upset about it all.'

Sarah nodded. 'I'm sure he is. But, as Mr Henderson said, Daniel is our only concern right now. Excuse me.'

Sarah expected to find Paul in his usual position, holding Daniel's hand and talking to him. Instead she found him slumped in the armchair, his face buried in his hands. She touched his shoulders gently.

'I don't know how much longer I can take this.' His voice was muffled but Sarah could hear the pain only too well. She wasn't sure what she said to try and comfort him but the words kept flowing as she

tried gently to massage some of the strain from
Paul's shoulders and neck. She was also not sure at
what point he fell asleep but she covered him with
a blanket and sighed with relief.

For a long time Sarah sat and watched Daniel.
She held his hand and talked quietly, willing his
fingers to twitch or the dark lashes against his
cheeks to flutter. The tube had been removed that
afternoon. Daniel's breathing was strong and
steady. The severe bruising around his eyes was
fading now, and he looked as though he were
merely asleep, the scruffy soft toy dog, so obviously
treasured, tucked in beside him.

'It's time to wake up now, Daniel,' Sarah said
softly.

The nurse who came in to check the equipment
at that point smiled sympathetically at Sarah. 'He
will,' she said encouragingly. 'The EKG was definitely picking up today. He's showing response to
stimuli and commands. It's just not voluntary yet.
He just needs a good incentive,' she added. 'It
won't be much longer.'

'It's already been too long,' Sarah said, glancing
over her shoulder at Paul. Even in sleep his face
looked grim, the deeply shadowed eyes and downward curve of his lips testimony to his emotional
trauma. She looked back at Daniel and then at the
nurse.

'I've got an idea,' she said slowly. 'I'm going to
need your help, though. And I need to make a few
phone calls.'

It was just over an hour later that Sarah was again
at Daniel's bedside. The nurse looked up from her

seat beside the bed. 'No change,' she reported and then smiled. 'In either of them.' She glanced at Paul. 'Did you get permission?'

Sarah nodded, biting her bottom lip as she smiled. One arm had been tucked inside her coat. She now pulled the garment open with her other hand to show the nurse what she held.

'I'll leave you to it,' the nurse said. 'Good luck.'

Sarah took a deep breath and sat on the edge of Daniel's bed. It had been one thing to take a duckling into a general paediatric ward but this was something much more serious, and approval had been given only grudgingly by the consultant. She didn't have much time. Carefully, she took the six-week-old retriever puppy and sat him on the bed beside Daniel's hand. She stroked it gently.

'Behave yourself,' she whispered sternly, 'or we'll both be in big trouble.' Raising her voice a little, Sarah spoke to Daniel.

'You've got a visitor, Daniel. His name is Luke.' She picked up Daniel's limp hand and, holding it in her own, stroked it over the puppy. 'He's one of the babies you've already met. Do you remember? Feel how soft he is. Can you feel his ears?' Luke obligingly licked Daniel's fingers and Sarah was careful to protect the IV line going into the back of his hand. She kept talking. 'Luke really likes you, Daniel. He'd really like you to say hello to him.'

There was no discernible response from the child and gradually Sarah fell silent. It had seemed like such a wonderful idea but it wasn't going to make any difference at all. Tired out from his late night adventure, Luke curled up and went to sleep. Sarah's eyes also drooped. She'd just rest for a minute and then she'd have to put the puppy back in the box in her car.

Her eyes jerked open when she felt a touch on her cheek. She found Paul, smiling, and her own lips curved in an instant response. She hadn't seen Paul really smile since the accident happened and she'd forgotten the warmth it created in her.

'It was a brilliant idea,' he murmured.

'It would have been—if it had worked.' Sarah's smile faded and she looked down. The puppy was still asleep, Daniel's hand resting on its back.

'Paul?'

'Yes, my love?' Paul was still watching Sarah, his hand now stroking her neck.

'Is it my imagination?'

'What's that?'

'That Daniel's fingers just moved.'

The hand froze on her neck. Sarah held her breath. She was genuinely unsure of what she'd seen. Perhaps it had been wishful thinking and maybe she was unwarranted in raising Paul's hopes. They both watched, transfixed, as Daniel's hand moved infinitely slowly towards the head of the puppy. As it began to track down the puppy's back again Sarah saw the flutter of eyelashes. Carefully, she eased herself off the bed and backed away. She didn't want to be the first person Daniel saw if he opened his eyes. She didn't see the actual moment it happened but she was still close enough to hear Daniel's first mumbled words.

'Hi, Dad. Is Luke going to be my puppy?'

There could have been no better indication that Daniel was going to be all right and that no serious brain damage had been sustained.

He remained in the intensive care unit for another two days and was then transferred to Sarah's old haunt, Ward 23. Angela and Judith promised to take special care of their new addition and even agreed to another smuggled visit by Luke. Sarah had deliberately kept a low profile since Daniel had come out of his coma and Paul hadn't objected—somewhat to her dismay.

'I'm reluctant to push anything just now,' he'd explained. 'I nearly lost my son and it's made me think hard about our future.'

Whose future? Sarah wondered. Paul and Daniel's or Paul's and her own? But Paul was happier to spend more time away from Daniel now. He had some urgent duties to attend to as manager but the rest of the time he spent with Sarah. They'd made love for the first time in over a week the night after Daniel had been transferred to the ward. It had been a time of exquisite gentleness—an act of healing as much as of passion. Life seemed to be beginning again but the emphasis had changed. Daniel's well-being still held top priority.

'He's been asking to see Luke again,' Paul told Sarah. 'I told him that it was up to you. That it had been your idea in the first place.'

Sarah nodded. 'I did have some help. The staff had to agree and Mum met me halfway to town with the puppy. Perhaps I should get Mum to visit him with Luke.'

'He'd like to see your mum,' Paul agreed, 'but I think you should bring the puppy in yourself.'

Sarah had to laugh. 'And I thought I was the only child psychologist around here.'

The visit was a huge success, despite the fact that Luke wet Daniel's bed and chewed up three get well cards. Sarah and Daniel talked dogs and Daniel's eyes were shining by the end of the visit, but he did look very tired.

'Dad said maybe I would be able to keep Luke, Sarah. Do you think it would be all right with your mum?'

'I'll let you talk to her about that yourself. She's going to come and visit you soon. But I'll tell her not to sell him to anybody.'

'Thanks, Sarah.' Daniel yawned. Sarah scooped up Luke and put him back in his box.

'I'll get Judith to bring you some clean sheets.' She smiled. 'Maybe next time we'd better play with Luke outside.'

It was an unusual few days for Sarah. She spent a lot of time in Ward 23 but not as a doctor. Daniel's recovery was proceeding well, though he still suffered from bad headaches and tired very easily. Cheryl was working with him daily to mobilise and strengthen his badly bruised leg.

Sarah was sitting with Daniel one afternoon during the rest period when the physiotherapist poked her head around the door. Daniel groaned when he saw her.

'Oh, no. Not again! We're busy.' Daniel waved at the mess on his bed. They were sifting through a stack of old magazines, cutting out all the pictures of dogs they could find.

'We've done your work for today.' Cheryl smiled. 'It was Sarah I was hoping to find. I've got someone who's very keen to say hello.' She stepped back and Michael eased into view. He was carrying the soccer ball under his arm.

'Hey, Michael!' Sarah was delighted to see him. 'Are you ready for that game?'

'Yeah.'

'I'll be right there. This is Daniel. Daniel—this is my friend, Michael.' Sarah turned to Daniel as she made the introduction and was surprised to find him scowling suspiciously.

'Sarah's visiting *me*,' he informed Michael.

Sarah suppressed more than a smile. The jealousy was almost palpable. For the first time Sarah felt she had won a place in Daniel's heart. He was responding to her love and that could only mean an assurance of what she desperately craved for her own future.

'Tell you what, Daniel. Let's put you in a wheelchair and you can come and help me play soccer with Michael. Would you like to be goalie?'

The scowl faded. 'Can I be on your goal?'

Sarah couldn't wait to tell Paul. She knew he was having meetings all afternoon to finalise new contract details with the cleaners' union. The stalemate had been broken while Daniel had been in his coma. Paul had been completely disinterested and Sarah knew he wouldn't have gained any satisfaction from bickering over any final details today.

Even so, she was surprised to find him looking so grim when she went to his office after five.

'How did it go?'

'I gave them pretty much what they wanted on the minor issues. They're happy.'

'So it's all settled?'

Paul nodded. He drummed his fingers on his desk. Sarah noticed how dark his eyes were and could find no hint of a smile when she searched his face.

'But there's still a problem?'

He nodded again.

'Are you going to tell me about it?'

Paul picked up the fax that he had been drumming his fingers on. He waved it in the air and then slapped it back onto the desk angrily.

'This message is from Catherine. My ex-wife,' he explained, as though Sarah might have forgotten who she was. 'Thanks to the publicity surrounding Daniel's accident, some well-meaning old friend decided she should know about it.'

'And?' Sarah sensed there was more to Paul's anger. Much more.

'She's planning to visit him. Arriving the day after tomorrow.'

'From where?'

'Washington, D.C. I have the flight details here.'

'How do you think Daniel will react?'

'I have no idea. But I'm about to find out.' Paul jerked to his feet. 'This is the last thing we need.'

Sarah nodded. The triumph of her breakthrough with Daniel that afternoon suddenly lost its significance. How could she compte with a 'real' mother?

'And that's not all,' Paul sighed angrily. 'She's informed me in this communication that she's planning to sue for custody of Daniel.'

'What?' Sarah's mouth dropped open.

'It's all couched in legal terms. Basically it says if I can't ensure the child's safety then I must be an unfit parent. She's going to take over the rest of his upbringing and can do it much more to his advantage, thanks to her stable remarriage, permanent house staff and position in society earned by a very successful career in law.'

'She hasn't got a prayer,' Sarah hissed. 'She abandoned him as a baby, for God's sake.'

'Eight-year-olds are much less demanding than babies,' Paul said bitterly, 'and much less likely to interfere with career ambitions. Especially when you can afford to pay other people to raise the child.' Paul screwed his eyes shut as he rubbed his face. 'Unfortunately, my solicitor thinks she has a case, particularly in view of the fact that I'm not providing what might be considered a nuclear family situation.'

'Meaning?'

'That I'm not married. He has no mother figure in his life.'

'Yes, he does,' Sarah argued. 'Me.'

Paul rested both hands on Sarah's shoulders. 'That isn't enough. Not yet. We're not married.'

'In the words of someone I know rather well...' Sarah smiled faintly. 'That can be arranged.'

Paul's grip on her shoulders tightened. 'You'd do that? You'd marry me to give me grounds to fight this custody case?'

Sarah looked him squarely in the eye. 'No, Paul. I'd do that because I love you. Because I also love Daniel. And especially because I'm not going to let anything—or anyone—destroy our future together.'

CHAPTER NINE

'I ALWAYS knew she'd come back. That's why I kept Spot.' Daniel was clutching the old soft toy excitedly. 'So she'd know I hadn't forgotten. How many hours is it now, Sarah?'

Sarah tried to smile. 'Sixteen,' she told him. If seemed that she'd been counting the hours for ever, but her anticipation of the event couldn't have been more different to Daniel's. She was dreading it. 'It's time you got some sleep. When you wake up it won't be long to wait.'

'I know.' Daniel sighed happily. 'Do you think she's missed me, Sarah?'

'I think she must be very concerned about you to be coming all this way,' Sarah said carefully. She began to straighten Daniel's bed. Paul had gone to find him a glass of water.

'Do you think she'll want to take me back with her?'

Daniel's query startled Sarah. Paul had told him only of the intended visit. No mention had been made of the bid for custody.

'That would mean leaving your dad,' she said quietly. 'I thought you guys were a team.'

'We are.' Daniel's face fell, then he brightened. 'He'd still have you, though, wouldn't he?'

'Oh, yes. He'd still have me.' Daniel made no objection as Sarah bent and kissed his forehead.

'But the team would be missing its most important member.'

'Who's the most important member?' Paul came in, carrying the glass of water.

Sarah looked at Daniel but it was clear he didn't want to discuss the matter any more.

'Are you going to be here in the morning, Dad? For when my mother gets here?'

'I'll be here.' Paul kissed his son. Then his gaze caught Sarah's and she read in him the same dread she felt enclosing herself. Once again their future seemed uncertain. Whatever the outcome of tomorrow's visit, the balance would be changed in some fashion. The rocky foundations of their lives at present seemed no base to be building on.

Catherine's flight was due in at ten a.m. the next day. Allowing for time to clear customs and get a taxi to the hospital, Catherine wasn't expected until at least eleven. Paul refused to meet his ex-wife at the airport.

'She wasn't invited. She's not wanted,' he said bitterly to Sarah. 'The sooner she gets that message the better.'

'Daniel seems to want her,' Sarah pointed out. 'He can think about nothing else.'

'Daniel wants a dream,' Paul said heavily. 'A fairy-tale ending to what he sees as the missing part of his life. When he meets Catherine that dream will be shattered. He won't find the love he craves. It never existed. She didn't want a baby. She refused to consider giving up her career, even for a few weeks. She wouldn't hear of breast-feeding. God, she wouldn't even hold him for three days.'

'Why did you marry her, Paul?'

'I'd known her for years. Off and on,' Paul said thoughtfully. 'I was nearly thirty. The initial drive for career success was beginning to fade. I recognised that I needed something more in my life. Catherine seemed to be in a similar position. She'd been made a partner in her law firm. She'd proved she could do it. Maybe she was ready for a new direction or maybe it was the idea that she was attracted to. It wasn't until she became pregnant that she realised it wasn't a choice she'd really considered. I had to work very hard to persuade her not to terminate the pregnancy. It was the beginning of the end as far as we were concerned.'

'So you don't think she really wants Daniel back?'

Paul snorted. 'Of course she doesn't. Perhaps it's an idea she's chasing again, without having considered the implications. Maybe she wants to have a final shot at me. Or maybe her conscience has been pricked at the reminder of the child she abandoned. Whatever her motives, I'm quite sure Daniel is going to end up hurt and I can't forgive her for that.'

'Perhaps it's something he has to go through,' Sarah suggested gently. 'While it's hard, not to be able to shield him from the pain, maybe it's necessary to heal an even greater hurt. All you can do is to be there for him. Help him through it and provide the security for him to build on afterwards.'

'Just like you're doing for me.' Paul smiled suddenly and Sarah felt his bitterness fade. 'What would I do without you, Sarah?'

'I hope you're never going to find out,' she replied seriously. 'Have you made the arrangements with the registry office?'

'Yes. Tomorrow at four.' Paul looked at Sarah with real concern. 'This isn't the way I wanted it to be, Sarah. For you—for us. Are you sure you don't want to invite your family?'

'No.' Sarah smiled wistfully. 'This is just between ourselves.' She laughed suddenly but without mirth. 'It's a bit ironic, isn't it?'

'Why?'

'You're seeing your ex-wife for the first time on the day you're going to remarry. Out with the old and in with the new?'

'Catherine was out of my life a very long time ago, Sarah. I just wish she'd stayed out. For Daniel's sake even more than my own.' Paul shook his head. Then he drew Sarah into his arms. 'And, just for the record, you're not ''new''. You've always been part of my life. It just took me a hell of a long time to find you.'

Sarah went shopping the next morning. It took her until well after eleven to find the dress she wanted to wear that afternoon. The soft apricot fabric was perfect for the autumn tones of her honey blonde hair and brown eyes. The simple design of the dress was casual but was transformed into elegance by the matching jacket. The accessories were easy to find but Sarah decided against a hat. A nearby florist provided a small bouquet of flowers in matching tones, making a buttonhole spray with the smallest blooms. Sarah had her hair trimmed and then took her purchases back to her flat.

It was now one o'clock and the tension she'd been trying to ignore became overriding. She rang Ward 23.

'Angela? It's me, Sarah. Is Daniel's mother still there with him?'

'No, she's not.'

Something in Angela's tone made Sarah catch her breath. 'What time did she leave? Is Daniel OK? Did she upset him?'

'No, Daniel's not OK and, yes, she did upset him. But not by what time she left.'

'Oh, God. What did she do?' Sarah felt suddenly cold. Angela sounded very angry.

'She didn't show up. That's what she did.'

'What do you mean? Is the flight delayed?' Sarah was bewildered.

'No. The flight was on time. She wasn't on it. Paul was here with Daniel, waiting. Paul rang the airport at eleven-thirty to check that the plane had come in on time. He rang again at twelve-thirty to find out whether she'd been on it. Apparently she didn't bother getting on at the other end.'

'Oh, no!' Sarah breathed. 'How's Daniel taking it?'

'He's not,' Angela replied shortly. 'He's sitting in a wheelchair, waiting, out by the lifts. He won't listen to anything anybody tells him. He's convinced she missed the flight and she'll be getting another one as soon as she can.'

'How's Paul?' Sarah was appalled at this turn of

events. How could that woman do this to her son?
She had never even met Catherine but right now
Sarah hated her.

'Worried. We all are. Daniel's overwrought. He
didn't sleep much last night and was nearly sick
with excitement all morning. It's hardly good for a
recovering head-injury victim. We're considering
giving him a hefty sedative right now.'

'I'm coming in,' Sarah told her friend. 'This is
just awful!'

Sarah expected to find Daniel still watching the
lift when she arrived but the area was deserted. The
rest period was not yet over and the atmosphere of
calm seemed inconsistent with the emotional
trauma Sarah knew had occurred. She found Paul
in Daniel's room. The curtains were closed and
even in the dim light she could see that the small
boy was deeply asleep. Paul and Sarah embraced
fiercely and wordlessly. Then Paul led her out of
the room and closed the door behind him.

'You heard, then?'

'I rang Angela. She said they were thinking of
sedating him. I can't believe Catherine's done this
to him, Paul.'

'I can,' Paul said harshly. 'It's all the proof
needed that she couldn't care less about her son but
Daniel won't—can't—accept that.'

A nurse approached the pair as they leaned
against the wall by Daniel's door.

'Mr Henderson? Your secretary just rang. She
says there's a fax for you from Washington. She
thought you'd like to know.'

'Thanks.' Paul straightened his back. 'I'll go and

get it. I'm interested to see what excuse she's come up with.'

'Would you like me to stay with Daniel.'

'No. He'll sleep for hours. We gave him enough of a sedative to knock out a small elephant. Judith said she'll be watching him.'

'Then I'll come with you,' Sarah said decisively.

The fax was an excuse—of sorts. Catherine stated she had decided to wait until the custody hearing had been dealt with so that her visit could coincide with taking Daniel back to the States.

'Over my dead body,' Paul muttered.

Sarah sighed. 'Has any date been set for a preliminary hearing with the family court?'

'Early next week, according to my solicitor. He's keen to get a copy of our marriage certificate on his desk tomorrow.'

'Oh, Paul. How can we? After this?'

'How can we not?' Paul was watching Sarah carefully. 'Daniel's devastated, Sarah. Perhaps you were right when you said he needed to get through this in order to heal the greater hurt and build a future. But he's going to need a lot of help and I can't do it on my own.'

'I'm not sure he'll accept my help,' Sarah said nervously. 'We've achieved a friendship but that may not be enough. Even the trust he's built in me so far could well have been destroyed by what must seem like a new rejection from his mother.'

'I'm not talking about your helping Daniel precisely,' Paul said slowly. 'I said I couldn't do it on my own. It's me that needs you as well, Sarah.'

'But...' Sarah shook her head in confusion. She

sat down on the edge of Paul's desk. 'I thought
that—because of the accident—your relationship
with Daniel had priority, that you weren't going to
jeopardise it by pushing him too far or too fast. I
thought you were marrying me to make sure you
win permanent custody.'

'No.' Paul almost shook Sarah when he gripped
her shoulders. 'How could you think that? Sure, I
might have been prepared to postpone our marriage
if that would have helped. I thought I was being
selfish. I blamed myself for Daniel's insecurity and
unhappiness. But you know who is really to blame?
His mother, that's who.' Paul's grip on Sarah's
shoulders loosened. 'And I'm not being selfish in
forcing you into Daniel's life. You know why?'

Sarah shook her head, her eyes fixed on Paul's
so close to her own.

'When you're in an aeroplane and they're giving
the safety demonstrations they show you how to use
the oxygen masks, don't they?'

Sarah nodded, bemused by the turn in the conversation.

'You know what they say to any parents? That
you have to attend to your own oxygen supply before you attend to the needs of your children. In
order to help them you have to ensure that you're
capable of doing it.' Paul's fingers traced the outline of Sarah's face. 'You're my oxygen supply. I
can't help Daniel without you in my life, and he's
going to need all the help I can give.'

'I'd like to help too,' Sarah whispered. 'Not just
for you—or us—but because I love Daniel too.'

'I know you do.' Paul's smile was as gentle as

the fingers that now lingered on the curve of her lips. 'That night when he was still in the coma. You thought I was asleep but I woke for a while and watched you. You were holding his hand and crying. I didn't disturb you because I could feel I wasn't a part of that moment. I could also feel your love. I thought you looked like you were his mother.'

'I felt like it,' Sarah admitted shyly.

'One day Daniel will feel like your son,' Paul told her. 'I'm quite sure of it.'

'I wish he was.' Sarah bit her lip. 'I hope it's just a matter of love. And time.'

'Time!' Paul's eyes widened. He looked at his watch. 'We'll have to run. I've got my suit here but…' His gaze travelled over Sarah's jeans and her favourite Bart Simpson sweatshirt. 'Well, I guess it's quite appropriate in a way.'

Sarah laughed. 'We'll stop by my apartment. I can change in ten minutes. What about Daniel?'

'Judith has my cellphone number but I'm sure he'll sleep through till morning. You've no idea how done in he was.'

'I can imagine.' Sarah took the hand Paul offered her and climbed off the desk. 'We're not going to let it happen again.' She tugged his hand. 'Come on, we'd better not be late.'

The service was simple, the witnesses the registry office staff. Sarah experienced one moment of panic when the celebrant asked for the rings. She had completely forgotten the need for them. Paul produced a small velvet box from his suit pocket, inside which were two matching gold bands—his and hers.

'How did you manage to get the size so perfect?' Sarah queried afterwards. 'I'm impressed.'

'I knew you had a good reason to let me borrow your engagement ring.' Paul's smile was poignant. 'It let me have a matching wedding band made in the same size. That's why I didn't give it back straight away.'

'And I thought you were just glad to be released from your obligations.'

'Fat chance!' Paul's smile widened. He touched his glass to Sarah's. 'Here's to the future, Mrs Henderson.' He looked around them. 'I hope I can offer you a little more than this.'

Sarah grinned. 'Oh, I don't know. It's quite appropriate, really. I should have changed back into my sweatshirt and jeans.'

They were sitting on the floor of Paul's office in a deserted administration block. Fish and chip wrappers were spread on the floor beside them, their champagne in the heavy tumblers from beside the water carafe. Paul had checked on Daniel briefly to find him still asleep but felt the need to stay in the hospital overnight. Sarah had agreed completely.

'It's not much of a wedding night,' Paul apologised yet again.

'Let's think of it as a practice run,' Sarah suggested. 'Why don't we do it all again in a few months when all this is behind us? We'll have a big party and I'll get a real wedding dress.'

'Daniel could be my groomsman,' Paul agreed.

'And Luke could be a flower-dog.'

'And we could have a honeymoon on a desert island with nothing to do but make love.'

'Mmm.' Sarah and Paul eyed each other.

'Sarah?'

'Yes?' She pressed her lips together and tried to match his serious expression.

'Do you think our marriage certificate will be valid in a court of law if it's unconsummated?'

Sarah tilted her head thoughtfully. 'I don't think so.'

'Perhaps we should do something about that.' Paul's face was close to hers. So close she could feel the movement of his lips as he spoke.

'Absolutely,' she murmured, just before speech became impossible. 'It's our duty.'

It was nearly dawn when Sarah let herself back into her apartment and hung up her now very crumpled dress and jacket. She decided against trying to sleep. A long, hot shower and a cup of strong coffee were all she needed. She found herself smiling.

'It might have been an unusual wedding night,' she told her empty apartment, 'but it was certainly memorable.'

Holding out her left hand, Sarah glanced at the rings. Paul had produced her engagement ring again and had insisted that she put it on. 'It wasn't the world's greatest engagement, was it?' he'd said ruefully.

'An engagement is only an entrée,' Sarah had replied. 'We never needed that, did we?'

'Don't ever take it off again,' Paul had warned.

'Perhaps I should—just for a while.' Sarah had frowned. 'Daniel's not going to be too happy about this.'

Paul had shaken his head. 'This is a new beginning. For all of us. No half-measures and no deception. Our relationship is the base that we're going to build our future on and that includes Daniel's future, I hope. What sort of message would it give him if it looks like it's up for negotiation or adjustment?'

Sarah nodded to herself now. He was absolutely right. She rinsed out her coffee-cup hurriedly. It was just as well she wasn't working at present. She was going to have a very busy few days.

The first priority was a visit to her family. Her parents' disappointment at the secrecy of her marriage was not completely dispelled by her explanation of the need for haste and the situation not being appropriate for a large celebration. Her mother was, however, mollified by the idea of a repeat ceremony in the near future.

'You could have it here in the garden,' Evelyn suggested. 'In spring, when all the bulbs and blossom are out.'

'Sounds great,' Sarah agreed. 'I've got a few other things to organise first, though. You don't know of any houses to rent out of town, do you? Not quite as far as this but we'll need plenty of room for Luke. And good fences.'

'I'll ask at the clinic,' Jack told her. 'My receptionist knows everybody for miles.'

'And I'll make a few phone calls,' Evelyn promised. 'There's bound to be a farm cottage empty somewhere.'

Having set those wheels in motion, Sarah made the trip back to town and to the hospital. Paul was in his office. The backlog of work from his time spent at Daniel's bedside was beginning to present problems.

'Daniel's angry now,' he told Sarah, 'but he's not ready to talk. I've been with him all morning but I had to get some work done and he kept telling me to go away and leave him alone.'

'Did you tell him about us, getting married?'

'Of course.'

'How did he take it?'

Paul shrugged. 'Hard to tell. He's angry with everything and everybody. You, me, himself and especially his mother. Not that he would admit it.'

'It's part of the grief process,' Sarah said. 'It's the death of a dream for him.'

'I know.' Paul sighed. 'But it's not easy to know how to help in the face of rejection.'

'Don't let it get to you,' Sarah advised. 'The most important thing is to weather the storm, be there for him and let him know how much you love him.'

Paul nodded. 'I'm doing my best, Doc.'

'How is he physically?'

'He looks terrible. Hung-over from the sedative and emotional grinder. He refused to do any physiotherapy. Cheryl was going to take him swimming. We've postponed the final scan as well. I think it'll be a few days before he can be discharged.'

'Good. I need time to organise somewhere for us

to live.' Sarah moved towards the office door. 'I'll go and see him now.'

The destruction of the bond that Sarah and Daniel had built was evident the moment Sarah entered the boy's room.

'Go away,' he told her. 'I'm busy.' His eyes were glued to the screen of the small television they had installed in his room. A cartoon show was playing. Loudly.

'Can I turn the TV down and talk to you for a minute?'

'No.' Daniel's head didn't turn. Sarah sat on the end of his bed. At least he couldn't have too much of a headache, Sarah decided, if he could stand the television at this volume. She wasn't surprised when Angela put her head through the doorway.

'Turn it down, thanks, Daniel. Or use the earplugs. You're disturbing some sick kids.'

With a theatrical sigh Daniel climbed out of his bed and put the earplug jack into the socket. He then began to untangle the long wire. Sarah took advantage of the sudden silence.

'I'm really sorry your mother didn't come, Daniel.'

'I'm not,' Daniel snapped. 'I don't care.'

'Well, I care,' Sarah told him. 'I can understand why you're angry and I want you to know that I care about how you feel.'

'Go away,' Daniel told her again. He had straightened the wire and he climbed back onto his bed as he inserted the earplugs. 'I don't need a mother,' he said loudly, unable to hear his own voice. 'And I don't want one.'

Sarah sat for a while but there was no communication possible. Daniel hunched himself up in the bed so that his back was towards her. His eyes were fixed on the television again and there was no way he could hear her. With a sigh Sarah stood up. She'd known it wouldn't be easy but she felt as though she were facing a brick wall. Her heart sank even further on leaving Daniel's room.

A rubbish bin stood beside the door. Along with a bunch of dead flowers and some screwed-up papers, a soft toy was wedged into the bin. A scruffy dog with black spots.

The location of a suitable cottage didn't present the obstacle Sarah had feared it might. The location was perfect, just out of the city limits, the fencing ideal to keep a young dog contained and the acre of garden and orchard a paradise for both a puppy and a child. The state of the long-unoccupied house was far from ideal.

That weekend saw Sarah, her parents, Helen and Holly and several friends involved in an intensive cleaning-up operation. Paul came for an hour or two when he could spare the time from work pressures and being with his son. He always seemed to arrive just when everyone was stopping for a meal or coffee-break, which caused some friendly ribbing.

'Start as you mean to go on, that's what I say,' Paul countered. 'I am a manager after all.'

'You'll keep,' Sarah warned him, going past with an armload of rotting curtains. Then she caught the look in Paul's eyes and bit her lip. She knew how increasingly frustrating he was finding his employment. He dreamed of returning to surgery but was convinced it would have to stay a dream.

'It's been too long now,' he'd told her sadly. 'I haven't even done a locum in more than a year. I'm out of touch. My confidence has gone.'

'It would come back,' Sarah had assured him. 'It's just a matter of taking that step.'

'No.' Paul had shaken his head. 'There's a lot more to it. Thanks to Daniel's accident. I felt so helpless when that happened. It's not just the victim's life that's hanging in the balance and dependent on medical skill. I was just as dependent on an emotional level. For each victim or patient there's a whole network of people affected. I just didn't realise how deep that could go. It makes the responsibility feel overwhelming. I don't think I could ever take it on again.'

Sarah had been unable to persuade Paul and had dropped the subject for the moment. Seeing the look in his eyes now made her determined to raise it again—soon. There had to be some way to make him change his mind and pursue the career he so desperately missed. Some way to give him back the confidence that Daniel's emergency had shaken out of him. Right at this moment, however, there were more urgent tasks. Sarah shoved the pile of rotten fabric into Paul's arms.

'Here. Manage these for me. They're to go on the trailer. Dad's doing a trip to the rubbish dump later.'

A muffled voice came from the depths of a kitchen cupboard.

'What's that, Mum?'

Evelyn backed away from her task, scrubbing brush in hand. 'I said I put the old curtains from our attic in the back of my car. See if you can find a set to fit. They're old, but they're clean.'

Holly came skipping down the wide hallway. 'There's a henhouse in the orchard.'

'Great.' Sarah smiled. 'Daniel will love that.' She grinned and waved at Angela who was washing the outside of the windows. 'Come in for coffee!' she called.

'I still can't believe you got married, without asking me.'

'You've grumbled about that ever since you got here Angela. I keep telling you we'll do it again.'

'Can I be a bridesmaid?' Holly spoke around a mouthful of muffin.

'You'd have to be Daniel's partner,' Sarah pointed out. 'And not wind him up.'

Holly considered this. 'That's cool,' she pronounced. 'I suppose he's part of the family now. I'll only wind him up on Saturdays.'

'So, when is it to be?' Angela persisted. 'I want to make a note in my diary.'

'Why?' Sarah grinned. 'So you don't get double-booked?'

Angela groaned. 'I wish. Still, my love life is not the issue. Let's see. You're too late for Easter and Christmas is too far away—'

'It doesn't matter,' Sarah interrupted. 'It'll be special whenever we do it.'

'I know.' Angela snapped her fingers. 'Mother's Day. You are becoming an instant mother after all.'

Sarah caught Paul's eye and they exchanged a

wry glance. She was about as far away from being Daniel's mother at present than she could ever be. His anger had faded, to be replaced by a sullen reserve. He had returned to clinging to his relationship with his father and made sure Sarah felt unwelcome whenever she came near. It was lucky she was simply too busy to let it get her down, Sarah thought. On top of the clean-up of the house, the apartments had had to be packed up. The removal trucks were due on Monday, the day before Daniel was going to be discharged.

Sarah and Paul had discussed the pros and cons of not taking Daniel back to his old home at great length. They'd decided that the length of time he'd been in hospital was going to mean adjustment in any case, and to settle him and then shift him again shortly afterwards would only add to his insecurity.

'It's part of the base,' Paul had reminded Sarah. 'Let's make sure it's secure.'

Angela broke into Sarah's thoughts. 'So? What do you think? A Mother's Day wedding?'

Evelyn came to Sarah's rescue. 'That's only three weeks away. I couldn't possibly organise anything by then. No, it has to be spring.'

Three weeks away. Sarah knew the date would hang over her much as the time of Catherine's planned visit had done—an event to mark how far away they were from being a real family.

An event to mark how she wasn't—and could never be—Daniel's mother.

CHAPTER TEN

'IF I SAY you can't then you can't. So there!'

'Maybe I don't want to.'

'You do too. And you can't.'

'Who said you're the boss?'

'I'm older than you. And you're just a nerd.'

'Well. You're a *girl*!'

The verdict was given with the tone of an ultimate insult and Sarah shook her head. The quarrel between the children was drifting in through the window of the kitchen where she and Evelyn were finishing the preparations for a family lunch. She sighed lightly and stopped rinsing the lettuce as the conversation faded. Then the voices rose again as Holly and Daniel came inside the house.

'We'll ask, then.'

'You won't be allowed. You just wait and see.'

The children entered the kitchen. Evelyn looked up from where she sat at the table, buttering bread rolls.

'I wouldn't put your nose that far up in the air if I were you, Holly. You'll leak when it rains.' Evelyn watched Daniel who stood with his eyes down. Luke sat on the floor beside him, stretching his shoelace to breaking point. 'What's the problem, Daniel?'

The boy glanced up. 'Holly says I'm not allowed

to call you Gran. She says that you're her grandmother and not mine.'

'Oh.' Evelyn Kendall put down her knife. 'As far
as I'm concerned, Daniel, you're as much a part of
my family now as Holly is. Would you like to call
me Gran?'

Daniel hesitated and then nodded slightly. Holly
looked put out but shrugged and flashed a cheeky
grin at Sarah.

'It's Saturday,' she pronounced. Evelyn gave her
a stern look but turned back to Daniel. 'Of course,
there are important things about having a gran that
you should know,' she told Daniel seriously.

Daniel's suspicious scowl was automatic.
'What's that?'

'They need lots of cuddles.'

Sarah held her breath as Evelyn opened her arms.
Her mouth dropped open a little as she saw Daniel
willingly go into her mother's embrace, and she
was aware of a wave of jealousy. How could it be
so easy for her mother to gain acceptance when
Daniel refused to let Sarah herself even try to get
close? She shook the lettuce leaves so vigorously
that the stalks snapped off as she stared out the
window, watching the children running back outside, the fat puppy waddling in their wake. Daniel
looked happier than she had seen him since—well,
since the day she'd brought him out to meet her
parents for the first time.

'How come it's so easy for you?' she asked
Evelyn wistfully. 'I'm trying so hard and he won't
even talk to me, let alone let me give him a cuddle.'

'Perhaps you're trying too hard,' Evelyn suggested. 'Relax a little. Children need to know their limits and they need a lot of love, that's all. Especially Daniel. He's going to need a lot of love for a long time.'

'I've got a lot to give him. He just won't accept it.' Sarah put the salad bowl on the table.

'He will,' Evelyn said complacently. 'He's desperate for it. I'm just safer, that's all. I'm not competing with him for his father's attention and he doesn't have to think about me as a mother figure.'

'Huh!' Sarah snorted. 'He thinks of me as simply a live-in maid. I asked him to pick up his clothes in the bathroom the other night and do you know what he said? "You do it—that's *your* job."'

'He's just testing the limits,' her mother told her. 'You need to be kind but firm. Children have to have limits so they can feel secure within them. If you're consistent and he can push so far and can't win or drive you away then he'll feel it's safe to accept you. Then the love can really begin.'

'It's not so much his rudeness to me that bothers me,' Sarah said. 'It's the way I get between him and Paul. He told Paul that he'd rather have a housekeeper because at least she would live somewhere else. Paul got angry and told him off and so the tension just keeps increasing.'

'It's only been three weeks,' Evelyn smiled.

'It feels like three years,' Sarah groaned. 'It's a bit easier since he's gone back to school, though. At least we have one thing in common now.'

'What's that?'

'The sense of relief when Paul gets home,' Sarah said sadly.

The shrieks of children's laughter from the orchard made them both smile. 'It's wonderful to see him looking so well,' Evelyn said.

Sarah nodded. 'The recovery power of kids never ceases to amaze me. He hasn't even had a headache since he came out of hospital, and with his hair growing back you'd never know it had happened.'

'That gives us two things to celebrate, then. Cheer up, love, and get the bubbly out of the fridge. I'll see if the others have the barbecue under control.'

Sarah took the cold bottle of champagne and began to undo the foil wrapping. The children were the only ones not to know the reason for this celebration lunch. Court proceedings had dragged on over the last three weeks but yesterday final ruling had been given. Catherine had no grounds on which to gain custody. Paul and Sarah had sole and permanent responsibility for Daniel's upbringing. Access visits had been offered but only within New Zealand. Much to everyone's relief, the offer had been declined.

'If she can't have it all, she won't want any of it,' Paul had commented. 'Thank God for that.'

The barbecue smelled wonderful and Sarah watched Daniel as he pointed out to Paul which sausages he wanted.

'I'll have that one. And that one with the burnt bits. You're the best cook, Dad.'

'I specialise in burnt bits,' Paul agreed. He grinned at Sarah and she responded, trying to quell the pang it gave her. Daniel only picked at any meals she created. She tried to conjure up some optimism as she continued to watch father and son, happily sorting the meats, but failed miserably. The day she had been dreading was almost upon them. Tomorrow was Mother's Day and she had made no progress at all with Daniel. If anything, their relationship had deteriorated.

The peaceful rural surroundings added to the air of anticipation as the meal preparations were completed. Sarah was beginning to pour the champagne when the peace was jarred by the distant roar of a vehicle.

Paul groaned. 'The louts are out.'

Jack shook his head with disbelief. 'If people had any sense at all they'd have some respect for gravel roads. Instead, we get idiots who think they're on some sort of car rally.'

They all stopped to listen as the crescendo of noise peaked and then began to fade.

'I hate to think what speed he was doing,' Paul began, when suddenly he stopped. The noise of the vehicle had cut out as though a switch had been flicked. A split second later there was an horrendous thump and a scraping noise.

'It's rolled,' Paul stated calmly. 'He was going too fast to take the bend.' He was already moving towards his car. Sarah was surprised to see him pull a solid case out of the boot of his car. 'I didn't know you kept an emergency kit,' she exclaimed.

Paul flashed her a wry smile as he started to run. 'I like to pretend I'm still a doctor,' he called back over his shoulder.

'Just as well,' Jack muttered. 'For once I haven't got mine with me.'

Sarah set off at a run to catch up with Paul. Jack went to his car, having told the others to stay put. By the time he'd negotiated the long driveway Sarah and Paul were already at the scene, having cut across the field. The car was back on its wheels, the roof heavily dented. The single occupant, a young male, was slumped over the top of the steering-wheel.

'No safety belt,' muttered Paul. He tried the driver's door but it was jammed. Jack arrived at that point and took a crowbar from his boot. The door came open with a metallic screech a few seconds later. Paul's hand went to the carotid artery on the victim's neck.

'He's alive,' he told Sarah. 'Call an ambulance.'

Sarah picked up the cellphone and spoke into it as she watched Paul. He held his hand in front of the man's nose and then leaned his own head in closer.

'Mild stridor,' he told Jack. He began gently feeling the victim's head and neck. 'No obvious fractures but we'll have to watch his neck. The bleeding seems to be superficial—from that scalp laceration.' Paul leaned closer again but the laboured breathing sounds could now be heard even by Sarah who was standing some distance away. Paul straightened briefly. 'We're going to have to get him out or he'll asphyxiate. Sarah, you and Jack will have to try and stabilise his head and neck while I lift out the lower half.'

Jack positioned himself beside Paul, and Sarah climbed into the passenger seat. Slowly and awkwardly they managed to move their patient, with

Sarah crawling over the seats as she tried to splint the neck with her hands.

'On the road,' Paul ordered breathlessly. 'We need a flat surface.' He stripped off his jersey, rolling it up and placing it under the hollow of the victim's neck. 'Find some more padding,' he directed Sarah. 'Try and get something right around his head.' Paul opened his emergency kit and quickly put on surgical gloves. Taking an oral airway, he inserted it into the patient's mouth but the laboured breathing continued unchanged.

'Look at that.' Paul touched the obvious bruising on the man's throat. He felt around the area carefully. 'I think he's fractured the hyoid bone. There's a lot of contusion. We're going to have to do a tracheostomy.'

Jack looked doubtful. 'Here? I don't think my skills are up to that.'

'Mine are.' Paul began to pull items from his kit as he spoke. 'You support his head. Don't extend the neck any further than it is now. Put one hand around the back of his head and one under his chin. Sarah, you hold the sides.'

Holding an alcohol swab in one hand, Paul carefully felt down the victim's neck. His fingers found the V-shaped depression at the top of the adam's apple, ran down and located the ring of cartilage beneath. He swabbed the area and reached for a scalpel and a large-gauge IV cannula. Sarah watched in admiration as Paul confidently made a stab incision just above the ring of cartilage and then deftly inserted the cannula. He removed the central part to leave a hollow tube.

'Grab the scissors, Sarah—get his shirt off.' Paul was checking the air flow of the tube. He reached for his stethoscope.

'There's several broken ribs on the right side,' Sarah informed him.

Paul was listening to the chest over the top of the collar-bones. 'He's got a broken right collar-bone and a pneumothorax.'

Jack groaned. He had his hand on the side of the victim's neck. 'Pulse rate's going up,' he commented.

Paul made a rapid survey. 'Doesn't look like any major limb fractures. How's his abdomen?'

'No obvious distension,' Sarah reported.

'Look at this.' Paul's attention went back to the man's chest. 'Surgical emphysema!'

Sarah touched the skin. Air under pressure had been forced into the subcutaneous tissue. It felt like the bubble paper used to wrap parcels. Even as she felt it she was aware of the increased efforts at respiration under her hand. Paul was checking the tracheostomy tube. He shook his head.

'He's losing it. It must be a tension pneumothorax.' He began to listen to the chest again, rapidly moving position from top to bottom and back again. 'Grab me another angiocath, Sarah. We can't do this from the side—I don't want to move him. We'll go for a high intercostal space.' Paul seemed to be talking to himself and Sarah was astonished at the speed and confidence with which he moved. Another stab incision was made between the patient's ribs and the internal part of the cannula again removed after insertion to provide a hollow tube. A

rush of air signalled the release of the trapped air
which had collapsed one lung and threatened the
function of the other.

'I'll put a three-way tap on this and a syringe,'
Paul stated. 'We can release any further air that
way.'

'Heart rate's dropping,' Jack said with relief.
'And the pulse volume's on the way up.'

Paul straightened. He flashed a grin at Sarah.
They could hear the wail of the ambulance in the
distance now.

'We'll get an IV line in and run in a litre of
haemaccel.'

Sarah handed him another swab and IV cannula.
'You're wasted in management,' she told him. 'You
belong back in Theatre.' She watched the excited
light in those dark blue eyes kindle.

'You know something? I think you're absolutely
right.'

The peaceful family atmosphere disintegrated following the accident. Paul went in the ambulance,
determined to manage his patient on the trip back
to town. Evelyn took Jack home to clean up. The
blood from the accident victim's scalp wound had
managed to spread itself over every item of clothing
he had been wearing. Helen and Holly stayed for a
while but, in the absence of Paul, Daniel's mood
suffered an abrupt decline. He and Holly ended up
in another argument. Of all things, it was about
Mother's Day.

'I'm going to take my mum breakfast in bed,'

Holly announced when Helen was safely out of ear-shot, washing dishes. 'I've made a card, too.'

Sarah looked up from her task of tidying the bar-becue. 'Good for you,' she told her niece. 'She'll love that.'

Sarah was moving back into the house when she heard Holly ask Daniel what he was going to do for Mother's Day.

'Why should I do anything?' The reply was sullen. 'I haven't got a mother.'

They were trading insults as Sarah retreated to the kitchen, but the silence was ominous when she returned for the last of the plates. Holly, clearly fed up with Daniel's attitude, nagged her mother until Helen gave in and took her home. Sarah understood how Holly felt.

She watched Daniel over what now seemed a very long afternoon as he played in a rather half-hearted fashion with Luke and wandered aimlessly around the property. He refused the meal Sarah pre-pared for him in the evening and it was difficult not to show a flash of real irritation. Perhaps her mother was right. She was going to have to stake out some limits. She had been too accepting of his rude be-haviour so far. Daniel responded by turning on the television and ignoring her.

They both waited for the return of Paul. He rang to tell her he was very keen to stay and observe the imminent surgery on his patient, having success-fully managed the difficult case himself on the way in. It was obvious he had gained enormous satis-faction from the successful resuscitation and any lack of confidence in his abilities had been completely erased. Sarah did her best to encourage the excitement he was allowing himself at the prospect of returning to surgery.

'It could be perfect timing,' he told Sarah during the phone call. 'There's a general surgical position coming up in a few months' time, I'm told. That would give me enough time to do some retraining.'

'You don't need it,' Sarah told him. 'And I think you should go for it. It's what you should have been doing all along.'

'But what about the longer hours? The on-call?' Paul reminded her. His tone held a plea that Sarah responded to firmly.

'We'll manage. I've told Martin Lynch I'll only work in his private practice during school hours and I need to have school holidays free as well. He's quite happy with that. Even if we have other children we can still work around that.'

'Not if. When,' Paul told her happily. 'Nothing can stop us now.'

Sarah hung up, feeling delighted that Paul was so excited about the future and the idea of returning to the work he loved. The atmosphere of the house, after terminating their contact, suddenly increased her own frustration, however. The prospect of having their own children should have been a very exciting one, but the way things were at present it wasn't possible to even contemplate the idea seriously.

She told Daniel that Paul was on his way home.

'Good,' he replied, his relief patent. He didn't look away from the television.

Sarah fed Luke and then put a tray of steak and

sausages left over from the barbecue into the oven
to reheat. Paul would be starving. She sighed loudly
as the laughter from the television show jarred her
mood. The volume had been annoying Sarah for
some time and she had been ignored twice in her
request to have it turned down. So much for my
ability to set limits, she thought miserably. When
the advertisement for the chocolates that promised
to be the perfect Mothers' Day gift came on, however, Sarah finally snapped. She marched into the
room, grabbed the remote control and pushed the
mute button. Daniel was enraged.

'Turn it back on! I was watching that!'

'No, I won't turn it back on, Daniel. I've had
enough. I asked you to turn it down twice and you
ignored me.'

'I don't have to do what you tell me.' Daniel's
eyes flashed. He looked exactly like his father had
the time Sarah accused him of having an affair with
her. Daniel scrambled to his knees, his fists
clenched, and Sarah stared down at the angry little
face. 'You can't tell me what to do,' he shouted up
at her. 'You're *not* my mother. I don't need a
mother.'

Sarah's anger fled. As she held the eye contact
with Daniel she could suddenly see past the surface
aggression. She could see the vulnerability and the
pain. She could see a small child desperately trying
to make sense of the emotional war in which he
was engaged. Sarah dropped to a crouch in front of
him, still holding the first direct eye contact they'd
had in a very long time.

'No, I'm not your mother, Daniel,' she said quietly. 'I didn't give birth to you. But there's more to being a mother than giving birth.' Sarah took a deep breath as Daniel looked away, but she wasn't going to stop now.

'It's about loving a child, caring very much about what happens to him. Being happy because he's happy. Being sad because he's sad. Trying to help him become the best person he can be and worrying about whether the choices made are the right ones. Especially just being there—no matter what. Maybe that's being a mum, rather than a mother.'

Daniel was sitting very still but his head was turned away. Sarah couldn't be sure he was even listening but she felt compelled to continue.

'You don't need a mother—but I think you would like to have a mum. You haven't had anybody you could trust enough to be that before. You have now. I'm not going anywhere, Daniel. I married your dad because I love him very, very much. I made a promise to stay with him and love him for the rest of my life. That promise included you. It doesn't matter if you give me a hard time and make life difficult for me. Well, it does matter because it makes all of us unhappy and stops us being a family, but it's not going to make me go away. Ever. We could be a family—that's up to you.'

Sarah sighed and sat down on the floor. She waited out the silence, hoping Daniel would say something. But the silence continued until Sarah broke it.

'You know, when a mother gives birth to a baby she feels an incredible joy—and anxiety. The first thing she wants to know is whether the baby's OK.

If it is she can feel all the hope for the future of that baby, the love she can give and receive and the excitement of knowing she can watch that baby grow up and become a special person.

'When you were so sick in hospital I sat and watched you and worried about whether you would be OK. When you woke up I felt so happy—as happy as the day I knew your dad loved me as much as I loved him. And I felt that hope for your future. And I knew I loved you.

'That love is there for you, Daniel. And you can choose whether you let it grow. It's like....' Sarah searched for an analogy. 'It's like training Luke. You have to start with the little things and then build on them. If you do it with love and understanding and can be consistent then one day you find you have an amazing bond. An obedience champion, maybe. Or a family.' Sarah bit her lip. She had run dry finally. She felt exhausted but relieved. She'd said all the things she'd been wanting to say for weeks. Had he listened? Or was it too much for an eight-year-old to take on board?

When it became apparent that Sarah had finally stopped talking Daniel moved. But not towards Sarah. Very slowly, he got to his feet and, without turning, he left the room. Sarah waited until she heard his bedroom door close quietly before she let the tears come.

'It'll come,' Paul told her later that night as she lay nestled in his arms in their bed. 'I'm sure it will.'

'I feel like I've given all I can,' Sarah said mournfully. 'But it still isn't enough.'

'It's more than enough for me,' Paul murmured. 'And I love you more than I ever thought it was possible to love anyone. Will that do for the moment? For me to love you enough for both of us?'

Sarah nestled closer but said nothing. What could she say? Paul's love was perfect, more than she had dreamed of sharing. But, no, it wasn't quite enough.

Mother's Day dawned bright and clear. Sarah awoke before Paul and lay listening to the chorus of birdsong outside their window. She gently extricated her limbs from the tangle they'd been in with Paul's. He stirred and opened his eyes slowly. Then he smiled.

'You've no idea how wonderful it is—you being the first thing I see each day.'

'Oh, yes, I do.' Sarah moved closer to give him a lingering kiss. Then she propped herself up on one elbow. The scuffling noise she heard in the hall probably meant Luke needed to be let out—if it wasn't already too late.

The bedroom door was slightly ajar. Sarah watched as it slowly opened further. It *was* Luke, but he had company. Daniel came into their room, carefully balancing a large wooden tray. Looking more serious than Sarah had ever seen him, he put the tray on her bedside table.

The glass of orange juice had spilled a little. The toast was more than a little burnt. But Sarah didn't even see the culinary offerings. The only thing she was aware of on the tray was the card—a folded sheet of cardboard with a magazine picture of a dog carefully glued to the front.

Sarah reached out her hand and slowly opened

the card. The message pencilled inside was simple.
It read, ''Happy Mum's Day.''

Sarah caught her bottom lip between her teeth as
she blinked hard to prevent the prickle of joyful
tears developing any further. She was aware of
Paul's face very close to her own as he read the
card over her shoulder.

With an effort, Sarah raised her eyes from the
message on the card to find Daniel's dark blue eyes
gazing at her solemnly. His expression was wary,
his anticipation of her reaction palpable. Sarah held
the eye contact but didn't smile.

'This is the best card I've ever, ever, had,' she
told him seriously.

Daniel's expression flickered but he remained
motionless—still waiting.

'Of course,' Sarah continued carefully, 'there are
important things about having a mum that you
should know.'

This time there was a hint of a smile in the small
face. 'Are they the same as about having a gran?'

Sarah nodded as her lips began to curve into a
smile.

'Well, I do know, then,' Daniel stated confidently.

'I don't.' Paul raised an eyebrow at his son.
'What are they?'

Daniel sighed with mild exasperation. 'They
need lots of hugs,' he explained patiently.

'Absolutely right.' Sarah sat up and held her
arms open.

She gently folded the small boy into her arms. It
was as though the gift she was receiving was too

precious to risk any damage. The hug was brief. Sarah felt suddenly nervous, not wanting to push things too fast or too far. An unfamiliar shyness swept over her and she could see the reaction reflected in Daniel's face. It was Paul who saved the moment from becoming awkward. He sat up and patted the space in the bed beside him commandingly.

'Come on. There's plenty of room and it's my turn for a cuddle.'

Daniel happily scrambled over Sarah's legs and climbed into the bed between them. Luke made an unsuccessful attempt to follow him. Paul wrapped his arm around his son's shoulders and then grinned at Sarah.

'Well?'

Sarah found four very dark blue eyes regarding her seriously.'

'Well, what?'

'Aren't you going to eat your breakfast?'

As Sarah carefully balanced the tray on her knees Luke made a successful attempt to join them, having launched himself at the bed from a greater distance. Daniel caught the enthusiastic puppy before he could bounce onto Sarah's tray. He looked worried.

'Is he allowed on the bed?'

'Of course,' Sarah replied. 'He's part of the family, isn't he?'

Daniel nodded, burying a happy grin in the puppy's neck.

Paul chuckled. 'He might even get a piece of

toast. I can see Daniel's inherited my cooking speciality.'

Daniel's face appeared again, looking anxious. 'What's wrong with the toast?'

'Nothing,' Sarah said firmly. 'And I'm the only one who gets to eat it.' She shut her eyes briefly as she held a piece of toast by its blackened crust and then she sighed happily.

'This is going to be the best breakfast I've ever, ever, had.'

Modern Romance™
...seduction and
passion guaranteed

Tender Romance™
...love affairs that
last a lifetime

Sensual Romance™
...sassy, sexy and
seductive

Blaze
...sultry days and
steamy nights

Medical Romance™
...medical drama on
the pulse

Historical Romance™
...rich, vivid and
passionate

MILLS & BOON®

Winner at

2001 **IDEA** INTERNATIONAL
DESIGN
EFFECTIVENESS
AWARDS

MAT5

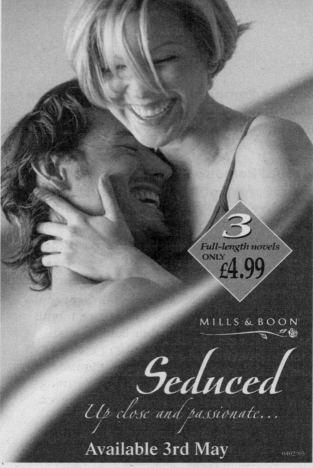

Coming in July

❧

The Ultimate Betty Neels Collection

❧

* A stunning 12 book collection beautifully packaged for you to collect each month from bestselling author Betty Neels.

* Loved by millions of women around the world, this collection of heartwarming stories will be a joy to treasure forever.

Available at most branches of WH Smith, Tesco, Martins, Borders, Eason, Sainsbury's and most good paperback bookshops.

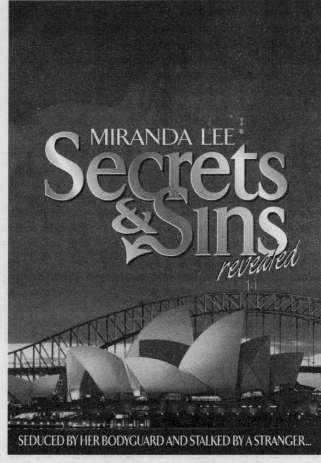

MIRANDA LEE

Secrets & Sins revealed

SEDUCED BY HER BODYGUARD AND STALKED BY A STRANGER...

Available from 15th March 2002

SANDRA MARTON

raising the stakes

When passion is a gamble...

Available from 19th April 2002

*Available at most branches of WH Smith,
Tesco, Martins, Borders, Eason, Sainsbury's
and most good paperback bookshops.*

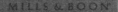

GIVE US YOUR THOUGHTS

Mills & Boon® want to give you the best possible read, so we have put together this short questionnaire to understand exactly what you enjoy reading.

Please tick the box that corresponds to how appealing you find each of the following storylines.

32 Richmond Square

They're fab, fashionable – and for rent. When the apartments in this central London location are let, the occupants find amazing things happen to their love lives. The mysterious landlord always makes sure that there's a happy ending for everyone who comes to live at number 32.

How much do you like this storyline?

❏ Strongly like   ❏ Like   ❏ Neutral – neither like nor dislike

❏ Dislike   ❏ Strongly dislike

Please give reasons for your preference:

_____

_____

The Marriage Broker

This city agency matches marriage partners for practical as well as emotional reasons. Upmarket, discreet and with an international clientele, The Marriage Broker offers a personal service to match clients' needs and situations.

How much do you like this storyline?

❏ Strongly like   ❏ Like   ❏ Neutral – neither like nor dislike

❏ Dislike   ❏ Strongly dislike

Please give reasons for your preference:

_____

_____

A Town Down Under

Meet the men of Paradise Creek, an Australian outback township, where temperatures and passions run high. These guys are rich, rugged and ripe for romance – because Paradise Creek needs eligible young women!

How much do you like this storyline?

❑ Strongly like ❑ Like ❑ Neutral – neither like nor dislike
❑ Dislike ❑ Strongly dislike

Please give reasons for your preference:
_____

_____

The Marriage Treatment

Welcome to Byblis, an exclusive spa resort in the beautiful English countryside. None of the guests have ever found the one person who would make their private lives complete…until the legend of Byblis works its magic – and marriage proves to be the ultimate treatment!

How much do you like this storyline?

❑ Strongly like ❑ Like ❑ Neutral – neither like nor dislike
❑ Dislike ❑ Strongly dislike

Please give reasons for your preference:
_____

_____

Name: _____

Address: _____

_____

Postcode: _____

Thank you for your help. Please return this to:

Mills & Boon (Publishers) Ltd
FREEPOST SEA 12282
RICHMOND, TW9 1BR

NO STAMP NEEDED – postage has been paid.

MILLS & BOON
STEEP/RTL/13
The STEEPWOOD Scandal
REGENCY DRAMA, INTRIGUE, MISCHIEF... AND MARRIAGE
A new collection of 16 linked Regency Romances, set in the villages surrounding Steepwood Abbey.
Book 13
Mr Rushford's Honour
by Meg Alexander
Available 3rd May
Available at most branches of WH Smith, Tesco, Martins, Borders, Eason, Sainsbury's, Woolworths and most good paperback bookshops.